DARN GOOD
COWBOY CHRISTMAS

CAROLYN
BROWN

sourcebooks
casablanca

Published by Sourcebooks Casablanca, an imprint of Sourcebooks, Inc.
P.O. Box 4410, Naperville, Illinois 60567-4410
(630) 961-3900
FAX: (630) 961-2168
www.sourcebooks.com

Printed and bound in the United States of America
QW 10 9 8 7 6 5 4 3 2 1

This one is for The Davis News *gals:*
Sharon Chadwick, Beverly McFarland,
and Alesha Chadwick Henley

Merry Christmas!

Chapter 1

IT WAS JUST A WHITE FRAME HOUSE AT THE END OF A long lane.

But it did not have wheels.

Liz squinted against the sun sinking in the west and imagined it with multicolored Christmas lights strung all around the porch, the windows, even in the cedar tree off to the left side. In her vision, it was a Griswold house from *Christmas Vacation* that lit up the whole state of Texas. She hoped that when she flipped the switch she didn't cause a major blackout because in a few weeks it was going to look like the house on that old movie that she loved.

Now where was the cowboy to complete the package?

Christmas lights on a house without wheels and a cowboy in tight fittin' jeans and in boots—that's what she asked for every year when her mother asked for her Christmas list. She didn't remember the place being so big when she visited her uncle those two times. Once when she was ten and then again when she was fourteen. But both of those times she'd been quite taken with the young cowboy next door and didn't pay much attention to the house itself. The brisk Texas wind whipped around ferociously as if saying that it could send her right back to east Texas if she didn't change her mind about the house.

"I don't think so," she giggled. "I know a thing or two

about Texas wind, and it'd take more than a class five tornado to get rid of me. This is what I've wanted all my life, and I think it's the prettiest house in Montague County. It's sittin' on a foundation, and oh, my God, he's left Hooter and Blister for me. Uncle Haskell, I could kiss you!"

The wind pushed its way into the truck, bringing a few fall leaves with it when she opened the truck door. Aunt Tressa would say that was an omen; the place was welcoming her into its arms. Her mother would say that the wind was blowing her back to the carnival where she belonged.

The old dog, Hooter, slowly came down off the porch, head down, wagging his tail. Blister, the black and white cat, eyed her suspiciously from the ladder-back chair on the tiny porch.

Her high heels sunk into the soft earth, leaving holes as she rushed across the yard toward the yellow dog. She squatted down, hugged the big yellow mutt, and scratched his ears. "You beautiful old boy. You are the icing on the cake. Now I've got animals and a house. This is a damn fine night."

The key was under the chair, tucked away in a faded ceramic frog, just where her Uncle Haskell said it would be when she talked to him earlier that afternoon. But he hadn't mentioned leaving the two animals. She'd thank him for that surprise when she called him later on.

She opened the wooden screen door and was about to put the key in the lock when the door swung open. And there he was! Raylen O'Donnell, all grown up and even sexier than she remembered. Her heart thumped so hard she could feel it pushing against her bra. Her hands were shaky and her knees weak, but she took a deep breath, willed her hands to be still, and locked her knees in place.

"If it's religion you're sellin' or anything else, we're not interested," Raylen said in a deep Texas drawl. He'd been pouring a glass of tea in the kitchen when he heard a noise. Hooter hadn't barked, so he figured it was just the wind, but when he opened the door he'd been more shocked than the woman standing there with wide eyes and a spooked expression on her face.

She wore skintight black jeans that looked like they'd been spray painted on her slim frame. Without those spike heels she would've barely come to his shoulder, and Raylen was the shortest of the three O'Donnell brothers, tipping the chart at five feet ten inches. Her jet-black hair had been twisted up and clipped, but strands had escaped the shiny silver clasp and found their way to her shoulder. Her eyes were so dark brown that they looked ebony.

"Raylen?" she said.

Her voice was husky, with a touch of gravel, adding to her exotic looks. It made Raylen think of rye whiskey with a teaspoon of honey and a twist of lemon. He'd heard that voice before. It had been branded on his brain for eleven years, but she couldn't be Haskell's niece. Liz wasn't supposed to be there until the first of the week at the earliest.

"That's right. Who are you?" he asked cautiously.

"I happen to own this place," she said with a flick of her hand.

"Liz?" Raylen started at her toes and let his gaze travel slowly all the way to her eyebrows. She'd been a pretty teenager, but now she was a stunning woman.

"Surprise! I guess this chunk of Texas dirt now belongs to me. What are you doing here?" she asked.

Could Raylen really be the cowboy Santa was going to leave under her Christmas tree? He'd sure enough been the one she had in mind when she asked for a cowboy. She'd visualized him in tight fittin' jeans and boots when she was younger. Lately, she'd changed it to nothing but a Santa hat and the boots.

His hair was still a rich, dark brown, almost black until the sunlight lit up the deep chestnut color. His eyes were exactly as she remembered: pale, icy blue rimmed with dark brown lashes. It all added up to a heady combination, enough to make her want to tangle her hands up in all that dark hair and kiss him until she swooned like a heroine in one of those old castle romances she'd read since she was a teenager. Speaking of kissing, where in the hell was the mistletoe when a woman needed it, anyway?

Cowboys have roots, not wings. Don't get involved with one or you'll smother to death in a remote backwoods farm or else die of boredom. Her mother's voice whispered so close to her ear that she turned to make sure Marva Jo Hanson hadn't followed her to Ringgold, Texas.

Raylen stood to one side. "I came to feed and water Hooter and Blister. Haskell asked me to do that until you got here. We met when we were kids, remember?"

"I do," she said. How could she forget? She'd been in love with Raylen O'Donnell since she was fourteen years old.

"Haskell said that if you didn't like it here, he'd sell me your twenty acres." Now that was a helluva thing to blurt out, but he couldn't very well say that she'd grown up to be the most exotic creature he'd ever laid eyes on. He'd thought she was cuter than any girl he'd ever seen when she was about fourteen or fifteen, but he hadn't realized that she'd only been the bud of the rose. The full-blown flower was standing before him right then, making him fidget like a little boy.

"I'm going to live here. Uncle Haskell said if I like it, he'll deed the place over to me in the spring. The place isn't for sale and won't be," she said.

"And do what? Ringgold isn't very big."

She shrugged. "I don't know. Pet the cat. Feed the dog."

"That won't make a living, lady," Raylen said.

She popped both hands on her hips. "I don't reckon what I do for a living is one damn bit of your business, cowboy. Do you intend to let me come into my house?"

Why in the hell was he arguing with her? Never in all the scenarios that she'd imagined did he cross her. He'd kissed her. He'd swept her off her feet and carried her to a big white pickup truck and they'd driven off into the sunset. He'd smiled and said that he remembered her well and she'd grown up into a beautiful woman. But he hadn't argued.

Raylen motioned her into the house with a wave of his hand. She brushed across his chest as she entered the house and was acutely aware of the sparks dancing all over the room but attributed it to anger or disappointment, maybe even a bitter dose of both. She'd had Raylen on a pedestal for more than a decade and he didn't even recognize her. He was probably married and had three or four kids too. That was just her luck!

When she fanned past him he got a whiff of a

sensuous perfume that went with her dark, gypsy looks, and he wanted to follow after her like a lost puppy dog.

"I'll take over feeding the cat and dog," she said.

"Okay, then here's the key Haskell gave me." He dug into his pocket and handed her an old key ring with two keys on it. "Welcome to Ringgold, Liz. I still live on the ranch that surrounds this land. Haskell sold me most of his ranch six months ago, all but the part the house sits on."

"He told me."

Raylen headed for the door, "The O'Donnells are your closest neighbors. Come around to see us sometime. Be seein' you."

She wanted to say something; she really did. But not one word would come out of her mouth. Raylen in her living room, looking even sexier than he had when he was seventeen and exercising the horses. Raylen, all grown up, a man instead of a lanky teenager, talking to her... it was such a shock and a surprise that she was speechless. And that was strange territory for Lizelle Hanson.

"Dammit!" she swore.

The noise of the truck engine filled the house for a moment then faded. She'd been so stunned to see him that she couldn't think straight. She hadn't known what to expect, but it sure wasn't what she got. She fished a cell phone from her jacket pocket and punched a speed dial number.

"I'm here," she said when her mother answered.

"And?"

Liz giggled nervously. "It's bigger than I remembered, and there's a sexy cowboy who lives next door but he's probably married and has six kids because no guy that pretty isn't taken. I'd forgotten how big the house is after living in the carnie trailer."

"Have you unpacked? You can turn around and come back right now. You could be here in time to take your shift tomorrow night, and my brother can sell it to those horse ranchers next door to him."

"Not yet. I was on my way in the house when Raylen opened the door and scared the hell out of me. Hooter and Blister are still alive and well. I'm not ready to throw in the towel yet."

"Raylen?" Marva Jo asked.

"The sexy cowboy. I met him both times I came to visit Uncle Haskell. Remember when I told you about the boy that tried to beat me walkin' the fence when I was ten? That was Raylen."

"You are right. He's probably married and has a couple of kids. I was hoping the house would be butt ugly to you."

"No, ma'am. I squinted real hard and even imagined it with Christmas lights. Looked pretty damn fine," Liz said.

"We'll be in Bowie in a few weeks. By then you'll be sick to death of boredom. You were born for the carnie and travel," Marva said.

"I will have the Christmas lights on the house when you get here," Liz said.

"A house not on wheels with Christmas lights and a cowboy." Marva laughed. "Be careful that the latter doesn't cut off your beautiful wings, because that part of the country produces a crop of hot cowboys every generation."

"Good night, Momma. I love you," Liz said.

"Love you too, kid. Go prove me right about getting bored to tears. It's only half an hour until time to tell fortunes and I still have to get my makeup on. Does that make you miss me?"

"Not yet. I only saw you this morning. Hug Aunt Tressa and I'll see you in a few weeks."

———

Raylen drove down the lane and stopped. The left blinker was on, but he couldn't make himself pull out onto the highway. The whole incident at Haskell's place had been surreal. Haskell said his niece, Liz, was going to take over the property. He remembered Liz very well. She was the ten-year-old who'd walked the rail fence better than him even though he was thirteen. She was the fourteen-year-old who rested her elbows on the same rail fence and watched him exercise the horses. Now she was so pretty she sucked every sane thought out of his brain.

He finally pulled out on Highway 81 and headed north a mile, then turned left into the O'Donnell horse ranch. She'd find out pretty quick that a person couldn't make a living by petting the cat and feeding the dog, and when she did he intended to be the first in line to buy her twenty acres. It was the only property for a three-mile stretch down the highway that didn't belong to the O'Donnells.

He parked in the backyard, crawled out of the truck, and sat down on the porch step to his folks' house. Dewar drove up, parked next to him, hopped out of his truck, and swaggered to the porch. Just a year older than Raylen, Dewar was taller by several inches. His hair was so black that it had a faint blue cast as the sunrays bounced off it. His eyes were a strange mossy shade of green and his face square. His Wranglers were tight and dusty; his boots were worn down at the heels and covered with mud.

"Y'all get those cattle worked at Rye's?" Raylen looked down at his own boots. They were just as worn down at the heels and covered with horseshit. His jeans had a hole in one knee and frayed hems on both pant legs. His shirt looked like it had been thrown out in the round horse corral for a solid week and then used for a dog bed a month after that. Damn it all to the devil and back again. He'd planned on at least meeting Liz the first time in clean duds, not looking like a bum off the streets.

"Yes, we did, and we would've got them done sooner if our younger brother would've helped," Dewar said.

"Aww, y'all didn't need me. And besides, if you worked harder and played with Rachel less, you'd get more done."

"Bullshit! You're just tryin' to find excuses." Dewar grinned.

Rachel was their oldest brother's new baby daughter, the first O'Donnell grandchild, and only a few months old. Her father, Rye, was Raylen and Dewar's oldest brother. Her mother, Austin, had been a Tulsa socialite until she inherited a watermelon farm across the river in Terral, Oklahoma, and fell in love with Rye. Rachel was getting to know her two uncles and it was an ongoing battle about which one would be the favorite.

"Want a beer? I swear I'm spittin' dust and hot summer is long since past," Dewar said.

"I'd drink a beer with you," Raylen said.

Dewar disappeared into the house and brought out two longneck bottles of Coors, and he handed one to Raylen. "So you got the chores done around here or am I going to have to do those too?"

"All finished. Everything with four legs has been fed and watered. Horses are all exercised, and even Haskell's dog and cat are fed. His niece is over there now. She can take care of Hooter and Blister." He turned up the bottle and downed a fourth of it before coming up for air and a burp.

Dewar plopped down on the porch step beside Raylen. "Is she going to keep the place or do you have a chance at buying it?"

"Says she is going to keep it. I asked her what she was going to do to make a living in Ringgold, Texas, and she said she was going to feed the dog and pet the cat. Hell, if Haskell gives her his money as well as that twenty acres, she won't have to do nothing but feed a dog and pet a cat."

"What's she look like?"

"Damn fine. Not a thing like old Haskell. She's got jet-black hair and the blackest eyes you've ever seen, and her skin is this light toast color that says she's got some kind of exotic blood in her. Build like a red brick outhouse without a single brick out of place."

"You took with her?"

"Hell, no!" Raylen said too quickly.

―~~―

Liz stood in the middle of the living room floor and turned around slowly. The room was bigger than the fifth wheel travel trailer where she'd lived her entire life. A stone fireplace with a real chimney was centered on the north end with a stone apron in the front. Two brown leather recliners flanked a sofa dated in the seventies with its wagon wheel arms and six brown corduroy cushions. The coffee table sat on a real cowhide area rug. A wheeled cart on the east side of the fireplace held a small television set, and as if something had to be used to balance the arrangement, a ladder-back chair was on the other side with a pot of silk greenery on it. That whole arrangement scarcely took up half of the big room.

The south end was covered with empty bookcases, floor to ceiling. Uncle Haskell had said that she'd have to start her own collection because he was taking all his beloved Westerns with him. Another sofa faced the bookcase. That one was orange and yellow floral velvet, had deep cushions and big round arms that begged for someone to settle in with a good book. A wagon wheel chandelier hung in the middle of the room over a library table with a set of horse head bookends and a well worn *Webster's Dictionary* in the middle. An antique oak business chair was set at an angle as if waiting for Uncle Haskell to come back and look up a word.

It wouldn't take a lot of rearranging to give the room a more open and less cut-up look. Take the table and put it in front of the bookcases. Move the floral sofa under the window to the east, and angle the fireplace arrangement.

"Oh, oh! And a Christmas tree right there with lots of presents under it, and garland looped around the ceiling caught up with Christmas bulbs. And cedar boughs strewn on the mantel with a nativity scene in the middle." Excitement filled the whole room as she pictured her first Christmas in her own home.

But that was another day's work. Right then she was hungry and she hadn't even thought about bringing groceries with her. She wandered into a country kitchen with cabinets making a U on three sides and a small maple table and four chairs set right in the middle. A picture of her, back when she was ten, was stuck to the front of the refrigerator. It had to have been taken that summer when she showed up Raylen by staying on the top of the fence longer than he did. That and when she was fourteen were the only two times her mother let her spend the day at Uncle Haskell's place.

She remembered her short, stocky uncle inviting her for the day and her mother shaking her head. "What can it hurt, Marva Jo? She just wants to see my new puppy. His name is Hooter and he loves little kids," Haskell had said. "Come on. I promise not to put fertilizer on her feet."

On the way to his house she'd asked him why he'd want to put fertilizer on her feet. "It's a joke, Lizelle. Your momma is afraid if you see how I live that you'll like it."

Later, when she was older, her mother had admitted that she had seriously never wanted her to get acquainted with the way the other side lived, for fear she'd want that instead of the carnie life.

"We were all born into the same family. All grew up in the carnival. But Haskell, the one who is supposed to be running this business, wanted roots. I don't want that for you, my child. I want freedom and wings for you.

And I've been afraid you'd get his genes and want the other side's life. He is like Momma. She stayed with the carnival because she loved Daddy, but she loved settling down for the winter months more than the traveling ones," Marva Jo had said.

Liz's stomach grumbled and she forgot about the picture of the dark-haired girl in the picture and looked inside the refrigerator. It was empty except for a chunk of cheddar cheese and a tall pitcher of sweet tea. She rustled up a glass from the cabinet and a tray of ice from the freezer. The tea was sweet, cold, and tasted wonderful. There was half a loaf of bread still within its date on the cabinet. She opened a pantry door to find a walk-in room with loaded shelves on three sides. Supper would be soup and cheese, and soon, because she was starving. She'd left Jefferson, Texas, that morning with butterflies the size of dragons in her stomach so she'd skipped lunch.

She heated a can of vegetable soup, leaned against the counter, and let the scene from two days ago replay in her mind. Marva had come into the trailer late and opened a can of beer. She'd propped a hip against the cabinet in the tiny kitchen and took a long gulp as she watched Liz remove her fortune-teller's makeup.

"What do you want for Christmas, kid?" Marva asked.

As if by rote, Liz grinned and said, "A house with no wheels and a sexy cowboy."

"Your Uncle Haskell called a couple of weeks ago. Poppa is ailing and needs full-time help these days. Tressa and I've been talkin' about one of us staying with him for the first half of the run next year, and then switching off, and the second one staying with him the last half. But Haskell drove out to visit him last week and came up with another idea. He says that he's used to living in one place and is ready to retire. He's already sold off most of his ranch. We talked about it and Poppa likes the idea of having his son nearby. So Haskell bought one of those prefab houses and had it moved on the land. It's built to be wheelchair accessible so if Poppa gets to where he can't get around or take care of himself with Haskell's help, then he can live there too. Now here's the rest of the story. The part that I don't like but Haskell and Poppa both say is the right thing." Marva Jo looked like she'd just come from a funeral, or worse yet was about to go to one.

Liz would never forget the pain in her mother's face. "Haskell is giving his house and the last twenty acres of his ranch to you. If you like it, come spring, he'll put the whole thing over in your name. We'll be in Bowie the last week in November just like always, so I will see you then. That's a month from now and by then I hope you have changed your mind about living in a real house. So it's up to you, kid. You really want a house with no wheels, or has it been a big joke between us all these years?"

Liz had whispered, "Holy hell! Yes, Momma, I want it."

"Then pack your bags, girl. You're leavin' in the morning. If you decide you want to come back to the carnival, you're always welcome, and the people next door to Haskell's have already said they are interested in buying the acres and the house. Me, I hope to hell that you hate the damn place in a week or even a day. I don't want you to go, but Haskell and Poppa are right. You are twenty-five. It's time for you to make your decision about being a carnie forever or quitting the business."

"And so here I am," Liz said aloud as she poured the soup into a bowl. "I guess Raylen is the one Momma was talkin' about buying my property. Well, ain't that the holy shits! I've wanted to see his pretty blue eyes again for eleven years and he wants my house and land. I got what I wanted, but it'll be a cold day in hell when he gets what he wants."

After she'd eaten two bowls of soup and a chunk of cheese, she washed up her dishes, a habit her mother had instilled in her from childhood. "In a trailer this size there's no room for clutter," she'd said so many times that Liz couldn't count them.

She went back to the living room, found the light switch, turned on the hall light, and started down the hall. Four doors opened off the hallway. Haskell's bedroom was the first on the right, across the hall from the bathroom, and swept clean. Not even a lonesome, old dust bunny scampered into the corner. The next two offered up two more bedrooms. One very small one was completely empty. She vaguely remembered a desk being in the room. She swung open the fourth door to find another bedroom with a four-poster bed, dresser with a big round mirror above it, and one of those old-time vanities with a velvet bench that pulled up to a three-sided mirror. The bed looked like it covered an acre and made her feel small when she kicked off her shoes and stretched out on it.

The wind brushed a tree limb across the window screen and Hooter set up a long, low, lonesome howl right under the window. It sounded as if he were mourning the loss of his master, which sent chill bumps dancing up and down Liz's arms. She threw her legs over the side of the bed and hurried back down the hall, through the kitchen, and slung open the back door.

"What is it, old boy?" she asked.

If dogs could grin, Hooter did. He lowered his head and marched into the house, across the kitchen floor, and to the recliner in the living room where he turned around three times before snuggling down on the cow skin rug. Liz had been so busy watching the process that she hadn't realized Blister had snuck in with Hooter until the cat brushed past her leg. She jumped straight up and let out a screech, her heart pounding so hard that she threw a hand on her chest to keep it from jumping out on the floor and shooting past her in a blaze that would rival the cat.

Blister slowed down before she reached the recliner and touched noses with Hooter before settling down on the back of the chair like a fur collar on a fancy winter coat.

They both looked up at her mournfully as if asking why she didn't join them, but she shook her head. "I've got to haul suitcases and boxes into the house. I don't have time to sit around and watch television, but thank you for the invitation. If it's still on after I unpack, maybe I'll take you up on it later this evening."

Put them outside. Do not pet them or let them stay in the house. You'll get attached and it will make leaving even harder. You know what happened that time I was gone for two days, and you hid that kitten in the trailer, her mother's voice argued with her.

"I'm not leaving, Momma. I wasn't teasing when I said I wanted a house and a cowboy for Christmas.

Every time we go into a new town, I wonder what it would be like to live in one of the houses in that town. Now I get to find out."

Hooter rolled his big, soulful eyes up at her as if asking what she was talking about. She reached down and scratched Hooter's ears as she walked past him and out into the night. She had two suitcases, a worn old fiddle case, and two boxes to unload. It wasn't much to show for twenty-five years, but when two people share a travel trailer, there's not room to collect junk. Only the very precious items could be saved, and they were in the boxes. She carried in the suitcases and set them inside the door and went back for the boxes.

She looked north but couldn't see anything but the moon and one star hanging in the sky. Raylen lived over there. She'd never seen the house, but Uncle Haskell said that his nearest neighbor lived a mile to the north. Was he over there with his wife and a house full of kids? Were they loading up in his truck or van or whatever his wife drove to go to town for fast food and a movie? Would she get bored by the end of the winter season and be ready to go back on the road with the carnival?

She sighed and carried her fiddle case inside, then the two small boxes. She was now officially moved in and it was exhilarating. The dog and cat looked up with soulful eyes and she told them, "Work first. Play later."

When she'd finished putting her crystal ball on the vanity, a snapshot of her mother and Tressa in full costume on the dresser, and her deck of worn Tarot cards on the bedside table, she felt more at home in the big room. She popped open the suitcases and hung jeans, flowing skirts, a few shirts, and a denim jacket in the closet; arranged underwear, pajamas, and three bright colored costumes in dresser drawers; and set several pair of high-heeled shoes, a pair of Nikes, and a pair of scuffed up cowboy boots on the closet floor.

"Work is done. Now I can play," she said.

She headed up the hallway. Blister opened one eye but didn't budge from the recliner. Hooter raised his head and looked toward the door.

"Already wanting to go back outside, are you?" The words were barely out of her mouth when someone knocked hard on the door.

She hadn't heard a vehicle and the dog hadn't stirred. Some watchdog Hooter was! She opened the door to find Raylen leaning on the jamb.

"Evenin'," he said in a deep Texas drawl.

"Good evenin'," she said.

"You goin' to invite me in?" he asked.

In carnival life few people came inside the trailer. When they knocked on the door, it usually came with an invitation to come outside, to eat supper at the community potluck, to take a walk around the grounds, or to pet the horses. It had to be pretty serious between two people for them to spend time inside a trailer together. Her mother had never brought a man, carnival worker or any other, inside the trailer. Tressa was the only person Liz could remember ever sitting at the small kitchen table with them.

"Well?" Raylen asked.

She stepped aside. If she was going to embrace a normal life she'd have to get used to the rules. "Come in. I'm sorry. I just got unpacked and my mind was off in la-la land."

Raylen grinned. "Been there."

He went straight for the recliner where Blister had taken up residence on the back and sunk into it. Hooter raised his head and wagged his tail. Raylen scratched his ears and then turned his attention to Blister.

"They miss Haskell. I'm glad you let them in the house."

"He was howling like he was dyin'. I opened the door to see what was going on, and they both came in," she said. Should she sit in the other recliner or the sofa? She finally crossed in front of him and claimed the other chair.

"They're good animals. Blister has a litter box in the utility room off the kitchen. The litter is in the cabinet beside the washer and dryer. Hooter would explode before he'd make a mess, so there's nothing to worry about them bein' inside. Haskell said they were good company and that Hooter knew all his secrets. He told me that he was glad the dog couldn't talk."

Liz smiled. "Too bad. He could tell me stories about my uncle, I'm sure."

"Yep, he could." Raylen grinned. When she smiled, he remembered that crazy feeling in his chest when they were teenagers. She'd smiled at him over the fence and his heart had done a couple of flip-flops. He wanted to do something fancy on the horse, like jump a hurdle, but his momma would have had his hide if he'd hurt her prize horse.

Liz inhaled deeply to ease the antsy feeling in her gut, but it didn't help. All she got was a lung full of Raylen's shaving lotion. Damn! The man had cleaned up in the last couple of hours. His boots were spit shined, his hair still glistened from a shower, and his Wranglers were starched and creased. He looked like sin on a stick all sweaty and dirty, but cleaned up—he just plumb made her mouth go dry.

Raylen rubbed Blister's fur and stole sideways glances at Liz. She'd taken the clip from her hair, and it fell below her shoulders. It was even blacker than Austin's, his brother's new wife of a little more than a year. Liz's dark eyes reminded him of a deep, dark hole that could swallow him up if he stared into them; as if they could see straight into his soul and tell him everything he'd ever thought or would think.

"So you are Uncle Haskell's nearest neighbor, now mine, I guess?" she asked.

He pointed toward the fireplace. "Less than a mile as the crow flies, straight that way. Haskell's house and ours is probably set on a plumb line, but to drive there, you have to go down to the highway, hang a left, drive a mile, turn left down the lane, and then back as far as your place is off the highway. But I jumped the fences and walked over tonight. Needed the exercise after Momma's supper."

I would shoot you between the eyes if you called me Momma. When I get a husband, even when I have kids, he's not calling me Momma, she thought.

He noticed the scowl on her face. *Lord, what did I say wrong?*

"How many fences?" she asked.

"Well, you leave the backyard fence but it's got a gate. Then the corral fence but it's got a gate too. After that there's the rail fence out into the horse pasture, but there's a stile over it, and then your fence. So I suppose I only actually jumped one fence." He grinned.

That grin was flirting. If he was her husband he'd be in the doghouse with Hooter for looking at another woman the way he was staring at her. Liz couldn't remember when she didn't work at the carnival in some capacity or another. And she'd seen men walking down the midway with their arm around one woman and eyeing another just like Raylen was doing.

Raylen saw the disgusted look cross her face and stood up so fast that Blister rolled down into the chair. "I came to invite you to Sunday dinner tomorrow. We do the big family thing on Sunday, and Grandma wants to have music." His palms were sweaty, and high color stung his neck.

She pointed. "One mile straight across there?"

"That's right. At noon. My sisters, Gemma and Colleen, will be there and my brother, Dewar. My other brother, Rye, and his wife and baby daughter, Rachel, live over in Terral, right across the river and they'll be coming too. And of course Grandma and Grandpa and Momma and Daddy."

Liz's dark eyebrows knit together in a frown. Did he live with his mother and father?

Well, you lived with your mother until yesterday, so don't be casting stones! Aunt Tressa's gravelly voice whispered so close that she turned to make sure she wasn't in the room.

"I'd love to come to dinner. At noon? Can I bring something? What's your wife's name?" she blurted out and wished she could cram the words right back in her mouth. God, that sounded so tacky.

"Wife?" he stammered.

"You didn't mention your wife's name. Rye, your

brother, is married to Austin. Are any of the rest of you married?" She might as well be hung for a full-fledged sheep as a little bitty lamb. She'd opened the can of worms. She might as well let them all out to wiggle.

"Hell, no! I wouldn't be over here askin' you to dinner if I was married. That wouldn't be right." The words shot out of his mouth like cannonball.

She cocked her head to one side. Were all the women in Ringgold, Texas, blind? Raylen filled out those Wranglers right well, and his biceps strained the seams on his Western-cut, plaid shirt. How in the devil had he outrun all the women?

"Do you have a husband?" he asked bluntly.

It was her turn to blush and shake her head emphatically. "Carnies aren't the marryin' type."

"Carnies?" He wondered if that was a family name.

"That's right. You sure I can't bring something?"

"We plan on music." He smiled. "If you play an instrument bring it along. If not, just bring a healthy appetite."

She walked him to the door. He turned and looked down into her eyes and felt himself falling. She moistened her full lips with the tip of her tongue and he leaned in to kiss her then jerked back.

Liz wanted that kiss and felt cheated, then cheap. A woman didn't let a man kiss her just because he asked her to Sunday dinner. She might be a carnie, but she wasn't trashy. She took a step back and looked over her shoulder at the dog and cat.

"I'll see you tomorrow then," she said hoarsely.

He cleared his throat and opened the screen door. "Be lookin' for you. Want me to drive over and get you?" he asked awkwardly.

"No, I'd either walk or bring my own truck," she said just as stiffly.

"Okay, then. Good night, Liz."

"'Night, Raylen." His name slipped off her tongue entirely too easy, and he did smell good and look good and that kiss would have been so, so good.

She plopped down in the recliner, and Hooter laid his head in her lap. Blister moved from the back of the chair to the arm and purred. The remnants of Raylen's shaving lotion surrounded her.

"I'd give you each a big T-bone if you could talk and tell me more about Raylen."

She dug her cell phone out of her purse and punched in the speed dial for her uncle. After five rings she was about to hang up when she heard his voice.

"Uncle Haskell. I'm here and I'm unpacked and I was so tickled to see Hooter and Blister. Do I really get to keep them? I've already made up my mind. I'm staying on the property and I promise I'll spoil them even worse than you did."

"Whoa, girl. Slow down," Haskell said. "Yes, you can keep Hooter and Blister. They wouldn't be happy anywhere but right there and I know you'll spoil them. But you haven't been there long enough to make up your mind, so you have to stay until March when the carnival pulls out of here before I sign it over to you legally. I told Raylen to water and feed Hooter and Blister. I guess he did?"

"Yes, he was in the house when I got here. He went home but he came back and invited me to the O'Donnell's for Sunday dinner. He said they're going to have music," Liz said.

"You'll enjoy that. That Raylen and Dewar both are good men, Lizelle. Take your fiddle and enjoy the day."

"Are you settling in out there?" Liz asked. It hadn't occurred to her in the flurry of excitement that her uncle might not be satisfied in Claude and might want to come back to Ringgold.

"Yes, I am. Poppa and I are getting along pretty good. I'm still unpacking my books, but we're getting a few boxes done each day. Poppa borrowed some yesterday. I may make a reader of him yet. He's anxious for Marva Jo and Tressa to get here though. He loves revamping the wagons every winter."

"I'm glad you are there, Uncle Haskell. He gets lonely. I promised Hooter and Blister some quality family time so I'm going to hang up and visit with them," Liz said.

"I'll be looking for reports at least once a week," Haskell said.

"You got 'em. Good night," Liz said.

Did that mean she could ask questions about Raylen once a week as well as give her uncle a report?

Chapter 2

LIZ PUT A MARTINA MCBRIDE CHRISTMAS CD IN THE truck player as she drove down her lane toward the highway and listened to "I'll Be Home for Christmas." So what if it was the middle of October and Christmas was still a couple of months away? Liz was home for Christmas. She could feel it in the peace and joy that surrounded her.

Martina sang that Christmas Eve would find her where the love light gleamed. Liz sang along with her and got cold chills down her back as she thought about love light gleaming on her by Christmas Eve.

"Maybe next Christmas Eve. It would take a miracle to have it this year," she said.

She and her mother liked country music. Tressa hated it. Liz wondered where her Uncle Haskell stood on the issue. Somehow she couldn't see her overall-clad uncle listening to the Irish melodies that Tressa loved. She'd bet her fiddle that he was a Willie Nelson and George Jones man.

Another three Christmas songs had played through when she made a left onto the O'Donnell property. She gasped when she saw the big, two-story white house and all the vehicles parked out front. She'd expected to find something more like her house, a small ranch-style place with a dog on the porch.

"Oh, stop it," she talked to herself. "You've been in

real houses before. You're acting worse than you did on your first date nine years ago. And this isn't even a date. Raylen said he didn't have a wife. He didn't say anything about a girlfriend. He's probably just being a good neighbor."

Folding chairs under a shade tree in the backyard had a guitar, banjo, and several other stringed instruments sitting on them. She wondered if she should add her fiddle to the mix but decided to leave it in the truck. Could be that she'd have enough normalcy by the time dinner was finished and be ready to get the hell out of Dodge.

The wind had died down from the night before, but a breeze whipped her long, flowing skirt around her ankles when she got out of the truck. She pulled her bright orange crocheted shawl around her shoulders and made her way to the door. Her finger headed for the doorbell but it didn't reach its mark. The big wooden door swung open and Raylen stood a foot from her. How in the devil did he do that? Did he have a sixth sense that knew when she was about to ring a doorbell or unlock a door?

His cologne reached her nose at the same time her eyes took in the sight of him in black Wranglers, a black pearl-snap shirt, and shiny black boots. The whole effect was enough to make her swoon like a heroine in the romance books she loved.

Raylen stood to one side and motioned for her to come inside. She wore a multicolored patchwork skirt that reached her ankles, high-heeled shoes, a turquoise knit shirt, and a bright orange shawl around her shoulders. The sunrays on her jet-black hair gave it a deep blue tint, and she chewed on her full bottom lip as if she were just a little bit nervous. He was so mesmerized by the sight that he didn't think he could utter a single word, but when he opened his mouth the words flowed. "Liz! I heard a door slam and hoped it was you. We're just about ready for Grandpa to say grace and then we can eat. I was afraid you wouldn't take me serious about the invitation, but I'm glad you are here."

"Hey, talk later. I'm starving," a dark-haired woman yelled as she made her way down the staircase.

"That's Gemma, my youngest sister," Raylen explained. "Let's have grace and then I'll introduce you to the family." He put his hand on her shoulder and steered her through the living room, dining room, and into the kitchen.

The living room was a huge square with lots of tall windows letting in natural light. A brown leather sofa with deep cushions and wide arms was on either end of the big, square room with rocking chairs and recliners thrown in here and there, with tables and lamps beside them. It was a room that invited family and friends to come right in and make themselves at home.

"We're all here, so Grandpa, would you say grace?" a man who looked a lot like Raylen asked.

Everyone bowed their heads.

Liz did the same but stood perfectly still. Raylen's touch sent vibes up and down her spine that she'd never felt before. She tried to listen to the words of thanks his grandfather delivered in a deep Texas drawl, not totally unlike Raylen's voice. But she couldn't concentrate on anything but the heat flowing from his hand, through the shawl and the knit shirt.

"Amen," Grandpa said.

Gemma extended her hand. "You must be our new

neighbor. We'll miss Haskell. He's been a wonderful neighbor."

Liz reached out and Gemma's shake was firm. She had black hair cut in short layers that framed an oval face, deep green eyes beneath arched dark eyebrows, heavy lashes, and a wide mouth. She took care of her short height with a pair of bright red three-inch high heels on a one-inch platform. She wore skintight jeans and a green shirt the same color as her eyes.

With a slight pressure on her back, Raylen turned her around to face more family. "This is my father, Cash O'Donnell, and my mother, Maddie."

Liz shook hands with Cash who was taller than Raylen. They shared the same hair color, but Raylen's eyes were clearer blue, and his face more square cut with a stronger chin.

Maddie bypassed her hand and hugged her. "Welcome to Ringgold, honey. We're here if you need anything. Come over if you get bored. Holler if you want company."

"Thank you," Liz said softly. Would the invitation still stand when they found out that she came from a long line of carnies? Or had Uncle Haskell told them about his sister's lifestyle?

Maddie had a few crow's feet around her bright blue eyes, but there wasn't a single gray strand in her chestnut-colored hair. She was taller than her daughters and slim as a model. Any twenty-year-old woman would have been delighted to look that good in snug jeans.

"I've got to get the last pan of hot rolls out of the oven, so excuse me, but remember what I said," Maddie said.

"Thank you, I will."

"My sister, Colleen," Raylen said.

Her hair was a strange burgundy color, and her face was slightly rounder than Gemma's angular planes, and her lips a wee bit wider. She was a little taller than Gemma but built on the same delicate frame.

"You have gorgeous hair," Liz said. She could imagine Colleen in a gypsy costume with a long scarf tied around her forehead and all that hair flowing down her back.

Colleen nodded but didn't offer to hug her or shake her hand. "What kind of job are you lookin' for, or are you going to farm that twenty acres?"

"I haven't thought that far. Are you offering me a job?" Liz asked. She'd been in catfights before, and Colleen's eyes said that she did not approve of her brother bringing a stray into the house for Sunday dinner.

"I work at the casino as a blackjack dealer up in Randlett, Oklahoma. I imagine I could put in a word for you if you're shopping around for a job," Colleen said.

"I'd rather have something closer," Liz said.

"Then go talk to Jasmine at Chicken Fried. She's going to need a waitress in a couple of days. I'm Austin, the sister-in-law, Rye's wife," a tall woman, with jet-black hair and beautiful blue eyes, said from behind Maddie. "And that baby that Maddie is takin' from my husband is Rachel, our daughter."

It was plain as a gold earring in a gypsy's ear that Rye and Raylen were brothers, only Rye was well past six feet tall. The baby that he was passing to his mother was a dark-haired little girl with her mother's eyes. Liz wondered if Rachel would be as tall as her mother too.

"I'm pleased to meet you," Liz said. "Who's Jasmine?"

A brunette in pink cowboy boots, jeans, and a cute, flowing top raised her hand. "That'll be me. And any-time you want to work come see me. I'm lookin' for a waitress at the Chicken Fried, my café just up the high-way. And I'm not a sister or kin. I got into the family on Austin's shirttails. Welcome to the area. I love it here."

An older woman slipped her arm around Liz's shoulders and knocked Raylen's off. "I'd be his grandmother, Franny, and that man with his plate loaded so high he needs sideboards is his grandfather, Tilman."

"And I'm Dewar, his other brother," another hand-some cowboy said.

Dewar wasn't quite as tall as Rye but taller than Raylen and his face was fuller. He also sported a deeper dimple in his chin and a scar on his cheek. "So are you getting unpacked over there? Got a truck coming in with your things? Need us to gather up a bunch of men and help you get it unloaded?"

"No, thank you, I'm handling it just fine." Liz smiled.

She bit back a giggle. If they'd seen how little she'd brought they'd have too many questions to answer in a lifetime. And was Dewar flirting with her?

"Well, you call us if you change your mind," Dewar said.

"You better stop yapping and get over here or I'm going to clean out the mashed potato bowl and you're goin' to be left out in the cold," Jasmine said.

"Got to go protect my dinner." Dewar headed to the bar separating the kitchen area from the dining room. Like the living room, it was one big, square room with the same come-right-on-in attitude.

Thank you, Jasmine, Raylen thought.

His brother's eyes had lit up entirely too bright when he saw Liz. And he was the next in line. Rye found Austin the year before and it was Dewar's turn if Cash's prophecy about his children all getting married in the order of their birth was to come true. Raylen didn't care if his brother got married or to whom, as long as it wasn't the new neighbor. He might not even like her once he got to know her, but that tingle in his hand every time he laid it on her shoulder sure made him want a chance.

Raylen dropped his arm back on her shoulder again. "We'd better elbow our way up to the bar or else we'll go hungry."

Liz wasn't ready for the sizzle of instant heat rushing out every nerve ending when Raylen touched her. She'd dated a few times. She'd been kissed. She'd had a few relationships that wound up in bed. But not even her dreams about Raylen prepared her for the attraction that almost had her panting right there in front of his family. She blinked three times to be sure she wasn't in another dream and looked up to see Colleen staring right at her.

She winked. It just came out, but it set Colleen's mouth in a firm frown instead of a smile. That woman would be something to deal with. But it would have to be later because Liz was hungry, and the house smelled like fried chicken and hot yeast rolls. Those kinds of meals didn't come along often, and she wasn't letting one sourpuss sister ruin it.

Rye handed her a plate. "Well, Miz Liz, how do you like Ringgold?"

"Haven't seen any of it except Uncle Haskell's place and this one. How big is the town anyway?"

Raylen chuckled. "If we round up everyone from the Red River to halfway between us and Bowie, we could probably roust up about a hundred people."

"Uncle Haskell said it was tiny and that the fire from a few years ago burned up a lot of it," she said.

Rye draped his arm around his wife. "That it did. I hope you like it."

"I already do," she answered with a bright smile.

"You Irish?" Grandma asked.

"No, ma'am. Not that I know about anyway. Are you?"

"Oh, yes, I am. I come from a long line of Irish. With your dark looks I thought I saw some Irish. Maddie was an O'Malley before she married Cash."

"I done good when I lassoed Maddie," Cash said. "Woman is what made this ranch what it is today. Good Irish woman is hard to come by."

"And we've all got the temper to prove it. And Raylen is the worst of the lot. That's why he's not married," Gemma said.

Colleen playfully poked her sister on the arm. "He'd be runnin' a close race to you and…"

"Don't say it." Dewar pointed.

"You got that right about my daughter." Grandma was piling her plate high. "Maddie can take a colt that's all gangly legs and turn it into a million-dollar racer."

Grandpa yelled from the dining room, "Got that from you, sugar."

Grandma grinned at Liz. "Got 'im fooled."

"Y'all come on over here and sit with us. Ain't room at that table to cuss a cat without gettin' a hair in your mouth," Dewar said when Raylen and Liz had their plates filled.

"You really interested in a job?" Jasmine asked when Liz sat down beside her.

"I could be."

Dewar reached out to steal Jasmine's hot roll and she aimed a fork at his fingers.

"Touch it and you are dead," she said.

"Don't be her friend, Liz. She's mean and hateful." Dewar grinned.

Jasmine shot right back. "Don't be his friend. He's a thief."

Liz picked up a chicken leg with her fingers and bit into it. She didn't whimper but she wanted to; it was the best chicken she'd ever eaten—crispy on the outside and tender and juicy on the inside.

Jasmine talked between bites. "Lucy usually supplies me with waitresses, but she's out of stock right now. You'd have to be there at six in the morning, but you're done about two so your afternoons and evenings would be free."

"Lucy?" Liz asked.

"It's a long story. Pearl, who's been my friend since we were toddlers, inherited a motel over in Henrietta, Texas. Short version is that she took in Lucy to help her out when Lucy's abusive husband whipped on her the last time. When Pearl and Wil married, she turned the motel over to Lucy to manage. She helps other abused women find work when they decide to get out of their bad relationships. But she doesn't have anyone to send to me right now, and Amber is leaving on Wednesday to live around her folks in northeast Arkansas."

Dewar eyed her bottle of beer, and Jasmine slapped his shoulder playfully. "You do not even want to think about touching my beer. I might stab you with my fork for messin' with my bread, but darlin', they won't even find your bones if you steal my beer."

"See," Dewar said, "I told you she was a mean old hussy."

Liz shrugged. "I'd say she's protectin' her property. Woman can't be lettin' a man come along and steal her property, can she?"

"You got that right," Jasmine said. "Me and you are going to get along just fine. So will you work for me?"

"Sure, I'll fill in until Lucy finds someone who needs a job." Liz wished she could reach up and snatch the words back into her mouth the minute they were out in the air. She should have at least slept on the idea before she took the job. She didn't need the money. She had plenty in her bank account to live a year without lifting a finger. But on the other hand, she would meet the local people, get to know them, and carve out a place in Montague County, Texas. Or else by the time the carnival was ready for another season, she'd be ready to give up her roots, slap on her wings, and fly away.

"Could you come in Tuesday and work with Amber to get the feel of it?" Jasmine asked.

"Sure. Where is it?" Liz asked.

"Right up the road a couple of miles. Same side of the highway. Next to Gemma's beauty shop," Jasmine said.

"Just waitress work, I hope. I don't cook worth a damn," Liz said.

"I do the cookin'. That's why I bought the café. Just need someone to serve it up and run a cash register. You ever done any waitressing?" Jasmine asked.

"Little bit," Liz answered. Well, running a concession

wagon was the same thing. She took orders. She served them. She took money and made change. There couldn't be a whole lot of difference.

"So tell me about your family. You from Texas?" Dewar asked.

"My whole life. Momma was born out near Amarillo, little town named Claude. I was born over in Jefferson, Texas. I guess I'm truly a third generation Texan. Just never thought about it like that until now."

"You didn't visit Haskell much, did you?" Dewar asked.

"He came to our winter place between Amarillo and Claude for Thanksgiving and Christmas every year, and we saw him in the fall of the year when we came through these parts. Grandma died when I was a little girl, but my grandfather is still alive and he's out in west Texas. But y'all knew that because that's where Uncle Haskell has relocated to help with Poppa. How long have the O'Donnells been in Ringgold?" She changed the subject.

Raylen yelled over the din of voices all talking at once. "Daddy, how long has the family been in Ringgold?"

"Hell, I don't know. Grandpa used to say we squatted in this area and they built the town around us. I expect we've been somewhere up and down the Red River border for a hundred years or more," Cash said.

"And the O'Malleys have been here every bit that long," Grandma said. "And if y'all don't eat your dinner, we ain't never goin' to get out there and do some playin'. I been lookin' forward to music all week, and all y'all want to do is jaw around. I guarantee you it's goin' to come up cold here pretty soon, what with Thanksgiving in a little more than a month, and we won't be able to play outside. Remember that year back in about ninety-one or ninety-two when the whole area iced up on Thanksgiving? Well, it can happen again. And spring is a long way off if we get an early winter."

"Yes, ma'am." Dewar grinned.

"Who are the musicians?" Liz asked.

With a wave of her hand, Jasmine took in the whole family. "They all play something or sing."

"Really? You?" She looked at Dewar.

"Dulcimer is my specialty, but I can fill in on an acoustic guitar if Rye gets tired, and I can play a little bit of fiddle," he said.

Gemma raised a hand. "Dobro and guitar."

"Colleen?" Liz asked.

"I'd be the banjo picker," she said.

"Grandma plays the dulcimer and the Dobro, and sometimes she can talk Grandpa into singing for us," Raylen said.

"Sounds like fun," Liz said.

"It is, darlin'," Grandma said, "especially if you like country music and good old Irish toe-stompin' tunes." She picked up her plate and headed for the kitchen with it. When she returned she walked right on past the dining room table and toward the door. "I'll just be warmin' up the dulcimer while y'all finish up," she said.

"She's usually not in this big of a hurry," Raylen said.

"I'm finished. I'm going on out there with her," Liz said.

"Speakin' of Thanksgiving, where are you going for the holiday?" Dewar looked at Jasmine.

"Momma would tack my scalp to the garage door if I didn't go home for the holidays. I'll close up the

Chicken Fried for the day and go have dinner with the family," Jasmine answered.

"You're welcome here if the weather gets bad," Dewar said.

"Maddie already said I was part of the family and didn't need any invitations to anything going on here, but thank you anyway. That's who I'm missin'! Where is Ace today?" Jasmine looked around the room.

Dewar chuckled. "He's over at Wil and Pearl's. Is that old ugly cowboy going to beat my time with you?"

Liz was already standing, plate in hand, but she stopped.

"You, darlin', ain't got no time to beat, and neither does Ace. He's just my friend, like you," she said.

Dewar threw a hand over his chest. "You break my heart, Jasmine."

"Yeah, right! You are full of pure, old horse hockey. Finish your dinner or Grandma is going to fuss at you," Jasmine said.

Raylen looked at Liz and explained, "Ace, Wil, and Rye were best friends. Rye and Austin got married last year in the summer, and Wil and Pearl were married in February."

"And Ace?" she asked.

"Oh, that cowboy is too pretty to settle down with one woman the rest of his life. And besides, the woman that got him would have to train him. He's not even housebroke." Jasmine laughed.

Liz smiled. That reminded her of what Aunt Tressa had said about Blaze.

He's too handsome to ever settle down. And your temper is too volatile to put up with women hanging on him and his flirting, so don't be thinking because you two aren't blood related that there could ever be a relation-ship there.

Raylen pushed back his chair, picked up his plate, and led the way to the kitchen. "I'm finished too. I'll go with you, Liz."

Grandma was warming up with "Bill Bailey." Liz sat down one of the two quilts that had been tossed out on the ground. Her skirt fluffed out around her, and Raylen sat down on the edge of it. When he tried to get up he stumbled and fell closer to her. Their feet tangled up together and both of them fell backwards with her landing in his arms up against his side like they'd been napping on the quilt.

"That was on purpose," Dewar yelled from the back porch.

Raylen moved to a sitting position. "I'm so sorry. I was trying to get off your skirt and…"

Liz laughed. "Forgiven. Accidents happen. You don't play one of those instruments?"

Raylen nodded. "Yes, I do, but I was just going to sit down here and visit with you until they all get here."

Grandma stopped playing the dulcimer and guffawed. "Don't be judgin' him too quick. He might be clumsy, but he can make a fiddle do everything but tell you a bedtime story."

Liz raised a dark eyebrow. "Oh, really. Care for a contest?"

Raylen's blue eyes bulged. "You play the fiddle? Want to show me what you've got? You can play my fiddle and I'll go in the house and get an old one."

She stood up. "Mine's in the truck. You told me if I played an instrument to bring it. You were serious, weren't you?"

"Hell, yeah, I was serious. That all you play?"

"Yep. How about you?"

Jasmine piped up from the edge of the quilt where she was settling down to listen. "Raylen is the one that can play all of them. I swear he could string up a stick with balin' wire and make it spit out a beautiful song. You sure you want to challenge him to a contest?"

"Yes, I'm sure." Liz smiled.

Raylen lost his heart that very minute when she smiled. If it hadn't been for his competitive nature born from being the third child and trying to keep up with two older brothers, that smile might have convinced him to let her win. But he just couldn't do it.

Liz brought her fiddle out of the truck. By the time she got back, Rye had handed Rachel off to Austin and picked up the guitar. Raylen adjusted the strings on a fiddle. Colleen had a banjo strapped around her neck, Gemma picked at the Dobro, Dewar had a mandolin in his arms, and Maddie had a harmonica up to her mouth running up and down it to get the feel for the right sound.

Liz tightened the strings on her fiddle, positioned it on her shoulder, and ran the bow down across them. She shook her head, made a few adjustments, and tried again. That time she was ready to play. Grandma raised an eyebrow at her and she nodded.

Rye struck up a chord, and they all fell in to begin the backyard concert with "Red River Valley," and followed that with "Bill Bailey." In the latter, Raylen had the lead and made the fiddle whine the melody.

Grandma stood up when they finished "Bill Bailey" and kissed Grandpa on the forehead. "Okay, honey. I'm goin' to sit this one out and we're goin' to have a fiddlin' contest. Liz, you know 'The Devil Went Down to Georgia'?"

Liz dragged the bow across the fiddle and the first chords of the song raised the hair on Raylen's arms. He could feel the fiery heat from hell's furnace in the chords and knew he'd met his match.

He moved closer to Liz and ran the bow across his strings. Their eyes met and the contest began with Gemma singing the song into the microphone as they fought it out without blinking. The sun held its place high in the sky, and nothing moved or breathed until the song was over and the applause began.

Liz had forgotten that there was anyone on the face of the earth but her and Raylen while she played. She'd gotten lost in his blue eyes as they played facing each other. For a minute, she wondered where the audience came from and why they were clapping, then she remembered and bowed gracefully as if she'd just finished a set on the Grand Ole Opry stage.

"You goin' to lay that fiddle on the ground since I'm better than you?" Raylen asked when the last of the notes settled.

"You lay your fiddle on the ground. I beat the devil out of you, cowboy," she said.

His blue eyes danced. "The hell you did. Ain't no one ever beat me on the fiddle."

She poked her bow at him. "Suck it up, cowboy. I beat you fair and square."

"I want a rematch," he said.

Grandma cackled. "I'd say it's a draw and we'll have a rematch next time. For now we're going to play some more. Don't be puttin' your fiddle down, girl. You're goin' to give him a run for his money the whole rest of the afternoon. Raylen, you don't get to play anything else today neither."

Grandpa nodded seriously. "The queen she-coon of Montague County has spoken. You don't mind her, and I'll hear about it all week."

Raylen shot a look at Liz.

She popped the fiddle on her shoulder and drug the bow across the strings in an old Irish song that put even a bigger smile on Grandma's face. "You sure you ain't Irish, darlin'?"

Liz winked at Grandma and kept playing.

Raylen raised an eyebrow at her and matched her note for note.

Rye picked up the tune on the guitar and Colleen did the same with the banjo. Grandma placed the dulcimer in her lap and began to strum. When that song ended Grandma went right into "Rye Whiskey," and Liz didn't miss a beat. She glanced over at Raylen and graced him with her brightest smile. The ploy didn't work. He didn't mess up.

You are flirting, Lizelle. She heard Aunt Tressa's voice and almost dropped her bow. *Less than twenty-four hours and you're letting a cowboy and a silly Christmas wish run your life, possibly even ruin it. You have the gift. I've told you that a million times, so why don't you stop fighting it and come back where you belong.*

She argued as she played. *I'm going to work on Tuesday morning. That should keep me away from him. And I'm not flirting, and I don't have any gift. I just watched you from the time I was born and learned to read people's expressions and emotions. It only takes a couple of well-placed questions and a pack of cards. There's nothing to it.*

Liz's shoulder ached by the time Granny finished the last fast tune and held up her hand. "I'm tired and ready for my Sunday nap now. You younguns can keep on playin' if you want to, but I'm retirin' to the bedroom for a rest."

Grandpa slowly made his way over to her side and held out a hand.

She passed the dulcimer off to Colleen, brushed back her gray hair, and looked up into his eyes. "Thank you, darlin'."

He looped her arm into his. "Anything for my sweetheart."

Aunt Tressa, where are you? Did you see that? That's what I want for Christmas: a love like theirs.

Before Aunt Tressa's voice could argue with her, Jasmine hollered from the quilt, "Hey, Liz. You want to follow me to the Chicken Fried? I'll show you around a little while it's empty, and you'll know where it is."

"Love to." Liz opened her fiddle case, loosened the strings, and put her instrument away.

Raylen could have strangled Jasmine King right there in front of Grandma, Dewar, and even God.

Chapter 3

THE BUFFET AT THE CAFÉ IN BOWIE WAS FILLED FROM one end to the other with comfort food. It was a very different café than the Chicken Fried where she and Jasmine had gone the day before. This was a buffet; Jasmine's place was an old-fashioned plate lunch type of café where people sat down, ordered from a menu, and waited for their food to be served.

Liz was hungry enough that the pinto beans cooked with ham, fried okra and crispy brown squash, hash brown casserole, corn bread, and roast beef all looked good. Marva Jo called it comfort food. Aunt Tressa called it sin on a plate. Uncle Haskell called it down home cooking.

When she placed her tray on a corner table for two people, she couldn't believe that she'd put so much food on it. There was enough there for her, Tressa, Marva, and even Blaze. And Blaze could eat a small cow when he was hungry. Thank goodness she'd paid at the door and it was all-you-can-eat, but still she blushed slightly when she unloaded the bowls and plates from the tray.

"Mind if I join you?" Raylen asked.

He was close enough that she could smell his after-shave and feel the warmth of his breath against the soft part of her neck right below her earlobe. She jerked her head around and looked right into his blue eyes, not a foot away.

"Raylen?"

"I'm not stalking you," he stammered.

She eased into her chair and motioned for him to sit across from her. "I didn't think you were."

He set his plate and bowls off the tray and reached to take hers. Their hands brushed in the transfer and she got that same feeling she'd had on Saturday night when he was close enough to kiss her, and on Sunday when he guided her through the O'Donnell house with his hand on her back. It was tingly enough to put butterflies in her stomach. And had enough electricity to paste a silly grin on her face that even biting her lip couldn't erase.

Raylen set the trays on a nearby cart and pulled out a chair across from her. He was twenty-eight years old and no one had ever affected him like Liz did. He'd dated a lot of drop-dead gorgeous cowgirls, and a few pretty ladies who didn't know the back end of a horse from the front end of a tractor. He'd even fancied himself in love a few times, but a jolt of pure desire had never heated him up when he touched one of those women's fingertips like it did when he just brushed against Liz.

"I was down here loading up on seed and fertilizer. What are you doing in Bowie?" he asked.

"I've got to stock up at Walmart," she said. "Basics like cleansers, and I'm going to buy five books today because I can put them on my bookcase and not have to donate them to the next library," she said.

"Why couldn't you keep them before now?"

"I've lived with my mother in a fifth wheel trailer my whole life. We don't have room except for the necessities. I was twenty-five this past August and was thinking about getting my own trailer. I already have a truck big

enough to pull it, and I can have a riggin' put in the bed
to hook up to with no problem. But Uncle Haskell left
me his land, and I'm talking too much." She blushed.

"I'll still buy that land anytime you want to sell,"
Raylen said.

"It's not for sale," she said.

"Okay, but just remember to call me if you change
your mind and decide to buy that trailer. So what did you
think of the café? Are you going to really take a waitress
job?" He changed the subject.

She nodded.

"It's tough work," he said.

"I'm a tough woman," she said.

Raylen chuckled.

"What's so funny?"

"You don't look so tough."

"Oh? What can you tell about me just by lookin'?"

He started at her forehead and scanned all the way to
where the table top met her breasts, then leaned back,
looked under the table, and let his eyes travel down
the length of her legs to her black high-heeled shoes.
It might be rude by any other standard, but she'd chal-
lenged him and that made it legal for him to look his fill.

He picked up her hands and turned them over to look
at the palms. Touching her hands proved that the air
around them did sizzle when they touched. He took his
time studying them so he didn't have to let go.

Finally, he said, "Okay, you don't work with your
hands. They don't have calluses like someone who
works hard for a living. They're also not dry and wrin-
kled like someone who's done a job that involved lots of
water like dishwashing. You are fit, so that means you

either work out at an expensive gym or do some kind of exercising. I'd say you come from a wealthy background and don't know jack shit about keeping house or taking care of twenty acres of land. How'd I do?"

He still had her hands in his when someone stopped at their table and laid her hand possessively on Raylen's shoulder. "Well, hello…" She drew both words out in a long southern drawl. "…Raylen O'Donnell. Where have you been keeping yourself, darlin'? I haven't seen you in weeks."

Raylen dropped Liz's hands. "Been busy, Becca."

Liz looked up at the hussy who'd just wrecked her palm reading. She'd liked the way her small hands fit into Raylen's big old rough cowboy hands, and she'd damn sure liked the sparks that shot every which way when he touched her. Liz wished that Becca, whoever the hell she was, would drop dead right there in the café.

The woman pushed back her blond hair but didn't take her hand off Raylen's shoulder. Dammit! Liz had asked if he was married and he'd stuttered like a ten-year-old who'd got caught with a *Playboy* magazine. But she hadn't asked if he was engaged or had a girl-friend. Dammit! Dammit!

Liz took better stock of the tall woman. Her blond hair was cut short, and she wore designer jeans, fancy cowboy boots, and an orange Western blouse that looked custom-made. Not a working cowgirl but a fancy one that would take a cowboy's eye. Double dammit!

The look Becca gave Liz said the war was on.

"Who's this?" Becca asked.

"I'm sorry," Raylen said. "This is my neighbor, Haskell's niece, Liz. She's moved into his place."

"Well, well, well," Becca said. "Has Raylen offered you market price on the place?"

"It's nice to meet you, and my place isn't for sale at any price," Liz said.

Becca leaned down and put her other hand, the one that wasn't on Raylen's shoulder, on the table in front of Liz. "I'll give you three times what the going price is for that land."

"Why? Is there gold or oil under the topsoil?" Liz asked.

Becca stood up straight and laughed aloud. "It's not what's under the dirt or even on top of the dirt that I'm interested in. It's what lives next door. See you around, Raylen." She blew Raylen a kiss as she left, hips swaying and hand-tooled boots tapping on the wood floor.

Liz looked across the table at Raylen.

"What?" Raylen asked.

Liz shrugged. "Guess I'm sitting on a gold mine since *you* live next door. If I sold, would I owe you a commission?"

Raylen's face registered shock. "Me?"

"Who else lives next door?"

"Dewar," Raylen said.

"So is Becca interested in Dewar? Does Jasmine know?"

Raylen threw both hands up. "Jasmine isn't Dewar's girlfriend. Becca has been my best friend since grade school. We're just good friends. She's a handful and speaks her mind, but she's just my friend."

"So then it's not a love triangle?"

Raylen stuttered and stammered, "A what?"

"Never mind. So why does she want my land?"

"She lives down close to Stoneburg on a cattle ranch. And since we're friends, I guess she wants to live close to my family. Hell, I didn't even know she was interested in buying land in Ringgold. Her daddy owns three fourths of Stoneburg," he said.

"I see," Liz said.

Becca didn't really love Raylen. She put on a show for some strange reason, but she didn't love him. Her hand had rested possessively on his shoulder, but her eyes did not glitter when she looked at him. They did not say that she could stretch him out on a plate like a Christmas ham and devour him like Liz could.

The image of Raylen without jeans, boots, and a shirt that strained at the arm seams made Liz so hot that her insides went all gushy and warm. She sipped ice cold sweet tea, but it didn't help much when she shut her eyes and caught an imaginary glimpse of him from behind wearing nothing but his sweat-stained straw work hat. She squeezed her eyes shut tightly and willed him to turn around in her vision, but he broke the spell when he spoke.

"Becca is my friend and she never likes..." he stopped himself before he said, "any of my girlfriends," then he took a long sip of tea and said, "any of my other girl type friends. Tell me about you. So you grew up in a travel trailer. Why?"

Her eyes snapped open and she was only slightly amazed to see him still dressed and pushing back his dinner plate. "I was born a carnie. My grandparents were carnies. My mother and her sister are carnies even yet. Didn't Uncle Haskell tell you?"

"Carnie? That a family name?"

Liz laughed. "Carnie as in carnival. Did you ever go to the carnival when it was in Bowie?"

Raylen cocked his head to one side. "Are you serious?"

"I am very serious. My grandparents owned the carnival. When Nanna died, Poppa, that's my grandfather, bought a small trailer to live in and gave it to his daughters since Uncle Haskell didn't want any part of that kind of life. He parked it on their land out in west Texas, not far from Amarillo, but he refuses to take the wheels off or skirt the thing. It's where we winter from the end of November until the first of March. We do maintenance, paint, grease, and whatever else is needed to put the show back on the road in the spring. Each year there's evidence that's Grandpa is growing roots, but he'll never admit it. The carnival was doing a gig in Jefferson, Texas, when Mother had me, so I've truly been a carnie all my life. If you came to the carnival in Bowie when you were a little boy, our paths have probably crossed in the past."

Raylen nodded. He'd thought his older brother, Rye, was crazy when he fell hard and fast for Austin, a big city girl with a big city job. There was no way Austin would ever leave everything she'd worked toward her entire life and move to tiny little Terral, Oklahoma, to run a watermelon farm. But Austin had roots. Liz had never had any at all, so chances of her falling for a deeply rooted rancher were slim and none.

"Haskell never showed interest in the carnival?" Raylen asked.

Liz smiled. "It was a sore spot between him and his sisters. One is my mother and the other is my aunt."

"Why?" Raylen asked.

"Uncle Haskell wanted to settle down when he met Aunt Sara. He left the carnival and bought that piece of property, then worked for a company in Nocona until they could make the ranch pay its way. They wanted a house full of kids, but Aunt Sara couldn't have any. I barely remember her. She died when I was about five, but she always came to the carnival in Bowie and brought me homemade cookies."

Raylen finished his dinner and sipped sweet tea. "I was eight when Miss Sara died. It was one of the first funerals I went to. I don't remember seeing you there."

"Aunt Tressa and Poppa came. Mother kept the carnival going."

"How did you go to school?" he asked.

"I didn't. Aunt Tressa and Momma homeschooled me just like their momma did them. I got my associate's degree in business online before my sixteenth birthday. Momma said I could stay off the carnival rounds a couple of years and get my bachelor's degree, but I didn't want to."

"So you ran the business end of the carnival?"

Liz shook her head. "I'm not strong enough to wrestle that from Aunt Tressa. She's the financial head. I'm Madam Lizelle, The Great Drabami."

"The great what?"

"Drabami. It's a gypsy word for fortune-teller. I tell fortunes, read your palm, lay out the cards, or look into the big crystal ball, and..." She took a deep breath. Might was well spit it all out and hold nothing back.

"And what?" Raylen asked.

"I belly dance," she said.

Raylen kept eating and didn't answer.

Liz wondered if he hadn't heard her before he finally said something.

"You are waiting for me to bite. I'm not going to. You're not going to catch me with that story." He grinned.

"It's the truth. Throw your palm out here."

Raylen wiped his hand on his jean leg and flipped it out on the table. She picked it up with her left hand and cradled it in her right. She'd held men's hands in hers since she was sixteen when she did her first reading, but nothing prepared her for the sparks that danced around the café when she traced the curve of his lifeline from the middle of his wrist around his thumb.

"You will have a long and productive life, Raylen O'Donnell. You will have one successful marriage and fate will play a big part in your choice of a partner." She almost stopped there because her mother had read her palm with the same words not a week before, but she gently traced another line and said, "You let your head rule and not your heart, but that will change. Don't be afraid. It's in your future and you will fear giving up control, but in the end you will see the wisdom in allowing love to come into your heart."

He pulled his hand back with a jerk. "That sounds like a bunch of hocus-pocus to me. So are you puttin' in a fortune tellin' shop in Ringgold?"

"Hell, no! I'm going to work for Jasmine starting tomorrow mornin'," she said.

He was careful to look at her full lips and not her black eyes. "I still think you are pulling my leg about that fortune tellin' business, but I do believe you about going to work for Jasmine. I'm glad. She needs help and she's my friend. You'll like working with her. Well, I've got to get back to work. See you around."

"Come over sometime and I'll get out the cards and

do a real reading for you. I might even put on my costume and dance for you," she said.

"Still not biting!" He waved over his shoulder.

She finished her tea and tossed a couple of bills on the table for a tip. She'd planned to grab a hamburger at the Dairy Queen and hit Walmart for supplies when she left Ringgold that morning. But she'd seen the café on the west side of the highway as she came into town, and there were two police cars as well as dozens of trucks in the parking lot. Any place where ranchers and police both ate had to be good, and she had not been disappointed. Besides, she'd just had lunch with Raylen.

She fished her phone from her purse and punched in the first number on speed dial. Blaze picked up on the first ring.

"Hey, so was I right? Are you on your way home?" he asked.

"Hell, no, you weren't right and you had no right to yell at me. But I couldn't wait for you to stop sulking to tell you about Raylen." She laughed and went on to tell him about Raylen being there and the past two days. "And I've got a job starting in the morning."

"You won't last," Blaze said. "Some people are born to be still. Others to travel. Me and you are travelers, sweetheart."

"Want to bet?" she asked.

"No, I don't want to take your money. You're goin' to need it to buy a trailer."

"I'm hanging up on that note. Good-bye, Blaze," she said.

"Bye, sweetheart," he said.

A warm wind blew up from the south, swirling leaves

around her truck tires. Black birds hopped around in search of free food but found very little. Liz wished she'd tucked the leftover corn bread into her purse to give them. Next time she'd remember that they were there.

She opened the door to the Silverado truck and slid into the driver's seat. She put in a Christmas CD called *Now That's What I Call a Country Christmas* that she'd gotten the year before. Kellie Pickler made Liz smile when she sang "Santa Baby" and talked about her Christmas list. Liz's list wasn't long. Maybe, just maybe, Santa would have time to throw that last item in the sleigh and she'd get her cowboy by Christmas.

She'd gone through the house and made a list of household items along with dog food, cat food, and laundry detergent. It would be strange to wash clothes at home. Monday morning was wash time in their carnival business. The crew tore down the carnival, got the animals into the trucks, and got everything ready to roll to the next location. Those who weren't busy with that job used the time to visit the local coin operated laundry. Tuesday and Wednesday were travel days, with the hopes of arriving at their next gig sometime before dark on Wednesday. From the time they pulled into the parking lot, pasture, or wherever they were paid to set up, a flurry of activity took place to get things ready for the opening night, which was usually Thursday. Then it was nonstop work until Sunday evening when they turned off the lights and started tearing down again.

Laundry day was the day that Liz had time to look through magazines. Even if they were years old, she loved poring over the pictures of the insides of houses, especially the before and after ones. Now she had a house of her own and she could redo it any way she wanted. But other than moving around the furniture, she wasn't sure she wanted to do anything at all to the house.

She talked to herself as she drove. "Nothing other than decorate it for Christmas with twinkling lights and lots of stuff. Plain old Christmas stuff that I can keep from one year to the next. I don't care if I have a whole room full of it. Right now there are two empty bedrooms and I can store it all there."

Walmart was all the way across town, but she wasn't in a big hurry so she drove slowly, taking a long look at the storefronts. She'd been in Bowie once a year ever since she was born. She knew where the grocery store was located, right along with Walmart, the old location and the new one, the laundry, and the Dairy Queen. Aside from that, until that day, nothing else mattered. But now she noticed a couple of furniture stores, a western wear store, banks, and several other places that looked interesting.

She snagged a parking place close to the door and checked the price of gas. It was two cents cheaper at the place next to Walmart than in town so she made a mental note to fill up before she left town. Tomorrow, she'd get up early and go to work at Jasmine's Chicken Fried café, but that afternoon she took her time in the store, looking at the new fall shirts and jackets before she started filling her cart with items from her list.

She didn't even see Becca until their carts came within an inch of crashing together as she rounded the end of an aisle and came face-to-face with her.

"Well, hello again, Libby," Becca said.

"It's Liz, not Libby. And hello to you," Liz said.

Becca leaned on her overloaded cart filled with

large bags of dog food. "So you all moved into Haskell's place?"

Liz pushed her cart to one side. "Yes, I am. It was nice seeing you again, Becca."

Becca reached out and grabbed the side of the cart. "Sure you don't want to sell?"

Liz shook her head. "I'm very sure. It's not even mine until spring. Uncle Haskell is letting me live there, but I still have the option of changing my mind."

"And if you stay?" Becca asked.

"Then it's my property," Liz said.

Blaze would like Becca for sure. He tended to go for women with blond hair and green eyes, and he really liked tall, tough women who dressed like Becca. Blaze and Becca... it even sounded good together. She fit all the criteria, but Blaze didn't stick with anyone more than a week or two, so the bubble in her imagination about Becca running off to help in a carnival burst with a loud bang.

"So what kind of work do you do?" Becca asked.

Becca was being downright nosy and it didn't sit well with Liz, who was tempted to blurt out her whole life story just to watch Becca's jaw hit the floor.

"Right now I'm going to work as a waitress at the Chicken Fried café for Jasmine. I start work in the morning," Liz answered.

"How long have you known Raylen?" Becca asked.

Now we get to the real reason she's created this cart wreck in the middle of the store. I would do the same thing for Blaze.

"If you count from the first time we met, about fifteen years. But I'd only seen him twice before I moved into Uncle Haskell's house," Liz said.

Aunt Tressa's advice was loud and clear in her mind. *Keep a poker face and don't give away jack shit. Watch their expressions and you'll learn enough to give you a good reading.*

Becca cocked her head to one side and frowned. *Confusion. Disbelief.*

Liz turned the tables and watched Becca's expressions. "So you went to school with him and you have always lived in this area?"

"That's right. Raylen and I have roots that go deep," Becca said. At the mention of his name her eyes should have lit up like a tilt-a-whirl, but they didn't. Her mouth said words; her eyes didn't back them up.

"Well, I'd better be going. I've got a ton of work to do before work time tomorrow morning," Liz said.

Becca didn't move her cart.

"Waitress, huh?" She smiled again. *Pure happiness.* Evidently she figured Raylen would never be interested in a waitress.

"That's right. You ever eat at Chicken Fried?" Liz asked.

"Oh, yeah. Love Jasmine's food. She has chocolate cream pie on Friday, so that's my regular day. Raylen loves it. He and Dewar usually drop by on that day. Raylen is a chicken fried steak guy and Dewar likes Jasmine's double cheeseburgers," Becca said.

Happiness brings about confidence, Aunt Tressa said. *Confidence loosens the tongue, and that's when you keep your mouth shut and listen.*

Liz nodded. "Maybe I'll see you there at the end of the week, then."

An upward tilt of the chin said she'd won the fight. "Oh, I'm sure you will. Raylen and I eat there pretty often."

Liz pushed her cart to the right and disappeared around the end of the next aisle as quickly as possible.

"Well, hello," Colleen said.

Liz flashed a brilliant smile but inside she was groaning. All she did was eat lunch with Raylen. It wasn't even a date. She'd paid for her own dinner and simply sat with him. Why did she feel like she was being punished?

Colleen studied her like she was a bug under a microscope. "I hear you had lunch with my brother."

Liz tried to keep a blank expression like she'd been taught, but it was impossible.

Colleen shrugged. "He called to tell me to pick up a few things since I'm already here."

"Well, rats! If I'd known you were shopping for the neighborhood, I'd have called you with my list," Liz teased.

Colleen shook her head. "It's only because he's my brother that he can weasel me into getting him dish soap and a bag of potatoes. Anything more and he'd be in here himself."

"Well, I've got to get back to the pet aisle. See you around," Liz said.

"You take that job at Jasmine's place?" Colleen asked.

Liz nodded.

"You always been a waitress?"

"Of sorts."

"Where?" Colleen asked.

"All over the state of Texas, some in Oklahoma, and over in Arkansas. We traveled a lot." Liz pushed her cart past Colleen's and hurried to the back of the store.

Her phone rang when she was safely hidden in the

aisle with the pet food. She dug it out of her purse, saw that it was her mother, and pushed the button to answer it.

"Hello, Momma," she said.

"We're on the move. Next stop is Bells, Texas. You always liked that little town. Why don't you meet us there and give up this notion of living like the rest of the world?"

"After only two days? No, thank you. Besides, I've got a job. I'm going to work at the Chicken Fried café in the morning." Liz picked up a dozen cans of fancy cat food and put them in her cart.

"Doing what?" Marva Jo asked.

"Waitress for minimum wage," Liz told her.

Marva Jo laughed so loud that Liz held the phone out from her ear.

"What's so funny?"

Marva hiccupped. "Now I know you'll come home to the carnival where you belong. You doing waitress work… girl, you haven't worked for that kind of money since you were fourteen. I couldn't have asked for a better job to teach you a lesson."

"I don't need the money, so it doesn't matter," Liz argued.

"Okay, let's talk about the cowboy next door. Did you tell him that you don't have to work, that you have an inheritance big enough to buy his piece of Texas dirt?" Marva changed the subject.

"I had lunch with him. And yesterday I went to his parent's house for Sunday dinner and music afterwards. And no, I didn't tell him anything about money. Why would I? I don't think it would be right to say, 'Hey, Raylen, I'm rich.' But he did damn near beat me in a fiddlin' contest," Liz said.

"Dammit!" Marva Jo exclaimed.

"Is that not as funny as the minimum wage?" Liz asked.

"No, it is not! You slow that wagon down, girl. You know very well that you don't belong with a *gadjo*."

Liz sucked in a lung full of air and got ready for the age old argument. "We are carnies, not gypsies. You married a *gadjo*. So what's to say if I fall in love with a *gadjo* that it…"

Aunt Tressa butted into the conversation. "Don't argue with your momma, and learn from her mistakes. She married a *gadjo* and it did not work. I don't care if you grow potatoes and marry a dirt farmer, but you will be nice to your momma. She misses you and wants you to come back where you belong. And Haskell might have mentioned that his niece has a nice big bank account, so be sure that *gadjo* isn't angling for more than twenty acres of tumbleweeds and chiggers."

"You riding with her, are you? And Raylen isn't that kind of man. If he loved a woman he wouldn't care if she had a dime or a million dollars," Liz said.

"Yes, I am, and you can't out-argue two old gypsy gals, so give it up."

"I'm hanging up and getting my shopping finished. Love you both. Oh, oh! I see the Christmas aisle. Can't wait to see you next month. I'm putting up the Christmas tree early so you can see it."

Chapter 4

LIZ UNLOADED ALL HER PURCHASES, WHICH INCLUDED three bags of Christmas ornaments for her tree. She laid them on the kitchen table and admired each and every one of the bright shiny bells and balls. She'd looked at a six-foot tree but couldn't make up her mind whether to get a tall skinny one or one of those huge fat ones. She left the kitchen and looked at the living room. If she scooted the sofa back, there would be plenty of room for a big, round tree with lots and lots of ornaments and a star on top.

She put her hand on her cheek and drew her eyes down, envisioning a real cedar tree in the spot. No, as long as she planned to leave a tree up, a real one would be entirely too messy. She went back to the kitchen and was stacking cans of cat and dog food in the pantry when the phone rang. Thinking it was her mother and Tressa again, she ignored it, but when it started again after less than a minute interval she fished it out of her purse.

"Hello," she said.

"Hey, kid. Thought I'd check on Hooter and Blister. I forgot to tell you that their vet papers are in the drawer beside the refrigerator. Hooter will need his shots in February and Blister gets hers in March," Haskell said.

"Okay, guess what? I bought ornaments for my Christmas tree today and there's plenty of room for me to store them, and do you have a fake tree hiding some-where or did you cut a real one every year, and..."

"Whoa!" Haskell laughed. "Slow down, Lizelle! You know how Sara liked Christmas, or maybe you didn't since you were so little. Them days, I always cut a real tree. But the last few years, I just put up a little bought one because the real ones shed so bad. Can't keep enough water in the pan to keep them happy."

"That's what I figured. I'm going to buy a big one and I'm going to have a house that puts the stars to shame," she said.

Haskell laughed. "Then, darlin', go out to the barn and look in the tack room and the loft. There's surprises out there for you."

"What barn?" Liz asked.

"The one behind the house."

"I thought that was O'Donnell property."

Haskell laughed again. "Kind of hard to picture twenty acres when you've lived in a trailer your whole life, isn't it?"

"I figured it went from fence to fence after I left the highway and then to the back side of the yard," she said.

"You're right until you get to the back side of the yard. Now go on back to the barn and then to the fence back behind that. Then you've got twenty acres. The Christmas stuff is in boxes, and they are all marked."

Liz squealed. "You mean I've got a whole barn to put stuff in? I may go back to Walmart this afternoon."

"So you like it there?" Haskell asked.

"Been here two days and I'm not ready to run yet," she said. "And I go to work tomorrow morning."

"Lizelle, you don't have to work," Haskell said.

"I know, but I want to. It'll get me acquainted with more folks than the O'Donnells. Did I tell you that I had Sunday dinner with them yesterday and I played my fiddle and Raylen and I had a contest? I beat that cowboy, but his grandma called it a tie," she said.

Haskell chuckled again. "They are good people, the O'Donnells. Been fine neighbors all these years. Raise some of the best horses in the whole state. You could be ridin' horses, exercising them for the O'Donnells instead of working at a café," he said.

"But I want to work at the café. I can't wait. It's going to be so much fun," Liz said.

"How's Blister and Hooter?" Haskell changed the subject.

"Spoiled and I'm making them even worse. How are you doing out there, Uncle Haskell? Tell me the truth."

"Much better than I thought. Dad and I are getting along and looking forward to the girls being here a couple of months. We're cleaning up the big barn so we can pull in a trailer at a time and do some serious repainting and repair. He's excited about all three of us being here together and he's even considering letting me underpin his trailer before serious winter sets in."

"Wow! That's a miracle." Liz breathed a very quiet sigh of relief. Uncle Haskell sounded busy and happy so he wouldn't want his land and house back in the spring, hopefully!

"I thought so too, but he's minding the cold more since he's older and I told him it would make his trailer warmer. Got to go now. I see him headed out to the repair barn. If I don't get out there soon, he'll do too much."

She barely had time to utter "love you" before Haskell cut the connection. She hurried to the kitchen window and looked out at the barn… her barn. She couldn't wait to snoop around, so she rushed back to her bedroom, kicked off her shoes, stomped her feet down into cowboy boots, and grabbed her denim jacket.

"Merry Christmas to me," she sang as she headed out the back door toward the big metal barn. Not only did she have a house without wheels, she had a barn, which meant that she didn't have to be careful about what she hauled onto the place because she had tons of storage room. Hell's bells, she could park the carnie trailer that she'd lived in her entire life inside that big building and have room left over.

She slid the door back and the smell of hay, feed, and leather all hit her nose at the same time. She'd grown up accustomed to that odor, only it came from a small pen where the riding ponies were kept. They'd had Shetland ponies when she was a little girl, but as they got too old for the carnival, Tressa had replaced them with Gypsy Vanner horses, and Liz had fallen in love with them. The extra tuft of hair on their feet made them look like they were flying when they pranced.

"I could have some right here. I could breed Gypsy Vanners and have baby colts. There's plenty of room for a pair." She wandered through the big building, discovering a riding lawn mower and a small tractor. And a momma cat with a litter of kittens hid in the back corner, but they were all so wild that she couldn't get near them.

Located in the northeast corner of the barn, the tack room was about the size of her living room. Shelves lined the walls, and the leather smell overpowered the hay and feed smell when she opened the door. Boxes of every size and shape were shoved in the shelves and were labeled in Haskell's spidery handwriting.

She pulled an old ladder-back chair with chipped paint over from the table where Haskell repaired and cleaned saddles, bits, and bridles. She hopped up on it and grabbed the first box she could reach. It wasn't heavy, but when she moved it the dust flew into her hair, her nose, and eyes. Once the box was on the table she opened it with a knife she found on a bottom shelf.

The squeal rivaled the one when she found out the barn was hers. Inside the box she found old-fashioned Christmas lights. The kind with big, multicolored bulbs, and they had been wrapped carefully around a cardboard tube. She wouldn't even have to waste hours and hours untangling them when she got ready to put them up.

"Bless your heart," Liz said as she looked up to see dozens of other boxes marked Christmas.

The next one she removed very gently so the dust didn't gag or blind her. It held more lights, as did the third, fourth, and fifth ones. The sixth one was filled with ornaments wrapped individually in newspaper. She undid each one, lining them up on the table as she did. The next one had a nativity scene that would look lovely on the mantel, just like she'd imagined.

"It's Christmas before Christmas," she said.

―――――

Glorious Danny Boy, a solid black quarter horse, pulled at the reins, but Raylen kept him to a steady trot the first time around the pasture. Danny Boy had put the O'Donnell Horse Ranch on the map that year, and when Maddie and Cash won the title again the next year with Major Jack, it became famous. Nowadays, Maddie and Cash raised horses but didn't race them. Glorious Danny

Boy and Major Jack had such sought after bloodlines that she was particular about what mares she'd even allowed to carry one of their colts. And each year, she sold half a dozen of her own prize colts sired by Danny Boy or Jack.

Raylen finally gave the big black stud enough rein to let him gallop around the pasture.

"Feel like you are back in the race, do you?" Raylen asked.

Danny Boy slowed down to a slow walk and went straight for the pasture fence. He neighed and several mares raised their heads.

"Checkin' on your harem? I can barely keep up with one woman at a time, old man." Raylen chuckled.

He hooked a leg over the saddle horn and let Danny Boy visit with his women for a spell while he thought of Liz. He remembered Wil telling him about the night his wife, Pearl, convinced him that her full name was Minnie Pearl Richland.

"Nice try, Liz Hanson. You might be a carnie but belly dancin'? Come on, lady, I didn't just fall off the hay wagon, and you are not going to snooker me like Pearl did Wil," he said.

Was Liz's last name Hanson? Haskell's last name was Hanson, so it stood to reason that her mother and aunt were Hansons. But if her mother was married, then Liz's name wouldn't be Hanson. She hadn't mentioned a father, not even when she was trying to make him believe that bunch of bullshit about belly dancing.

"I bet if I'd said I'd be over at six thirty for a belly dancin' demonstration she would have backtracked, by damn," he said.

Danny Boy took a step backwards. His mares were all fine and there was a fence between him and them so he was ready to run some more. Raylen had just made the second round in the pasture when he noticed the barn door over at Haskell's place was wide open. He reined in and dismounted.

"My turn," he told the horse as he looped the reins to the rail fence.

He jumped the fence and was almost to the barn when he heard a squeal. He picked up the pace and followed the next scream to the tack room. It was most likely fear of a mouse, but it could be that she'd fallen or hurt herself. He slung open the door to find her with half a dozen open boxes surrounding her on the floor as well as on the table.

"Liz, are you okay?" he asked.

She jumped and squealed again. "Dammit! Raylen, you scared the hell out of me."

"Well, you scared me. I heard you yelp and thought you were hurt," he said.

"It was excitement, not hurt," she said. "I found all these gorgeous old decorations so I can make my house pretty for Christmas. Want to help me?"

He raised an eyebrow. "Tonight?"

"No, but before Thanksgiving. Momma and Aunt Tressa are coming the week before Thanksgiving and I want it decorated by then." She held up a gold ornament to glitter in the light from the window.

"Sure," he said.

"What are you doing over here? Have you been riding?"

"Exercising horses. That's my afternoon job several days a week. Why? Do I smell like a horse?"

"Little bit. I'll trade off help. You help me get my house decorated by the time my family gets here, and after Thanksgiving I'll help you exercise the horses. I love horses."

"You ride?" That was as believable as belly dancing.

She laid her ornaments to the side. "Our carnival has pony rides for the kids. We used to have Shetlands, but now we have Gypsy Vanners. Ever heard of them? I ride in the winter months every single day. And Poppa has bigger horses out on the property, the ones that we can't use for the carnival but he can't bring himself to sell. So, yes, I ride."

He threw up his palms. "Sorry I doubted you. And yes, I've heard of Gypsy Vanners. Dewar could talk for hours about Vanner horses. He's been buggin' Momma to invest in a pair, but she won't have none of it. She told him if he wanted to play with the fancy horses then to go ahead, but to keep them on his property. And I'll take you up on that offer. I'll help decorate the house if you'll help me exercise the horses," Raylen said.

"Good. Dewar will have to come to the carnival and see Aunt Tressa's four Vanners. They're spoiled rotten, and she treats them like babies."

Liz's pulse picked up the tempo and her hands began to sweat. If Raylen O'Donnell knew how many times she'd whispered his name in the past eleven years, he'd scoot right back across the fence and never come back. Back when she was fourteen she'd wanted him to kiss her so bad that she dreamed about it. And now the feeling was back with all the ache and pain that went with it.

Raylen leaned on the edge of the table and pretended interest in the boxes. But what really made his blood race was Liz in those cowboy boots and snug fitting jeans. She'd been dressed like that when they were both teenagers that fall when he'd exercised Major Jack, getting him ready for the big race. He'd wanted to be a jockey but even though he was the shortest O'Donnell brother at five feet ten inches, he was still too big to qualify as a jockey. But what he'd wanted more than that was to show off for the pretty girl who hung on the fence rail and watched him. Her eyes had mesmerized him even then, and he'd wanted so badly to taste those sexy lips.

"Well, I left my horse out back, tied up to the fence. Saw the barn door open and thought I'd better check on things," Raylen said.

Liz moved around the table. "I'll walk with you. Is it the same horse you rode back when we were kids?"

He nodded.

She fell into step beside him. "Uncle Haskell said y'all have two over there that folks stand in line to get a chance at their bloodlines. He told me their names but I forgot."

"Glorious Danny Boy. That'd be him right there." Raylen pointed. "And Major Jack. They both won the Texas Heritage Stakes and made the ranch what it is today. O'Donnell Ranch has a dozen blue blooded mares that Momma and Daddy use to raise colts from those two. She's got a long list of folks interested in buying a colt from either one of them."

Liz reached up and ran her hand down the length of his nose and he nuzzled her hair.

"He's a beauty," she said.

"You like horses, do you?"

She nodded. "And cats and dogs and cows."

"Tell me the truth. You were raised on a ranch out in west Texas, weren't you?"

She looked up into his sexy blue eyes. "I was raised in a carnival. I tell fortunes and do some belly dancin' to bring in the crowd when Aunt Tressa or Momma is telling fortunes. We winter out near Claude, Texas, from the last of November until the first week March, and Poppa likes animals."

He leaned forward and fell into the depths of her dark eyes. She moistened her upper lip with the tip of her tongue and his pulse raced.

It was a slow-motion experience. The closer his mouth got to hers, the hotter the liquid in the pits of her belly got. When his lips claimed hers in a hard kiss she kissed back with all the passion in her soul.

Dear Lord, if he'd have kissed me like this when I was fourteen, I'd have never left Uncle Haskell's place, she thought when he broke the kiss and took a step back.

"I been wantin' to do that for eleven years," he said and walked away whistling.

She watched him mount up and gallop off like a cowboy in an old Western movie. When there wasn't even a dot on the horizon left, she reached up and touched her lips. They felt like they'd just sucked on a jalapeno pepper, but they were cool as a snowball.

Chapter 5

LIZ SAT STRAIGHT UP IN BED AND SLAPPED THE ALARM clock so hard that it bounced off the far bedroom wall and still kept buzzing. What was she thinking, telling Jasmine that she'd be at the café at six o'clock in the morning? Somewhere in the Good Book, there had to be a verse that said, "Thou shalt never see the pearly gates if thou riseth out of thy bed whilst it is still dark outside."

She threw herself back on the pillows, but the alarm clock sounded even louder, pitching a buzzing hissy upside down on the hardwood floor. Finally, she threw off the covers and crossed the room, picked up the indestructible varmint, and pushed the off button. She trudged to the bathroom, flipped on the light, and covered her eyes with the back of her hand.

It was a cardinal sin to be awake at five o'clock, and a glance toward the mirror proved it. Liz's black hair looked like a whole nest of rats had had a hell of a party in it while she slept. She grabbed a brush and went to work, sweeping it up into a ponytail and twisting it into a sloppy bun. She slapped on barely enough makeup to be presentable in public and went back to the bedroom. Jasmine said jeans and a T-shirt was fine and that she provided aprons.

Her eyes were still half shut when she picked up her purse and keys from the kitchen table and stumbled out into the darkness. Hooter looked up from the corner of the porch with mournful eyes, and Blister ran to her empty food dish.

"Well, shit! I can't leave until I feed the livestock," Liz grumbled as she went back inside the house.

She filled the food dishes and made sure there was fresh water and headed toward her pickup truck again.

"Good mornin'," Raylen said cheerfully as he hopped over the fence in a swift movement.

Liz glared at him. "It's five thirty in the morning. What is good about that?"

"Going to be a beautiful day. Sun will be rising in another hour. Thought I'd stop by and tell you good luck on your first day at work. I'm getting ready to plow that field right there." He pointed toward the tractor sitting on the other side of the fence.

Too damn bad Hooter and Blister won't eat green stuff right off the land, she thought.

"Thank you for the good luck," she said.

He hurried to the truck and opened the door for her. "Have a good day."

"How can you be so happy at this time of day?" she asked.

"I'm an early riser. Love the morning when things are just waking up," he answered.

She brushed against him and the electricity between them woke her up so fast it made her head swim. So the fire in his kiss wasn't a one-time episode.

"See you later. Have a good day," he said as he slammed her truck door shut.

—⁓—

Liz drove out to the end of the lane and turned north. It

was a good thing he hadn't kissed her or she'd have been tempted to drag him back into the house for a romp in that big old soft bed. By the carnie Bible she was already sinning by getting up before the sun; she might as well go to hell for a big sin as a little one. She had a smile on her face when she opened the door to the café and found Jasmine in the kitchen.

"Hey, come on back here and get a cup of coffee. It'll be about ten or fifteen minutes before the crowd starts wandering in," Jasmine yelled.

Liz followed the aroma of coffee blended with bacon and sausage through the dining room and into the kitchen. Jasmine pointed at the coffee machine and the cups stacked up beside it. Liz helped herself.

"Your breakfast and dinner comes with the job. So if you want a sausage biscuit, help yourself." Jasmine pointed toward a plate with several already made up.

Liz picked up one. "I hate to cook. I may be your waitress until my dying day."

A young woman, not as old as Liz, rushed through the door and into the dining room. She poured a cup of coffee, then added two heaping scoops of sugar and enough cream to turn it pale tan. Then she picked up a sausage biscuit and wolfed it down before grabbing another one.

While she nibbled at the second one, she dug in her jeans pocket and handed Liz a piece of paper. "I'm sorry. I was hungry and thought I was late. I'm Amber. I made a list of the way I do things to help you out. Before I leave in the evenings, I put out the breakfast menus and make sure the table is ready for the next day. That'd be full salt and pepper shakers, ketchup bottle, and pepper sauce. I get the coffee pots all ready so all we have to do is turn them on. Breakfast rush is from about six to eight thirty, and then there's a few drifters up to eleven when lunch starts. Then it's a madhouse until two."

"Pleased to meet you, and thank you for the notes," Liz said.

"I hate to leave. I've loved working here, but Momma is ailin' and I need to go home," Amber said.

"Whatever brought you to Texas anyway?" Liz asked.

"Worthless sumbitch I met in a café up in Rogers, Arkansas. He was a truck driver and I was doin' waitress work. I'd just got out of a bad marriage and got right back into one even worse than the first one. Momma told me, but I wouldn't listen," Amber said.

"I'm sorry," Liz said.

"Me too. Could've saved myself a lot of pain and misery," Amber said. "But that's all behind me now and I got a grip on life. I won't make the same mistake a third time, thanks to Lucy over at the Longhorn Inn. That woman is a saint, let me tell you. She gives talks at the shelters around here and finds jobs for those of us who need them. I've been livin' in the motel and helpin' her out some in the evenin's to pay for my room for the last six months. A saint, I tell you, and Jasmine here ain't far behind her."

"I don't do nothin'. You worked for every dime you made here," Jasmine said.

Amber had thin lips, but when she smiled her whole face lit up. "Yep, I did, and I learned more than how to fill up salt shakers. What's your story, Liz?"

"My Uncle Haskell gave me his house and twenty acres if I want it," she said.

"Haskell Hanson? Love that old feller. Wondered why we hadn't seen him in the café the last week. Is he sickly?" Amber asked.

"No, but my grandpa is, so Uncle Haskell moved one of those prefab houses onto the property out in west Texas. He's going to take care of Grandpa."

"That where you are from—out there in west Texas?" Amber asked.

Liz sipped her coffee. "No, I'm from all over the state, the lower half of Oklahoma, and even some of Arkansas. My mother and aunt own a carnival, so I grew up traveling."

"Well, that sure sounds like fun." She nodded toward the porch. "Looks like Slade Luckadeau and his grandma and aunt are our first customers today."

Liz looked up to see two elderly women and a handsome cowboy coming through the doors.

"I'll get it," she said.

"Okay, go get your feet wet, Miss Carnival." Amber giggled.

"Good morning, folks. What can I get you this morning?" Liz asked as she whipped the strings of a white apron around her waist and tied them in the front.

"These two old grouchy women didn't want to cook this morning, so we're eating before we go to a farm auction down in Chico," Slade said. He was a tall, blond, blue-eyed cowboy.

"Don't you be callin' us grouchy," one of the women said. "You're the one who was bitchin' about gettin' up too damn early. I'm Ellen and this is my sister, Nellie, and that's her grandson, Slade. We have to keep an eye on him or he'll be buyin' nothing but culls. He's married to a woman who helps him buy good horse stock, but me and Nellie have to help him out with the cows."

"Don't listen to them two. They're just grumblin' around," Nellie said. "They're both so happy to be goin' somewhere today they could just dance a jig in a pig trough. I want the big breakfast, the one that comes on a platter with scrambled eggs, pancakes, sausage, and biscuits and gravy." She was tall and slim, wore jeans and boots, and had gray hair cut in a short easy-to-take-care-of style.

"Me too," Ellen said. "Only I don't give a shit about cholesterol so bring me two pieces of sausage." She was shorter than her sister, had dyed hair swept up in a ratted hairdo popular in the seventies, and wore a sweeping, multicolored skirt with a bright orange ruffled top.

"Make mine with bacon instead of sausage," Slade said.

Liz wrote everything down and carried the order to the kitchen. "That's one sexy cowboy out there."

"Yep, if he wasn't married I'd be on the other side of this business flirtin' with him," Jasmine said.

Liz leaned against the doorjamb and kept an eye out for more customers.

Jasmine went on. "I'm just teasing. I'm not getting involved with anyone for a while. I don't have good sense when it comes to the opposite sex."

Amber nodded, her expression stone cold serious.

Liz cocked her head to one side and frowned.

Jasmine cracked eggs into a bowl. "But if I ever trust another man it's goin' to be someone like Slade. He's so in love with his wife, Jane, that he don't even see other women. I swear, Angelina Jolie could walk right up to him and whisper in his ear and it wouldn't affect him.

Jane is his whole life. Well, Jane and those two little girls they have."

"Is there any more Luckadeaus?" Liz asked.

"What would you be askin' that for? Raylen acted like he was almighty interested at Sunday dinner," Jasmine said.

"No, he isn't," Liz argued.

"Blush on your face says he is," Jasmine said.

"More customers. Today, you take the orders and I'll deliver them and we'll split the tips," Amber said.

"I'm in the learnin' stage. You keep the tips for your trip," Liz said.

"You are a good woman. Jasmine, you keep her long as you can," Amber said.

Liz took orders from the first table and turned around to see another group who'd pulled up chairs around the table next to the door. She made a quick trip to the kitchen and hurried back out.

"Just coffee for all of us," a man said.

"Except I'll take a slice of whatever pie Jasmine has back there," Becca said.

"Well, hello again." Liz's tone was as flat as west Texas countryside.

"Hello to you. Don't matter what kind of pie it is. I had breakfast in the bunkhouse with the guys, but I'm wantin' something sweet." Becca dismissed her with a wave of her hand.

Liz took the two orders to the back, filled four coffee cups and set them on a dark brown tray, picked up a slice of chocolate cream pie, and carried it out. Becca didn't say a word, not even "thank you" when Liz set the pie in front of her.

As she carried the tray back to the kitchen she met Amber coming out with an armload of orders.

"Watch that woman over there with all those men. She's downright mean. I don't like her. She treats me like dirt," Amber said out the side of her mouth and kept walking.

"Why don't Amber like Becca, and why would she treat her like dirt?" Liz asked Jasmine as she waited for customers to arrive.

Jasmine cracked four eggs into a bowl and whipped them until they were frothy. "Becca comes from money. Her dad owns the biggest spread in the county over around Stoneburg. She's got an ego bigger than Dallas and pretty much gets what she wants."

"I get the feeling she doesn't know what she wants," Liz said.

"You've met her?"

"At lunch yesterday. Raylen introduced her."

"I'll expect to hear more of that story when we aren't busy. She and Raylen are a strange pair, but they've been friends since they were babies. To my way of thinkin', she's got roundheelitis, but someday she expects to walk down the aisle with Raylen or Dewar. Her daddy don't really care which one," Jasmine said.

"Roundheel-whatis?" Liz asked.

"Man winks at her and her round heels get off balance and she falls back on the bed and takes the man with her. It's a disease that antibiotics won't cure." Jasmine laughed.

Liz laughed with her. "Sounds serious. Is it contagious?"

"I don't know. Don't plan on getting close enough to her to find out, but she'd better think again if she's going to hoodwink one of my friends into marriage," Jasmine said.

"Got a deadline as to when she's going to do the hoodwinkin'?"

"Her daddy is putting the pressure on her, but she likes the chase too well to be tied down, and rumor has it she has the hots for the new foreman out on her daddy's ranch," Jasmine said.

Liz took a long, steady look at the cowboy sitting beside Becca. Dark hair that hung down on his shirt collar. Even though it had an unkempt look about it, Liz knew a high-dollar haircut and the result of hair product when she saw it. Blaze had the same look about him, and his hair was his crowning glory.

The cowboy said something and Becca handed him her fork. He ate a few bites of her pie and pushed it back. She made a show out of licking the fork clean before she started eating with it. Her eyes were sparkling and her body language spelled love in all capital letters.

"Where is your mind?" Jasmine asked.

"Out in la-la land. More customers?"

"No yet, but I heard someone coming up on the porch," Jasmine said.

"Hey Slade, what are you doin' out this early with such good-lookin' chicks? Does Jane know you're out cheatin' on her?" Ace yelled as he shut the door behind him.

"Don't you go tellin' on me," Slade said.

Ellen, the shorter one, crooked a finger at Ace. "Come on over here and sit with us, darlin'. For that sweet lie, I'll buy you breakfast. If you'll let me drive that truck of yours, I'll buy you dinner, too."

"Now Miz Ellen, I done heard how you drive too fast and drink too much. You are way too much of a party girl for me. Hey, Amber, bring me… you're not Amber," Ace said. His eyes did a slow scan from Liz's toes to her hair.

He was a pretty cowboy with his blond curls and blue eyes, almost as handsome as Slade, but his flirting eyes did nothing to heat up her insides like a glance from Raylen did.

"I'm Liz. Amber is leaving tomorrow and I'm taking her place. What can I get you?" she asked.

"Well, honey, how about dinner tomorrow night since Miz Ellen is too much woman for me to handle?" Ace said in a slow Texas drawl.

But it didn't make Liz's underpants start crawling down toward her ankles like Raylen's voice did.

"Darlin', you couldn't handle me either. You want the big breakfast or just coffee?" Liz asked.

"Girl after my heart." Ellen giggled. "Reminds me of myself when I was young."

"Hell, Ellen, you never did have black hair unless it come out of a bottle."

"Now don't go givin' away the family secrets, Nellie." Ellen giggled.

Jasmine came out to the table. "All Ace wants is coffee. Those fellows out in his bunkhouse cook a mean breakfast for him every morning, but he can't stay away from Chicken Fried because he likes to flirt."

"Mornin', Jazzy. You want to go to dinner with me tomorrow night so my pride won't be wounded? Miz Ellen here is too fast for me and your new waitress is just downright mean," Ace teased.

"Woman has to be mean around you. I saved you a slice of lemon pie. You want it now or later?" Jasmine asked.

"Right now. If I don't eat it in a hurry, Slade will talk you out of it," Ace said.

Liz went to the kitchen, poured a cup of coffee, and put the last piece of lemon pie on a saucer. The place was full of good-natured cowboys, both bad boys and good guys, but not a one of them appealed to her. However, all she had to do was conjure up a vision of Raylen and they all disappeared. Was there really such a thing as love at first sight or even lust at first sight?

She carried the coffee and pie out to Ace and set it before him, deliberately brushing his shoulder. Not a single spark or ember fired up. Nothing. Nada!

"I heard that Haskell gave you his place. You want to sell it?" Ace asked.

"I do not! Why would you want it, anyway?" Liz asked.

"Raylen would pay me triple what I gave you for it. He wants that land so damn bad he'd drop down on one knee and propose to you to get it." Ace laughed.

"Well, it's not for sale. I'm going to live there forever," Liz said.

Her bubble popped with a loud cracking sound inside her head. While she'd been floating around in the land of passionate kisses, Raylen had been sweet-talking his way into buying her twenty acres. Well, it would take a hell of a lot more than one steamy hot kiss and a five o'clock good morning to get her land. Even if she had been in love with the man since she was a kid, he would squat and fall backwards before he worked that angle on her.

All men have an angle. They either want your money,

they want to get in your underpants, or they want both. Aunt Tressa's words echoed in her head as she fell to earth with a hard thump.

"Dammit!" she whispered as she followed Jasmine back to the kitchen.

"So what'd you think of Ace?" Jasmine asked.

"He's a bad boy lookin' for a woman with that disease Becca has got. I notice that she doesn't even look at him but flirts with every other man in the house," Liz said.

Jasmine laughed out loud. "They dated some in high school. He went away to college, and the breakup was not a nice one."

"Do you know everything about everybody?" Liz asked.

"Almost. I've been here since last February, and a small café is almost as good a gossip place as a beauty shop. What I don't hear, Gemma does, and we trade off," Jasmine said.

Amber carried a pile of dirty dishes to the sink and started rinsing them before loading the dishwasher. "So what was it you did in the carnival?" she asked.

"I told fortunes and did some belly dancin'," Liz said.

"Well, I'll be damned. I'd have figured you for the one who tamed the lions," Jasmine said.

"It's a carnival, Jasmine, not a circus."

Amber giggled. "Y'all talkin' about this place? Well, it's a circus right now. Slade's aunt and granny are arguing as usual. Becca is flirting with the cowboy right next to her, and Raylen and Gemma are on their way in the door. It's fixin' to heat up out there."

Liz waited until they were seated before she went back out to the dining room. "Good mornin'. What can I get you two?" she asked.

"Pancakes for me. Raylen didn't cook this mornin', and then I had to drag him off the tractor to get him to feed me. And it was his morning to cook," Gemma said. "And coffee, black as sin and strong as hell."

"Same for me. Gemma is a big girl, and she didn't want to get up early, so if I had cooked, it would have been cold so she can't bitch," Raylen said.

"You two live together?" Liz asked.

Gemma nodded. "Last year when I put in the shop the folks said I could live with them and I did for a couple of weeks. But then Raylen said I could use one of his spare bedrooms so I moved in with him. Momma is a better cook."

"But Momma is a hell of a lot nosier, ain't she?" Raylen smiled.

"Yep, she is," Ace said from the table behind them. "But you gotta love her 'cause she's your momma."

"See," Ellen said. "It's the law. You got to love your momma, your granny, and your aunt who is a hell of a lot younger than your granny."

Slade rolled his eyes. "How are things at the O'Donnell place? Y'all ready to sell Glorious Danny Boy yet? Jane would give you a blank check for that horse."

Raylen shook his head. "Momma wouldn't sell Danny Boy for half the gold in Fort Knox. She raised him up from a colt. She'd sell Gemma before she would Danny Boy."

Gemma slapped him on the shoulder. "No she wouldn't. I'm the baby daughter. She'd probably sell you though. You're just a worthless old third son."

Liz had started back to the kitchen when Raylen

reached out and touched her arm. "What are you doin' when you get off work?"

"I'm going back out to the barn and getting into more Christmas boxes so I'll know what I've got and what to buy."

Gemma clapped her hands. "Can I come to your house and play? I love Christmas. Are they those old lights and ornaments?"

"They look like they belonged to Aunt Sara's grandma. She must've liked Christmas because there's boxes and boxes that I haven't even opened."

"My last appointment is at three. I'll be over soon as I get her out the door," Gemma said.

"Come right on. Soon as I take stock of what's out there, I intend to start putting up the lights. I want it all done before Thanksgiving. Momma and Aunt Tressa are coming the week before because they've got a gig in Bowie. I'll take all the help I can get. Raylen is coming too. We made a deal. He's going to help me do the Christmas stuff and then I'm going to exercise horses as payback." Liz fought the urge to rub the spot where Raylen's hand had touched her wrist. It was hotter 'n a barbed wire fence at the front gates of hell, but she didn't touch it.

"What's that?" Becca crossed the floor in long strides.

"I'm putting up Christmas before Thanksgiving. Want to come help?" Liz asked icily.

"Hell, no! I've got better things to do and so do you." Becca touched Raylen on the shoulder.

Raylen shrugged off her hand. "Maybe so, but I'm going to help out a neighbor and then the whole month of December when I'm busy as the devil she's going to be exercising horses."

Becca pulled out a chair to sit at their table. "You are an idiot, my friend."

"Be careful. You might not want to be friends with an idiot," Raylen teased.

Liz left them to their bantering and took their order to Jasmine.

"That hussy better not steal my help this afternoon," Liz mumbled.

"Help with what?" Jasmine asked.

"He said he'd help get my Christmas boxes down from the shelves in the barn and she's out there working her wiles on him," Liz said.

Jasmine shook her head. "Don't pay any attention to her, Liz. The show is all for Ellen and Nellie's benefit. They'll play cards on Friday night with her great-aunt from down in Chico and tell that they saw her flirting with Raylen. Great-aunt will call Becca's daddy and tell him. He'll be happy that she's not seriously interested in his new foreman, who is that guy out there with the dark hair and the come-hither-to-bed look in his eyes. And all will be good on that ranch. Meanwhile, back at the soap opera, she'll be spending her nights in the bunkhouse with the hired help while Daddy entertains visions of merging two big ranches."

"A female Blaze, only Aunt Tressa don't care who he marries or if he's a playboy the rest of his life," Liz said.

"Who is Blaze?" Amber asked.

"He's a crack-jack mechanic who takes care of the carnival equipment. He's so sexy that he ought to be a carnival attraction. Women flock to him like flies on a fresh cow patty. And that's exactly what he is: a bunch of bullshit! But he's a nice piece of eye candy and he can charm the hair off a frog's ass, so women don't have much chance when he smiles at them. He's my best friend and when Blaze gets here, Miss Becca's liable to get an acute case of roundheelitis and fall into his bed."

"How about your bed? Raylen going to warm it up?" Amber asked as she loaded a tray of dishes into the dishwasher.

"What in the hell made you ask that?" Liz asked.

"A blind person could see the vibes between you two." Amber giggled. "And not every man in Montague County would offer to haul old boxes down off a shelf. You might be the fortune-teller, but you can't see what's right in front of your face."

"You want a job with a traveling carnival? With that kind of imagination, Aunt Tressa could turn you into a fortune-teller in no time." Liz teased.

Amber shook her head. "No thank you. I'm goin' home."

Chapter 6

L<small>IZ</small> <small>TURNED SLOWLY AND SURE ENOUGH,</small> R<small>AYLEN WAS</small> leaning against the doorjamb leading into the tack room. Her sixth sense hadn't failed her, or maybe she should call it her lust sense because every time he was anywhere near, a warm liquid feeling oozed down into her stomach. Smudges of dirt were smeared across his forehead, he had hat hair and a band on his forehead where his straw cowboy hat had rested all day, and his jeans were dusty and his chambray shirt sweaty. And her pulse still quickened at the sight of him.

"Gemma said to tell you she's sorry. Ellen and Nellie walked in just as she was finishin' up with her last old gal and asked if she had time to cut Nellie's hair and style Ellen's, so she won't be here for another couple of hours," Raylen drawled. "I'm also supposed to tell you we're havin' a party next Monday night in my barn. We do it every year for Halloween. Gemma loves the holidays. We have Halloween at my place. Then Thanksgiving and Christmas is at the folks'."

His deep voice sent that lust sense into overdrive. She raised a dark eyebrow and flirted a little. "Is that an invitation?"

"Yes, it is, and Gemma seems to believe you about that fortune telling stuff, so she's going to ask you to tell fortunes for everyone so bring your crystal ball or your cards or whatever other hocus-pocus you need," he said.

"You want me to dance, too?" she asked.

"Sure I do." He grinned. "How about a demonstration right here and now just for me? You got a skimpy little outfit to put on? Can I tell Gemma you said yes?"

"Yes, I'd love to tell fortunes, and yes, I'd love to go to a Halloween party. Never been to one. Is it dress up? I'll wear my belly dancing costume and you can stop doubting me, Raylen O'Donnell."

A gray cobweb had circled around the top of her hair like a filmy halo. But Lizelle didn't remind Raylen of an angel, more like a devil woman haunting his dreams and firing up his desire. She wore the same jeans and shirt she'd worn at work all day and still smelled like a mixture of food and leftover exotic perfume. The combination was so heady that all he wanted to do right then was kiss her again and see where it could or would lead.

"Yes, ma'am, it is dress up. I'm going as a cowboy, and you sure can come as a belly dancer." He rocked forward on his tiptoes and reached for a box on the third shelf.

"I can do that." She smiled.

"I don't think so. I can barely reach it without a ladder."

She giggled. "I'm not talking about getting to that box up there. I'm talking about wearing one of my costumes to the party. Should I wear orange, turquoise, or hot pink?"

He set the box on the table and pointed toward the ceiling. "Whichever one you want to wear, and I'll believe it when I see it. This isn't all of the decorations. The loft is full of stuff. Your Aunt Sara loved Christmas, and every year Haskell made her one thing new to go out in the yard. Even after she was gone, he kept on making a new piece every year. He kept them up there, all covered up with tarps. Want to go take a look? There's probably enough to reach from here to the road."

Liz forgot all about the costumes. "Are you serious? Uncle Haskell mentioned more stuff, but I figured it was like this."

"Yes, I am serious. After she died he didn't put the stuff out in the yard, but he kept making one thing a year. I found him up there once when I was a teenager painting a funny lookin' wagon pulled by four horses. It was all painted in wild colors, but it had Santa sitting on the driver's seat and the top was covered with toys. I asked him what he was making and he explained to me about how Sara had always liked for him to make her one wooden cutout a year and the wagon was his gift to her that year. Come on. I'll show you. There's got to be thirty or more of them up there," Raylen said.

The wooden ladder went straight up with only room for one person at a time. Raylen stood to one side and let her go before he did, waited until she was more than halfway up, and then put his boot on the bottom rung. His eyes naturally went to her well-rounded fanny, and his thoughts to something a helluva lot more fun than uncovering wooden Christmas lawn decorations.

The loft was half as big as the barn and swept clean. Buckets of paint were arranged on shelves on the north side with brushes standing, handle down, in Mason jars. Everything was organized and very clean.

"This reminds me of our barn in west Texas. Grandpa does that. Keeps his paint all lined up by color and his brushes cleaned and in jars ready to use. He works hard from the first of December to the first of March every year redoing our wagons. I love to watch him paint. His hands are so steady and his combination of colors is breathtaking." Her voice had a faraway sound as if she were homesick.

"You miss it, don't you?" Raylen whispered.

"Miss what?"

"Being a carnie."

"Of course I miss it. Would you miss ranchin' if suddenly you lived in the middle of Dallas?"

His expression changed to dead serious. "I couldn't survive without ranchin' and horses and tractors. Missin' it wouldn't even cover the feelings. I'd probably wither up and die in the big city. Is that what you're going to do here, Liz? Wither up and die?"

Liz turned around and met his eyes in a determined stare. "No, I am not. I've wanted this forever and I'm going to grow roots. But I'll always miss a portion of carnie life. It's what my family is, not just what they do. Uncle Haskell was the only one who ever quit the business and even then when he came home for the holidays at Christmas, he helped Grandpa paint."

Raylen heard the freedom in her voice. It was an elusive thing that he couldn't put into words, but it was there. There wasn't enough good rich Red River dirt to grow roots on Liz's heart. Like she said, the carnival and constant movement is what her family was, not just what they did. And Hanson blood flowed in her veins. It was what she was and that involved wings that flew from one place to the other.

He removed the tarp from the first wooden cutout and revealed a dark-haired woman in a bright orange harem-looking outfit sitting in the fork of a Saguaro cactus. She was barefoot and had a Santa stocking on her head. The cactus had Christmas garland wrapped around it and holes drilled in it for lights.

"Guess this year's decoration is in celebration of you taking over the house. I hadn't seen it before but that is you, Liz. You look like a dark-haired *I Dream of Jeannie*. Evidently, I was wrong about the dancing costumes. Is that the one you are going to wear to the party?"

His heart did a nose-dive into his boots. Every cowboy in the whole damn county would be panting after her like a bull in the springtime. He wouldn't have a snowball's chance in hell of getting a date with her and he'd taunted her into wearing that skimpy thing.

"Yes, it is, Raylen. It's my orange belly dancing outfit, and I think I will wear it to the Halloween party. Orange goes with Halloween, doesn't it?"

Liz folded her arms across her chest and studied the piece of art. It was definitely a rendition of her in her orange belly dancing outfit. Uncle Haskell had always liked it better than the pink or the turquoise. But why did he place her on a cactus and not on a wagon pulled by reindeer, or sitting beside Santa?

"There's holes in the cactus for Christmas lights." Raylen couldn't take his eyes off the costume.

"Well, that does make it a little more Christmas-like. Let's look at the rest." She'd think about the significance of the cactus later. A prickly old cactus had nothing to do with Christmas.

"Present to past or past to present?"

"You mean they're organized?"

Raylen pointed to the bits of paper thumbtacked on

the wall above the tarps around the room. Each one had five years penciled on it beginning with 1975–1979.

"Past to present," she said.

Raylen moved past her and dropped a dusty tarp from a group of flat wooden cutouts. The first one was Santa Claus in a cowboy hat and boots, and Mrs. Claus in an apron holding up her dress tail to reveal bright red cowboy boots.

Liz moved closer and held the other end as she peered behind it. "Look, there's a date on the back that says 1975, and what's this?"

She peeled off a thick envelope that had been stapled to the backside of the cutout. "It's got my name on the front," she said.

"Then I guess you can open it." Raylen would have rather been holding her than propping up Mr. and Mrs. Claus on the only wall of the loft that wasn't filled with tarp covered ornaments.

She plopped down on the floor, sitting cross-legged like a little girl, and opened the letter. "He says that he doesn't have time to tell me all about each piece over the phone and if he writes it all down I can keep it and think about it later. This piece is the first Christmas he and Sara were together on the ranch and he was working at Nocona for a boot company and he made her a pair of red boots and this thing as a funny joke to put out in the yard. She loved it so much that she said he had to build one every year of something that happened in their lives."

"Okay, ready for 1976?" Raylen set Mr. and Mrs. Santa to one side to reveal the next one.

It was a four-by-eight-foot nativity scene so realistic

that she reached up to touch the woolly lamb beside the shepherd. She had to stare at baby Jesus in the manger a full minute before she was convinced his little chest wasn't moving with each breath. Haskell had captured the love in Mary's and Joseph's eyes, as they looked down on the newborn so well that Liz wondered why he hadn't taken up professional portrait painting.

"He's even better with a paintbrush than I remembered," she said. "This is because Aunt Sara wanted something that represented the reason for the season, as she said."

"He's an artist, alright," Raylen agreed.

"He doesn't say what kind of reaction she had to his gifts. I would love to know if she got excited and clapped her hands or if she hugged him and danced around the living room because she was so happy," Liz said.

Raylen moved the nativity over and revealed the next piece. "I suppose that was private and he doesn't want to share those memories."

Liz laid the letter down and pointed. "That's a pumper. But I didn't see oil wells on the property. Look closely, Raylen. There are elves peeking out from the bottom."

"There aren't any oil wells on his land," Raylen said.

Liz read a while before she looked up to find Raylen staring at her. "Aunt Sara inherited land that year from a great-aunt down near Beaumont. It had oil wells on it and she had a share of the royalties. That was the year Uncle Haskell quit the factory and started ranchin' full time. Look, there's holes for lights in the pumper. No wonder there are boxes and boxes of lights in the tack room."

Two hours later the sun was going down and they

weren't even halfway through uncovering the beautiful artwork or reading about it.

"So," Raylen held out a hand to help her up off the floor, "if you put all this stuff up it's going to look like one of those Christmas light drives."

"Won't that be wonderful! Every year when we are in a town that has a light exhibit, Momma and I take a drive through it. Is there one around here?"

"The prettiest one is up in Chickasha, Oklahoma. But if you put up all this, you can bet folks will come from miles around to drive down your lane," he said.

"I'll sit on the porch in the evening and hand out candy canes when they turn around." She remembered the time that they'd gone through one in east Texas and there had been a donation booth at the end for a charity. The lady there had worn a Mrs. Claus suit and gave out candy canes. Did she have time to buy a costume like that? What would she look like in a white wig?

"You goin' to wear a belly dancin' outfit while you hand out candy canes?" Raylen teased as he pulled her up to her feet.

"Of course, and if anyone wants to put ten dollars in my jar, I'll do a dance out in the yard for them," she shot back.

His face went as still as stone, but he didn't let go of her hand once she was standing. "You can't do that. This is a small town, Liz, but that would draw idiots from everywhere and you might get hurt. Promise me you won't do that, or if you do that I can come over to protect you."

"I was teasing. I was thinking about a Mrs. Claus costume. You want to be Santa?" she said quickly.

"Thank God and no, thank you."

He drew her closer, looking down into her dark eyes, trying to find the faint glimmer of something stationary that would not fly away. But he couldn't see anything but a reflection of his own immediate wants and needs—and that was to kiss her.

His mouth lowered to hers, and she rolled up on her toes to meet him halfway. Lips devoured lips when they met in a clash of passion. She wrapped her arms around his back, her fingers digging into the tight muscles and broad shoulders. He pulled her shirt loose from her jeans and ran his hands up her back to the bra level, his fingers enjoying the softness of her bare flesh. The raw heat that flowed between them was intoxicating and addictive. Liz had never experienced anything like it before, and she instantly wanted more.

"Hey, anyone here?" Gemma's voice came from the doorway.

Liz stepped out of Raylen's embrace and blushed.

"We're in the loft. Be down in a minute," Raylen called down.

"I've got food," Gemma singsonged back up.

Raylen pulled Liz back into his embrace and brushed a feathery soft kiss across her mouth. "You have the sweetest lips," he whispered.

"You say that to all the girls?"

He hugged her tightly and traced her jawline with his forefinger. "Only the belly dancers. You are so beautiful, Liz."

"You say that to all the girls, too?"

He sighed. "Only the ones who can walk the fence better than me."

Gemma yelled from the bottom of the ladder, "What are y'all doin' up there?"

"Putting the ornaments all back. We're on our way down," Raylen hollered.

"Well, hurry up. Food is getting cold and I don't like cold mashed potatoes," Gemma said.

"We're on our way." Liz pushed away from Raylen and started down the ladder. "What kind of food have you got?"

"I brought leftovers from Chicken Fried. Jasmine said she'd have to toss them so I figured we could eat while we look through boxes. Today's special was roast and potatoes, so she sent a container of that, some gravy, some green beans, and a few yeast rolls. It's still warm, so hurry up. You two can play Santa Claus if you want, but I'm starving," Gemma said.

Liz didn't think she could swallow a bite what with the pent up red hot fire in her belly and the nervous jitters flitting around in her stomach. It was a good thing Gemma interrupted them or Liz would have tossed caution out the loft window and turned passion loose right there in the barn with baby Jesus looking on from the nativity scene.

"So what all did you find up there?" Gemma asked.

"You'd never believe it. Uncle Haskell made a huge lawn piece for Aunt Sara every year they were married, and when she passed away he kept on making one a year. They are gorgeous and I'm putting all of them out this year. That's sweet of Jasmine to send food." Words came out of her mouth but her body, mind, and soul still relived Raylen's kisses.

"She said it was going to the garbage if we didn't want it," Gemma said. "How many pieces are up there?"

"About thirty-five, near as we can figure, and there's lights for every one of them. Big lights like the old-time ones they used years ago. It's going to look like the Griswolds live here."

And all the lights won't make as bright a light as went off in my head when Raylen touched my bare skin or kissed me. I'm still too giddy to swallow food and too wound up to sit still.

Gemma nodded between bites. "You can count on me and Raylen and Dewar to help you get them up. It will be fun to help, won't it, Raylen? Daddy and Momma put up lights around the house and an enormous wreath on the door, and sometimes she makes Daddy drag those wire reindeer things out of the barn to go in the yard. Dewar has one of those pre-lit trees that sometimes he shoves in a corner and sometimes he forgets all about."

Raylen could have strangled his younger sister. He'd already entertained visions of just him and Liz doing the decorating and all the lusty kisses that would come as a result of working together.

"You really think you can rope Dewar into helping?" Raylen asked.

"Sure, he'll help. And I'll get Jasmine and Ace, too. The more hands, the quicker the work will get done. I think Dewar likes Liz, don't you?" Gemma said. "The way he was flirting around with her was kind of cute. And he is the next one in line."

"In line for what?" Liz asked. Was there a *gadjo* ritual that she didn't know about?

"Daddy says we have to get married in the order of our birth. Me and Colleen have been tryin' to find wives for these guys for years because we don't want to be eighty and pushin' a walker with our wedding bouquets roped to the front of it down the aisle. Now it's Dewar's turn and…"

"Things don't have to happen that way. Daddy was teasing," Raylen said quickly.

Gemma peeled back aluminum foil from the disposable trays and began to heap food onto her paper plate. "We'll see. Come on and fill up a plate. I brought paper ones from the beauty shop and even had enough plastic forks. Tell me about the artwork up there. Is it wood?"

The tack room soon filled with the aroma of good food intermingled with the normal smells of leather, hay, and dust. Raylen and Gemma lit into the supper like two hungry coyote pups. Liz was still combating the effects of the make-out session. She drained the tall plastic takeout cup of sweet tea and could have drunk another one, but she barely nibbled around the edges of the small piece of roast she put on her plate.

"It's wood and painted. Uncle Haskell made it realistic, too. The nativity is so real that the sheep looks woolly," Liz said.

Gemma talked between bites. "I hated to miss all the fun, but I can't ever turn down Nellie and Ellen. They are a hoot. They get to arguing about some wild thing Ellen did in the past and bickering, and it's a helluva lot better than Comedy Central. I tried to get them to come to the Halloween party next week, but they'd have none of it. Said they were keeping the kids so Slade and Jane could come over to it," Gemma said.

"What kind of stories?" Liz asked. One thing that outsiders did more than carnies was discuss their lives with anyone who'd listen.

"Real life. When Ellen was young, she was a real hellcat. She liked to drive fast, flirt, date, and drive men wild. And she just loves to relive the stories. I like to listen, so we make a pair. She was tellin' today about the last time she got to drive any kind of vehicle. I'd heard the story before, but she always puts in a few more details and it's a hoot to listen to her tell it," Gemma said.

Liz looked over at Raylen and wanted to lick that fleck of potato from the corner of his mouth. When his tongue flicked out and caught it, she gasped and hurriedly covered it with a fake cough in her napkin.

"I'd love to hear the story. Entertain me while we eat," Liz said to take her mind off Raylen.

"Nobody can tell that story like Ellen," Raylen said. He didn't want to listen to his sister's voice. He'd rather Liz talked about the carnival, her job, or hell's bells, she could talk about the weather and the fall leaves, as long as he could hear her voice.

"But now my curiosity is aroused, so tell me what it's about anyway," Liz said.

Aroused, Raylen thought. *More than my curiosity is aroused right now. I need a cold shower or maybe a hot one with you all naked and slippery right beside me. Shit! I've got to rein in those thoughts or embarrass myself right here in the tack room!*

"Okay," Gemma said. "We've all heard the story a hundred times, but every time they tell it, Ellen embellishes it even more. Ellen said she was fifty, but Nellie raised an eyebrow and mouthed behind her back that she was past sixty. Anyway, she was in a vintage Corvette with this guy. She couldn't remember if it was a '55 or '56 model, but it was one of those cute little red things according to her. He'd been smartin' off about how no woman was ever drivin' his 'vette. When he got out at a service station to go to the men's room, Ellen noticed that he'd left the keys dangling in the ignition.

"She said he was a stupid sumbitch to trust her like that, and he deserved to be taught a lesson. She also admitted that she'd already had more than her share of a fifth of Jack Daniel's whiskey. She got about half a mile down the road when she lost control on a patch of gravel. She said she went ass over teakettle for a while, and when everything stopped moving, she was sitting on her ass in the edge of a farm pond where cows watered, and there was manure and dirty water up to her waist."

Gemma was laughing so hard the last words came out one at a time in the midst of guffaws. Liz and Raylen caught the infection, and they all three wiped at their eyes with paper napkins.

Liz's hiccupped. "Was she hurt?"

Gemma swallowed hard three times. "That's the first thing I asked, but Nellie picked up the story there and said that she didn't even get a broken bone. But the front of that Corvette had kissed a pecan tree, and if Ellen hadn't been drunk as a skunk and limber as a wet rag, she would have been killed. Ellen said that Jack Daniel's saved her life and she'd kept a bottle in the house the rest of her life. She came up sputtering and spitting filthy water and cussin' a bloody blue streak about getting mud and cow manure on her new boots. The owner of the car had called the police and reported his vehicle stolen and his girlfriend kidnapped. When they arrived a few minutes later, she was sitting beside the car with what was left of the bottle of Jack in her hands. Neither the bottle nor Ellen had a scratch. She offered the cops a drink for coming to her aid, but the sorry bastards hauled her ass off to jail for stealing an automobile, driving while intoxicated, and a few more trumped-up charges. She said she was surprised they didn't throw in stealing cow shit along with all the other charges, since she took a fair share of it to jail with her in her boots."

Liz laughed but kept Raylen in her peripheral vision. He chuckled at all the funny parts of the story, but his blue eyes kept undressing her and every piece of clothing that he mentally removed caused her to shiver and want more.

Oblivious to anything but the story, Gemma went on, "Nellie said it wasn't all that funny because she was the one who had to get up at two o'clock in the morning and go to Chico to get her. Ellen said that she wasn't about to use that public toilet in the corner of the jail cell, and all that whiskey hit her bladder at one time, so she was dancing in her cow shit boots by the time Nellie arrived. And all Nellie wanted to do was cuss and rant at her. Nellie paid the fines, for the car damage and the whole shebang. And you know what Ellen is still bitchin' about after umpteen years?"

Liz shook her head.

"That she thought the judge was hot and left her phone number on the table right in front of him, and he never did call her."

"I've got to get to know these women better. Do they come into the café often?" Liz asked.

"At least once a week. Ellen gets her hair fixed every week, and Nellie gets a cut about once a month. I tried to get them to come to the party and bring the kids, but

Ellen said she was dressing up like a hooker. Nellie says she's not letting her out of the house," Gemma said.

"What are you dressing up like?" Liz asked Gemma.

"Depends. If Creed says he's coming I might dress up like Daisy Duke. God, but that boy is pretty and the less clothes I have on the less he has to take off," Gemma said.

"He's too damn young for you!" Raylen said.

"He's twenty-four, Brother. And I'm only twenty-five, and I didn't say I was going to marry him. I just thought I'd make his job easier if we did hook up," Gemma said.

"Jesus, Mary, and…"

"Forget Joseph. I'd rather have Creed." Gemma giggled.

"You…" Raylen couldn't find words.

Gemma slapped his finger when he brought it up to shake at her. "Right back at you. Just remember what's good for the goose is good for the gander. You O'Donnell guys can be wild, but us girls are supposed to be sweet little lilies? It don't work that way, Brother. If I want to take off my Daisy Duke cutoff jeans for Creed, then I will do so and you can't stop me."

Liz had always wanted a sibling so she could argue just like Raylen and Gemma were doing right then. She switched her empty tea glass with Raylen's and sipped at his full one while they bickered.

So the O'Donnell guys had a reputation for being a little on the rough side, did they? She'd bet dollars to funnel cakes that not a one of them could outdo Blaze. And if Gemma liked them wild and woolly, maybe she'd be the one to tame Blaze. Too bad he wouldn't be in

Bowie over Halloween. Liz would have wrangled an invitation for him to the party and watched all the women flock around him.

Gemma poked her on the arm. "I asked what you were going to dress up like. What were you thinkin' about?"

"Blaze," Liz said honestly.

"You are dressing up like fire?" Raylen forgot about the argument and jerked his head around to look at Liz. So she was going to come to the party as fire. Well, that seemed right fitting the way she'd heated him up with those sexy-as-hell kisses.

"No, I'm not. Blaze is… well, he works for the carnival. His momma was Aunt Tressa's winter friend in west Texas. It's a long story, but her friend died when Blaze was fourteen so Tressa took him in and taught him the carnie business. He's kind of like a surrogate son to her. I was thirteen that year so we were brought up together, kind of…"

"Kind of like a brother?" Raylen asked.

Liz busied herself with a box of ornaments. "Not at all. More like a best friend."

Gemma sat down on a stool close to Liz. "Tell me more."

"He's tall. Blond hair. Strange eyes that are almost gold like a wildcat's eyes. And he has this animal magnetism that draws women to him like he has supernatural powers or something. He's a lot of fun and I can't wait for you all to meet him," Liz said.

"You going to marry him someday?" Gemma asked bluntly.

"Hell, no! Not Blaze. I'm not so sure any one woman could rope him in on a full-time contract. He's my friend, not my boyfriend." Liz laughed.

"Man, I'd like to try," Gemma said with a sigh. "Well, I've got to go. I promised Momma after I delivered supper and made sure things were going all right here that I'd come over to the house and cut her hair. She didn't have time to get in to the shop today and she has that horse meeting in Wichita Falls tomorrow. I'll see you tomorrow at the café, Liz."

"Thanks for the food. Now that I know why there are so many boxes up there, I don't need to look in every one of them. I'll start putting things out right after Halloween. I want it all lit up so Momma can see it. I'll take pictures to send Uncle Haskell," Liz said.

Gemma headed toward the door. "Then we'll plan to work on it in the evenings after the big party. If you see me lookin' like Daisy Duke, then you'll know Creed is there. Dewar better hang a tag around your neck that says for everyone to back off or those Riley boys will gather round you like a bunch of struttin' Banty roosters."

"More like vultures," Raylen grumbled.

"What did you say?" Liz asked.

He wiped his hands on a paper towel and shook his head. "I was askin' if you want me to help put any boxes back before I go. I've still got some chores to do at home."

"No, they can all stay right here and I'll clean up. Thanks for showing me where the lawn things were hidden away, Raylen. I appreciate it."

Everything had felt so right in the hayloft when she was in his arms and kissing him, but now that Blaze had been set loose, along with a cowboy named Creed and his brothers, there was an awkwardness between them every bit as big as a full-grown Angus bull.

"Be seein' you around then. Are you really dressing up like a belly dancer?" Raylen headed for the door and then turned abruptly.

"Guess I am. What other women are coming besides Gemma, Colleen, and Slade's wife?"

"Whole area comes to the party. Becca will be there."

Liz's tone was colder than a Texas blue norther when she asked, "And what does she usually wear?"

Raylen grinned. "As little as the law allows. Holler if you decide to get any of that stuff off the loft. It has to be lowered by rope out the door to get it out of there. Haskell cut them out and painted them right on the spot. I told him once that it reminded me of building a boat in a basement. He told me that he'd lower it down with ropes when he got ready to put it outside."

Liz nodded. She heard what he was saying, but "as little as the law allows" was playing through her mind like a marching band on a continuous loop. Damn that Becca anyway! She was just playing with Raylen. She loved that hired hand with the pretty haircut.

Raylen waved and left her with a plate full of uneaten food and dusty boxes of decorations. She waved back, but wished Becca would suffer a strange virus brought on by roundheelitis that slapped her big tall butt in bed for at least twenty-four hours on Halloween night.

She pushed all the leftovers into one aluminum tray, turned out the barn lights, and carried the food to the house where she set it on the porch for Hooter and Blister to fight over. She was still muttering about Becca when she went into the house. She turned on the lights and the house phone rang at the same time.

"Hello," she said. Next week she was buying a new phone that had Caller ID on it and getting in touch with the phone company to have that feature, along with Internet, put on the telephone plan.

"Hi, kiddo. How'd your first day at work go?" Uncle Haskell asked.

"It was great. I met Slade and his granny and her sister," she said.

"Nellie and Ellen. Two great old gals. They'll talk your ear off and entertain you with their stories. That Ellen was a rounder in her day. Did she tell you the Corvette story yet?"

"No, but she told Gemma and Gemma told me. And there's this girl named Becca," Liz said cautiously.

"Don't worry about that filly. She's going to flit all around the roses and land on a pile of pure old cow shit one of these days. She's all flirt and no substance," Haskell told her. "So how'd you like Jasmine?"

"She's great and I liked Amber, but she's leaving tomorrow morning, so we didn't have time to be real friends. But I really do like Gemma. I don't think Colleen is going to be friendly, though."

"Colleen is a strange one. Gemma is more outgoing. How about Raylen and Dewar?" Haskell laughed.

Liz paused. "Raylen helped me tonight and he's promised to help put up all the cutout pieces. Then after Thanksgiving, I'm going to help him exercise horses to pay him back. It's a pretty good business deal. We found all the things you made for Christmas. I'm going to put them all up this year between here and the road. Is there enough power to turn on all the lights?"

"You bet there is. That's why I called tonight, to tell you all about that stuff. You'll have the gaudiest house in Montague County. So Raylen helped you, did he? I figured Dewar would have offered."

"Why?" Liz asked.

"I don't know. Well, here's Dad. We're watching *NCIS* on television tonight. He likes that show, and I made him banana pudding with whipped cream. Have fun, and I'm glad you are making friends. There's good people in Ringgold. You'll fit right in with them."

"Uncle Haskell, I love all the pretty things in the barn," she said. She wanted him to stay on the phone and tell her more about her neighbors and new friends.

"I knew you would. Sara always wished she could've had you rather than God giving you to Marva Jo. But life does have a bunch of twists and turns. Call me and send pictures when you get all that situated." He chuckled. "Bye now."

"Good night, Uncle Haskell," she said.

A warm feeling settled around her like a tightly crocheted shawl on a cold winter night. She wrapped her arms around her body to hold it closer and jumped when someone knocked on the door.

She opened it a crack and looked out to see Raylen standing with his hands shoved down in the pockets of his jeans, then she slung it open.

"Sorry, I just didn't want to scare you. I hopped over the fence and was in my yard before I remembered that I drove my truck over this morning and parked out by your barn. I was afraid you'd hear the engine and think someone was trying to steal your Christmas stuff." He grinned.

"Come on in," she said. She was learning the art of being grounded and rooted pretty damn fast.

"Can't. Still got some chores. Just wanted to let you know about the truck. Don't know what in the devil I was thinking," he said. He wasn't about to own up to the fact that he was thinking about how tough it was going to be if Dewar did set his cap for Liz when he left the barn.

She opened the screen door and stepped out on the porch. "Thanks."

He cupped her face in his hands and looked deeply into her brown eyes. "You really are very beautiful, Liz, and I don't say that to all the girls."

She didn't have time to answer before his lips found hers in blaze that burned every thought of anyone or anything from her mind. All too soon, it was over and he stepped back.

"Good night, Liz," he whispered and disappeared into the night.

Chapter 7

THE NIGHT WAS CLEAR WITH THE FAINTEST HINT OF a crisp fall breeze. Wispy clouds strung out like spun strings of cotton candy over a waning moon that promised werewolves, witches, goblins, and maybe even shape-shifters later on in the evening. Across the river bridge in Terral, little children were at the community center eating hotdogs and nachos before their parents loaded them on the back of hay wagons and took them trick or treating. Some would even ride across the river bridge to Ringgold in their cute costumes to hold out their bags to aunts and uncles, grandmothers and friends. Excitement had danced in the air all day, and Liz was more excited than the trick-or-treaters as she thought about her very first Halloween party.

She wore her orange belly dancing outfit, pulled her dark hair up into a ponytail, and stretched a two-inch wide jeweled hair clip around the base. She artfully applied her stage makeup, which included extra eye shadow, liner, and a deep, dark burgundy lip liner and lipstick, then very carefully affixed the headpiece, a double row of dangling, sparkling crystals with a pear-cut topaz resting between her eyes.

A circlet of bangles that sounded like wind chimes when she walked clipped around each ankle, with matching ones around her wrists. Shoes were nothing more than thin leather soles kept on her feet with the tiniest strap of leather across her toes. She removed them before she danced, because Aunt Tressa had taught her to feel the rhythm with her feet. However, it was only a costume that night. She was a fortune-teller, and no one had asked her to dance.

The orange costume was her very first grown-up dancer's outfit. Aunt Tressa gave it to her for her eighteenth birthday and she'd worn it when she danced that night on the small porch attached to the fortune-teller's wagon. After her dance, people had lined up for two blocks waiting to have their fortune told by the Egyptian Dharma. The bra top was covered in bright, shiny rhinestones and sequins, creating a pattern that glistened from every angle when she moved. A fringe cascade below her bustline hung at varying lengths, drawing the eye downward toward her belly button and the intricate belt topping off a sheer, handkerchief hem skirt. The wide, V-shaped belt matched the bra with sequins and rhinestones.

She affixed a rhinestone the size of a lima bean to her belly button and picked up the most important piece of her costume—a two-by-six-foot length of chiffon, scattered with rhinestones and bangle beads, that served as both a veil and a shawl around her shoulders.

Raylen had offered to come for her, but she'd opted to take herself so that she could leave if she wanted. She slipped her leather jacket over her outfit and was careful not to shut her skirt tail or her shawl in the truck door when she left. A Texas Highway Patrol fell in behind her when she pulled out onto the highway.

"Now that would take some explaining if he pulled me over for speeding. Yes, sir, Mr. Patrolman, I'm a real belly dancer and I'm on my way to tell fortunes. Flip your hand out here and I'll be glad to tell you how long you will live. Oh, my, you are going to have a very short life unless you let me go without even a warning." She giggled nervously as she turned into the O'Donnell's lane. The highway patrol turned with her.

"Dammit! What is he doing?" She kept a check in her rearview mirror.

She drove past the two-story house and made a left turn, following the two ruts that made a path toward the big, lit-up barn which would have been no more than half a mile from her house if she'd walked straight west. She passed a log cabin and slowed down to a crawl. Light pouring through the windows cast a yellow glow on the shrubs. A hound dog was silhouetted on the porch, and while she eased past what had to be Raylen's house the lights suddenly went out, the front door opened, and the dog yipped. Gemma stepped out and waved at Liz, who put on the brakes.

Gemma trotted over to the truck and swung the door open for Liz. "Wow, girl, when you dress up, you do it right! Hey, Sammy, are you in costume or not?"

Liz stepped out and asked, "Is he for real?"

The patrolman waved. "Not. I just came by for a minute to see how things were going. Who's your friend?"

"New neighbor. She's tellin' fortunes tonight. You sure you can't stay?"

"No, I'm on duty. Ten minutes tops and that's my break time," Sammy said.

Gemma turned her attention back to Liz. "Where did you get that getup?"

"Just one of my carnie costumes. I guess Creed isn't here tonight or you'd be Daisy Duke." Liz grinned.

Gemma was a witch in a short-tailed outfit with a low neckline that scooped low enough to show a couple of inches of cleavage. Her pointed hat was covered in black sequins and glittered in the dark.

Gemma frowned, drawing her dark brows down until they were almost a solid line. "Oh, he's here, but I got word early that he was bringing along some girl he met in college. They are Mickey and Minnie Mouse. She's crazy, I'm tellin' you, just plumb crazy. Creed is so damn fine he should be Tarzan or Fabio, not Mickey Mouse. And he's crazy for letting her dress him tonight. I'd never dress something as sexy as Creed up like a damned old Disney character. I might dress him up like a stud bull, but shit! Mickey Mouse?" Gemma fussed the whole way to the barn.

"Hell, Ace could pull off a Mickey costume better than Creed. Never did see what all the women saw in Ace anyway, but his brothers are a different matter with all that dark hair and those big old, soulful blue eyes. Dalton and Ryder are too young for me, but what does a year matter? That's all the older I am than Creed."

"Wow!" Liz said when she stepped inside the barn.

"We do get carried away. We buy new things every year and add them to what we have in storage, so each year gets better. Jasmine is running the bar for the next hour and then I have to relieve her. You've got to tell fortunes for us tonight so choose a spot."

"Palms or cards?" Liz asked. At least Gemma hadn't asked her to dance in front of the whole crowd. Dancing before strangers was easy; doing so before her newly found friends wouldn't be.

"I don't care if you read tea leaves, but when Becca

gets here, you tell her that she's going to be dirt poor and wind up living in a trailer house with six kids and four hound dogs," Gemma whispered. "I do not want her for a sister-in-law."

"But what if she's destined to be an O'Donnell?" Liz asked.

"Then change her destiny." Gemma laughed. "I'm going to check on Jasmine. Grab a beer or a plate of food and mingle. You got about thirty minutes before fortunes begin."

———

Raylen had been watching the door for the past half hour. Becca had arrived and made a splash as Annie Oakley in jeans cut off so short that an inch of her butt cheek showed when she was standing upright and hung lower on her hips than a bikini. When she bent over a table, even more of her cheek peeked out, but there was not a single cellulite cell anywhere. She wore a sequined hat, had rhinestone encrusted .38s strapped low around her hips and tied to her thigh with velvet ribbons, and a pearl-snap Western shirt. It was tied up under her breasts, leaving her entire midriff bare. Her boots were as shiny as her hat and sparkled every time she took a step.

When Gemma and Liz came through the doors, and Liz removed her leather jacket, Raylen's breath caught in his chest. Someone yelled at Gemma from across the barn and she headed in that direction. Liz looked up and saw Raylen, waved, and made a beeline toward him. He was glad for the few seconds to collect his thoughts before she reached him.

"Well, good evening, Indiana Jones," Liz said.

Raylen sported two days' worth of stubble, a hat

like the one Harrison Ford wore in the movie, and he'd rolled the sleeves up on his gray work shirt, unbuttoned the first three buttons to show a little chest hair, and wore faded work pants rather than jeans. A leather whip circled around his left shoulder.

"And what do I call you?" Raylen touched her shawl gently.

"Madam Drabami. I'm here to tell fortunes to those who aren't faint of heart," she said.

"Did you figure out that he's Indiana Jones?" Dewar walked up behind her. "That's his costume every year. I keep tellin' him that he looks more like Crocodile Dundee."

"Oh, no, Crocodile Dundee wasn't near as handsome," Liz said.

Raylen popped his brother on the shoulder playfully.

"Him, handsome? Did you leave your contacts out tonight? Let me show you around." Dewar grinned.

Raylen looped Liz's arm through his and said, "Sorry, Brother. Indiana Jones knows more about Egyptian princesses than a pirate does."

"Are we going to find a lost treasure?" Liz asked. "Please tell me we won't have to go into a cave where there are snakes or rats."

"You afraid of snakes and rats? Hell, woman, I figured something as beautiful as you could charm anything on the earth."

Liz laughed. "You are a silver-tongued rogue, not Indiana Jones. I bet there ain't even a treasure in here."

Raylen chuckled. "Oh, yeah there is and I've got it on my arm. A drink for Madam Damagamy?"

Liz giggled. "Drabami. It's the gypsy word for fortune-teller. But she would love a cold beer."

He pushed back a strand of fake cobwebs and led her toward the bar, where six-foot black cat cutouts with green flashing eyes stood propped at each end. Cauldrons with billowing smoke sat on the bar and were scattered around the room on tables.

Ace reached up and grabbed Raylen's arm as they passed his table. "Hey, hey, you goin' to share or do we have to have a duel? My pistol can outdo your whip for the harem lady."

Ace had been in and out of the café all week. He and Jasmine were best friends and he reminded Liz so much of Blaze it wasn't even funny. He had that confident swagger about his walk like Blaze, curly blond hair, and he flirted with every woman he met. The one thing that was different was the eyes. Ace had crystal clear blue eyes, not totally unlike Raylen's. But when he sized Liz up with those eyes, it didn't do a damn thing for her. Not one single bell or whistle went off like they did when Raylen graced her with a look and a smile.

Raylen grinned. "I'm pretty good with a bullwhip, pard'ner."

"Ace, get your sorry butt behind this bar and help me." Jasmine yelled and crooked her finger at him. "You are my backup and I'm swamped."

Ace strutted over to the bar. "You've been saved by the sexy bartender who is begging for my help."

"Who is he supposed to be?" Liz whispered to Raylen.

"John Wayne," Raylen answered.

"Yes?" Ace turned quickly. "Did someone call my name? Is there a cowgirl in distress?"

"Not right here. This is Madam Dammagrammy," Raylen said.

"Madam Drabami," Liz corrected him with a giggle.

"Well, I guess Indiana will have to save her. John Wayne don't have no truck with anything but cowgirls," Ace winked.

"Two bottles of Coors, please, miz bartender," Raylen said.

Jasmine popped the lids off two longnecks and set them on the bar. "Liz, can you really do the dance that goes with that getup?"

Liz nodded. "But not to George Strait."

"Guess we're slap out of luck then because all these cowboys listen to is country." Jasmine smiled.

"What can I get you, Becca?" Ace asked.

Liz bit back the groan before it escaped her lips.

"I'm not Becca. I'm Annie Oakley and I bet I can outshoot and outdance you." Becca's eyes were on the cowboy at the end of the bar: Taylor, the foreman of her father's ranch.

"Well, Annie Oakley darlin', what can this slow cowboy get you to drink?" Ace played along.

"I'll have a whiskey and Coke," Becca said and turned around, popped her elbows on the bar, and leaned back, straining the snaps on her shirt. "So you're the fortune-teller tonight? Are you going to look into the crystal ball and tell me that I'll be walking down the aisle with Raylen in six months?"

"I don't use the ball. I use cards and your palm and I'll tell you whatever it says," Liz said.

"You really believe all that shit?" Becca asked.

"Do you read your horoscope every day?" Liz asked right back.

Becca readjusted her position and claimed a bar

stool. "Hell, yeah, and it comes true about fifty percent of the time."

"Hey, Raylen, are you going to introduce me to your lady?" A man dressed like a pirate bellied up to the bar.

"Liz, this is Dalton Riley. He's Ace's younger brother. And Dalton, this is my new neighbor, Liz," Raylen said.

Dalton got to his feet and bowed over Liz's hand. He brought it to his lips and gently kissed her fingertips. "May I have the next dance, Miz Liz?"

"Of course you can," Liz said. "But right now Raylen and I are headed to the food table."

"I'll hold you to that dance," Dalton said.

Becca reached out and touched Raylen on the arm. "Be a sweetheart and get me a plate of nachos. Libby can sit here beside me and we'll talk about the stars."

Raylen tilted his head and looked at Liz. "Her name is Liz, not Libby. You'll have to get your own nachos. Liz is supposed to start telling fortunes in fifteen minutes so we're going to eat."

"You ain't no fun and not even a good friend tonight, Raylen," Becca pouted.

Raylen ignored her and steered Liz toward the long food table with a hand on the small of her back. Bare, rough cowboy hand against cool flesh created enough heat to burn hell to the ground. Her body hummed with the excitement of his touch, and she wondered if she'd be able to read the cards or even see a lifeline on a palm.

All the strange people, the party atmosphere, the decorations, and the night air reminded her of opening night at the carnival: new faces eager to win a stuffed animal, little children clamoring to ride the ponies or the Ferris wheel, the smell of funnel cakes and cotton candy, the hawkers drawing in the crowds, and Liz dancing to bring in people to the fortune telling wagon.

She missed it all.

Liz wasn't a spectator. She was a player. She liked to dance. She liked to be in the midst of the carnival. She liked to tell fortunes and watch the people and children. What in the hell ever made her think that she could settle down and never roam again?

Raylen pulled out a chair for her and sat close enough that he could drape his arm over her shoulders. Liz looked out across the people laughing, talking, milling about from one group to the other. The energy wasn't as electric as opening night at the carnival, but it was there and it fed the atmosphere.

"Would you go steal a candle from one of those tables, Raylen? And ask Jasmine if I can have one of her smoky cauldrons, and then I want a handful of dirt in one of those orange paper plates," she said.

"Why?" Raylen asked.

"Props," she whispered.

He raised an eyebrow.

"Earth, wind, and fire. I'll call on the spirits to steer me to the right future for the people," she said.

"Hocus-pocus." He chuckled.

"Spirits." She smiled.

He could easily move earth, wind, and fire for her when she smiled like that. Hell, he could talk the angels out of their wings and the devil out of his horns if Liz wanted them for her hocus-pocus.

"Why are you stealing my candle?" Becca looked

away from Taylor when she noticed Raylen picking up the candle.

"Fire. Madam Drabami told me to bring her fire, and her wish is my command," he said.

"You're goin' to get burned," Becca said.

"Not if I don't stick my fingers in the jar." He laughed.

He set the candle on the table. "There you go, Madam."

She smiled up at him. For another smile, he'd damn sure find her some wind and earth. He picked up an orange plate on his way outside and scooped up a handful of dirt.

"What in the hell are you doing?" Colleen asked.

"Taking earth to the gypsy fortune-teller," he said.

"You are crazy and you're goin' to get hurt," she said.

"Not if someone like you don't blow hot air across my dirt and get it in my eyes," he said.

He passed the bar and picked up a cauldron.

"Hey!" Jasmine yelled.

"Got to have wind if the folks want their fortunes told," he said.

"Then take it and be off with you, knight-in-shining-Indiana-hat." She waved him away.

When he returned, Liz had a deck of cards in her hands, shuffling them. He'd never seen such quick hands or such speed. Colleen couldn't even put on a show like that and she was a professional blackjack dealer.

Liz spread the cards on the table, quickly picked them back up, and did an air shuffle that reminded her of Blaze. She looked across the table and pictured him sitting there beside Raylen.

She blinked and it was gone, but she couldn't stop thinking about Blaze. They had shared everything, including one kiss along the way. She was eighteen and both of them had had one too many beers that evening. They'd been scraping and painting wagons all day with Grandpa and they were tired and sweaty from the work inside the warm barn. She'd reached for a beer at the same time he did, and their hands and eyes met somewhere in the middle. Looking back, it was inevitable since they were thrown together so much, but it had been awkward instead of passionate.

When it was over, she wondered why the women acted like momma cats in heat every time they were around him. And he'd wiped the kiss away with the back of his hand.

"I don't kiss that bad," she'd said.

"No, but I feel like I just kissed my best friend, or worse yet, my sister." Blaze laughed.

"Yep, that's what it felt like," Liz said.

"Guess we know now that we ain't meant to be together no matter what Tressa and Marva Jo think," he'd said.

"Guess so," Liz had told him.

And that was that. From then on, they talked every night about everything. She heard about his women. He heard about her crushes. She knew when he thought he was in real love with that woman from Amarillo. He knew when she lost her virginity to the son of an air conditioner repairman right there in Claude, Texas, during the winter months. Blaze had held her hair back while she threw up after drinking too much the night she broke up with the boy, and Blaze was the only person in the whole world who knew that she'd harbored a long-time crush on Raylen O'Donnell.

"I'd give a whole quarter for your thoughts right now instead of a penny," Raylen said.

"Sorry, I was thinking about fortunes," she said.

Well, she was in a way.

Her future and Blaze's, anyway.

Creed Riley drew up a chair across the table from Liz and right beside Raylen. "Is it time for the palm reading to begin? My girlfriend just went to the bathroom, but she wants to be first so she sent me to hold her place in line. You don't look like a witch. And why do you need old Indiana Jones to protect you? If you could really see the future then you'd know if you were in trouble with this feller around you."

Liz looked up and giggled. "I'm not a witch. I'm a Drabami, that's gypsy for fortune-teller. There's a big difference. And Indiana isn't protecting me; he's my wingman."

Creed couldn't have looked less like Ace's brother. He had brown hair, green eyes and towered above his older brother. "So why do you need a wingman?"

"I don't tell people what they want to hear. I tell them what I see, and sometimes they'd just as soon no one else heard what I have to say, so my wingman keeps everyone back about ten feet and turns them loose one at a time. Kind of like one of those good-lookin' doormen at a fancy big-city club," she said.

Creed laughed.

His girlfriend, Macy, sat down at the table and plopped her hand out in front of Liz. "Tell me that cowboy is going to make a wonderful husband." She had a high squeaky voice and blond hair peeking out from behind the Minnie Mouse wig.

Liz fanned the air above the cauldron. "Wind, earth, and fire, descend on us and give us your power to see the future. Show us what lies in the morrow as well as in the distant future." She shuffled her cards one more time.

"Macy, cut them and then lay out the top card on the table."

The woman laid out the wine card and Liz said, "You will soon have a cheerful experience. Your birthday must be nearing."

"Let's hope the wine means a party before then. My birthday isn't until the end of March," Macy said.

"You will have a wonderful, exciting year beginning next spring. You'll have parties to attend and I see long-distance travel in your future with a new love interest that you will find in one of your trips. There's a jackpot in your money sector if you take advantage of the financial opportunities. If not, you will find happiness but it won't be ecstatic happiness."

"I'm not sure I like this fortune tellin'. It sounds like I'm going to find my true love away from Ringgold," Macy said.

Liz nodded. "You will be happy if you decide to stay in Montague County but your real happiness and wealth awaits outside of Texas."

"Now I know this is all bullshit. I'm going to marry Creed and live on a cattle ranch," she said.

Liz smiled. "Just remember what I said when you travel."

At midnight Liz had read everyone's palm except Raylen's, and she didn't want to read his or lay out the cards for him either. She'd told Slade's wife that she would have a third pregnancy which would produce twin boys and Rye's wife, Austin, that she would have a big family in the next ten years. Colleen's fortune said that she would marry someone who would take her to faraway places and make her an exotic princess.

"Now what do we do with earth, wind, and fire?" Raylen asked when the party finally broke up.

Liz shuffled her cards and returned them to her pocket. "We return earth to earth, blow out the fire, and turn off the wind with the button on the bottom of the cauldron."

Gemma sat down and propped her feet up on the table. "Well, darlin', you made the party tonight. It was the best we've ever had. Everyone was talking about what you said. Creed said he'd prove you wrong because his girlfriend was going to marry a cowboy, and Colleen says you are full of shit because she's never leaving this area."

"We'll see." Liz smiled.

"Me, I want to believe you, darlin'. I want to think that by next Christmas I'll have found my own special cowboy. Matter-of-fact, I'm going to be damn good this whole year so Santa can bring him to me. I want him to show up on Christmas day wearing nothing but one of those cute little Santa hats and cowboy boots. Whooo-wee, that makes my little hormones whine just thinkin' about it," Gemma said.

"God Almighty, Gemma!" Raylen said.

"Yep, he is, but Santa might be almighty too if he can bring me that by next Christmas. I'm goin' home. We'll pack up and clean up tomorrow night. Jasmine and Colleen are helping. You want to?" Gemma looked at Liz.

"Sure."

"Supper is on the house for anyone who helps. It's

leftover party food and whatever Jasmine brings," Gemma said. "See you tomorrow."

"I'll drive you home." Raylen looked at Liz.

"No need. I drove myself," she said.

"Then let me drive your truck home and I'll walk back through the pasture," he said.

"I didn't see any devils or blackbirds in the cards." Liz laughed.

"Blackbirds?" Raylen frowned.

"They signify dire misfortune," she said.

"Well, there's crows between here and your place so I better see you to the door." He laughed.

"Okay," she agreed. "But that Dalton fellow really should be taking me home since I promised him a dance and got so busy that I never did dance with anyone."

Gemma took her feet off the table and stood up. "Hey, girl, let Raylen take you home. Dewar got hooked up with Angie Sutter and took her home. I really did think you and him would hit it off but guess I was wrong. Remember what you told him?"

Liz nodded. "That love was on its way to meet him."

"What'd you tell Raylen? I didn't hear his fortune," Gemma asked.

"Didn't do his. He was my wingman and we didn't have time to see what the earth, wind, and fire could conjure up for him. We'll have to read his cards next time around. Good night and thanks for inviting me."

"It's me who's thankin' you. See you tomorrow at the café," Gemma said.

Liz and Raylen were both quiet on the way to her house. Raylen had seen the glow around her as she read palms and told fortunes. It was exciting and exotic. He'd be a complete fool to think that she'd ever give up a life like that to be a waitress in Ringgold, Texas, the rest of her life or settle down with a horse rancher either. She belonged in a carnival, not on a Texas ranch.

The evening had plumb worn Liz out. When she worked at the carnival, her hours were different. She worked until midnight, spent an hour locking everything up, another one talking to Blaze or Tressa and her mother, and then slept until midmorning. Tomorrow the alarm would go off at five. It didn't give a damn if she'd told fortunes until midnight or if she'd gone to bed at ten o'clock. The café opened at six, and customers were usually sitting in their cars waiting for the doors to be unlocked.

Raylen parked the truck and walked Liz to the door, waited while she opened it, and stepped inside without being asked.

"Raylen, it's late," she said.

"I want three minutes of your time," he said.

She cocked her head to one side. "What?"

"I want you to dance for me," he said.

"You've never seen a belly dancer perform?"

He shook his head. "You are so beautiful and I've imagined you dancing all evening. Please?"

"Okay," she agreed.

She picked out a CD, put it into the CD player, and pushed a button. Raylen settled into one recliner while Blister claimed the other and Hooter slept on the floor in between.

Liz went to the middle of the floor and turned her back. When the music started, her hands were up with her shawl tangled up in them and one leg slightly cocked outward. Her body and the music became one entity.

She moved close to him and popped a hip out to brush against his hand.

He smiled.

Putting a hand on each side of the recliner, she did several torso rolls, the sequins and fringe becoming a sparkling blur in constant movement. She knew that she was putting more sexiness into the dance than she had ever done before. It was belly dance and pole dance combined, but she loved the hot desire in his eyes.

His eyes locked with hers and a fine bead of sweat popped out on his upper lip.

She stood up, locked her fingers above her head, and turned her back to him, hips rolling from one side to the other. So he was hot, was he? Well, her skin was on fire from the way his eyes had gone all soft and dreamy. If his eyes could do that to her, she could hardly imagine what sex would be like.

Raylen was so aroused by that time that he was aching. He reached out to touch her, but she moved away and his fingertips barely got a taste of what he wanted.

She swirled in front of his eyes, the scarf becoming fairy wings. One minute it flirted with his face and then was gone before he could capture it with his lips. Another moment it snaked across the pulsating bulge behind his zipper, and even though he couldn't really feel it, it was a blowtorch that heated him up even more.

All he could hear was the tinkling of her bracelets and the bells on her ankles, a sound that filled his ears with music. She said she couldn't play anything but a fiddle, but that wasn't true. She was doing a fine job with silver bracelets and little brass bells strung on an ankle chain.

When the music ended, the shawl was dragging behind her and their eyes were locked together in a heated gaze that said only one thing would ever put the fire out. He grabbed her hand, pulled her to him, and using every bit of willpower he could conjure up, he undressed her without tearing her costume to shreds.

He covered her mouth with his in a series of steaming kisses that just made him hotter and hotter, and every time he opened his eyes, her gaze drew him into her soul even deeper. She undid his belt buckle and unzipped his pants and he settled her onto his erection.

Three thrusts later he groaned, "Liz," and burst inside her.

"Oh, my God," he said when he could breathe. Damn it all to hell! She would think he was horrible. He'd practically ripped her clothes off, hadn't even let her finish undressing him, and then went off like a blasted bottle rocket in less than a minute. Hell, he'd done a better job than that when he was fifteen.

"I'm so sorry." He buried his face into her hair.

"Round two won't be so furious," she whispered.

He covered her mouth with his, his tongue tasting the salty sweat on her upper lip.

"You are amazing," he whispered hoarsely, already aroused again.

She tangled her fingers in his thick dark hair and lost herself in his kisses. She could feel his hardness and he groaned when she wiggled. She slowly unbuttoned his shirt, taking time to run her palms over the soft, brown chest hair and gently massage his nipples.

"You are killing me, Liz," he said.

"Consider it payback for those hot kisses that you

gave me and then walked away," she whispered softly in his ear, her breath warm, and her voice seductive.

He groaned and pulled her back to his mouth for another long, lingering kiss.

He groaned. "Liz, I…"

"What?" she whispered as she ran her tongue around his earlobe.

He ran his rough palms over her back. His touch was hellfire and North Pole ice at the same time. "Cold hands, warm heart" came to her mind, but it didn't hang around. Nothing did. All she could think about was the aching desire right where the belly button diamond had been a few minutes before that wild and furious ride. She arched her back and gasped at the sensation.

She pulled his shirttail the rest of the way from his pants and ran her hands down across his chest, down through the thin line of soft dark hair that extended from taut nipples to belly button.

"My God, that feels good," he whispered.

"Yes, it does," she said. "Smooth as silk. Hard as steel."

He kissed her hard, their bodies melting into each other so tightly that a ray of light couldn't find its way from one side to the other.

"Bedroom?" he asked.

"Oh, yes."

He stood up and she wrapped her legs around him, but it didn't keep him inside. She told herself that it didn't matter. She would reclaim him in a few minutes, but she missed the connection all the way to the bedroom.

Without breaking the steaming kisses, he carried her to the bedroom. She'd been in a hurry that morning and the bed was a jumble of covers, but somehow he managed to throw them all on the floor, leaving only the fitted sheet on the mattress.

He laid her down and quickly kicked his boots off, removed his jeans, and threw them along with his shirt in the corner. She watched him in amazement. His body was so hard, so muscular, and so damn sexy. He stretched out beside her and gathered her close to his side. It was his turn to tease and make her as hot as he had been and was again.

"You feel good, Liz," he said.

"So do you, Raylen," she answered, her voice deep with desire.

His fingers danced down her rib cage. His tongue wrapped around a nipple and brought it to full attention before he moved to the other breast, all the time letting his fingers move like feathers down her body, stopping to massage, to tease, to caress until she was nothing but one big ache that only Raylen could satisfy.

She arched against him and thought that she was going to explode like he did before he could even get started. Her dance could not have made him as hot as he was making her. If it had, he would have gone up in spontaneous combustion, taking the recliner with him. But she wasn't going to beg, not yet.

He stretched out on top of her, his erection hard against her belly, and made love to her lips, tongue, and mouth in scorching kisses that left her panting.

"Please," she whispered.

"Are you sure?"

"Oh, yes," she gasped.

With a firm thrust he started a rhythm that was too fast, too slow, too passionate, that took her breath from her body. She wrapped her arms around his back and rocked with him as she raked her nails across his flesh. Nothing had ever felt so right in her whole life. Not the first time she'd had sex or any of the few casual affairs she'd had since then. Raylen was the cowboy she'd been waiting for her whole life and…

In that moment she had a flash of sheer, unadulterated fear. What if he thought she was a slutty carnie who went to bed with anyone? What if she'd just ruined her chances of happiness with him?

His mouth covered hers in a string of passionate kisses that fanned the flames already sending her up in blazes and erased every thought from her mind. She arched her back against him and gave herself to the red-hot fire and forgot about what-ifs.

Raylen wanted it to last until the break of dawn, but the long night and too many beers brought it to an end faster than he wanted. Still, it made up for that first disaster.

He gasped at the same time she called out his name and with a shudder collapsed on top of her. Then he rolled to one side but kept her in his arms. She reached across him and picked up the top sheet from the floor and tossed it over them.

He brushed a sweet kiss across her forehead. "Wow!"

"That barely covers it," she said.

He tipped her chin up. "I've wanted to do that since we were teenagers too. I dreamed of you more than once. And you made me so damn hot with that dance that I disgraced all manhood. Oh my God, I didn't even think about protection, Liz."

"I take care of that with a little shot a couple of times

a year. Don't worry." She cuddled up next to him and felt as if she were sitting in the middle of a beautiful flame, the glow surrounding her without scorching her wings.

Was it possible to have wings and have roots too?

"It wasn't that bad. Kind of like an appetizer to whet the appetite before the main course," she whispered. "Raylen, I'm not..." She couldn't find the words to tell him that she wasn't like Becca who had that round-heelitis disease.

"Not what?" he asked.

"I'm not a slut. I don't fall into bed with any man that winks at me."

He kissed her forehead. "I know that, Liz. I can see it in your eyes."

She searched his face and his eyes. "I believe you. Then, this is not a one-night stand?"

"Hell, no!" He hugged her tighter. "Darlin', it's the beginning of something wonderful. But you can't dance like that for another man. Promise me! I'm not bossy about a lot of things, but I couldn't stand for another man to see you dance like that."

"I've danced for years, Raylen, but that was a special dance and I promise," she said as she drifted off into a dreamy half sleep.

Raylen pulled a sheet up over them and hoped that she felt the same way he did because he never wanted to let her go.

Chapter 8

LIZ PICKED A CLEAN APRON FROM A DRAWER AND wrapped it around her waist, bringing the ties back around to tie in the front. She loaded the pocket with an order pad and two pens, poured a cup of black coffee, and sat down at the table.

Jasmine slipped a pink cap over her brown hair, pulled the ponytail out the back, and gave Liz a once-over. "You look like warmed over sin, girl. Did they keep you telling fortunes all night?"

Liz covered a yawn with her hand. "Midnight."

"And then?" Jasmine asked.

"And then I did a stupid, stupid thing," Liz said.

"Dewar or Raylen?" Jasmine asked.

Liz swallowed fast to keep from spewing coffee across the kitchen. "What makes you ask that? It could have been one of Ace's brothers or even Ace."

"No, it was either Dewar or Raylen, and I think it was Raylen. He's the one that can't keep his eyes off you. Dewar notices because he's a man. Raylen's looks go deeper. Only a blind man would have trouble seeing that."

Liz sipped the coffee. Maybe the clock hand would miraculously spin around ten times and she'd be saved by customers.

It didn't happen.

"Well? You better talk fast because doors open in

ten minutes." Jasmine's green eyes twinkled. "Dewar or Raylen?"

"Raylen. It's always been Raylen. Since I was fourteen, it's been Raylen. I measured every boy and later every man by Raylen. He's so high up on a pedestal that even God looks up to him," Liz said.

Jasmine sat down in one of the three chairs surrounding the small table in the center of the kitchen. It was a work station when she and Liz folded napkins, a resting station at the end of the day, and a place for her to set up shop for the business end of the café once a week.

"Tell me about it. Raylen might be a sweetheart, but there ain't a man livin' who deserves to be on a pedestal that damn high," Jasmine said.

She took a sip of coffee and her phone rang.

Jasmine pointed. "If it ain't God, then get rid of them. I'm dying to hear what happened."

"Hello," Liz said.

"Okay, okay, you are forgiven for running away, but I still want you to come back to your real home," Blaze said on the other end of the line.

"Blaze, darlin'! I can't wait to tell you everything that's happened, but I've got to work in ten minutes."

Blaze's deep laughter filled her ear and the empty hole in her heart. "I'm just crawling into my trailer. Last night's woman was beautiful but turned out to be a whiner, so that won't happen again. When I got home I had to call and tell you that. The rest can wait until I wake up. Call me in the middle of the afternoon."

"Oh, I will, and I've got so much to tell you," Liz said.

"You know I love you," he said.

"And I love you. Good night, darlin'."

Jasmine's expression was one of acute confusion. "You love Blaze but Raylen's on a pedestal?"

"That's right. I told you about Blaze. He's my best friend, kind of like Pearl is to you. We were the only two kids on the carnival rounds since I was thirteen and he was fourteen. And he's my confidant like Gemma is yours, and then he's like my brother and my cousin. Blaze wears lots of different hats. But he's not Raylen."

Jasmine poured a cup of coffee and sat down at the table. "Did Raylen spend the night?"

"Not quite all of it." Liz blushed.

"I watched you telling fortunes last night, girl. You miss that life. Your eyes were all glittery and you loved what you were doing. I can get a new waitress when you get bored in Montague County. Raylen's heart is a different matter," Jasmine said.

"I told you it was a stupid, stupid thing," Liz said.

"It could be, or it could be a brilliant thing," Jasmine said. "Like Ellen says, it's all in how you look at it and what comes out of it in the end. It's time to unlock the door. You ready?"

Liz nodded. "I reckon I'd better be."

There was a steady stream of regular morning coffee drinkers before Gemma showed up at eight o'clock. She snagged the last table in the corner and ordered biscuits and sausage gravy with a side order of hash browns. She wore her usual tight jeans, sneakers, and a T-shirt with her beauty shop logo on the back. Her dark hair was pulled up into a ponytail, and her makeup did little to cover the dark circles under her eyes.

"It ought to be a sin to look like you do after last night," Gemma told Liz when she brought her food.

"Oh?" Liz fought down the high color creeping up on her neck.

"I danced and flirted. You told fortunes. Both of which would tire a woman out, and what did we get for our efforts? Not a damn thing. We both slept alone and I don't know about you, but I got up cranky as hell. It ain't fair, I tell you. And then of all the things, you tell me I got to wait a whole year before my knight-in-shining-new-Chevrolet-truck is going to come carry me off. Hell, you could have shuffled them damn cards different and he could be on his way right now to drop down on one knee and propose to me," Gemma said.

"Can't manipulate the cards." Liz giggled.

Gemma picked up her fork and started eating. "Can't manipulate my brother either. You could have told him that if he didn't cook my breakfast every day between now and next Christmas you were going to put an evil spell on him, but oh, no, you didn't even lay the cards out for him. That sorry sucker was still snoring when I left a while ago. He put a note on the kitchen table that said he was sleeping in and then going to work on the barn when he woke up."

Liz pointed toward a group of deer hunters dressed in camouflage and made her escape toward them. "I'll be over after work to help you with cleanup," she told Gemma.

"I've got appointments until six. It'll be you and Raylen and maybe Dewar if you can rope him into helping until I get there," Gemma hollered across the room.

—∼∼∼—

Raylen carefully removed the fake cobwebs from the walls and ceiling and packed it between layers of tissue in the cardboard boxes where it belonged. He'd almost finished that part of the job when Dewar showed up close to noon.

"Hungry?" he hollered. His voice echoed in the enormous barn where they held annual horse sales. The atmosphere was all different then with the horses prancing around in the circle, and the buyers all lined up around the top balconies.

Raylen stopped what he was doing and wiped his hands on his jeans. "Starving. Want to go up to Chicken Fried?"

"No, Momma sent me to get you. She made dumplin's and pumpkin pies."

Raylen nodded and headed for the barn door. Part of him was damn glad that his momma had chosen that day to make his favorite dinner; that was the sensible part that needed more time to process the night before. The other part, the section that controlled his heart, longed to see Liz again, to make sure an awkwardness had not sprung up between them that would send her scooting back to her carnival.

"Good party last night. Lots of people. That Liz was a hit with her fortunes," Dewar said as they walked side-by-side a quarter of a mile back to the house.

"Yep," Raylen answered.

"She looked like that woman in *I Dream of Jeannie*. Remember when we used to watch those reruns when we were kids?"

"Yep."

"If she'd had blond hair instead of black, she'd have looked like her."

"Yep."

"You stuck on that word or do you know another one?" Dewar asked.

"Liz ain't as tall as that actress was and she's prettier. That enough words for you?"

"You got a thing for her?" Dewar asked.

"Why are you askin'?"

"Remember when we all went out to Wil's and took him coon huntin' with us?" Dewar asked.

Raylen remembered the night very well. True, they'd gone coon hunting that night, but it was more than that. They went to railroad Wil into admitting that he had feelings for Pearl and it had worked.

"Yep."

"Well?" Dewar stopped at the back porch.

"Deep subject." Raylen grinned and hurried inside the house.

Dinner was on the table with Maddie, Cash, Colleen, and the grandparents already seated and waiting. Grandpa said the blessing as soon as Dewar and Raylen sat down and Cash began to pass the dishes.

"Got to go wash up," Raylen said. "Didn't want to hold up dinner since you were all already sittin' down. Colleen, you leave me some chicken!"

Colleen threw her deep red hair over her shoulder and grinned at her brother. "Yeah, right!"

He washed his hands and face and took time to comb his dark hair straight back. The man looking at him in the mirror didn't look any different than the one who'd looked at him the morning before, but he damn sure felt different. How could having sex one time with a woman change a man so much, and yet no one else could even see it?

When he returned to the table everyone was talking, mostly about the party the night before. Grandpa looked up and winked as if he knew something, and Raylen felt a slow heat crawling up his neck. Then Grandpa pointed to Colleen's plate and Raylen saw the all the extra chicken beside her dumplings.

Raylen sat down beside her and loaded his plate with dumplings and then deftly, while his sister was talking to Grandma, forked the chicken from her plate and raked part of his dumplings over it.

"Hey, where's my chicken?" she said when she looked down. "Raylen!"

"Don't look at me. I was in the bathroom. Dewar probably stole it."

Dewar threw up both palms defensively. "I'm innocent."

Colleen narrowed her dark green eyes and looked from one brother to the other. "Raylen, you did it. You can't hide nothing."

Raylen grinned and shoved food into his mouth.

"He's got the hots for our new neighbor and he's hidin' that pretty dang good," Dewar said.

The grin vanished and he shot his brother a dirty look.

"She's a pretty woman, but you'd best be careful," Grandma said. "She's like a butterfly. They look so pretty flittin' around out there among the roses, but if you catch one and put it in a jar, it'll die."

"She'll get tired of plain livin'. She's a…" Colleen said.

"A carnie," Raylen finished for her. "Once a rancher, always a rancher. Maybe that don't hold true for a carnie."

"I'll bet you it does," Dewar put in his two cents.

"I'll take that bet. Ten bucks says she stays," Raylen said.

"Ten says she goes before Christmas." Dewar stuck out his hand and they shook over the table.

"Twenty says she's gone by December fifteenth," Colleen said.

Raylen looked at Colleen. "You don't think anyone can change?"

"Person is raised one way, chances are they'll stay that way. Am I going to get your twenty or not? I won't ever marry anyone but a rancher. It's in my blood."

"I'll put twenty on it." Raylen sipped his iced tea. "So you're sayin' if a man walked up on our porch, say, sellin' Bibles, and you looked at him and fell in love in an instant like Rye did when he looked at Austin, that you wouldn't be happy sellin' Bibles with him?"

Colleen giggled, then laughed aloud, then grabbed her napkin to wipe the tears. "Me sellin' Bibles? That ain't never goin' to happen, Brother. I'm marryin' a cowboy when I get around to fallin' in love. One who lives on a big ranch."

"Good girl," Maddie said.

"Never say never," Raylen said. "Gets a person in trouble every time."

Chapter 9

Liz sat in the truck for a full five minutes just looking at the barn. It was a big, square, metal building with enormous sliding doors on the east side. One of them was open about three feet, and she had no doubt that Raylen was cleaning up after last night's party. She had her hand on the door handle when her cell phone rang and she jerked back as if she'd been burned. She answered it without even checking ID, figuring that Raylen was calling to give her a hard time about dragging her feet.

"I just woke up. I miss you. Come home," Blaze said.

"I am home. I love it here and I can't wait for you to see this. It's as big as the winter place and I've got a barn and a dog and cat and enough Christmas decorations to light up half of Texas. And Raylen is next door and he's not married, Blaze. And I'm sitting here in my truck looking at the barn where we had a dress-up Halloween party last night, and I'm going to help Raylen with cleaning it all up this afternoon. I have a job and I love it."

Blaze laughed. "That sounds like you are trying to convince yourself. What did you say you did last night?"

"There was a party at the neighbors'. A Halloween party with a live band and open bar and I told fortunes," she said.

"Did you wear the turquoise?"

"No, orange."

"And?" Blaze pressed.

"And Raylen took me home afterwards," she said.

"Damn, Lizelle. Tell me what happened. I feel like I'm pulling teeth," he said.

For the first time Liz couldn't tell Blaze what had happened. It was too personal, too intimate. "I set earth, wind, and fire, and it was so easy because they had cauldrons with dry ice in them so they were smokin' and that made the wind, and fire came from a candle, and Raylen went outside and got me some dirt on a paper Halloween plate and I set all three around me. Then I either did their palm or laid out the cards or both. You showed up in one of the readings."

He took the bait. "Oh, tell me who you were reading for."

Liz bit back a giggle. "Her name is Colleen and she's Irish to the bone. She's got strange colored red hair that is almost burgundy and deep green eyes. You'll meet her when you come to visit at the Bowie gig. She's Raylen's sister and she works as a blackjack dealer at a casino over the border in Oklahoma."

"And what card did you see?" Blaze's voice said that he was wide awake.

"Oh, no! I don't kiss and tell, not even to you, when it comes to cards. It was her personal future. If you want me to read the cards for you then come see me," Liz teased.

"Tressa can do it anytime I want." His tone said he was pouting.

"Yes, she can. I don't think you'd like Colleen anyway. She's independent as hell and doesn't stutter when she speaks her mind. And she wouldn't put up with one minute of your bullshit. The first time you looked at another woman she'd tie your carcass to an altar and cut off your balls. The cards must've been wrong to even suggest that you'd meet her in the future, or else they were right and you'd better go on down to the funeral home in Claude and get fitted for a casket."

"That's morbid, but you've got my curiosity roused. Besides, you know I like red hair. Are you just tellin' me this crock of bull to keep from talkin' more about you and Raylen?"

"I am not doing any such thing. And just to prove it I will introduce you, but rest assured it would never, ever work between you two. If she caught you flirting, I'm serious, she'd cut your balls off, deep-fry them, and feed them to her cat."

"Shit! That made shivers up my back. Did you turn over the card that says I'm to run from her?"

"I told you, I don't kiss and tell," Liz said. "And now I've got to go help clean up the mess. It's a neighbor thing. I'm helping them today, and starting tomorrow they're going to help me put up all my decorations so it will be all pretty when y'all get here."

"Lizelle, don't get too involved with Raylen. He's just a kid you met briefly and built into a superhero. He's a real person, sweetheart, and real people aren't gods or heroes. Your heart will always be a wanderer. You know that old sayin' in the church about giving them a child until they are six and they'll never change. It works the same in lots of things."

Liz sighed. "You were fourteen."

"Yes, but my mother was a flower child and I loved the carnival my whole life, even if I didn't get to join it until I was fourteen. I'd stand by the fence and watch y'all leave in the spring, and my heart would hurt to go with you. We're carnies at heart, sweetheart. We'll never change."

"Gotta run. Time to go earn my help puttin' up decorations," she said.

"Did you sleep with him already?" Blaze asked bluntly.

"Losing connection. Tell Momma hi," Liz said and flipped the phone shut.

Liz was halfway to the barn when Raylen stepped out.

"Already done?" she called out.

"You ain't that lucky. I've got the cobwebs down and part of the tables cleared off." He grinned.

If a heart could do a belly dance, hers did. Complete with jangling music and tinkling bells.

She swallowed twice and said, "Well, I'm here to help. Tell me what to do."

Colleen appeared right behind Raylen. "I'll tell you what to do. Come right on in. You can strip down the tables and I'll wash them. Then Raylen can fold the tables up and stack them on the rack. I bet Gemma took extra appointments today on purpose, that rat!"

Raylen winked slyly at Liz. "We'll make her work extra hard when we start putting up Christmas decorations tomorrow night, won't we?"

"Oh, yeah," Liz said. "You going to help us too, Colleen?"

"Can't. This is my only day off this week and then I'm dealing blackjack for seven nights in a row. Six at night until six in the morning," she said.

Liz followed them into the barn. "Lord, you'll be wiped completely out."

"Didn't you work seven nights a week at the carnival?" Colleen asked.

"Guess I did in one capacity or the other. We were set up and running four nights a week. I did fortunes two or three of those. We were usually tearing down and moving two days and setting up one day. Those days it was all hands on deck from daylight to way past midnight. We slept and ate when we could," Liz said.

"Miss it?" Colleen asked but she looked at Raylen.

"Of course. Would you miss blackjack?"

"Yes, I would. I'd miss the excitement. There's something about people who gamble. They are..." Colleen stopped.

"Electric," Liz finished for her.

"That's it. There's static in the air and excitement," Colleen said.

"Carnival inside a building." Liz smiled.

"And you can leave all that behind for a dog and a cat and a waitress job?" Colleen pressed on as she stripped a table of its orange plastic cloth, wadding it up and tossing it in an oversized trash can.

"What would it take for you to leave your job behind?" Liz cleared cups, plates, and napkins from the next table.

Raylen bit back a grin as he worked. Liz was holding her own against his most pessimistic sister. Not that Colleen would ever let him get away with calling her that. No sir, she'd say that she wasn't pessimistic, she was realistic.

Colleen stripped off another tablecloth and shoved it into the trash can before she answered. "I'm not sure, but it would have to be huge."

"How huge?" It was Liz's turn to press.

"Bigger than a waitress job at the Chicken Fried and

an old dog with arthritis and a temperamental momma cat," Colleen said.

"In my world my job, Hooter, and Blister are huge," Liz said.

She didn't add Raylen or her house and land into the mix, but they were a hell of a lot bigger than Hooter, Blister, or Chicken Fried. Raylen had winked at her when she arrived, but that's all she got, which wasn't a lot after the hottest sex on the face of the earth. Maybe he wanted a friend with benefits as Blaze called some of his women. He could wish in one hand and spit in the other and see which one filled up fastest, if that's what he had in mind. Liz wanted a whole lot more than that.

Colleen's cell phone rang and she dug it out of her hip pocket. "Hello... yes, I can... be there as soon as I can... good-bye."

She flipped it shut and put it back in her pocket. "Sorry, but that was my boss. Girl who was working tonight has the flu so I'm drawing down some serious overtime. Have fun. Gemma should be here soon," she said on her way out the door.

Liz heard the truck engine pull away from the barn before she crossed the floor of the arena and popped her hands on her hips.

"I won't be a friend with benefits," she spit out.

"I didn't ask you to," he said.

"Then why did you act like last night didn't even happen?"

He grinned. "It was the hardest thing I've ever done, but I didn't know how you wanted to play it. If you want me to, I'll crawl up on the barn roof and shout loud enough they can hear me over in Oklahoma that we slept together last night."

She tried to bite back the giggle but it wasn't possible. It erupted into a full-fledged guffaw that left her mascara running and her sides aching. "You. Wouldn't. Dare."

He took a step toward her. "Don't ever dare an O'Donnell. Besides, I'm not ashamed that I had sex with you, darlin'. Are you? If you want me to show you the steps to get to the roof I'll be right glad to do so. We can both do some yellin'," he teased.

Not to be outdone, she moved closer until she was nose to nose with him. "I'm not quite ready for that," she whispered as she moistened her lips.

One look at those delicious lips and he was lost. He circled her waist with his hands. She shut her eyes and rolled up on her toes to meet his slightly parted lips as they sought hers.

Hot desire filled every inch of her body as he made love to her mouth like he had the night before. Without breaking the kiss, he pulled her hips closer to him. She gave a little hop and wrapped her legs around his waist, his belt buckle pressing into her pelvic bone. She shifted and what was below the buckle was just as hard and pressed even more.

"Tack room?" he whispered.

She barely nodded and wrapped her arms tighter around his neck. She'd been in a relationship half a dozen times in her twenty-five years, but none of them had been as hot and steamy as one of Raylen's kisses. None had made her throw common sense to the wind and agree to a wild romp in a tack room.

The kisses grew deeper and more passionate, each one turning up the heat more than the last one until she thought that steam was surely blowing out her ears. Her jeans were hot against her skin, her bikini underwear was sticky, and her bra suddenly felt two sizes too small.

She heard the tack room door open and then he kicked it shut with his boot heel. She fumbled with his belt, unzipped his jeans, and pushed her jeans and underpants down to her ankles. She shifted her weight until he was inside her. He braced her against the wall and kept his lips on hers, their tongues doing an ancient mating dance while she hung on during the fury of burning heat.

She'd had sex, but it had always been in a motel bed with the man on top. Never had she had a ride so wild or so passionate. She'd sure never felt the kind of heat that made her arch her back against the wall and beg for more. And she'd never wanted to do it again as soon as it was over.

"Hot damn!" she said.

"I take that as you are happy," Raylen panted as he raked a table clean with a forearm and laid her down on it.

"Yes," she panted.

He collapsed beside her, pulling her as close to his side as he could get her.

"Ready to go to the rooftop?" he asked.

"Damn near."

His lips found hers with a fierce, hot kiss that got her ready for another round. He ran his palms from her chin, up across her cheeks, and tangled his hands in her hair.

"You..." he whispered.

"You…" she whispered back.

His hands were everywhere—on her hips, her thighs, probing, finding spots that made her forget everything but how much she wanted him.

"I want more," he whispered hoarsely into her hair.

"Me too," she said.

"When I touch you, the world disappears," he said.

His eyes were dreamy and scorching hot at the same time. She stretched enough to brush a kiss against each of his eyelids and he moaned. Until that moment she wasn't aware that a man could groan in a Texas drawl or that it would turn her heat knob up to high.

Raylen had never felt raw passion before that moment. He shifted his position and suddenly she was under him on the rough table. He ran a hand down her ribs and up her back, unfastening her bra. His touch made her gasp and arch her back for more.

"Please," she begged.

With a long, slow, gentle thrust Raylen began a rhythm that drove her crazy and brought her to the edge of a climax. Then he slowed down until she thought she'd die with desire, and at the very moment when she could stand no more, she dug her fingernails into his back and said, "Now, please, Raylen."

"Liz!" he said hoarsely.

The heat had melted them together on the narrow table when they heard a truck headed their way. They frantically searched for clothes and pulled them over their sweaty bodies, barely getting the job done before they heard Gemma yelling.

"Hey, anybody here?"

Raylen eased the tack room door open and gave the

room a once-over. "I'm in here making room to store things," he hollered.

"Is Liz with you?"

"Isn't she out there?" Raylen asked.

"Don't see her," Gemma said.

"Guess she took a load of trash out the back door. We've been loading it in the bed of my truck and I'll take it to the dump when we are finished."

Liz looked at him with wide eyes and he winked. He laced his fingers in hers and led her to a door on the other side of the tack room and very gently opened it so it wouldn't creak.

"Go on out and circle the barn and come back in the front door," he whispered as he brushed a kiss across her lips. "Unless you want us to go out there together and start bragging about what we did."

She slipped her hand from his and eased out the door, blowing him a kiss on the way. "Thank you," she mouthed. But she missed that special time afterward, like the night before when they'd cuddled before she fell asleep.

Chapter 10

FALL IN TEXAS CAN BE COLDER THAN A BRASS MONKEY on the North Pole or hot enough to go swimming in the lake, sometimes both within a three-day span. It's that time of year when folks turn on the heat in the morning but by midafternoon they've switched it to air-conditioning.

The afternoon that Liz called in the troops to help put up yard decorations was one of the hot days and felt nothing like Christmas. The day before had hovered down around forty degrees, but a southerly wind picked up and warmed Ringgold up to eighty degrees and she'd turned on the air-conditioning when she got home that afternoon. There was cold beer in the refrigerator. She made a pitcher of iced tea, a pot of coffee, and arranged store-bought chocolate chip cookies on a plate. And then she set a small CD player on the porch with a Christmas CD in it, put it on repeat so that the songs would keep coming. She turned it up as high as it would go and waited for the army to come help her do battle with her decorations.

They all arrived at the same time: Gemma, Raylen, Dewar, Jasmine, and Ace. The three guys grabbed a cold beer and went right to the barn while the ladies had a glass of tea, cookies, and half an hour of gossip.

"Reckon they got it figured out?" Gemma asked.

"What?"

"Men folks are different than us girls. They have

to scratch their heads and measure and talk something to death before they get it done, right, Jasmine?" Gemma said.

"You got it. Then after they've done cussed and discussed, they do what we would have done to start with. They ought to be gettin' the stuff down out of the loft about now so we'll go on out and start loading lights," Jasmine said.

Liz laughed. "It's universal. You ought to be in the carnie business."

The guys were still measuring the opening when they finally got to the barn.

"Guess we didn't give them long enough," Gemma said. "Let's get the lights loaded on Liz's truck while they play like engineers."

Two hours later they'd figured it out enough that everyone was out of the loft, and all the pieces were unloaded up against the fence on the south side of the property. Now it was time for more head scratching and measuring.

"You're the boss lady. You tell us where to put it," Ace said.

"How many are there in all?" Liz asked.

"Thirty-six," Raylen said.

"Then we'll divide them. Eighteen on each side."

"By theme, color, or what?" Dewar asked.

"Let's lay them all out on the ground and then decide where to put them," Ace suggested.

Liz swiped her hand across her forehead, smearing dirt and sweat from one side to the other. "That would take until next Christmas."

She wore cutoff jeans and a faded T-shirt with Tinker

Bell on the front; her hair was parted down the middle and pulled up into dog ears that bounced when she turned from one side to the other. Raylen thought she was cute as a new baby kitten and wished he could kiss her right then and there. But that would bring the decorating to a damn halt because when their lips met, it never was long until they were shedding clothes.

"How do they stand up when a strong wind hits?" Gemma asked.

Raylen flipped a snowman around and pointed to the bottom. "See that board with the holes in it? Stakes go through the holes and then two feet into the ground. Plus there's a prop, kind of like the back side of an easel, that keeps them steady. We've got hundreds of stakes in the back of the truck yet. Haskell had them all cut and in two boxes. Looks like he did that this year because the cuts are fresh."

Liz had thought she'd know exactly where to put each one. It was supposed to come to her like divine intervention. The grouping of snowmen would go there and the nativity scene there, but it didn't work that way. She was totally bewildered.

"Help!" she said.

Jasmine pushed her brown hair behind her ears. "You really want a Griswold effect?"

Liz nodded.

"Okay, then take every other one and put it on the other side of the lane. Don't pay a bit of attention to themes or content. Just arrange them haphazardly like you said."

"Okay. That's the way we'll do it. But remember to fix them so one isn't back behind another so they are all as visible as possible from the road and from the lane," Liz said.

Ace picked up Betty Boop standing in front of a Christmas tree and carried it to the other side of the lane. Raylen grabbed a four-by-eight piece of plywood with a painting of three snowmen and a yellow puppy playing at their base.

"That must've been the year he got Hooter," Liz said.

"And that's this year, right?" Jasmine pointed to the cactus with the belly dancer sitting in the fork.

"You got it." Liz grinned.

Dewar got a firm grip on Santa's sleigh. "I'll come back and get the reindeer that hooks up to this soon as I haul this little fat man to the other side of the lane."

"Y'all take the ones that are left behind and arrange them where you want us to set them up. While we do that you can arrange on this side and then you can begin to string the lights while we set up that side," Raylen said.

"Mr. Organization," Gemma said.

"Miz Smart Mouth," Dewar taunted.

"Oh, hush! You'd agree with him just because it's guys against gals," she told him.

Jasmine touched Liz on the shoulder. "They argue like that all the time. It wasn't easy for me to get used to since I'm an only child. Pearl and I were friends and we argued some but not a lot. These O'Donnells fight like…"

"Irishmen." Gemma giggled. "It's fun. You ought to try it."

"I know exactly what you are talking about." Liz remembered the fights she had with Blaze. He hated to be wrong almost as much as she did, and their arguments could get heated. He was Irish too. Maybe that was the explanation. Their worst argument had been when he couldn't talk her out of leaving the carnival and then he stayed in his trailer and refused to come out to wave good-bye to her.

"Okay, then, let's put Mr. and Mrs. Claus with their welcome sign way back at the house. That way, when the folks get to the end, the old couple will be saying, 'come right on in and have a cup of hot chocolate,' and then..." Gemma started.

Liz was shaking her head emphatically. "No! I want them right here at the very front of the property to welcome everyone to the whole light show. Not way back there where you can't even see them. Put them right here in the corner."

"I disagree," Jasmine said. "I think they should go in the other corner since most people are right-handed, and that's where they'll look first."

Liz moved to the corner beside the cattle guard and crossed her arms over her chest. "I want it right here."

Jasmine and Gemma both cracked up.

"What is so damn funny?" Liz asked.

"You argued with us. I'm proud of you, girl. You might make an O'Donnell yet!" Gemma said.

"You two are..."

"Pigs from hell?" Jasmine asked. "Ever see *Steel Magnolias*? I love that line."

"Yes, I did and love it. And that's exactly what you are," Liz said. "I've argued with an expert and you two barely qualify as amateurs."

"You hear that, Raylen? She says she can out-argue us," Gemma said.

"When hell freezes over," he shot across the lane.

"Well, get ready for icicles on Lucifer's boogers!" Liz smarted off.

Raylen stopped and locked eyes with her. "I don't think so, darlin'."

"I don't give a rat's ass what you think."

Gemma cackled. "She's pretty good, Raylen. You've met your match on the fiddle and in a fight, too."

He grinned and carried a decorated Christmas tree to the other side. His arm brushed against Liz's as they passed each other. He caught her eye and winked. All the arguing left her in an instant and desire flooded her body. She wanted to send her friends home and drag Raylen behind those snowmen for a session of wild, passionate sex. That session against the wall in the tack room the day before had sent her mind into a whirlwind. Now every place she saw became a place for seducing Raylen.

She chose a spot for the next lawn ornament, stuck a twig in the soft earth to mark it, and helped Jasmine and Gemma place it. But her thoughts stayed on the tingling place on her arm where Raylen had touched her. Did he think she was easy? Would he get tired of her? Or worse yet, did he have an ulterior motive like Dewar said in the café? Just how badly did he want her twenty acres?

"You are frowning," Jasmine said. "This is supposed to be fun, not a chore."

"It is." Liz forced a smile. "I was wondering if we have enough to cover all the land as close as we're positioning them."

"You were thinking about Raylen," Jasmine whispered. "I saw the way you looked at him and that wink he gave you. Did he make you mad?"

"No, shhh," Liz said.

"Hey, I'm not tellin' anybody," Jasmine said.

"It's just that it's…"

Jasmine zipped her mouth shut and then laughed out loud.

"What's so funny over there?" Gemma asked.

"This place is going to make Griswold's look puny," Jasmine said quickly.

When they finished with the placement on that side, the guys had hauled the other half to the north side of the lane and the ladies changed places with them. That side went faster and they started stringing lights before the guys finished staking and propping the south side of the lane's decorations.

"I'm glad Uncle Haskell marked the boxes for me." Liz pulled a box with "Mr. and Mrs. Claus lights" written in big bold letters on the top from the back of her truck.

"Are they all like that?" Jasmine asked.

"Yes, they are," Liz answered. "We'll just have to dig through the boxes. Hey, you know what we should do? Put each box by the cutout where it goes rather than digging through them all."

"You sound just like Raylen. Y'all might be kin to each other as organized as you are. Your Uncle Haskell is probably his great-great-seventeen-times-back-cousin or something," Gemma said.

"God, I hope not," Liz said quickly and then looked up to see if she'd really said the words aloud.

"Why? Don't you want to be kin to the O'Donnells?" Gemma asked.

"No, ma'am. Y'all argue too much for me," Liz joked.

"It's Dewar, isn't it? I knew it from the first. You've got a crush on Dewar," Gemma whispered.

"Hell, no!" Liz said.

"Well, crap!" Gemma sighed. "I did want you to fall for him. We've got to get him married, and then Raylen." Gemma crossed herself and went on, "God forbid, but then Colleen. I'm not sure there's a man on the earth I can bribe into takin' her off our hands."

"Why?" Liz asked.

Gemma picked up a box of lights and carried them over to Betty Boop. "Because she's so outspoken and pessimistic."

"Not why about Colleen. Why do you have to worry about your brothers and sisters falling in love?" Liz asked.

Jasmine stacked one box on the top of the other and carried them across the lane. "Because according to Cash, they have to get married in the order of their birth."

"I thought that was a joke," Liz said.

"I heard y'all," Dewar raised his voice. "And you might as well give it up, Gemma. I'm not being rail-roaded to the altar."

"We could drug him and pay the girl," Jasmine whispered.

"What was that?" Dewar asked.

"I heard her," Ace said. "She said she was going to help Gemma drug you and pay some old gal to marry you."

"Better bring your lunch because it'll be an all-day job," Dewar said.

Jasmine pointed a long, slim finger at him. "Darlin', I could put something in your chicken fried steak and you'd wake up next to some old hussy wearing a wedding band. We would make her sign a prenup so she couldn't sue you for the farm in the divorce. We'd do that much for you. You'd better think about that when Gemma starts lookin' at wedding books. Us girls got to stick together."

Raylen caught Liz's eye and the look that passed between them sizzled. He made love to her with his eyes and she shivered. She could imagine his hands on her body as he slowly went from her shoes to her lips and lingered there.

"I'd say you'd better be out girl huntin', or else hire you a taster like they did in the old days every time you go anywhere near these witchy women. I think they're acting like they are jokin', but they are all dead serious," Ace said.

Jasmine narrowed her eyes at him. "You'd better be careful. I can have you at the altar in a heartbeat. I know lots of women who'd take your sorry old hide any way they could get it. And if you aren't nice to me I'll forget to have them sign the prenup."

"Dammit! Look what you got me into, Dewar. I was mindin' my own business drivin' stakes and now I got to watch my back." He pointed at a barbed wire tat around his upper left arm. "You see this? Me and Rye got them to protect us against witchy women. Austin got over or under Rye's barbed wire, but ain't no woman never goin' to get me to drop down on one knee. It ain't happenin', Jasmine darlin'. Not even you got that much power."

"Power ain't got nothing to do with drugs," Jasmine told him. "But you'd best take me on home. I've got to make peach cobblers before I go to bed tonight, and it's startin' to get dark, and you've got chores to do. Your hired help was fussin' yesterday about you getting' lazy."

"They were not! They know I work harder than any of them out there on that ranch," he protested.

Jasmine pointed her forefinger at him and pretended to shoot him. "Gotcha! But seriously I do need to get back to the café."

"Us too," Dewar said to Gemma.

"Yep, I got to make a run to the beauty supply over in Wichita Falls before they close at eight. Got two dye jobs and a perm in the morning," Gemma said. "Want to go with me, Liz?"

"No, I'm going to call it a day and do some house cleaning. Got to get everything beautiful for my mother and aunt. We're planning a pre-Thanksgiving potluck dinner in the barn before they go on to Claude for the winter. Start spreading the word. Everyone is invited," she said.

Ace unloaded two more boxes of stakes from the bed of his truck before he held the passenger's door open for Jasmine. They waved and drove off down the lane, honking when they reached the end. Dewar and Gemma got into his truck and fell in behind Ace's truck when they turned north toward Ringgold.

Raylen looked over at Liz and opened his arms. She walked into them and they closed around her. She looked up to find his eyes closed and his lips coming toward hers. She snapped her eyes shut and moistened her lips with the tip of her tongue. The kiss was hard and fiery and crackled the air around them.

"I can't stay. Momma and Daddy are expecting me to go over books with them tonight, but I had to kiss you. You ready to stand on the barn and tell everyone that we're dating?"

"But we aren't," she said. "We haven't been on a single date."

Raylen brushed soft kisses across her eyelids and forehead. "That can be fixed real quick. This is Wednesday. Tomorrow we'll finish this job. Friday, I've got to be in Wichita Falls for a horse meeting. So Miz Liz, would you have dinner with me on Saturday night? You don't have to work on Sunday so we won't have to be home early."

"Yes, I would."

"Then on Sunday afternoon, we'll go shopping for a tree and then have dinner or else have dinner and then shop for the tree. Monday we can put it up and get it decorated. If you want a real cedar one we'll go to the woods, but if you want a fake one then we'll go to the mall and find just the right size and style for you," he said.

She leaned back and looked at him. "You *are* organized."

"That's what they say, but I want you to have a perfect Christmas, even if it is the week before Thanksgiving." He couldn't tell her that he was falling for her entirely too fast and he wanted her to have more than a perfect Christmas. She deserved a perfect life, not just one perfect day a year.

He kissed her one more time, and she swore she heard bells and whistles off in the distance. He didn't want to leave, but his brain was a ball of mush and he couldn't think of an excuse Maddie would buy.

"Now I really have to go. Momma said seven and it's five minutes 'til. See you tomorrow after work."

Liz wished that Raylen wasn't so punctual or organized.

Chapter 11

JASMINE HAD TO MAKE A GROCERY STORE RUN TO Bowie for the café after work on Thursday so she couldn't go play Christmas with Liz. Gemma had three late appointments that would keep her tied up until dark. Dewar had promised Rye that he'd go with him to Breckenridge to look at a new longhorn bull he wanted to buy for rodeo stock, and they wouldn't be back until bedtime. Ace was up to his elbows in tractor repair and didn't even have time to come to the Chicken Fried for a hamburger.

That left Raylen and Liz to finish stringing lights.

He crawled out of his truck in her front yard and shook the legs of his dusty jeans down over his scuffed up cowboy boots. His chambray shirt was open down the front with a sweat-stained gauze muscle shirt underneath. He removed his straw cowboy hat, brim turned down deep in the back and front and curled up on the sides, and wiped sweat from his forehead with his shirtsleeve. The hat looked like it had survived a Texas wildfire and been through a couple of cattle runs, all a hundred years before.

Liz had rushed home from work with intentions of taking a shower to get the grease smell from her hair, but she'd barely made it to the porch when Raylen's truck pulled up. Her work T-shirt was stained where grease had splattered on her, and her makeup had long since gone.

"Where's the rest of the crew? I knew Dewar was going with Rye, but we were supposed to have some help," he said.

If he'd known he was working alone with Liz, he damn sure would've taken time for a quick shower and a change of clothes.

"Jasmine has to go buy groceries. Gemma had late appointments. Ace called Jasmine and said he didn't even have time to run by the café for a burger," she explained.

"Well, I guess it's a two-man crew, then. You ready to get this job done? We've got a helluva lot of work to do, Mrs. Claus."

She did not miss the way his sexier-than-hell blue eyes looked at her. What did they see? A messy waitress who'd just come from work? A neighbor in need? She'd love to be able to dive into those eyes like they were pretty blue ocean water and find the answers. With a slight nod, she led the way out to the cutouts. "It's even more than it looks like, Raylen. I want to have presents under the tree for everyone on the night of my party, so that means some shopping."

"For everyone? How do you do that when you don't even know how many will be there or what they'd like?"

"Boxes of candy and tins of popcorn. Everyone likes that, and it's fun to have a present."

He tucked her hand in his and paced his step to match hers. Hooter stretched and followed five feet behind them. Blister had a sudden burst of energy and bounded off the porch to run ahead of them.

The spark was definitely still there. It hadn't died overnight. Two days of fantastic sex and then a day without. But the old adage "out of sight, out of mind" must not apply to sexual attractions. The sizzling tingle was as strong as ever, and even though she smelled like grease and onions, he wanted to kiss her.

She wasn't a bit amazed at the gushy warmth spreading all over her body when he took her hand. It was there every time he touched her. He didn't even have to touch her; just catching him staring at her from across the yard or the room made her hotter'n a drop of water on the café griddle.

He squeezed her hand and swung her around to face him. "I've been putting hay in the barn all day and…"

She took two steps forward and wrapped her arms around his neck. "I've been working around food all day but I want to kiss you."

Her lips were like water to a man who'd walked thirty miles in the desert without a canteen. He couldn't get enough of them. One long, steaming hot kiss led to another and then a dozen, fueling a sexual bonfire before Raylen pulled back.

"Another minute like that and these lights aren't going to be working when your carnival gets here, darlin'," he whispered into her hair.

"Right now I'm all for instant gratification and working until midnight a few nights," she said.

"Me too, but when your family and friends arrive I want everything to be perfect. I think it'd be great if they took pictures to Haskell and showed him that all his artwork is on display this year," Raylen said.

They'd barely begun putting the lights on a piece when Liz's phone rang. She checked Caller ID and answered it. "Hi, Blaze! You just wakin' up? I've already put in a day at the… oh my God! What is it? Blister just ran down a field mouse and she's eating it from the nose, yuk, to the tail and I can hear the bones crunching."

Raylen looked up with a quizzical expression, removed his hat, and hung it on a snowman as he wiped away sweat again. That time he wasn't sure if it was from the weather or the inward heat.

"It's Blaze," she said as if that was all the explanation he needed.

Liz sat down on the ground beside the eight-foot-tall wooden Christmas tree. "Yes, I live in the country and yes, I really have a cat. I just told you that she's eating a mouse right now. So how did your day go?"

Raylen couldn't hear what Blaze said and didn't want to. A surge of jealousy shot through him and brought blistering angry steam out of his ears. It's a good thing he'd taken his favorite hat off or it would have been scorched. She could have said that she was working, that her brand new boyfriend had come over to help her and that she'd talk to him later, but oh, no, she just sat down like she was going to talk for a whole hour and ignored Raylen.

"That is so funny! You almost got yourself in a bind. You'd better check IDs before you go to flirtin' anymore. That was jailbait and could have landed your sorry ass in jail," she said.

Raylen finished stringing the lights on the tree, fastening them down with clips so the wind wouldn't blow them halfway to the coast. He went on to the snowman display and opened the box of lights for them. According to the positioning of the clips, they were to be strung all around the outside perimeter of each of the three snowmen.

"So you're on the way to Denton for the next-to-last gig of the year. Are you getting excited about sitting still for the winter?" she asked.

Raylen didn't give a damn about Blaze. He'd looked forward to spending time alone with Liz all day, and his Irish temper was only a notch below the boiling stage.

You are being a big baby. She misses him like a brother, and if you were in her shoes and Gemma called, you damn sure wouldn't tell her to hang up and call back later, his conscience scolded him.

Yes, I would. If she cared as much about me as I do her, then she'd want to spend what precious time she could with me. And if that was Becca, she'd be as mad as I am, he argued.

"You are kidding me. Tell me what happened and don't leave out a single detail," Liz said.

Raylen is working by himself, her conscience said bluntly. *Hang up!*

But I haven't talked to Blaze in two days and he's telling me about Tressa being sick, she argued.

She looked up to tell Raylen that she'd be finished in a minute and saw anger shooting out his eyes, his mouth set in a firm line, and the slight cleft in his chin deepening in a frown.

"What?" she mouthed.

His jaws worked like he was chewing gum, but nothing came out. Finally, he turned around and took two steps toward the house.

"Gotta go. Call you later," she told Blaze and snapped the phone shut.

"Raylen, dammit, turn around."

He kept walking.

She grabbed his hat and threw it at him. "Then go!"

The hat sailed over his head and hit the ground in front of him. He picked it up, slapped the dirt and grass from it, and settled it on his head before he turned around and said with gritted teeth, "Do not ever treat my hat like that."

She jogged to him, grabbed his hat off the top of his head, slammed it down on the ground, and stomped on it. "There's what I think of your damned hat."

He was too mad to speak so he picked up the hat, punched it back into shape, crammed it on his head, and kept walking. She took a deep breath and watched him go. His eyes were set straight ahead when he drove down the lane.

"Dammit! I wasn't through with this fight!" she said.

The phone rang, and hoping it was Raylen, she answered before she looked at the ID. "You pompous bastard. Don't you walk away from me when we are fighting."

Blaze laughed loudly in her ear. "I've been called pompous and my parents weren't married so I guess that part is right. But I didn't walk away from you. I do believe you hung up on me so I don't think this is about me. I called back to make sure you are all right."

"Hell no! I'm pissed. I'm not all right and I'm going to fix it right now. Tell me the rest about Tressa and make it quick because I'm so damned mad my cussin' is liable to fry out my cell phone."

Blaze barely kept the laughter down enough to say, "It's just a cold. She got a shot, some antibiotics, and Marva Jo ran the fortune-telling wagon one night. Tressa about went crazy, though. It was the first time since I've been with the carnival that she was too sick to work.

She says she's well enough to take over the fortunes in Denton and that, by damn, you are coming back to do them in Bowie."

"Okay, okay," Liz said. "I'll be there every night after I get off work, but right now I've got to go see what the hell put a burr in Raylen's saddle."

"Trouble in paradise?" Blaze asked.

"Damn straight, and he's not getting mad at me for throwing his hat on the ground," she said.

"Whoa! You threw a cowboy's hat on the ground? Darlin', that's a sin worse than coveting your neighbor's ass. Did you pick it up and hand it back to him nicely?"

"Hell no! I stomped it flat. So I guess I don't get to go to heaven today. Call me later." She flipped the phone shut. Covet her neighbor's ass! Well, she'd already done that more times than she could count since she'd come to Ringgold, so throwing Raylen's hat in the dirt could just be written down on the list with her other sins.

Raylen felt really stupid by the time he got home. He was glad that Gemma wasn't there so he could wallow in his self-proclaimed pity pool as long as he wanted. Liz missed her carnie life. She missed her friend, Blaze, who she probably belonged with more than she did with an old cowboy like Raylen. And she'd proven every bit of it by stomping on his hat. God Almighty! That was the ultimate insult.

He hung his poor, abused hat on the rack beside the door along with his black felt dress hat and his good straw hat, shucked out of his jeans in the living room, threw his dirty shirt over a rocking chair, and kicked his boots off in the hallway. When he reached the bathroom, he was wearing nothing but his socks. He wadded those up in a ball and slung them at the far wall.

"Damn women anyway," he muttered as he turned on the shower and waited for the water to warm.

"Nobody falls in love with their soul mate when they are kids. I don't give a damn if she could have walked a barbed wire fence instead of a rail one in her damned bare feet. I've been a fool to think that she was the one for me. Shit, any other woman wouldn't leave me standing cold while they talked to their best friend. How would she feel if I left her sitting there while I talked to Ace about coon huntin'? Hell, I wouldn't do that to her. I like her too damn much to talk coon huntin' when I could be spending time with her. And I would never, ever throw her favorite hat in the dirt and then step on it." He fumed as he got into the shower and soaped up his body.

She didn't even knock on his door but plowed right inside without an invitation, then took a look at the string of clothes leading down the hallway and the hats on the rack beside the door. She grabbed the one she'd stomped on and crammed it down on her head. It was too big, so she adjusted it to fit on the back of her head and then followed the noise of the shower. She might as well take the damn thing with her to the next fight since she'd offended it in the first one.

One minute Raylen was mumbling about women. The next the shower curtain flew open and there was Liz, her hands on her hips, anger flashing from her dark eyes, and his hat on her head. That shut up the tirade instantly.

"What the hell was that all about?" she asked.

"What the hell are you doing in my house and why are you wearing my hat?"

"Having a fight with you, you mule-headed jackass! The door was open and I followed the trail of clothes. And evidently this damn hat means more to you than I do, and since it started the fight, I figured it should be here for the next one. Now answer me." She raised her voice two notches.

"Don't you treat me like shit and then yell at me. I didn't cause this problem, lady. You did when you'd rather talk to your carnie boyfriend as me! And you can damn well go put my hat back on the rack. This steam will get it all out of shape."

"You are a jealous horse's ass. I wasn't talking to a boyfriend. That was Blaze. I told you that he is my friend, and Tressa's been sick. And this hat is so damned ugly it would take more than a stomping or steam to get it out of shape. It already looks like shit," she said.

"Oh, sure. Make an excuse. I heard you talking about him almost going out with a teenager. What kind of friends do you have that would be attracted to a little girl? And don't talk about my hat like that."

Liz narrowed her eyes. "The girl was seventeen, not a little girl. And she didn't look like a child, either. And don't be hateful! This is your fault, Raylen O'Donnell. Your Irish temper put you in this pot of boiling water."

"You put me in this pot, not my temper. You'd rather talk to your carnie friend than me? Well, go on and talk to him. And put my hat back and don't let the door hit you in the ass on the way out."

She glared at him and tried to stay angry but it didn't work. How could she be mad when he was standing there all wet and naked.

He glared back at her and tried his best not to grin but his eyes sparkled. She was just so damned cute when she was mad.

He reached out with both hands, slipped them under her armpits, and picked her up as easily as he would a feather pillow. He quickly removed his hat and pitched it out onto the vanity, set her down, clothes, shoes and all, under the shower spray, and kissed her hard.

One kiss and he was instantly aroused. Two and he throbbed.

One kiss and she forgot all about fighting or his damned hat and wrapped her arms around his neck and her legs around his waist. Damn, but that warm water felt good on her sweaty neck. Two kisses and she unfastened her jeans.

"Ever done it in a shower?" he whispered as he slipped his hands down inside her panties.

She gasped and shook her head. "There's a first time for everything."

He braced against the back of the shower and she leaned back far enough he could remove her top and bra. He licked the water from each breast and removed her jeans and underpants. There was no way to pull them off her hips without putting her feet on the floor, but they didn't waste a moment of time. In seconds he cupped her bare, wet butt and she hopped back into his arms.

Being wet made it easier than it had been in the tack room. She reached down and guided him inside and the water kept everything lubricated. She discovered that wet kisses were exciting as hell and wondered what sex would be like in a big old hot tub or Jacuzzi with all the bubbles.

He braced her against the wall and in a few hard thrusts brought both of them to a climax. She tightened her legs around his waist and he eased down to a sitting position in the shower with her still wrapped around him.

"Damn! My legs feel like rubber," he said.

"Oh, it's a rainbow," she said.

He opened one eye but didn't see a rainbow.

"Water and afterglow. Beautiful rainbow in your blue eyes," she said breathlessly on her way for another long, wet kiss.

After several minutes, he reached up for the soap and made a lather in his palms. Then he slowly bathed her using nothing but his hands. When he finished, he grabbed a towel from the rack right outside the shower, wrapped her in it, and carried her down the hallway to his bedroom.

He laid her on the bed and stretched out beside her. She cuddled up to his side and threw a leg over him. "We'll get your sheets all wet."

"There's more in the linen closet. Are we okay?"

"Was that what they call makeup sex?"

He chuckled. "It could be."

"Then let's fight every day because that was mind-boggling," she said.

He kissed her wet hair and pulled the edge of the bedspread over them. "Are you sure you aren't Irish?"

"I'll convert. Is there classes I have to take?" she teased.

"Not that I know of. Want to go finish those lights?"

"Hell, no! And just so you know, I left my cell phone in the truck."

He ran a hand down her back and she shivered.

"I'm still a little bit mad," she said.

"And my hat still has its feelings hurt," he whispered.

"Reckon we'd better have some more makin' up?" Her eyes glittered.

"I'd rather you danced for me first," he said.

"I will dance for you on Thursday," she said.

"Is that a promise?"

"It is. The carnival will be here and I'll be dancing on the stage and you can watch," she said.

"You promised you wouldn't dance for another man," he said.

"I won't be. I'll just be doing a plain old belly dance."

"Then I won't be there," he told her.

"Why?"

"Even a plain old belly dance would turn me on so hot that I wouldn't be able to walk."

She smiled up at him. "Then I will dance on Thursday, after the carnival, in my living room for you. Is your hat feelin' better?"

"Yes, ma'am," he drawled.

"I'm glad. It bothers me when your hat is mad at me," she teased.

The house phone beside his bed rang.

He kissed her on the end of the nose. "Sorry, darlin', but I couldn't leave it in the truck."

He answered it, jumped out of bed, and grabbed a pair of pants from his closet, motioning to her the whole time. When he hung up, he said, "Here's a T-shirt. I'll bring your wet things over to your house later. That was Dewar. Glorious Danny Boy has gotten out of the barn again. That horny horse takes off anytime he gets a chance. We've got to get him chased down, or Momma will have a heart attack."

"Call me later?" she said.

"Yes, I will, and you promised to dance for me on the Thursday of the carnival. You won't forget?"

"I'll be thinking about it every minute. Don't you forget," she teased.

"Honey, I won't be able to keep my mind off it, and believe me, when I think about it, I will be very uncomfortable."

Chapter 12

IT WASN'T LIZ'S FIRST DATE.

But it was her first date after sex three times as a prelude and she was as nervous as a momma cat in heat. Going to the Halloween party had been easy; she'd dressed up in one of her costumes. But going to dinner with Raylen and then shopping... with Raylen... for a Christmas tree and then coming home to after-date kisses and maybe hot, steamy sex... with Raylen... that was a whole different matter.

She looked at all the clothes in her closet and threw herself back on the bed. She should have made time for a trip to Bowie. She needed something new and exciting to wear that night on her first date with Raylen. Something that would make his eyes go all dreamy, like they did in the shower right after sex, when she'd seen the rainbow in them.

"I need something in red. No, that's not the exact lyrics. She said that she was looking for something in red that was cut down to here." She remembered the old Lorrie Morgan song from a few years back. The singer had talked about looking for a red dress that would knock her feller's eyes out in the first verse. Then she wanted something in white in the second, something in blue for a new baby boy in the third, and back to something in red in the fourth. Liz hummed the song as she pulled the filmy turquoise dancing outfit off the rack and held it up to her body. She imagined what it would look like without the top of her black lacy panties showing above the encrusted belt and without her black lace bra peeking out above the fancy sequined top.

"I'm looking for something in turquoise. If I met him at the door in this and did three minutes of dance, I bet we'd forget about leaving the house and I wouldn't be worrying about our first date," she told the reflection in the mirror.

She hung it back up and picked up her robe. Maybe if she walked away from the closet and stopped fretting, everything would fall into place. She shoved her arms down into the black satin robe and headed toward the living room. Liz, Hooter, and Blister had walked down to the end of the lane and back four times on Friday evening, and she'd sent pictures from her phone to Blaze, her mother, and Haskell.

She put a Christmas CD into the machine and leaned back in the recliner, picturing the way everything was going to look when her carnie family arrived. The phone rang and she picked it up to see Haskell's name on the ID.

"Hello, we've got those gorgeous ornaments out on the lawn and it's going to be beautiful and why did you ever put me in an old cactus?"

"Because it's your first year in the house, living in Ringgold, and making a lot of prickly decisions," he said.

"Well, I'm going to need one a year, so you better keep working out there in Claude. What are you making me next year?" she asked.

"Next year you get a manger scene with baby Jesus in it and a new puppy and a whole litter of multicolored kittens around the cradle," he said.

"Why?"

"By then you will know," he said.

"Come on, Uncle Haskell, why would you do that?"

"Maybe because I want you to have a new baby by then, and old Hooter could use a new puppy if you are going to stay there, and there's always kittens in the spring."

She giggled. "That would take a miracle."

"Who said the days of miracles were over?" Haskell asked.

She shut her eyes tightly and pictured one star in the sky and made a wish that Haskell was right.

"I called to tell you to send me a picture when you get it all done. Now I've talked enough. Poppa is coming over for supper," he said.

"I love you, Uncle Haskell," she said.

"I've always loved you, Liz."

She hung up and stood at the door looking out at the show. An adage that she'd heard for years came to mind. It said that when a person looks back on their life, it wouldn't be what they did that they would regret but what they didn't do. If she didn't get her butt into jeans and her feet into boots or shoes, she wouldn't be going on a real date with Raylen, and in twenty years she'd regret that decision.

She went back to the closet, pulled out a pair of designer hip hugging jeans, a black shirt with rhinestone buttons and long, fitted lace sleeves ending in a wide ruffle at the wrist, and a pair of black spike heels. When Raylen knocked on the door, she'd just finished running a brush through her hair one final time.

It had been a long day for Raylen. He awoke after erotic dreams of Liz dancing in a field of clover. He was sprawled out on a quilt and she danced for him in that orange costume. The bells on her ankle bracelets jingled in his ears, and her body moved to music that they shared in their minds.

He was fully aroused, and it took a long time under a cold shower to cool him down. He plowed that morning, but flashes of her dancing, sending out waves of that exotic perfume, caused a big problem behind his zipper several times.

He picked up the first CD in a stack he kept in the tractor and put it in the player, only to get an earful of Carrie Underwood singing Christmas songs. That brought a flashback of her in the tack room with cobwebs in her hair.

"Hell's bells," he swore. "This is miserable."

He got through dinner at his grandmother's without thinking about her more than a dozen times and left there headed for the barn to exercise horses until time for their date.

Sitting in a saddle with a throbbing arousal was painful, so he handed off the exercising to Dewar and offered to muck out stalls. By the time the day ended and he got to her front door, he was ready to jump right into bed. But that's not the way a real date started, so he knocked on the door and waited... impatiently.

Raylen didn't even look at what she was wearing until after he'd cupped her cheeks in his big hands and planted a sexy kiss right on her lips. Then he laced his fingers in her hands and stepped back to scan her from toes to eyes.

"Beautiful doesn't begin to describe you, Liz. Your perfume makes me think of an exotic woman in a sexy orange outfit doing a belly dance. And you taste like something the angels brewed up," he said.

"You are a romantic, sir, and you are purely sex on a stick," she said.

"On a stick?" He grinned.

"On a stick like ice cream. Lick on it until it melts."

He swallowed hard. "Darlin', we'd better get out of here after that remark or else we're going to wind up in bed and there'll be no Christmas tree when your momma arrives, but thank you, my Madam Dammybammy, for saying that I look like that," he said.

His jeans were starched, creased, and bunched up just right over his boots that were shined to a high gloss. He smelled like Stetson aftershave and tasted like something the devil brewed up. He was just too damn sexy for anything to do with an angel.

"Drabami." She laughed.

He'd said, *my madam*, and that was as warm as cuddling up to him after a long bout of sex.

"So are we ready to go? I'm starving. Haven't had anything since lunch and I've been looking forward to this date all day."

"I'm ready. Do I need a jacket?"

"Not now, but you will by the time we get home. Weather says there's a cold front on the way. Won't drop us down to freezing, but the wind is fixin' to be out of the north," he said.

She picked up her black leather jacket and purse. He kept her hand tucked into his the whole way out to his truck.

"Do you like Italian food?" he asked.

"Love it."

"Good. It was a toss-up between the Texas Roadhouse for steaks or the Olive Garden for Italian," he said as he helped her into the passenger's seat.

"I've never eaten at the Olive Garden but I love Italian. Blaze makes amazing lasagna," she said when he was buckled in and driving down the lane.

The mention of Blaze's name shot a jealous streak through Raylen's veins. His jaws worked in anger and his hands gripped the steering wheel so hard that his knuckles turned white.

"I can't wait for you to meet Blaze. You are going to like him. He's a lot like Ace."

She didn't miss his jaws clenching and unclenching or his grip on the steering wheel, or even the way his back went suddenly ramrod straight. It might not be the best time to bring up Blaze's name, but she hadn't done it intentionally. His name had just popped out when she thought about his cooking. And anyway, she wasn't going to walk on eggshells... not even for Raylen.

"Ace?" Raylen's tone was coated in a layer of ice.

Liz unhooked the seat belt and scooted across the bench seat to sit close to him. "Oh, yeah! He has blond hair like Ace and he's about that size and always flirting. He's got a woman in every place we stop, and if he doesn't have one, there's a dozen waiting in line for a chance at him. Like Ace! I could never fall for a man like that. Every woman I ran into in Walmart or the Dairy Queen might be one of his conquests. I think men like Blaze ought to have a permanent tattoo marker that they stamp their women with. That way when other women see how many there are they steer clear of him."

Raylen chuckled at first, then it turned into a full-fledged laugh that erased all the angry tension. "Ace would have to go back to the store for more tattoo ink if he had to stamp his women."

"Blaze would probably have to buy out the factory. One time we both had one too many beers and wound up kissing. I don't know what the women see in him. I felt like I'd just kissed my brother and he actually wiped my kiss from his lips with the back of his hand. Said he felt like he'd kissed a sister."

Another jab of jealousy hit Raylen's heart like a dagger.

"You ever kiss anyone that felt like that?" Liz asked.

"Becca," he said too quickly. "When we were in eighth grade, we were at a Valentine's party and got locked in a closet together after a game of spin the bottle. I don't know if I kissed her or if she kissed me, but it was like kissing a sister. Never did ask her out or kiss her again."

Liz actually felt green jealousy infiltrating her veins. Why in the hell had he brought up her name?

She clamped her mouth shut and counted to ten. It didn't work.

She counted to ten again. Still didn't work.

On the tenth time, she'd cooled down enough to point out the window and change the subject. "Look at those wire reindeer. I want some of those. Where can you buy them? Oh, look, there's a horse pulling a carriage out of that stuff, too. They are open and airy so they'd look good in among all the wood things."

She didn't want to talk about Becca or Blaze anymore.

"You can buy those things at Hobby Lobby or some-times at Big Lots or in the Walmart garden center," he said. "I thought we'd start at Hobby Lobby looking for a tree since you decided on an artificial one, so you can check there first."

"I want a real one, but Momma reminded me that I'm allergic to cedar and pine trees. Do you think they'll have one that doesn't look perfect? I want it to look real even if it's not."

"They'll have dozens. We can always lop off a limb or two to make it look real," he teased.

She slapped him playfully on the shoulder. "Don't tease me. This is important."

"Why?"

She swallowed hard and decided to be truthful. "Momma asked me every year what I wanted for Christmas and I told her that I wanted a house without wheels. When I was a teenager I added one more thing to my list and that was a sexy cowboy. So this year I've got my house with no wheels and I want it to be special."

"And the cowboy?" Raylen turned to look into her dark eyes.

She met his gaze and didn't blink. "The jury is still out on that one, and besides, it's not Christmas until December 25th. I might have a cowboy by then."

"After Thanksgiving, Santa Claus will be at the mall. You might have to sit on his lap and ask for a cowboy," Raylen teased.

"Been doin' that every year since I was four. Uncle Haskell says it takes a long time to make a house with no wheels and a cowboy. They aren't like Barbie dolls or skateboards. Oh, look at those." She pointed while they were stopped at a red light in Henrietta. "I want a swing in my yard like that so I can string lights around it at Christmas."

Raylen put on the blinker and pulled over to the display of picnic tables, benches, and one swing with room for two people.

"What are you doing?" Liz asked.

"Let's look at them. Can't get one tonight because we'll have your tree and your wire reindeer in the truck so we won't have room, but we can find out if he's here all the time or if he's ever over in Bowie." He was out of the truck and had her door open before she could blink.

"Evenin', kids. What can I talk you into buyin'? Missus interested in a picnic table? I'll make you a great deal. Picnickin' season is over and I'm tryin' to get rid of the rest of my stock." The man had two days' worth of white whiskers on his round face, a bald head, and bright blue eyes. He wore bib overalls and a long sleeved thermal shirt. His denim jacket hung on the back of a chair.

"How long you goin' to be set up in Henrietta?" Raylen asked.

"I live up the road a piece. I'll be here until Thanksgiving if there's anything left to sell. That's so I'll be out of Momma's hair while she fixes up the holiday dinner. Kids are all comin' home this year. Got six and it'll be a zoo at our house with them and all the grandkids," he said.

Raylen ran a hand over the swing. It was sturdy and well built. "What are you askin' for it?"

"Summer price is three hundred but it's the last one, and I've got it down to two hundred. I'd throw in one of them Adirondack chairs for that price too, just to get rid of the stock. You want one of them picnic tables for

your backyard too? More you buy the better the price.
I knock twenty-five off each big piece when you buy
two or more," the man said. "I know you. You're one of
Cash's boys, ain't you? He bought a set of them rockers
over there for Maddie's Christmas. I'm haulin' it out to
hide it in his barn on Monday while she's over at the
beauty shop. Want me to haul any of this stuff for you?"

"I'm his third son, Raylen. Guess I won't be needin'
anything right now since Daddy already bought the
rockers," he said.

"How 'bout you, missus?"

"Not tonight. Maybe I'll be back in a couple of days.
I really do like that swing," Liz said.

"Well, darlin', you and the husband, there, y'all have
a seat in it for a few minutes. You'll really want it when
you see how good it sets," he said.

Liz smiled. "I better not or Raylen will throw me out
beside the road for griping about how much I want it all
the way to Wichita Falls."

"We might stop back sometime." Raylen steered Liz
toward the pickup.

"That is some sturdy furniture. I really, really like that
swing," Liz said.

"Well, dammit!" Raylen said when he'd settled Liz
into the truck. "I left my keys on the table over there.
Laid them down to run my hand over the wood. Be
right back."

The old fellow looked up and grinned. "Which pieces
you want me to put in the barn, son?"

"The picnic table, the swing, and two of those chairs."

"I'll just charge you for the table and the swing.
Throw them two chairs in like I said I would. Go on now

and you can pay me when I deliver them on Tuesday. I knowed you'd come back. She can swing the new babies in that swing and your grandbabies will eat off that table. I don't do no shabby work," he said.

"Thank you." Raylen picked up his keys and whistled all the way back to the truck.

Liz looked across the seat at him. "Old fellow must get lonely. He sure likes to talk."

"Reminds me of my grandpa. What does your grandpa look like?" Raylen asked.

"He's six feet tall and thin as a rail. Totally unlike Uncle Haskell who took after Granny. She was short and round. Pictures tell a different story about her though. When she and my grandpa got married, she was built like a movie star of the forties. She had dark, wavy hair and this big, pretty smile. You could tell by the way he looked at her that Poppa always saw her as that gorgeous woman that he was lucky to get."

"Were they always carnival folks?" Raylen asked.

She nodded. "My great-grandparents started it up in the thirties when times were tough. It was cheap entertainment, and folks needed that. Then they retired and gave it to Poppa about the time he and Granny got married. You know the rest. Haskell decided he didn't want that kind of life but Momma and Aunt Tressa thrived on it."

She pointed out a western furniture store between Jolly and Wichita Falls. "I want to go there sometime. It's closed now, but when I get ready to redo the house I'd like to look at their stock."

"What have you got in mind for the house?" Raylen asked.

"Comfortable western or maybe early attic," she said.

He raised an eyebrow.

"Momma and I lived in a trailer my whole life. We don't use travel trailers or RVs because we'd have to take it into town every time we had to make a grocery or laundry run. We use fifth wheelers that hook into our pickup. I've never had space like I've got in the house, and I love it. Early attic is junk you'd find in estate sales. We never got to go to things like that or have anything that wasn't necessary. So I might decorate with early attic just so I can buy junk," she said.

"Then next spring, you and Granny can hit the estate sales. She loves to go and Grandpa hates them," Raylen said.

"That would be great," she said. "Is that the Olive Garden we're going to? There's a mall and a Ross store and a Hobby Lobby. I'm in love."

The waitress seated them in a corner booth right away, took their drink order, and handed them menus. While they made their selections she brought Raylen a beer and Liz a Diet Coke.

"I'll have the chicken fettuccine," Liz said.

"And I'll have spaghetti with meatballs," Raylen said.

"I'll be right back with your salad and bread. Hey, aren't you Raylen O'Donnell? I've seen you in here with Ace. Where is that cowboy? Haven't seen him in months. He used to come in once a week," the waitress said.

"Been busy. Lost his grandpa and inherited a ranch to run. Doesn't stray as far from home as he used to," Raylen said.

"Well, you tell him Katrina said hello." She hurried off to the kitchen with their order.

"Tat stamp, I swear," Liz said.

Raylen looked at her with a question on his face then remembered their previous conversation and smiled.

"I like this place. It's got a nice atmosphere," she said.

"Food is pretty good, too."

It was on the tip of her tongue to say she'd reserve judgment until she tasted it. Then she'd tell him if it was as good as what Blaze cooked, but as much as she liked makeup sex, she really didn't want to fight with Raylen. So far, other than having to cool her jealousy by counting, the date had been wonderful. Conversation had been good. Stopping on a whim to look at outdoor furniture had been fun. The kiss had been steaming damn fine.

Raylen reached across the table and covered her hands with his. "Did I tell you that you look pretty tonight?"

"Yes, sir, you surely did. I think the words were beautiful, exotic, and something to do with heavenly."

"Did I tell you that your eyes fascinate me? That I thought of them all the time after that year when you were leaning on the fence watching me ride?"

She smiled and her dark eyes glittered. "No, but I sure like that talk so you can keep right on with it."

"Well, well, well, lookee who's out on the town tonight."

Liz looked up slowly, hoping she'd been wrong about that voice, but she wasn't.

"Hello, Becca," she said.

God hated her! Or maybe it was the devil messing with her life. Whichever one it was, she wished they'd go on back to passing down judgment or stokin' up hell's furnace and forget all about Liz Hanson.

Becca slid into the booth with Raylen, plastering her side against his. "I bet I can tell you what Raylen ordered. He's a plain old spaghetti and meatball man. Never does try anything new. That's his life. He'll never go out on a limb and put something new in his life."

Liz didn't need to stay up all night reading *Catfights for Dummies* to figure out Becca's underlying message. She was telling her that in the end Raylen would settle down with a woman from that area that he'd known his whole life, that he didn't have the nerve or the balls to fall for someone new.

Becca patted him on the arm. "Steady old reliable Raylen. Course, he'll be just the ticket for some woman. She can trust him and never fear that he'll cheat on her. Might bore her to death, but he wouldn't be unfaithful."

"Lord, I'd hate to have you for an enemy," Liz said.

Becca's smile faded. Her back straightened ramrod stiff and she toyed with her bracelet as she shot daggers across the table. "Why'd you say that?"

"Because all you've done is put Raylen down since you sat down. If you're his lifetime friend and you do that, God only knows what you'd do if you were his enemy," Liz said.

Raylen squeezed Liz's hands.

"You talk big for someone your size," Becca said.

"I just tell the truth. Size ain't got a lot to do with it."

A tall, lanky cowboy stopped by their booth and held out his hand to Becca. "They've got a table for us now. Hello, Raylen. Hi, Liz. Nice to see you."

"Brandon." Raylen nodded.

"Y'all have a nice evenin'. We're off to the movies soon as we get something to eat," Brandon said.

"Have fun," Liz said.

When they were seated across the room, Raylen said,

"That was interesting. Never had a woman take up for me before."

"She always that bitchy?" Liz asked.

"No, she's really not. She's usually a lot of fun."

"Then she just plain don't like me."

Raylen shrugged. "Don't take it personal. She doesn't like anyone I go out with. And she really hates Jasmine. She thinks Ace has a thing for Jasmine because he's always goin' in there after the café is shut down and she and Ace were an item back in high school."

"That was years ago, and besides, I'm there most of the time when Ace comes in. He and Jasmine are the best friends ever." She caught herself before she said, "Like me and Blaze."

Chapter 13

THE HOBBY LOBBY STORE BUZZED WITH EXCITEMENT. Anything that had to do with Halloween was fifty percent off, and Thanksgiving items were displayed on two long aisles. But Christmas was what took Liz's eye. Several aisles displayed thousands of bright, sparkly ornaments that hung from the floor to above Raylen's head. Pretty paper, shiny ribbons, glittery garland, and beautiful tree toppers were on another aisle, and Liz could have all she wanted of everything that year. In years past, Marva Jo had set up a two-foot tree on the kitchen table and scattered the presents around it. They'd always put lights on the trees outside Poppa's trailer, and sometimes he even had a small tree, but nothing that went from floor to ceiling. She'd always wanted to buy lots of pretty decorations and that night she had the basket full before she and Raylen even turned into the Christmas tree aisle.

"From the look in your pretty eyes, maybe we should've brought a horse trailer to get all your purchases back to Ringgold," Raylen said.

She pointed at the biggest tree on display. "Oh, oh! Look at that big one. Will it fit in the truck?"

He hugged her tightly to his side. "They come dismantled and in a box so the answer is yes; however, you might want to reconsider. It says right here this tree is ten feet tall. It's eight feet from your floor to your ceiling. We'll have to cut at least two or three feet out of the top of that one," he said.

She cocked her head to one side. "You are saying I should buy a six foot tree in order to get the topper on it?"

He brushed a sweet kiss across her lips and wished he could have more than a taste. "That's right, but look at all the different six footers. There's the skinny one that doesn't take up much room, and there's a fat one that'll cover a quarter of your living room." He pointed as he spoke.

Liz pushed her cart toward the six footers, folded her arms, and studied each one. "I want the fat one. I don't care how much room it takes up. It looks like one we'd really cut down out in the woods. And I want some of that pine smellin' spray stuff to go on it so it will smell real. And…" She hesitated.

"And what?" Raylen asked.

"Can we cut a real tree down tomorrow and put it up in the barn? That's where we'll have our carnie dinner on Wednesday night. And I'd like to have a tree in the corner and presents for everyone who is there, and we could put up a cedar in the barn because I'd only be out there a little while, and besides, we could open the big doors and…"

Raylen drew her close to his side, liking the way she fit so perfectly next to him. "We'll go cut down a tree tomorrow and decorate one in the barn and one in the house." She grabbed his cheeks with her hands and rolled up on her toes. The kiss was supposed to be quick and no one was supposed to see it, but it lingered and grew more passionate by the second.

"Wow!"

"Yep," he said.

"Did that really happen? Did anyone see us?"

"I believe it did. I don't think anyone was around, but I bet they saw the smoke risin' off the fire we created. Do you picture that tree with a star or an angel on top?"

She smiled. "I know this cowboy with a cute butt that I might get to help me put a big star right on top of it. A star on the one in the house and an angel with fluffy wings on the one in the barn."

"Oh, really?"

She looped her arm through his. "You reckon you are strong enough to chop down a cedar tree?"

"Just how cute is my butt?"

Liz hugged up close to him and whispered, "Mighty fine when it's soakin' wet in the shower and pretty damn fine the way it fills out a pair of tight fittin' Wranglers."

Raylen planted a kiss on the top of her head. "If Madam Dallydinger will keep up that kind of talk, this cowboy just might even help her get the lights on her house tomorrow while she hangs half a gazillion ornaments on her two trees, and Sunday we can chop down a cedar tree and Thursday, you are going to dance for me again, remember?"

"Madam Drabami isn't going to be hanging balls on the tree, but she'd rather be outside watching her handsome cowboy's butt as he puts up lights. Now let's go find some wrapping paper. I've got dozens and dozens of boxes of candy and cans of popcorn to wrap. And yes, I'm going to dance for you on Thursday night. I'm looking forward to it, darlin'."

"Candy? You was serious?"

"Darlin', if you can't eat it, wear it out, or use it up in

a few weeks, you don't give it to a carnie. They have no place to put it," she explained as she led the way to the wrapping paper and bows. "Is my sexy cowboy going to help me wrap presents too? And after the big carnie Christmas party, we'll go shopping again so I can buy presents for Jasmine and Gemma and your momma and even Ellen and Nellie. I'm so excited about Christmas that I could dance…"

"Oh, no, not here!"

She giggled. "I was going to say dance a jig, not a belly dance."

"Okay, but don't put me down for any wrapping. I'm all thumbs when it comes to wrapping, and tape comes to life and attacks me every time I get around the stuff."

"Then I guess I'd better buy you those soft little black velvet handcuffs instead of duct tape for Christmas," she teased.

"I'd rather use that fancy scarf thing you dance with," he whispered so close that the warmth of his breath kissed that soft spot right under her ear.

She shivered. "You are cheating."

"All's fair in love and war, Madam."

Chapter 14

LIZ CARRIED SACKS FILLED WITH BOXES OF ASSORTED chocolates and cookies along with tins of popcorn painted with Christmas scenes into the house. Raylen unloaded the Christmas tree into the living room and put all the new wire ornaments on the porch until he ran out of room and had to set up the rest on the lawn. Then he helped Liz tote in the rest of the sacks.

When they finished, the two empty bedrooms were filled with sacks, wrapping paper, tape, ribbons, candy, and popcorn. She covered a yawn with her hand as she made her way back outside and noticed that it was two thirty in the morning. It had been a fantastic first date. She loved Olive Garden and couldn't wait to tell Blaze about it. Raylen had been so patient in Walmart while she wiped the shelves free of boxes of chocolates and tins of butter cookies and popcorn that he deserved a big gold metal on a velvet Christmas ribbon.

"All done!" He made it to the recliner where he plopped down.

"Thank you," she said.

"You are very welcome. Shall we talk about those handcuffs now?"

She sat down in his lap and yawned again. "Rain check, please. I'm wiped plumb out."

He pulled her closer and kissed her forehead. "Thank God! I'm too tired to move."

She pulled her knees up and snuggled down into his chest. "Pop up the footrest and push back so we can rest."

I wonder what sex in a recliner would be like. Oh, hush, I'm so tired, a bout of hot sex would kill me dead. And besides, I think Raylen is already dozing.

She meant to shut her eyes for only a minute. Just rest them long enough to garner enough energy to kiss Raylen good night. All good dates ended with a hot and heavy kiss that promised he would call again. At least they did in the movies. When she opened her eyes, sunlight was streaming in the window and Gemma was standing beside the recliner with her hands on her hips and a grin as big as Dallas on her face.

"Good morning?" Liz said weakly.

"Looks like it!" A smile covered Gemma's face and her eyes twinkled.

Raylen opened his eyes slowly. "Guess we fell asleep. What are you doing here?"

"Lookin' for you."

"Why?" Raylen asked.

"Because you didn't come home last night and there wasn't a note or a message on the machine. Remember what we agreed? We are adults and we don't have to answer to each other for our time, but if we aren't coming home then leave a message so the other one doesn't worry," she said. "So this is who you had a date with?"

"Yep," Raylen said.

"A date or dating?" Gemma asked.

"I promised to leave a message. For not doing that, I'm sorry. The rest is my business," Raylen said.

"I don't like it," Gemma said.

"Get over it," Raylen told her.

"Why?" Liz looked at Gemma.

"Because it complicates *our* friendship, Liz. You can't tell me details of your dates since it's my brother," Gemma answered.

Liz grinned but she didn't move from Raylen's lap. "You want details? We went to the Olive Garden, and I had fettuccine and Raylen had spaghetti, and Becca showed up and she doesn't like me, but that's okay because I understand because Raylen doesn't like Blaze either, and I'm not sure Blaze is going to like Raylen." Liz stopped and caught her breath. "And then we shopped at Hobby Lobby, where I bought that tree over there in the box. And then we went to Walmart, where I bought a truck load of presents. Are you any good at wrapping? You can help me get them done later today if you are. And then we came home and unloaded it all and fell asleep. Did I leave anything out, Raylen?"

"I kissed you in Hobby Lobby. I think if we kissed in Hobby Lobby, it's dating, not a date, isn't it?"

He squeezed her tightly to his chest. Part of what he said was a joke, part was truth. He wanted to be dating Liz, not just have had a single date with her.

Liz's expression went dead serious. "There's a sign on the Hobby Lobby door right under the one with the hours the store is open. It's written in that little bitty print that no one hardly ever reads, but I did before we went in."

Gemma butted in, "What are you talking about?"

Liz held up a palm. "Let me finish. The print says anyone not dating will be charged with a misdemeanor and a hundred dollar fine if they are caught kissing in Hobby Lobby. But since Raylen didn't see the sign, maybe it isn't a law. I'm not sure if both parties have to see it or not."

"Okay, Gemma, would you please go out in the barn, get the ladder, crawl up on the roof of the house, and yell that I'm dating Liz. That way all the other cowboys in Montague County can crawl off behind a mesquite tree and lick their wounds," Raylen said.

"You two are nuts! I don't think you are dating at all. You heard me coming and you staged this just to tease me, didn't you? I'm going home to get ready for church. I'll be back after dinner. But just to pay you back, I intend to tell the whole family that you two are an item, and I may tell Becca too, since she never misses Sunday morning services," Gemma said.

"Becca would be there if she had to crawl on her knees through six feet of snow, and all she had to wear was a little black lace teddy. She has to pray for a crop failure." Liz's tone was frosty.

Raylen leaned back and drew his eyebrows down. "Crop failure?"

"Standard practice for those who sow wild oats on Friday and Saturday nights. They go to church on Sunday and pray for a crop failure," Liz answered.

Gemma sat down on the sofa. "Well, damn! I didn't know I could do that."

"Now you know, so go do some serious praying. And if you would tell Becca it will save me a phone call," Raylen said.

"If I give you Blaze's number, will you call him? But not until after church. He'll be breaking at least one heart this morning before he gets busy tearing down the equipment to move it to Bowie," Liz said.

Gemma shook her head. "You two can do your own announcing, but I am telling the family at dinner unless y'all beat me to it. So if this is a joke you'd better tell me now before I get to the door, or you're going to have some big explaining to do."

"Have fun. We're going to be out cutting down a tree for the barn," Raylen said.

Gemma stood up and headed for the door. "On that note, I'm leaving. I don't even want to know why you are putting a tree in the barn."

When she was gone, Raylen hugged Liz even tighter. "Good morning, beautiful girlfriend."

Liz wiggled down tighter into his embrace. "I like the way that sounds."

"So do I, but darlin', it's gettin' to the imperative stage that I get to the bathroom."

She giggled and stood up, surprised that she didn't feel like a pretzel after sleeping for hours in his arms with her knees all drawn up. Raylen pushed the footrest down and made his way down the hallway. When he returned she was opening the Christmas tree box with a kitchen knife.

"Hey, I'll do that later. Right now I'm going home, get a quick shower, and change into work clothes so we can go hunt down the best real tree in the county," he said.

"You could shower here," she said with a wicked gleam in her dark eyes.

He wrapped his arms around her and kissed her hard, his lips lingering on hers for so long that she thought for sure they were headed for another bout of shower sex. Her toes tingled, hot liquid desire turned her insides to mush, and chill bumps the size of mountains crept up her backbone in anticipation.

"If I shower here, there will be no tree because we'll spend the day in bed," he said softly. "And there'll be no lights on the house or wire Santa Claus on the roof, or tree in the barn. Your choice, new girlfriend."

"Shit!" she mumbled.

"That wasn't an option," he said.

"How about when it's all done?" she asked.

"That is a promise!" He let go of her. "Be back in half an hour with an ax."

"I'll be ready. The scarf will be tied to my bedpost."

"Girl, you are evil," he said.

"Just don't let Becca change your mind when you call her," she told him.

He pulled her back into his arms and kissed her again, his tongue teasing and tempting her until she was moaning. "When you call Playboy Blaze, you tell him how you feel right now this minute."

Liz hadn't been prepared for so many cedar trees. She'd thought it would be like the Hobby Lobby store. A couple of dozen trees to choose from, and she'd stand back, eye them all at once, and pick out the one she wanted. But they'd traipsed through wooded areas with acres of mesquite and a cedar tree tossed in every few hundred yards, to scrub oak with a few more cedars fighting for a place, and then to an area that had dozens and dozens of trees.

Finally, she found one that appealed to her. She walked around the enormous tree and looked it up and down. With the decorations in the tack room and what she'd bought in her spare bedroom, she had plenty to decorate one that size plus the new one in the house.

"You'd have to get the ladder out to put the topper on it, but then I could see your sexy butt even better," she said.

"Is my butt cute enough for that job?" he asked.

"I'm not sure. Maybe you better bare it and let me make sure," she answered.

"Not in this cold wind, but later we'll talk about that idea. Is this the one?"

"Yes, it is. It's the one I want." She looked up and saw a tiny room on stilts. "What is that?"

"That is Rye's deer blind," he said.

"A what?"

"It's what Rye sits in and waits for a deer to come by so he can shoot it. See the slits in the side there? That's where you slip the rifle out," he explained as he slung the tote bag from his back and removed a chain saw.

"I thought you were bringing an ax," she said.

"This will do the job faster."

"How do we get this thing back to the truck?"

He revved up the chain saw and yelled above the noise. "Drag it, darlin'."

While he removed a few lower limbs and then cut the tree down, she meandered over to the deer blind. It didn't seem like a fair hunt to hide up in a place like that, and then shoot the deer when it wasn't looking. A true hunter should have to chase it and give it a fighting chance. She climbed the ladder to the landing and slung open the door. It was empty except for a folding chair in one corner with what looked like a sleeping bag thrown over it.

Raylen watched the cedar tumble to its side and hoped he hadn't broken any branches. Even if he dreaded meeting Blaze and her carnie family, he wanted everything to be perfect for their visit to Liz's house.

"Okay, now it's time to take it home," he said as he put the chain saw back in the case and looked around.

"Liz?" he yelled.

"Up here in the tree house," she said. "Come on up here. You can see all the way to the truck."

He made his way up the ladder and inside where she was staring out the small, rectangular window.

"Why didn't you bring me up here to find the tree? I can see hundreds of them from here."

He wrapped his arms around her waist and snuggled up against her back. "Because your perspective is all off. How big does that one I just cut down look from this angle?"

"About three feet."

She turned quickly and their lips met in a clash of passion.

"I wanted to do that the whole time we've been in the woods," she whispered. "Your lips are cold but they make my insides feel all bubbling hot."

"I know," he said.

He smothered her with more kisses, each one hotter than the last. When she tugged at his coat and began to unbutton his shirt, he helped her and then together they quickly undressed Liz. He folded his naked body around hers and started another series of searing kisses.

"The sleeping bag," he mumbled and walked her backwards until he could reach it. It almost covered the floor and there was enough to pull up over them when he laid her down.

He ducked under the covers of the bag and kissed her belly, her thighs, and even her knees.

"Whew, didn't know that knees could be sexy," she said.

"Everything about you is sexy." His voice was muffled under the down-filled bag.

The room swayed and she wasn't sure if it was real or her imagination. "Will this thing collapse if we…"

His head popped out of the camouflage bag at her neck level. He buried his face in the softness of her breasts and inhaled deeply. The last remnants of that exotic perfume she wore, plus coconut shampoo and the scent of Liz, aroused him to the painful level.

"The legs are set in two feet of concrete. It's not going anywhere," he said hoarsely.

A niggling thought in the back of Liz's mind said that she needed to slow things down. Sure, he'd said they were dating and he'd called her his girlfriend, but everything about their relationship was a whirlwind. Liz pulled out an imaginary pistol and shot the niggling thought deader than a poor little deer walking close to the deer stand. She didn't want to slow anything down. She loved the way things were progressing and hoped that he was still her cowboy on Christmas day.

On the inside, her body was a pool of hot lava. On the outside it was cool, but his touch turned up the temperature so fast she was panting. Tucked inside the sleeping bag, they were face to face and one hand stayed on her back but the other wandered, caressing and jacking up the heat even higher.

The hardness pressing against her belly told Liz that Raylen was every bit as hot as she was. The tremble in his fingertips said that it wasn't easy to hold back. One of her arms was pinned under him, but she let her free hand roam over his chest and down to his erection, wrapping her cool hands around it.

"Wow," he mumbled.

Both of them were so hot that smoke should have been rolling out the tiny slits in the side of the stand when he finally settled in between her legs.

"Our first time in a dating relationship," he said with the first thrust.

"And it's just as sexy as it was when we were just having plain old sex." She pulled his face down to hers for another series of kisses. "Can we come out here every day?"

"Why?"

"You can't get away from me, and nobody bothers us," she answered.

He chuckled and increased the speed until they were both covered in sweat, in spite of the cold surrounding them. He liked taking her to the very apex of the climax but not over the top. He liked the dreamy look in her dark eyes when she was hot and thinking of nothing but him almost as much as he enjoyed that final moment, when she hung on to him so tightly and dug her nails into his back. When she gasped and her eyes went from dreamy to demanding, he knew that she was ready and gave one final thrust.

"Hell's bells," she panted.

"I heard them ringing too," he said as he rolled to one side.

"Look at that. Even in a deer blind with the sun shining there's a rainbow in your eyes."

"Darlin', there is heaven in your eyes. Angels with fiddles and…"

"Angels have harps, not fiddles."

"Not in your eyes. They have fiddles. That's what makes the devil red. Because he's so mad that he can't have those fiddles."

"You see that in my eyes?" She kissed him on the chin.

"I see heaven, hell, and all in between in your eyes."

"Whew! You should be a fortune-teller. Crap! Raylen! Do you say that to all the girls?" She frowned.

"No, darlin'. Just the ones who entice me up to a deer blind."

"And that would be?"

"One so far," he teased.

She giggled and buried her face in his shoulder. "I could sleep for six hours."

He covered his yawn with a hand. "We've got more than six hours' worth of work to do on these trees and the house. Aren't they coming to Bowie tomorrow?"

"Yes, but not to my house until next Monday. You are a party pooper. I wasn't thinkin' about a tree but a nice long nap all wrapped up in this bag with you."

"Your choice, darlin'. Tree and house, or nap."

"Kiss me one more time and I'll get my clothes back on," she whispered.

Chapter 15

THE TREE WAS TOO BIG FOR THE HOLDER THEY FOUND in the tack room so Raylen nailed a cross bar on the bottom, stuck the whole thing down in a galvanized wash tub, and filled it half full of water.

"That should keep it from drying out for a week," he said.

Liz clapped her hands and hugged him right in front of Ace, Jasmine, Gemma, and Dewar. "It's beautiful. I'll wrap the bottom with an old quilt to cover the wash tub and then use a couple more quilts for the tree skirt. You are a genius."

"Whoa! You'll swell up his ego until the rest of us plain old cowboys won't be able to endure his struttin' around like a Banty rooster," Ace said.

Jasmine slapped the air in front of his face. "Honey, there ain't an ego in Montague County as big as yours. And you strut in your sleep, so don't you be callin' the pot black. Now you guys go get a couple of ladders. You can put the lights on the top and us girls will take care of the bottom half. When we get this one decorated we'll go in the house and do that one, then you fellers can take care of the outside lights while we wrap presents."

Ace poked her on the arm. "I'm going to work up an appetite."

Jasmine gave him a half smile. "I figured you'd say that so I'm prepared. We'll all go to the café and grill some burgers and make some fries after everything is done. I've got half a chocolate cake and two pecan pies left over from yesterday."

"For pecan pie I will string lights from here to the North Pole," Ace said.

Liz led the way to the tack room. The ladies each picked up one box and the guys stacked up two each. Dewar and Ace crawled up on ladders and worked together, clipping the strands of lights to the tree as Raylen fed the wires up to them. Jasmine started at the bottom of the tree, Liz began her strands a foot up from Jasmine, and Gemma started about two feet up from the bottom.

When they'd finished that job, Dewar said, "While we are up here we might as well put the garland on. Raylen, you can keep it coming just like you did the lights."

"And they accused me of being too organized," Raylen said.

"You got a girlfriend now. That erases all the sane thoughts from your head so me and Dewar get to wear the crown for organization," Ace said.

Jasmine started around the bottom of the tree with wide gold garland. "I'm damn sure glad dating doesn't affect women like that."

"Hey, now," Raylen said.

"I still can't believe you two are an item," Gemma said. "Are you sure y'all ain't just putting on a show to tease us?"

"I told Becca," Raylen said.

"Well, it damn sure ain't a joke then," Ace said.

"And?" Jasmine asked.

"She thinks I'm crazy," Raylen answered honestly.

"I can believe that's what she'd think. She was saving you for the last hurrah, Raylen. When she got ready to buy that wedding dress, she was going to land in your arms," Gemma said.

"Now she'll have to land in Dewar's or Ace's," Raylen said.

"Hey, what'd we do to piss you off?" Ace asked.

"Not me. Brandon can have her," Dewar said.

Gemma blushed. "Brandon?"

"That's who Raylen said she was with last night," Ace said.

Gemma clamped her jaw tightly shut and kept looping gold tinsel over the cedar limbs, but a blind man could tell she was about to explode.

"Okay, Gemma, what's this about Brandon?" Liz asked.

"Nothing!" Gemma snapped.

Jasmine shook her head at Liz.

"Nope, I'm not going to ignore it. Gemma, what's wrong?" Liz asked.

"I'm mad as hell. I could tear this tree down and beat the hell out of Becca with it. She's known for years that I had a thing for Brandon and that we'd been out a few times in the last month. I thought she was my friend as well as Raylen's. I guess not."

Liz finished her garland and went back for another length. "You ever think that maybe he asked her out and she's showing you that he's not the one for you? Maybe she is your friend."

Raylen's ears were hearing things! Surely Liz hadn't just taken up for Becca. Lord, if she could have heard the fit Becca threw when he called her that morning before Gemma spit out the news in church, she would be all for stringing the woman up by the thumbs. She damn sure wouldn't be giving her the benefit of a doubt.

"If it wasn't her going out with him then it could be someone else. I didn't see a cowboy from this area in your cards when I read them so Brandon ain't the one, honey," Liz said.

Gemma eyes softened. "Sorry sumbitch. I hope she winds up with him. It would serve him right. I'm not high maintenance like her."

"The hell you ain't," Dewar said.

She pointed up. "You hush or I'll rattle your sorry old ass off that ladder. Now tell me again what you saw in my cards while I get some more garland out of the box."

"I saw a blond cowboy. Tall, blond, and sexy. And he adored you." She didn't tell Gemma that the cowboy could very well be Ace because she couldn't see his face at all in her vision and the cards hadn't given her an exact description.

Gemma laughed out loud. "I think that card reading is a bunch of horseshit but I need something to hang on to. By next Christmas, right?"

"In my vision, I definitely saw a Christmas tree," Liz said.

"Well, then go to hell, Brandon, noel, noel, noel!" Gemma sang.

"Deck the halls with lots of bullshit," Jasmine chimed in.

"Rockin' around the Christmas tree and it ain't with you," Liz singsonged.

They all three cracked up in giggles and looped their arms together to go back to the tack room to bring out the ornaments.

"You understand any of that?" Raylen whispered.

"Hell no!" Ace said.

"Don't look at me. Women aren't meant to be understood," Dewar said.

When they set the boxes down, Gemma shook her finger at Raylen. "Don't be scratchin' your heads and measuring things. Shove a whole box up to Dewar and Ace. They can balance it on the ladder tops and get the top part done. You can help us work on the part we can't reach."

In thirty minutes, the tree was covered with ornaments, and Liz brought out the angel for the top. It reminded her of what her mother had said about not letting anyone cut off her wings. She decided to use it on the barn tree to show her mother that she could have wings and roots both.

Dewar and Ace got down off the ladders and motioned for Liz. She carried the porcelain piece carefully and settled her down on the branches, being sure she was secured before climbing back down the ladder into Raylen's waiting arms. He held her a minute longer than necessary, not wanting to let go but knowing better than to kiss her because there was no way he could stop with one.

A flicker of her dancing in front of the Christmas tree surfaced. Even though it took every ounce of willpower he had, he kept it at bay. One minute of entertaining that sight and he'd be in big trouble... again.

"And now for the finishing touch." Liz handed everyone a full box of silver icicles. "Come on, Raylen. We'll do the top and give Ace and Dewar a break."

"Oh, no! You are not going up on that ladder again,"

Ace said. "If you fell, Raylen would come gunnin' for us because we didn't talk you out of it."

When the tree was all aglitter with silver icicles, Raylen plugged in the lights and Liz sucked air. It was more beautiful than any tree she'd ever seen in the windows of real houses or even in the malls she'd visited on her travels from one place to the other.

"Like it?" Raylen asked.

"Love it. I hope the one in the house is half as pretty," she said.

Jasmine clapped her hands three times. "Okay, one down. One to go. Load up the rest of the boxes and let's go to the house."

Ace poked her on the arm. "You sure are bossy."

Jasmine laid a hand on his shoulder. "Think pecan pie."

The tree in the house didn't take nearly as long because it was prelit. They strung garland, with Dewar doing the top without a ladder, hung bulbs and icicles, and then Ace plugged it in. Raylen had his arm around Liz and hoped that she wasn't disappointed after the big tree in the barn.

"Oh!" she gasped. "It's just as fantastic as the other one, but in a different way. I love it and I'm glad you were with me or I'd have bought the ten-foot one." She brushed a kiss across Raylen's lips and blushed at the thoughts it provoked.

Jasmine pointed at the empty tree box. "Ace, you take that to the spare room so she can store her tree in it after the holidays. Raylen, you and Dewar take all these empty boxes and follow him. We're going to wrap up presents now and you three are off to the rooftops, ho, ho, ho!"

"Noel, noel, noel," Gemma said.

Raylen hugged Liz tightly. The day had been so near perfect that it scared the devil out of him. The other shoe would drop, and he was afraid that it would be in the form of Liz fluffing out her wings like the tree topper once the excitement of Christmas was over. For the first time he fully understood the way Rye must have felt every time Austin drove out of Terral on her way back to Tulsa.

Liz twisted her head from one side to the other and then turned around to look out the back window as Raylen drove down the lane. Jasmine and Ace were right ahead of them and Gemma and Dewar in the truck in front of them. If Liz had had her way, she would have put Gemma in the truck with Ace, and Jasmine in with Dewar, but it hadn't worked out that way.

"It's beautiful." She bounced around in the cab of the truck like a sugared up six-year-old on her way to see Santa Claus. The reindeer pulled Santa's sleigh into the night up on top of her house, and Rudolph even had a blinking red nose. It was even more beautiful than she'd pictured, but the picture that flashed through her mind as they turned north on the highway didn't have anything to do with blinking lights but with a deer blind and a sleeping bag.

"Just be glad that Haskell put in lots of high-powered wiring to provide the juice to run all that stuff. I bet the electricity meter is going so fast that it looks like a blur," Raylen said.

"I don't care how much it costs. It's worth every dime. I cannot believe we got it all done."

Raylen put his arm around her and drove with one hand. "You can thank Jasmine for that. Gemma told her what we were doing and she rounded up the posse."

She slid over closer to him and laid a hand on his thigh.

"Your touch is fire," he said.

"Well, darlin', yours damn sure ain't ice cold. Are we going to burn the house down and then be finished with the relationship?" she asked.

"What are you talking about?" he asked.

"Our relationship. It's so hot right now we can't get enough of each other. Is it going to burn down the house? On the other side of the ashes are we going to figure out we don't even like each other?" she asked.

"Nope. We're going to feed the fire for a long time with them hot kisses and then when we're old and gray we're going to sit back in the ashes and remember the good times," he answered.

Jasmine had already unlocked the café and turned on the lights when he parked and turned off the engine.

"I keep thinking about that deer blind," Raylen whispered before he covered Liz's mouth with his.

Gemma knocked on the window and pointed toward the café.

"Maybe we should've kept our relationship a secret a lot longer," Liz said.

"Didn't have a choice. We got caught," Raylen said. His heart swelled when she said "our relationship." It sounded so much better than simple dating.

Liz hugged him one more time and slid across the seat. "Got to admit, I am hungry. I've used up every bit of the energy from those peanut butter sandwiches we had for lunch."

He hurried around the truck to open her door. "Honey, we used up that energy in the deer blind before we ever ate lunch."

"Want to go back there? We could dash away, dash away, dash away all. I betcha they'd never find us up there," she suggested wistfully.

"Yes, I do want to go back, but I'm starving. So food first?" He gave her a quick kiss and tucked her hand into his.

The fire lit under the grill and deep fryer when they reached the kitchen. Jasmine organized everyone and everything. Ace chopped a head of lettuce while Gemma sliced tomatoes. Dewar peeled potatoes and motioned to Raylen to pick up the other knife. Jasmine did not allow frozen potatoes in her kitchen; that was a well-known fact.

"What can I do?" Liz asked.

"You can make up a dozen hamburger patties. Meat is in the fridge."

Ace stopped chopping. "Only a dozen. God, woman, I almost fell off that roof. I think I'm due more than two burgers."

"Eighteen?" Liz asked.

"Okay, but if you don't eat them all, I'll shove them down your throat. I'm not wasting good food," Jasmine said.

Ace started chopping again. "Not to worry. I'd take them home to the guys before I wasted a single piece of the best burgers in the state of Texas."

When the burgers and fries were done, the guys pulled chairs in from the dining room and they all crowded around the dining room table. Liz filled six disposable cups with ice and took drink orders before everyone began to build their own burgers. Jasmine dumped the hot fries right out of the basket onto a brown paper bag in the middle of the table and set a ketchup bottle on each end.

"Like I said, best burgers in Texas. What do you do that's different?" Ace piled lettuce, tomatoes, pickles, and onions and squirted mustard on the top bun before he smashed it down on the burger.

"I never buy the frozen patties or frozen potatoes. Use fresh meat and real potatoes. You can tell the difference once you've had the real thing. I went to a place down in Florida called Five Guys several years ago. It was the best burger I'd ever eaten and they use fresh meat and potatoes. The walls in their restaurant are lined with hundred-pound bags of potatoes and they use them as they need 'em. That's where I got the idea," Jasmine said.

Ace held up his iced tea glass. "Well, here's to Florida and Five Guys."

Jasmine dipped a hot fry in a pile of ketchup and remembered what Liz said that day when she asked her if it was Raylen or Dewar.

It's always been Raylen.

Everyone went silent as they ate.

Jasmine continued to think about how cute Liz was when she looked at Raylen. Gemma fought back a jealous streak because she wanted a cowboy of her own so badly. Dewar had been attracted to Liz that first day but his brother was in love with the woman. Ace bit back a chuckle. No way was he ever falling that hard for a woman.

Liz looked up to see everyone staring at her with

different expressions on their faces. "What's going on? Do I have ketchup on my face?"

Gemma giggled. "No, you don't. Why'd you ask?"

"Everyone was staring," Liz said.

"Darlin' they know beautiful when they see it," Raylen whispered and suddenly everyone started talking at once.

Chapter 16

THE DINING ROOM HAD THINNED OUT TO ONLY ONE table of elderly men who were deep into a heated discussion concerning politics. That brought up the idea of imports and exports and whether they'd have to bring in hay from another place that fall or if they'd have to buy any in the winter or if they had plenty of small bales in the barns and big round bales in the pasture to last.

Liz had long since removed their dinner plates, dessert plates, and kept their coffee cups filled as they solved the problems of the country. They were discussing gun control again with each of them telling how many guns were in their arsenal when she made one more pass with the coffee pot.

"Hey, Liz," Gemma called out from the door with Colleen right behind her.

Liz looked up, forced a smile, and bit back a groan. "Hi, y'all. Hungry?"

"Starving," Colleen said. "Got any of the special left?"

"We do. How about you, Gemma?"

"I'm not in the mood for turkey and dressin'. I'm saving that for Thanksgiving. Bring me a bacon cheeseburger basket," she answered.

Liz turned the order into Jasmine and waited in the kitchen.

"I'll holler when it's ready," Jasmine said.

"I'm procrastinating. Let's talk about what we're

going to do to decorate this place for Christmas. I've got lots of decorations left at my house. Let's put a big old stuffed Santa in a rocking chair out on the porch and hang ornaments in different lengths from the ceiling on ribbon… no, on jute twine because I saw some I want to buy at the Walmart store that were horses, steer horns, and horseshoes. We can make this a countrified Christmas in here. I saw one of those rough wood signs that we can hang above Santa on the porch that says, 'countrified and satisfied.' We can figure out who made it and commission them to make us one that says, 'countrified and satisfied' and right under it put 'have a Chicken Fried Christmas.'"

"Whoa, girl. I like all those ideas, and we can do them right after Thanksgiving. I'd planned to put up a little garland and a few lights the Sunday after Thanksgiving, but if you are offering your decorations, why not make it gaudy as hell. Who knows? We might get all kinds of traffic down this way for your light drive, and if they see everything lit up here, they'll drop by and give me some business. Now why are you procrastinating?"

"Colleen knows. I can see disapproval in her face."

Jasmine patted Liz on the back. "She was the same way with Austin. She loves her brothers, and I guess it's working with gamblers all the time that makes her not as trusting as Gemma. Besides, you've had it too good. You need some speed bumps."

"Speed bumps?" Liz asked.

"Life is like a highway. Got to have a few curves and speed bumps, or else you start to take things for granted."

"I'll remind you of that when your road is too straight and perfect," Liz said.

Jasmine flipped a burger and added a slice of cheese to the top of the cooked side. "I bet you do!"

"Let's talk Christmas decorations some more," Liz said.

Jasmine pointed toward the dining room.

The elderly men had evidently finished their executive committee meeting, because they were leaving when Liz went back out. She glanced at the table and almost went in that direction. She could clean it, pocket the tip, and make the job last until Gemma and Colleen's food was ready to serve. But if she didn't clean it right then, it would be waiting as an excuse if the speed bumps got too dangerous.

She decided on the latter and sat down at the table with the O'Donnell sisters. "So what brings you to town on a Tuesday, Colleen?"

"My hair. It was too long and needed some layers. Gemma just finished cutting it," Colleen said.

"Looks good. Anyone ever ask you to model for their hair products?" Liz asked. Colleen hadn't whipped out a six-shooter and pointed it at her so maybe Gemma hadn't had time to spread the news.

"Not yet. Raylen told me that y'all are dating," Colleen said.

"I guess so," Liz said.

Colleen stared right into Liz's eyes. "Don't break his heart."

Liz didn't blink. "I won't."

Liz expected more but Colleen looked out the window at the truck pulling into the parking lot. "I'm staying at the ranch tonight. Raylen says your place looks like the Griswold house. I'm looking forward to seeing it."

"It's the most beautiful thing you've ever seen. I've

got presents under the tree, and it's huge. Oh, I've been meanin' to ask you if we could borrow your tables next Wednesday night, Gemma. Colleen, did Gemma tell you everyone is invited? I can't wait for y'all to meet all my carnie family," Liz said.

"Wow!" Colleen said.

"Is that sarcasm?" Liz asked.

Colleen tilted her head toward the door. "Hell, no! Look! I ain't seen nothing like…"

"Blaze!" Liz shouted, crossed the floor in a dead run, and jumped into his waiting arms.

"Hi, sweetheart! Who is that gorgeous redhead?" he whispered.

Liz's answer was somewhere between a laugh and a groan. Colleen and Blaze! The devil would be line dancing in heaven to Charlie Daniels's "Devil Went Down to Georgia" before Texas was big enough for that combination.

"There's two women back there. You sure you're lookin' at the redhead?"

He spun her around and set her down. "That gorgeous one with the dark red hair and the jean jacket is who I'm seeing. Introduce me if you know her," he said.

"I planned on it." She picked up his hand and led him to the table. "Gemma and Colleen, this is my best friend, my surrogate brother and cousin, and part of my carnie family, Blaze. Darlin', meet Gemma and Colleen, Raylen's two sisters."

Colleen held out her hand. "It's a pleasure to meet you."

Blaze's eyes never left her green ones as he shook her hand, holding it longer than necessary before letting go and turning to Gemma. "I understand you've been a big help in getting everything ready for Lizelle's Christmas party."

"We just call her Liz." Gemma looked from Colleen to Blaze.

The man was dressed in black jeans and a black T-shirt that hugged a six-pack of hard abs and strained at the bulging biceps. His hair was blond, in need of a decent cut, and his eyes as dark as Liz's. He had two days' worth of light brown scuff that matched his eyebrows, a slight dent in his chin, and dimples when he smiled.

He wasn't a bit sexier than Ace or even Wil, but Colleen looked like she could see underneath all that black and could eat him instead of turkey and dressing for lunch.

"Order up!" Jasmine yelled.

Liz grabbed Blaze's arm. "Come on. You've got to meet Jasmine and…"

"Hey, y'all! Got any special left? I'm starving!" Raylen yelled as he came through the door.

"And Raylen," Liz finished.

They were like two tomcats that had just jumped on the yard fence at the same time. Time stood still. The sun was afraid to move. The clock stopped dead. Liz could see their fur fluffing out and their tails straighten up as they met in the middle of the café floor.

Raylen extended a hand. "You have to be Blaze. Liz wasn't expecting to see you until this evening. It's nice of you to drive up here and surprise her."

Blaze intended to crunch Raylen's hand, but he'd met his match. The cowboy's handshake was as firm as his. "I couldn't wait to see my favorite girl."

"Order up!" Jasmine called again.

"Gotta go work. You want the special, Raylen?"

He dropped Blaze's hand.

"Yes, darlin', I want the special." He brushed a quick kiss across her lips.

Then he turned back to Blaze. "Come on and sit with me and my sisters. I'll buy your lunch. Want some turkey and dressin' or one of the best burgers in the world?"

"I'd like one of those famous chicken fried steaks," Blaze said.

Raylen led the way to the table. "They're really good."

Liz plowed through tension as thick as a rangy old bull's hide all the way to the kitchen. She leaned on the doorjamb a minute before she picked up the tray. "Colleen was just barely a speed bump."

"It's all relative. I'd say she was the speed bump that got you ready for the big hairpin curve." Jasmine laughed. "He's pretty, but he doesn't make me have to go change my panties. Go on out there and sit with them. I'll bring out the guy's orders when they are done and meet him."

Liz whispered, "Colleen might need to buy some new underbritches or borrow a pair of yours."

Jasmine leaned away from the grill and peeked out at the table. "Well, I'll be damned."

"I know. Raylen will kill me or worse yet break up with me. Blaze can charm the hair off a frog's ass. Colleen doesn't have a chance. And he'll be gone in a week."

Jasmine shook her head slowly. "It'll take more than a tight shirt and dimples to get Colleen's britches wet."

Liz put on her best smile and carried out Colleen's and Gemma's orders. "Turkey and dressing for you, and bacon cheeseburger basket for you. Jasmine said she'd bring y'alls on out when it's done."

Raylen pulled a chair from an empty table and wedged it in between him and Gemma. When Liz was seated he brushed a kiss across her forehead and sat down beside her, taking her hand in his and resting their laced fingers on top of the table.

"Is everyone busy getting set up at the carnival?" she asked Blaze.

"They were getting positioned. Marva Jo has been antsy for two days. She's missed you. Is that your place south of here that looks like a North Pole store?" Blaze asked.

"That's it. Uncle Haskell made most of it," she answered.

"So you grew up next door to Uncle Haskell?" Blaze asked Colleen.

She had a mouth full of food so she nodded.

Liz glanced at Raylen. If looks could kill, Blaze would be a pile of cold bones on the café floor right then. And she didn't even blame him. She'd told him about Blaze and his conquests and there he was, flirting blatantly with Colleen.

"What do you think of Liz's place?" Blaze asked Colleen.

"Haven't seen it since she moved in. I thought I'd drop by tonight and look at it. It's all Raylen and Gemma have talked about all week," Colleen said.

"I'm going to help with the setup and see Momma, but I should be back by nine," Liz told Colleen.

"Orders for the guys," Jasmine said at Liz's elbow. "I've heard a lot about you, Blaze. Are you looking forward to a long, slow winter?" She set their food on the table, dragged a chair from the nearest table, and sat down.

"Liz has talked about all of you. And yes, I'm looking forward to the winter this year but I'll miss Liz. Thank goodness for cell phones so we can talk every night." He turned his attention back to Colleen. "Will you be takin' in the carnival?"

"I haven't been to a carnival since I was a kid."

"They keep a body young." He smiled.

Liz rolled her eyes at Jasmine. Colleen was a sheep being led to the slaughter by a wolf.

"I'd think all those terrifying rides would scare a few years off a person," Colleen said.

Liz cut her eyes around to Colleen. There was heat when she looked at Blaze but something else. Rock hard steel in her eyes said that she was attracted but she wasn't rolling back on her heels and falling into a motel bed with him. If he liked what he saw, he was going to work for it.

Gemma bounced a knee off Liz's and winked when Liz looked her way. Suddenly everything looked much better. Raylen wouldn't kill Blaze or break up with her. Blaze, bless his heart, didn't have any idea that the gorgeous redhead was a panther, and he'd only tamed little house kittens.

Blaze ate fast, complimented Jasmine on her cooking, flirted with Colleen, kissed Liz on the cheek, and told them all to come on out to the carnival and he'd see to it they had free armbands, so they could ride anything all evening without paying. Then he was gone and the static electricity in the café settled down.

"Is he your aunt's son or what?" Colleen asked.

"It's a long story but I'll give y'all the short version. We winter about halfway between Amarillo and Claude, Texas. We're sixteen miles from Amarillo and fourteen from Claude. My mother's people had a lot of land in that area when the depression hit, and they sold it to buy a small carnival. They kept enough to park the carnival for the winter months, and that's where we've always gone the week before Thanksgiving. The nearest neighbor is half a mile up the road and they had a daughter, Mary Lou, who was friends with Aunt Tressa. She got mixed up with a hippy group that decided to go to Wyoming and grow their own food when she was about eighteen. That lasted until she got pregnant and decided she'd rather grow longhorns than tomatoes. She came home and had the baby. Her folks died the year after he was born in a small plane crash going to Brownsville. Her dad had a heart attack at the controls and it went down. Then she got cancer and died when Blaze was fourteen. Aunt Tressa took him to raise. So he's not blood kin but just heart kin as Aunt Tressa says."

"What about the ranch where he lived?" Gemma asked.

"By the time Mary Lou died, she'd sold it off to pay for medical bills until all that was left was a small trailer and two acres. Aunt Tressa sold that and put it in a trust for Blaze, gave him a job, and he's been a carnie ever since."

"How did he feel about being jerked out of one world and tossed into another?" Colleen asked.

"He loved it from day one. He told me that he used to hang on the fence out by their place as we drove away in the spring and wish he could go with us. He's got that hippy blood in him from his biological father, I guess."

"Who was?" Gemma asked.

"His name was Jamey."

"Why'd she name her baby something like Blaze?" Jasmine asked.

"I asked Aunt Tressa that back before he came to live with us. She said Mary Lou didn't want him to have a common name. She was going to name him Phoenix like the bird that rose from the ashes. But when she was in labor she said it was like blazing fire, so that's what she named him. And there's no middle name. Just Blaze McIntire."

Gemma dropped the spoon she'd been fiddling with. "He's Irish?"

"To the bone. Mary Lou was an O'Riley and Jamey was a McIntire."

"Imagine that." Colleen smiled.

Chapter 17

LIZ FELT LIKE SHE'D GONE HOME WHEN SHE WALKED onto the grounds. Everyone waved, yelled, or came out to hug her, tell her how much they'd missed her and/or ask when she was coming back. It was half an hour before she reached the middle of the concession row where Tressa helped Joe and Linda, a couple that had been with the carnival for twenty years, set up the awning to the side of the funnel cake wagon.

Liz hugged all three and asked, "Where's Momma?"

"She just headed into the Porta-Potty. She'll be out in a minute. Hold up this pole," Tressa said.

Tressa had flaming red hair and aqua-colored eyes. She was taller than Liz but at fifty-six, she still had the same slim build. She wore jeans, a denim jacket, and lace-up work boots with steel toes. Joe was a tall, lanky man with a crop of gray hair that always needed cutting. Linda was a short woman with mousy brown hair and big green eyes.

Liz held up the poles while they stretched the awning. When they finished, they all headed to a semitrailer to bring folding tables and chairs to set up under the awning. Rain or shine, folks liked to sit and visit while they ate, and it brought more sales.

Liz leaned on the funnel wagon and watched for her mother.

"Hey, kid!" Marva Jo said.

Liz turned and wrapped her arms around her mother. "I was lookin' the wrong way. You snuck up on me. I missed you so bad."

She hugged Liz close to her and then stepped back to give a thorough once-over. "You have put on five pounds. Much more, and your belly dancing belt will be too tight."

Blaze appeared out of nowhere. "Is she tellin' you about that cowboy who won't let her out of his sight and all her new girlfriends? She doesn't miss us a bit. Don't let her lie to you."

Liz shot daggers at him. "You will always be in my life even if you are not in my sight and even if I'm mad at you."

"Mad at me! I came all the way up to Podunk, Texas, to see you and you're mad at *me*?" Blaze asked.

"I'm mad at you for saying that about not missin' my momma. I'm so mad at you that I might even stomp on your hat," she said.

"You never did tell me what happened about that. See, she doesn't even confide in me anymore, Marva Jo. She doesn't love any of us," Blaze teased.

"Children, this is no time to fight. We've got work to do and lots of it," Tressa said. "Blaze, get back to the Ferris wheel. And you, young lady, come help your momma work on the fortune wagon so we can visit. We've got to have this show up and ready before we go to bed tomorrow night, because the people will arrive at ten o'clock on Thursday."

Liz took a deep breath. She'd missed the smells of setting up, the oil and the dust. She'd missed the sounds of the drills and hammers, the horses complaining about being cooped up in a truck, and the people all talking at once as they worked. But most of all, she'd missed her mother. She looped her arm through Marva Jo's and they headed off toward the brightly colored fortune telling wagon together.

"All we have to do is check the electricity and snap down the wires," Marva Jo said. "Blaze couldn't wait to see you. He says your friends are okay, that one named Colleen is knock-down gorgeous, and that Raylen is not what he expected."

Liz waved at everyone they passed: vendors, hawkers, ride managers, and the maintenance crews. She knew them all by name. Knew their kids' and grandkids' names. Knew where they went home to winter after they had parked their wagons in Claude the week before Thanksgiving. And she'd missed every one of them.

"Did you hear me, Lizelle?" Marva Jo asked.

"Why did you full-name me? I was listenin'. I just want to see everything and everyone and can't do that and talk, too. What did Blaze expect out of Raylen?"

Marva Jo was six inches taller than her daughter, had strawberry blond hair and blue eyes. She was heavier than her sister but still looked damn fine in tight jeans and a fitted Levi's jacket.

"The way you've talked about him, Blaze said he thought he'd be six feet tall, bulletproof, and sitting on a big white horse." Marva Jo threw an arm around Liz's shoulders.

"He's five feet ten inches tall, has dark hair with red highlights when he gets in the sun, the clearest blue eyes you've ever seen, even lighter than yours, and he fell off his pedestal the first time we had a big fight," Liz said.

"And what was that over?" Marva asked.

"Blaze. I was talking to him on the phone and ignored Raylen who was putting up my Christmas lawn things so everything would be beautiful for y'all. And he forgot his hat and I threw it at him. He got mad because of his damned precious hat so I stomped it too!"

Marva Jo laughed. "And I bet you dropped down on your knees and apologized and made nice, didn't you?"

"Hell, no! I plowed right into his house and told him he was a horse's ass. His best friend is this bitchy woman that hates me. At least Blaze didn't act like he was better than Raylen like Becca does me."

Marva Jo laughed even harder. "How'd he react to a woman calling him names?"

Liz had backed herself into a corner. She took a deep breath and spit it out. "When I went into his house I saw that damned precious hat so I slapped it on my head and plowed right into the bathroom like a bulldozer. He was in the shower, so I jerked the curtain back and we had our fight right there. When I got my piece said, he jerked me in the shower, clothes and all, and kissed me."

Marva Jo really guffawed. "Now that's a man I could like. He'll keep you on your toes. What happened to the hat?"

"He pitched it on the vanity before he jerked me in the shower."

Marva Jo couldn't stop laughing.

"What did Blaze tell you about Colleen?" Liz asked.

Marva Jo swiped at her eyes with the cuff of her jacket. "He is smitten. Something I never thought I'd say about him, but after he told us about where you work, that girl was all he wanted to talk about. Here we are. I'll run the cord out to the main box and plug it in. You check the inside and out for burned bulbs. If it's all good, we'll snap it down."

Liz knew exactly what to do, and when she'd made sure everything worked, she yelled out across the lawn where Marva Jo was talking to Tressa, "It's all good. Where we goin' next?"

"To the midway. Fred needs someone to unpack and hang stuffed animals," Marva Jo said.

Liz hopped down from the porch where she'd danced at least twice a week for the past decade and walked with her mother toward the middle of the grounds. She'd always liked the Bowie gig. They had lots of room, and the grass was nice. She didn't like playing in Denton where they set up on concrete. Spilled drinks and food were messier to clean up on concrete than grass so they had to hose it down every morning. When they set up on dirt and grass there was little cleanup except for picking up paper. The birds ate what food was dropped, and the ground soaked up the liquids.

Marva Jo hopped up into the back of a semi and handed Liz a cardboard box. "Are you smitten with Raylen?"

"Maybe. Stack another one on top."

"What are you going to do about it? You've got to be honest with him, Lizelle."

She shrugged her shoulders. "See what happens. Right now I'm just happy where we are. We're having fun being together. I'm not in a hurry."

"That's good. Maybe you'll decide to come home. I'm thinkin' about shooting my brother." Marva Jo dragged three boxes to the edge of the truck and jumped down. She added another one to Liz's and then picked up the remaining two and led the way to the gallery.

"Stock is getting low," Liz said.

"It's right where I want it for the last gig of the year. We've got a couple of extra backup boxes, but I think we ordered supplies just about right last spring. We're going home with trucks that are almost empty. You going to dance and cover the wagon on Thursday and Friday to give Tressa a rest?"

Liz nodded. "I'm not going to dance, but I'm lookin' forward to tellin' fortunes. Did I tell you that I told fortunes at Gemma's Halloween party? And I saw a blond-haired cowboy in Colleen's future."

"Well, glory be! You did say cowboy?"

Liz gasped. "Oh no! He had blond hair and…"

"He didn't have boots or a hat," Marva Jo whispered.

"It's just a reading," Liz whispered.

"What?" Tressa ripped the tape from the top of a box and handed Liz small stuffed animals to hang on the wire at the back of the gallery.

"She saw a blond-haired man in Colleen's future," Marva Jo said.

"Well, shit!"

"It's probably not Blaze. Lord, he won't ever settle down. You said it yourself," Liz said.

"I read his cards last night just for fun. I saw a red-headed girl in his future and I turned over the wedding card," Tressa said.

"Dammit!" Liz said.

"Hurt yourself?" Raylen poked his head around the end of the gallery.

"Raylen! What are you doing here?"

"I came to meet your carnie family and to help," he said.

Maybe it hadn't been such a good idea to surprise her like that. But dammit! Tomorrow night was the night she was going to dance for him again. He'd wanted so many times to ask her not to prolong it but to do it sooner.

Every time he thought about her promise, his mouth went dry, his heart beat fast, and he had to fight down an arousal. If they ever got together on a permanent basis, she'd have to burn that damn costume or they'd never leave the house.

Liz leaned out the booth window and kissed him, quickly putting his fears to an end.

"Well, you got here at just the right time. You can meet Momma and Aunt Tressa at the same time. This is my mother, Marva Jo."

Raylen shook her hand. "Where did Liz get black hair and dark eyes?"

"From her father who was Latino. His name was Eddie Garcia. I gave her our family name when she was born because he was already dead, and it simplified matters," Marva Jo answered.

"And Aunt Tressa," Liz said.

He dropped Marva Jo's hand and held it out to Tressa. "My sister, Colleen, has red hair. Not the same shade as yours but still red. It's a pleasure to meet you both."

Tressa started at his scuffed up work boots, slowly took in his clean but faded jeans and chambray shirt, up to his eyes and hair. "You said you'd come to help? Why?"

"Thought you could use it and I'm caught up on my plowing for today," he said.

"Good. I like a man who's willin' to work. Come with

me and I'll show you what to do. I expect you can use a drill and hammer, right?"

"Yes, ma'am," Raylen said.

"Good, you can help Blaze put up the Ferris wheel."

"But…" Liz stammered. Raylen hadn't come to the carnival to help Blaze. He'd come to spend time with her. Was Aunt Tressa just plain stupid?

Marva Jo laid a hand on Liz's and shook her head. "Let it be," she whispered.

"Why?"

"If he survives tonight, he'll pass the test."

⚜

Blaze had just busted a knuckle when a stubby screwdriver bounced off the platform leading up to the Ferris wheel. He was cussing a blue streak and holding one hand with the other when Raylen and Tressa walked up.

Tressa grabbed his hand and pulled a tissue from her jacket pocket. "Hold it tight and shut up the caterwaulin'. That won't make it stop hurtin' or bleedin'."

"It'll damn sure make me feel better." Blaze clamped it down on his knuckle tightly. He glared at Raylen who glared right back. He wanted to tell the cowboy to go back to his dirt and leave him the hell alone but he couldn't. Not when Colleen had been on his mind all afternoon, and the man standing there in front of him was her brother.

"Raylen came to see Liz, but I stole him. He's going to help you. Looks like you need it if you can't even get the ramp up," Tressa said.

Blaze gritted his teeth. "The screwdriver slipped."

"Well, be careful. Raylen, do whatever he says. Two

strappin' fellows like you ought to have this Ferris wheel up and runnin' by bedtime," Tressa said as she walked away.

"You any good with mechanics?" Blaze asked.

"I can tear down a tractor and put it back together."

"Then I reckon you'll do. Right now we just got to get this ramp put together and then bring the seats out of the truck and fasten them into place. Motor is runnin' good. I'll do maintenance on it when we get to Claude, but it's run good this year."

Raylen was surprised after the dirty looks that Blaze would talk so much. "Got an extra screwdriver? I didn't bring my toolbox."

Blaze nodded toward a red metal box sitting about three feet from Raylen. "I'll hold this end up if you'll get that one fastened down. After this board, we can use the electric drill and it'll go faster. I'm determined to figure out a way to build a ramp that won't require teardown for next year. But right now it's got to be dismantled, or else we'd have to buy a forklift to get it from here to the semi."

Raylen leaned on the screwdriver and the three-inch screw went right into the place. "I can see where that one would be a real bitch, up underneath like that."

Blaze chuckled. "You got that right. Rest will go fast and easy, then we'll start on the…" He stopped dead in the middle of the sentence.

Raylen looked up to see him staring and frowned. Dammit to hell and back on a silver poker! They said they were going to Walmart, but he didn't think they'd show up at the carnival.

"They want to see Liz's house all lit up. Maybe they

came to get a key so they can see the tree in the barn," Raylen said.

Colleen and Gemma stopped at the shooting gallery and met Marva Jo, then she disappeared and they started handing toys to Liz. When that job was done, they all three trooped over to the Ferris wheel.

Liz kissed Raylen on the cheek. "I'm going to show the girls the fortune wagon, and then we're going to set up toys in the dart gallery. When you get this done, come and find us. We want the trial ride on the wheel."

Blaze couldn't take his eyes off Colleen. Standing up she was even more stunning than she'd been sitting down at the café. She was taller than Gemma but not by much, putting her at just about five feet four inches. Just the right height for him to walk beside comfortably with his arm around her shoulders. Kind of like how Raylen and Liz fit together. He shook that picture out of his mind. He didn't want to like Raylen, and he didn't want Liz to really fall for the cowboy even if he did know how to use a screwdriver. He wanted her to come back to the carnival, not put down any more roots in Ringgold.

Both men watched the women walk away. Raylen itched to slip his arm around Liz's waist and let his hand drop to cup her butt. Blaze's mouth went dry just looking at the way Colleen filled out those tight jeans and the way her hips rotated with every step in those cowboy boots.

"Well, guess we'd best get to work," Raylen said hoarsely.

"Yep," Blaze agreed, glad that Raylen couldn't read his mind. If he'd known how Blaze was looking at his sister, he'd use that screwdriver in his hand for a helluva lot more than putting a ramp together.

Chapter 18

THURSDAY NIGHT OF A CARNIVAL WAS USUALLY THE slowest one. Friday night business picked up and Saturday night it was booming. The Bowie gig was always touch-and-go with the weather. It rained and was so cold that only the brave at heart succumbed to their whining children and brought them to the carnival; or else it was unseasonably warm and everyone wanted one last fling before winter set in. Feast or famine was what Tressa called it.

Liz could hardly sleep on Wednesday night and awoke long before the alarm clock went off on Thursday. Like every opening day, her first thought was weather. She raised the blinds in her bedroom to nothing but darkness and groaned. The sun hadn't even started to rise yet. She checked her laptop for the weather update to find that it hadn't changed since the night before. Eighty percent chance of rain, cold front moving in, and enough wind to bring the chill factor down.

And there were voices in her house!

She tiptoed down the hallway to the kitchen to find Hooter and Blister following Raylen's every move. "What are you doing here?"

"You talkin' to me or the livestock?" Raylen asked.

She sat down at the kitchen table. "You."

"You've been on the go so much this week that I haven't got to see you except when there was a hundred people around us. I'm making coffee. I was going to bring it to you in bed," he said.

She hugged him from behind. "That's so sweet. I missed you too."

He turned around, dropped a kiss on the top of her head, and led her by the hand to the table where he sat down and pulled her into his lap. "So what's the agenda for tonight?"

"Have you heard a weather forecast?" she asked.

"What's that got to do with anything?"

Tonight was the night and he felt like a kid on the way to the candy store. Surely to hell the weather wasn't going to prevent her from doing that dance again.

"In the carnival business, everything," she answered.

"Guess it's more like ranchin' than I thought. I was plannin' on plowin' up the last forty acres surrounding you today, but there is already a fine mist out there, and the weatherman says rain all day, and the temperature is supposed to be around fifty with a wind chill factor of forty degrees," he said. "What does that mean for you?"

"It means business will be slow," she said.

He stood up with her in his arms and set her in another chair. "Coffee is ready. Weather-wise, the rain stops at noon tomorrow and the sun pops out. The cold front we've got today won't move out until Sunday, so the weather is staying in the high fifties with a wind chill five to ten degrees below that."

She sighed. "Slow carnival this week."

He put a mug of hot coffee in front of her and pulled his chair around so they would be closer. She left her coffee sitting and curled up on his lap, wrapping her arms around him and snuggling so close that she could listen to his heartbeat. Forget the carnival, forget the café. Peace enfolded her like soft, feathery wings and she wanted to stay right there forever.

"You promised me a dance tonight. Rain got anything to do with that?" Raylen asked hoarsely.

"I've been looking forward to dancing for you for days," she whispered into his ear.

His lips found hers in a passionate kiss that melted the peace and replaced it with red-hot desire. He slipped a cool hand under her knit pajama top and gently massaged her back before moving around to cup a breast.

She gasped and pulled back. "Raylen, much as I'd like to go where this would lead us, darlin', I've got to get ready for work."

He nuzzled down into her hair. "Five more minutes."

A quick glance over his shoulder at the clock said it wasn't happening. "Can't or I'll be late."

She pushed away, stood up, and bent down to plant a steaming hot kiss on his lips where tongue met tongue, producing enough heat to burn away the rain and clouds. When she stood up, Hooter was staring at them, head cocked off to one side. Blister had jumped up on the counter, not six inches from Raylen's ear, and meowed loudly.

Liz giggled. "I think they're tellin' us that we'd best stop now or else I'll get fired."

"I am very fired up." Raylen looked down.

"So am I, but…"

He scooped her up and carried her to the bedroom, quickly stripped her pajama bottoms off while she unbuckled his belt and unzipped his jeans. "A quickie, Madam Bellybammy?"

"Oh, yes!" She jerked his jeans down and guided him into her.

A dozen thrusts later he collapsed on her. She wiggled from under him in one easy move and jogged to the bathroom, started the shower water, threw off her pajama top, and stepped into the tub before the water was quite warm enough. She took the fastest shower she'd ever had in her life and had a towel around her when the door opened.

"Cold shower. Didn't you…?" he asked.

"Oh yes, darlin', very much so, but I've got to rush."

He wasn't helping, standing there naked. Broad chest inviting her to snuggle up to it; muscular biceps to hold her tightly; lips to kiss until she was panting; sexy eyes to sink into as he made love to her. One touch. One kiss. One word and they could spend the rainy day in bed.

"Okay, kiss me and I'll see you tonight," he said.

She tiptoed and the towel fell off.

He ran hands down her sides, stopping at her waist and bending to kiss her sweetly. "I want to hug you but you are all clean and I smell like hot sex. I'll see you tonight. Mind if I use your shower?"

"Not at all." She remembered the shower sex at his place and wished she could get right back in there with him.

She made it to the café five minutes before opening, grabbed a cup of coffee, and wolfed down two bacon biscuits.

"Does rain mean a slow day in the café business like it does in the carnie world?"

Jasmine poured a cup of coffee. "Not at all. If the ranchers can't work, they come to the café to talk ranchin', religion, and politics. So get ready for a very busy morning. I've got extra biscuits on the pans ready to put in the oven. They'll be orderin' sausage gravy and eggs to get the chill off. What happens to the carnival?"

"If it's rainy and cold, folks stay home. No amount of whining or begging from their kids can get them out in the nasty weather. We'll have a slow night and, according to the weatherman, the rest of the week is going to be chilly. If it's not raining, we might have a fairly decent weekend to finish up the year," she explained.

"You said 'we,' Liz. You're not completely cut away from it, are you?" Jasmine said.

"No, but I'm workin' on it. I've been growing these wings for twenty-five years. I can't get rid of them in a month," she said.

"That's understandable and honest. Time to open the door. The parking lot is already half full. Get ready for a rush," Jasmine said.

Liz picked up her apron and tied it around her waist. She wondered if Raylen was still in her house, if he'd left Hooter and Blister inside, if he ever told Becca about their sex life. That made her frown. Surely he didn't tell personal things, even if Becca was his friend. She damn sure wasn't sharing the intimate things about their relationship with Blaze, and he'd asked plenty of questions.

It was a hectic morning that gave way to a busy lunch rush. Closing time came before Liz realized that she hadn't seen Ace, Colleen, or Gemma all day. Colleen had said she'd only come over from Randlett for the day so that wasn't a surprise, but Ace and Gemma always ran through at least once a day.

Liz grabbed the broom after she'd wiped down all

the tables and made sure the salt, pepper, sugar, and pepper sauce bottles were refilled. She swept and Jasmine mopped.

"You don't have to do this," Liz said.

"You need to get out of here and spend time with your family. I'll get my cakes done for tomorrow's dessert and then us girls are coming to the carnival," Jasmine said.

"Really! I can't wait for you to meet Momma and Aunt Tressa. Colleen and Gemma came by last night and helped me stock the midway. And Aunt Tressa made Raylen work with Blaze on the Ferris wheel."

Jasmine stopped and leaned on the mop. "Talk while you sweep. I knew they were all coming, but we've been too busy to gossip."

"I was afraid they'd kill each other. I sure wouldn't want to have to work with Becca, like Raylen had to work with Blaze, but they got along all right. Then when they got it finished, all five of us did the debut ride. Tressa ran the controls and let us go around about a dozen times before she declared it was ready for use."

"Keep going. Who rode in each bucket?" Jasmine asked.

"Blaze rigged it so that he and Colleen sat together," Liz said. "I'm worried about that. I've told you about him and his womanizing."

"Who sat with you?"

"Raylen on one side and Gemma on the other," Liz said.

"You want someone interfering with you and Raylen?" Jasmine asked.

"Hell, no!"

"Then leave Colleen and Blaze alone. They're both

grown; and trust me, Colleen can take care of herself. Would you break up with Raylen if you had a brother who took to Becca?" Jasmine went back to mopping.

"No, but I'd sure think about shooting Becca grave-yard dead," Liz said.

"I rest my case," Jasmine told her.

Liz felt right at home in the travel trailer, sitting at the table with her makeup kit and mirrors around her. She wore a long, flowing multicolored skirt, a yellow blouse with billowing sleeves, with a turquoise scarf and beaded sandals. When she finished her makeup, she slipped six strands of different colored beads around her neck, a dozen silver bangle bracelets on one arm, and a tinkling charm bracelet on the other. Then she wrapped a long scarf around her head, tying it in a double knot right above her left ear and letting the ends fall over her breasts.

She was checking her reflection when her mother stepped into the trailer. "You forgot something."

"I did?"

"Ah, my child. One month and you are already becoming a *gadjo*."

"I'm not an outsider, Momma. What did I forget?"

Marva Jo pointed at her feet. "Your ankle bracelets. Got to have the tinkling to give the illusion."

"Thank you," Liz said.

Marva Jo went to the refrigerator and took out a Diet Coke. "I like your Raylen. He reminds me of your father except that your father had jet-black hair and eyes, like you have. And he was much shorter than Raylen."

"Then what makes him remind you of my father?" Liz asked.

"The way he looks at you. Just remember we are exotic to a *gadjo* for a little while. It didn't last with your father. It won't last with Raylen. Enjoy it while you have it and then let it go. Kind of like a butterfly on a pretty red flower. Stay until you tire of it and then fly away," Marva Jo said.

"What if I don't get tired of it?" Liz fastened charm bracelets with little brass bells around her ankles.

"It's not up to you. He'll get tired of it and then you'll find out that the place for you is in the bosom of the carnie. He's the only reason you went there and the only thing that holds you. When it's over, you'll come home. History repeats itself."

"What if it's five years down the road and we're in a committed relationship?" Liz asked.

Marva Jo kissed her on the forehead, being careful not to mess up her makeup. "What ifs could go on all night. You haven't forgotten the business like you did your ankle bracelets, have you? I wish you could dance tonight, but from what the weatherman says, it's going to be too cold. Such is life this late in the year. Sometimes it's nice and warm, and sometimes we don't even make enough to pay the electricity bill."

"What did you think of Colleen and Gemma?" Liz asked.

"I liked them but Colleen the best."

"You got to be shittin' me!" Liz said.

"No, I'm not shittin' you and that's a *gadjo* phrase which proves my point. Now get out of here and go do your job. You've got just enough time to get settled into the wagon and turn on the crystal ball light before your first customer."

She was on her way from the trailer to the carnival and had just waved at Blaze who was working the controls at the Ferris wheel when she heard someone yell her name. She was surprised to see Austin and Rye not five feet from her.

"I almost didn't recognize you," Austin said.

"It's me in living color. I'm telling fortunes tonight. Tomorrow night they've got me working the shooting gallery and Aunt Tressa is working the fortunes, then Saturday night I'm back at fortunes. Y'all are brave souls in this weather."

"This is the only night we get to come, and I love carnivals. Rye took me to a carnival on one of our first dates. I make him take me to one whenever it's close enough. Maddie is keeping Rachel for us," Austin said. "I don't care if I get wet. I've got dry clothes at home. And you didn't look like that at the Halloween party. You wore a genie outfit."

Liz smiled. "You're going to have to tell me the story of your romance when I have more time. Maybe we can all get together for a girls' night out sometime. And that outfit was my belly dancing outfit; this is my official fortune telling costume."

"Name the place and time. Maybe we can have it at my house and you can teach us how to belly dance," Austin said.

Rye's grin covered his face. "Can the guys have a guys' night out and watch?"

Austin kissed him soundly and giggled. "No, but you'll reap the benefits of our learning, I'm sure." She herded Rye off toward the Ferris wheel.

Liz noticed the paint was beginning to chip on the fortune-teller's wagon when she slipped inside and got it ready for business. She flipped a switch that turned on the recessed dim lights and another one that lit up the iridescent bulb at the base of the crystal ball. She struck a match and fired up two incense cones, and in a few seconds, the wagon smelled like sandalwood. Then she sat down and touched a button under the table that flipped a sign on the door to "ENTER." While she was with a customer, she would touch the button again and the sign would flip over to say, "DO NOT DISTURB."

She *had* missed the business. She'd missed the feeling of waiting for the first customer, the smell of the incense, the tinkling bells when she crossed and uncrossed her legs, and the pretty light in the crystal ball. And most of all the excitement in the faces of those who got their fortunes told.

Excitement!

That reminded her of Raylen that morning and the intensity of quick sex. They'd never had slam, bam, thank you ma'am sex. But then she'd never made love in a shower or against the wall either. Raylen was a complex, exciting man that kept her on her toes. She looked into the crystal ball and saw her own distorted face smiling back at her.

Chapter 19

THE DOOR SWUNG OPEN AND LIZ LOOKED UP AT HER first customer of the evening.

"Hello. Welcome to Madam Drabami's Fortunes," Liz said in a low voice.

Becca took two steps and sat down across the small table from Liz. "I came to see if you'd changed your mind about my fortune."

"Cards, ball, or palm?" Liz strained to keep her tone professional.

"What's the difference?"

"Palm is five dollars, cards and ball are twenty."

Suddenly, Liz didn't miss fortune telling at all. She wanted to strip out of the costume, then go home to her dog and cat and Christmas decorations.

Becca threw a twenty on the table. "Give me the works. Tell me that I'm going to marry Raylen when you move on and I pick up the pieces."

"I'll tell you exactly what I see, not necessarily what you want to hear. Do you want to change your mind before I start?"

Becca leaned across the table and said, "I don't like you. You are a fake and you're going to hurt Raylen."

"The works it is," Liz said. "Please lay your hands, palms up, on the table."

Becca laid them out with a thump. "Didn't you hear me?"

"I did, but you didn't put twenty dollars on the table to fight with me. You laid it out for a fortune. We can fight later. I don't charge for that." Liz picked up her hand. "I see a long, long life ahead of you. This line says you will be married for many years and this short one here suggests that you'll marry again after that, but it won't last long. I would think the first time you marry it will be for love, and when that love has passed on in your old age, you will look for it again and not find it."

Liz picked up the cards and shuffled them.

"That could be anyone's future," Becca said.

"It could be and it probably is for lots of people, but it is yours today," Liz said.

"I'll cut the cards and turn them. I don't want you to cheat," Becca said.

Liz handed the deck to her.

Becca reshuffled them, cut them, and then laid the deck on the table. She turned over the top card.

"Turn three side-by-side. One card can mean one thing but next to another one it takes on a very different meaning," Liz said.

Becca laid out two more cards and crossed her arms over her chest. "What does that mean?"

"You will have exceptionally good luck for a little while and then a reasonable measure of success, but you are walking on the edge of the cliff when it comes to your romantic side, and one misstep can put you over the edge. Be careful, or you will trade true love and happiness for contentment."

Becca shivered. "Okay, now the ball."

Liz rubbed her hands over the glass ball and looked closely into it.

Becca leaned in, but she saw nothing but her own face.

"I see you at a birthday party. Is it yours?" Liz asked.

"Could be. My birthday is the first week in November," Becca said.

Liz kept her eyes on the ball. Becca was a Scorpio. No wonder she was so biting with a scorpion for a zodiac sign.

"You thrive under intensity. You like adversity, but your dreams are bearing down on you, and you have an ongoing thorn in your side right now. Balance is not easy for you. You are drawn like a moth to the flame when it comes to drama. You like to stir up trouble and you are good at it. You need to let go of the control issue in your life and let your heart lead you. Your mind and those around you want one thing, but your heart wants something different, Becca. The reason you are in conflict between heart and head is because you are walking close to the cliff when you give in to your head. Let your heart lead you away from the edge of that cliff, and success in romance, business, and life will be yours."

Becca was listening to the words and the soft tinkle of bells so intensely that she didn't even hear the soft click. When a chilly wind circled around her, she thought it was the fortune hitting a home run to her heart. She pushed the chair back with so much force that she had to catch it before it fell as she stood up.

"I don't love Raylen," she said bluntly. "I love him as a friend with all my heart. I'd kill for him as a friend, but I don't want to marry him. Daddy has given me until June or he's going to cut me off."

"Sit down." Liz turned off the cold air.

"How much more?" Becca opened her purse. Her face was ashen and tears welled up behind her eyelashes.

"Nothing. This is not for sale at any price. I was raised in the carnival. I love it, but something in my heart keeps pointing me to another way of life. It's not easy. I want both but that's not an option. Momma says I have wings, not roots. Pulling the feathers out of my wings is not easy, but I do it every day because I'm determined to put down roots. Listen to your heart, Becca."

"I don't want to be poor," she whispered.

"It's the foreman, isn't it?" Liz asked.

Becca dabbed at her eyes with a tissue she pulled from her purse. "Taylor is his name. He's ten years older than I am, and he asked me to marry him. Daddy will fire him on the spot and cut me off."

"You sure about that? Talk to your dad. Can't do any more damage than what you've already worked up in your mind. Take Taylor with you and have an adult conversation with your father. Tell him you are ready to start working instead of playing. I bet you have a good head for organization and figures. It goes with the Scorpio sign," Liz said.

"Thank you," Becca said. "Don't tell Raylen."

"You'll tell him when the time is right," Liz said.

Becca left and Liz pinched her nose between her thumb and forefinger for a full minute before she flipped the switch under the table that shot out a blast of chilly air and the one that turned the door sign to ENTER.

––––∞––––

Liz applied cold cream to her face after she'd removed her costume and dressed in jeans, a T-shirt, and lined denim jacket. She'd shut down the fortune telling business at ten and took a long look out across the midway:

not much happening there. The Ferris wheel was still, and only the tilt-a-whirl was operating. There weren't twenty people milling around, and no one had looked like they were interested in palm readings or crystal balls.

She stomped her bare feet down into cowboy boots and hoped that the gyro wagon was still making sandwiches because she was hungry. It was her lucky night. She ordered two and a Diet Coke, found a seat under the awning, and sat down for a late supper. Before she could remove the paper wrapping from the first one and take a bite, Blaze had parked himself right beside her.

"Thought I'd find you here. Hope it picks up tomorrow night, or we might as well pack it up and go on to west Texas," he said.

"Oh, no! You are coming to my house on Monday and staying until Thursday. Tuesday is rest up day and Wednesday night we've got a Christmas party in the barn. It's all planned and invitations have already been given," she said.

"Who all has been invited?" he asked.

"All the O'Donnell family. They've been good to me. And Ace and his hired help, which is four guys, and Wil and Pearl and their foreman, Jack and Jack's family, and then Austin and Rye are coming with their baby girl, and Slade and his wife and girls and his granny and aunt. You've got to meet Ellen. She's the grown-up, eighty-year-old version of the women you like," Liz said.

Blaze smiled brightly. "Darlin', I wouldn't miss your party for anything. Now talk to me about this O'Donnell family some more."

"The family or Colleen?" she asked.

Blaze laughed. "You know me too well."

"Yes, I do."

"And I know you just as well. You are in love, but is it real love or are you in love with the idea of being in love? That's the question you need to ponder in the crystal ball." He pushed his wet hair back out of his gold-flecked eyes.

Unlike most blonds, he had to shave every day or he had a heavy scruff. That night he'd shaved smooth and Liz caught a whiff of his most expensive shaving lotion.

"So who's the lucky lady who'll be picking you up at midnight tonight?" She looked around.

"Could have a date. Don't have a date. Catching up on sleep tonight. Maybe tomorrow night someone will come along that takes my eye," he said.

Liz polished off her first gyro and unwrapped the second one. "I don't know if she's coming or not. Did you see Gemma tonight?"

"Yes, with your boss lady. They rode the wheel twice and ate Indian tacos and cotton candy. I heard her tell Jasmine that Colleen was going to love the tacos tomorrow night." Blaze grinned.

"She has roots. Deep ones," Liz said.

"You have wings. Big ones," he shot back.

"Be careful, Blaze."

"I can't. Not this time or I'll lose what my heart really wants, and you can't say a word because you're floating the same boat as I am," he said.

"Yes, I am," she admitted.

He held up a beer. "Here's to roots and wings. May they both have the ability to change."

"Last week you wouldn't have said that. You were begging me to give my house back to Uncle Haskell and come back to the carnival. And love at first sight is…"

He poked her playfully on the arm. "Love at first sight is bullshit. But the heart can reach out and know its soul mate at first sight, and then the love can come later."

Liz wadded up her papers and put them in the trash can at the end of the table. "Blaze, you are a romantic. Next thing you know, you'll be sprouting roots."

"No I'm not, but I can hope someone else will sprout wings someday. Got to run. Tressa is motioning to me. I think she's about to call it a night and shut up an hour early. See you tomorrow night?"

"Oh, yeah. I'm running the dart gallery. Colleen ought to love it when she sees me hawking for customers," she groaned.

"We are what we are." Blaze waved good-bye to her.

Raylen opened the door when she walked up on the porch. Candles glimmered in the background and Christmas music floated out to meet her. He wore flannel pajama bottoms, no shirt, and he was barefoot.

That much turned her into a whining bag of hormones. When he pulled her inside, kicked the door shut with his bare foot, and started a long series of long, lingering passionate kisses, she groaned.

"Stop!"

"Why?"

"One more kiss and we're going to bed and forgetting all dancing except for the horizontal kind," she said.

He took two steps back. "I've pictured this for days. I want the dance."

She took him by the hand and led him to the recliner. "Sit right here and I'll be back in a few minutes."

He wiggled.

He squirmed.

His hands were clammy, so he wiped them on his pajama legs.

A fine bead of sweat broke out on his forehead. He wiped that away with a tissue from the box on the end table.

He wanted her. He didn't care if she danced or not.

But she'd said she was looking forward to the dance and God only knew how bad it had affected him all week, so he waited.

"Wait is a four-letter word," he grumbled.

He leaned his head back and stared at the ceiling. Sugarland was singing "Winter Wonderland." He listened to the lyrics that said that a new bird was there to stay, that he sang a love song as they walked in a winter wonderland. Well, he and Liz had been listening to a new love song and they damn sure had a winter wonderland out there in the front yard.

The music changed right in the middle of the singer talking about facing the plans they'd made, unafraid, as they walked in a wonderland. Suddenly it sounded like snake charmer music, and Liz appeared out of the darkness, taking tiny steps toward the center of the room as her arms moved to the flute music, as if she were truly charming a snake.

The drums started and she did a one-foot spin, landing on both feet so close to him that he gasped. Then she slowly turned around, her arms beckoning to him and her belly muscles rolling. The tempo picked up, and she leaned backwards until her black hair touched the floor, and she was looking at him upside down. When the flute took center stage again she rolled back up, each graceful move as subtle as it was sexy.

She wore a different outfit that night and if possible, it was even sexier than the orange one. Turquoise hip-slung pants hugged her legs to the knees where ruffles in silver and lighter blue flirted with him every time she moved. A shimmering skirt was attached to the hip band and flowed down the back, and the bra was covered with beads that shook every time she shimmied.

The music changed slightly, bringing in a piano and she did another one-foot spin and removed the skirt. Raylen had no idea where the long silver scarf came from, but when she wrapped it around her hips and kept time to the music with hip clicks and belly rolls, he could hardly sit still.

The dance was so different than the orange one. The piano added a salsa flavor that had him sweating bullets by the time she started winding down with baby steps and shimmies that brought her closer and closer to him.

When the last drum rolled and the flute stopped, she bent down and claimed his lips in a kiss so passionate that he couldn't wait another minute to touch her. He wrapped his arms around her to find that she was heaving from all the exertion.

"Hard work," she panted.

"Hard everything," he gasped.

Sizzling hot kisses started when he picked her up and carried her toward the bedroom. He laid her on the bed and fumbled with the tight pants until she reached behind her and unfastened a zipper. He tugged them off and tossed them to one side, without taking his lips from hers. He jerked his flannel bottoms off and was on top of her before she could even think about removing her hair jewelry or her bra.

Less than a minute later he drawled, "Liz," and burst inside her.

"Oh, my God," he said when he could breathe. "It happened again. Darlin', I'm so, so sorry!"

She giggled. "Guess we'd best save dancing for very special occasions or we'll burn ourselves down like a wild grass fire."

"We'll never need to buy a Viagra pill. When I'm old all I'll have to do is look at that costume and bingo," he whispered.

"If I remember right, the appetizer last time didn't do a damn thing to satisfy our appetites and we had to have a main course."

When I am old, she thought. He'd said that they would be together when he was old, and she liked that so much that she would have danced for him again right then.

"I do believe we did." He grinned.

He rolled to one side and started a long, serious session of foreplay that included removing her headpiece, setting her up in the middle of the bed, and brushing her long hair while his other hand carefully unhooked the bra, then without breaking a single bead, he laid it on the end table.

"Oh, oh, that feels good," she said.

No one had brushed her hair since she'd gotten independent enough to take care of it all by herself at the age of six. She had no idea so many sensual nerve endings could be found by a naked cowboy with a hairbrush.

When she was totally naked, he moved her around to sit in front of him on her knees. "Now kissing but no touching anywhere else."

"Why?"

"You will see," he said.

She leaned forward and he did the same.

The kisses started out sweet and deepened gradually until they were both panting.

"Now one hand only and above the waist," he said.

"God, Raylen, you are killing me," she said.

"Not any more than you are me, but we are going to savor each moment of this night, Liz."

His right hand inched to her breasts and gently touched them as if he weren't sure he should be there. He looked deep into her eyes, asking for permission to touch her without saying a word.

The fingers of her right hand combed his chest hair and she did not blink as she begged him to love her and never break her heart.

Five minutes later he said, "Both hands and full body."

"Thank God!" she mumbled.

A few minutes after that she was arching against him and whimpering. "Please, Raylen. Take me now."

He settled in for a long haul with a firm thrust, but when she used some of those belly dancing moves in a horizontal position fifteen minutes later, he cupped both of her hips in his hands and with one final thrust reached a climax so strong that it knocked the breath right out of him.

"Wow!" she said when she could speak.

"Oh, yeah," he said between gasps.

"Hold me. I see stars and hear music."

He rolled to one side, wrapped her tightly in his arms, and buried his face in her black hair. No sir, he would never need those little blue pills, even if he and Liz lived to be a hundred.

"Promise me one more time that I'm the only man you'll ever dance for like that," he said.

"You got it," she said. "Only for you and only on special occasions."

"Like my birthday, Christmas, and our anniversary?"

She smiled. He was thinking they'd have anniversaries.

"And maybe July Fourth. We'll make our own fireworks."

Friday night was a little warmer and the stars were shining. Liz wore jeans and a carnie logo black shirt, tied a money apron around her waist, and worked the crowd. She'd just made a hundred dollars from a man who'd been determined to win his girlfriend the biggest teddy bear on the rack. If he'd been throwing for doughnuts, he wouldn't have even gotten the hole. He did finally hit one balloon and Liz gave the lady her choice of the medium-sized animals as a consolation prize for all the money he'd spent.

She turned around to pick up a balloon to blow up and there was Raylen in the galley with her, sitting on a small stool at the end of the stuffed animal display. He'd already blown up a bright red balloon and tied a knot on the end.

"Tressa said I could work with you tonight," he said.

Liz smiled and kissed him soundly right smack on the lips. "I missed you today. What have you been doing?"

"Exercised the horses and then cleaned out their stalls. Work before play." He grinned back at her. "Last night, I worked with your momma in the cinnamon roll wagon. It was quite an experience. I barely beat you home and got a shower before you came to dance for me."

Liz jerked her head around. "You were here? Why didn't you come find me?"

"Because I was working on one end of the carnival and you were holed up on the other end. I left at ten because your momma said it was slow."

"Why'd you work again?"

He pulled her down onto his lap. "Best way to get to know someone is to work along beside them. That's what Grandpa taught me when I was a boy."

"We gettin' to know each other tonight?" she asked.

"Guess so. There's a customer eyeing the big bear. You going to reel him in or want me to try?"

"Give it your best shot." She stood up.

"Hey, mister, your pretty girlfriend sure would like to take our big bear home with her. You can start to win it with only three darts. Three little darts to hit three balloons out of five and that gets you the first stuffed animal of your choice. Trade it back in and buy three more darts for the next size until you make it all the way to the big bear. What do you say? Three darts for two bucks or twenty for a five dollar bill."

The man shook his head.

"Well, sweetheart, I guess you don't get that bear tonight. Or else you'll have to find another cowboy to win it for you," Raylen said.

The man walked straight to the gallery and laid out a five dollar bill. It took every one of them but he popped three balloons. Liz blew up three more and Raylen tacked them to the corkboard.

"Keep it or try again?" Raylen said.

He shook his head.

The lady looked at the bear and stuck out her lower

lip in a fake pout. Liz had seen that ploy before and it worked about eighty percent of the time. The next step would be squeezing her boob right up to his arm and whispering something in his ear.

He laid out another five and popped the last balloon with the tenth dart. The woman traded her tiny piglet for a medium-sized zebra.

"That's it, Misty. You can either keep the zebra and go dancin' tomorrow night at the club, or else we'll try for the bear," he said.

Misty kissed the zebra and they walked off.

"Fish just flipped back into the water," Liz said.

Raylen squeezed her hand. "Your turn. If you put another hundred in your pocket before the next fish gets off the hook, I'll make you breakfast in bed."

"And if I don't?"

"Then you are breakfast in bed, and I'm not talking about food."

"I guess you mean to spend the night with me?"

He chuckled and tilted his head toward a soldier in uniform hugged up to his girlfriend. "I see a big fish, and are you askin' me to sleep over at your house tonight?"

"You're damn right," she whispered and handed the soldier a handful of darts for his five dollar bill.

Twenty dollars later the soldier handed the big bear to his girlfriend.

"Lucky SOB," Liz said.

"Not as lucky as I am," Raylen answered.

"What if we are too tired?" She yawned.

"I didn't say we had to collect on the bet tomorrow or even the day after. There's lots of mornings left in our life if we live to be three score and ten." He slung an arm round her shoulders and kissed her on the cheek.

Chapter 20

On Sunday morning, Liz's eyes popped open at five o'clock. She had one leg thrown over the edge of the bed when she remembered it was Sunday and she didn't have to go to work. She threw herself back down on the bed and shut her eyes, but she couldn't force herself to go to sleep.

Raylen turned over in his sleep, slipped one arm under her and another over the top, and snuggled up next to her, burying his face in her hair. Lying in his arms the past two nights, even without sex, felt so right, but right then she wanted to kick him out of her bed and run back to Bowie. She wanted to call Uncle Haskell and tell him to sell Raylen the land and put Ringgold, Texas, out of her mind forever.

Marva Jo's words played through her mind in a continuous loop. *Just remember we are exotic to a gadjo for a little while. It didn't last with your father. It won't last with Raylen. Enjoy it while you have it and then let it go. Kind of like a butterfly on a pretty red flower. Stay until you tire of it and then fly away.*

Flying away now would break her heart, but if they ever got married like her mother and father, and then it didn't last, she'd die of a broken heart. Marva Jo had been down the road and had hit all the speed bumps. She knew men much better than Liz did.

Give it until Christmas, Uncle Haskell's voice

argued. *You'll know by Christmas if you want to give up the land, and you can tell me when you come home to Claude for the holiday. Don't make a rash decision until then. You've only been there a month, and you've just had four days of carnival. See how you feel when they're gone and you're back in your normal schedule.*

Haskell was giving her an inheritance. Maybe because Aunt Sara had often wished that she was Liz's mother. Maybe because he knew how it felt to want to settle down. But she owed him a few more weeks. Besides, a broken heart was a broken heart whether it was the week before Thanksgiving or the day after Christmas.

She eased out of Raylen's arms and padded barefoot to the kitchen where she put on a pot of coffee. She popped open a can of cinnamon rolls, put them in a pan, and slid them in the oven. While they cooked she laid half a pound of bacon over a stand-up rack and stuck that into the microwave.

"I thought we were going to sleep in," Raylen said from the doorway.

"I woke up and couldn't go back to sleep, so I decided to make good on my loss and cook breakfast for you," she said.

"The bet was I'd bring you breakfast in bed, and if you lost you had to be breakfast in bed." He grinned. "You lost so let's go back to bed."

"Can't. Cinnamon rolls and bacon will burn," she said.

He slipped his arms around her and pulled her back to his chest. "I liked having you next to me in bed the last two nights, even if we were too tired for a romp."

His phone rang before she could answer. He picked

it up from the counter where he'd dropped it the night before and frowned.

"I'm on my way." He was already putting on his jeans before he flipped the phone shut.

"What?" Liz asked.

"Glorious Danny Boy got out of the barn and jumped a fence or two. He's the horniest old stud in the world. He gets to wanting a mare, and there ain't a lock he won't break. Damned horse anyway. We've got one mare we're watching close. We put her out to pasture a year ago because Momma said she's too old to bear any more colts to him, but he must really have a hankering for her. She's going to drop a foal before long and we're just hoping it don't kill her. Dewar followed his footprints to the woods back behind our place. I've got to go help find him. We're hoping to bring him home before Momma even knows he's gone. Dewar has already called the vet to be on standby. I'm sorry, darlin', but…" He left the sentence hanging.

"Do you need me to help?"

"Thanks, but no thanks. He's going to be spooky out there in strange land. It'll be best if Dewar and I take care of it. Are you going to help with the carnival teardown?" Raylen asked.

"Yes. Call me as soon as you find him, please?"

He gave her a quick kiss and stomped his feet down into cowboy boots. "I promise to keep you updated. See you later."

The microwave dinged as Raylen left, letting in Hooter and Blister at the same time. She pulled the bacon out and checked the cinnamon rolls. They were almost done, and the coffee had stopped dripping. She poured a cup and ate a piece of bacon while she waited on the rolls.

Blister jumped up on the counter and meowed. Hooter looked up at her and yipped.

"Hungry, are you?" She shook dog food from the big bag into Hooter's dish and opened a can of cat food for Blister.

The cat bailed off the cabinet, smelled the food, and rubbed around Liz's legs. Hooter ate one bite before he sat down in front of the microwave and looked up. Liz reached down to rub Blister's ears, and the cat licked her fingers. Hooter yipped again and Liz finally understood.

"You spoiled rotten critters. You're wanting bacon, aren't you? Guess you might as well help me eat it since a bigger critter done stole my feller this morning." She gave them each one piece and watched Hooter gulp his down in one swallow while Blister ate hers as daintily as English royalty at a tea party.

She opened the oven door and got a whiff on hot cinnamon. That was the Sunday morning breakfast in the trailer. Her mother would have bacon in the microwave and canned cinnamon rolls in the oven when she woke up. They'd each get a fork and eat them right out of the pan and then they'd go outside and start tearing down.

The rolls were toasted to a light brown when she removed them, cut a hole in the end of the plastic container of icing, drizzled it over the top, and ate out of the pan. And they were wonderful.

Everything was still lazy when Liz reached the carnival. Blaze was sitting on his metal door step with a can of

Pepsi in one hand and a toaster pastry in the other. He had pulled a lightweight jacket over a gray thermal undershirt. His flannel pajama bottoms were the ones Liz had given him for Christmas five years ago and had hot chili peppers printed on them.

"Sit down, sweetheart, and tell me your week has been better than mine. Want some breakfast?" he asked.

She scrunched in beside him. "I had hot cinnamon rolls and bacon. What are you whining about? My feller got called away to help find a runaway horse this morning while the bacon was still cookin'."

"I'm whinin' because Colleen just breezed in and out of my life and I want to know her better and life is not fair," Blaze said in a high-pitched little boy whine.

Liz laughed. "Aunt Tressa didn't sign a contract that life would be fair when she took you to raise. I think the one that the two of you worked up had something to do with lots of work, good pay, and you didn't have to go to public school. And besides, you've still got until Thursday morning before you leave this part of the state."

"You got a feller and I found my soul mate and I didn't even get to sleep with her." Blaze kept up the whiny little boy voice.

"You'll be at my place until Thursday morning. There's a big barn with a nice loft. She'll be around if she's interested. Have you lost your charm? Did the warranty run out on the charm and you forgot to renew it? Come on, Blaze, if she's your soul mate, it will work. If she's not, there's lots of fishes in the sea," Liz said.

Blaze finished the pastry and licked his fingers. "I

don't want to fish anymore. I want a soul mate like you got in Raylen."

"How do you know that?" Liz asked.

"It's in the eyes and the way you look at each other," he answered.

"That's a load of romantic crap. I've seen women look at you the same way since you joined the carnival."

Blaze threw an arm around her and hugged her up to his side. No bells or whistles sounded in her ears. Not a single spark sizzled in the air around her. No fireworks popped off in the distance.

"It's more than lust, Lizelle. It's something that can't be described. I knew when I looked at Colleen that she's my soul mate."

"I heard that about what was her name? Oh, yeah, Janet. And then there was Ophelia."

"Those were just wannabes. Third time is the charm anyway and this time it's real. I haven't been to bed with anyone since I laid eyes on her."

"Good God, Blaze. You are worse than…"

"You?" he asked.

"Far worse. I didn't know a man could have such a romantic side."

"We got that side, but we don't admit it to just anyone. We damn sure wouldn't tell it in a bar full of other men. Don't leave. I'm goin' to get dressed and then we'll start taking down the Ferris wheel. The place is starting to wake up. Pretty soon everyone will have the takedown fever," he said.

She stood up so he could open the door into his trailer and waited until he was inside with the door shut before she sat back down. Other doors began to shut around her, and folks began to head toward the median or the rides to get the Sunday job done. The pickup trucks with trailers behind them were pulled up in a line at the back side of the property with enough room to unhitch and get out if they needed to do so. The semis and flatbed trucks were parked behind them. They carried the equipment, the rides and the vendor's wagons. Five wagons to a flatbed, ponies in the horse trailer down at the end of the semis, stuff, stuff and more stuff in the big trucks. Vendors drove the trucks, and their wives drove the pickup trucks with the travel trailers hooked on the backs.

The next day they would leave, leaving nothing, not even a candy wrapper, in their wake. This year instead of heading due west, they'd go fifteen miles north to Liz's place. She had plenty of room for them to park and rest until Thursday morning when they'd be off to Claude. Poppa would be standing on the porch looking for them to stream onto the land by suppertime. Only this year, Uncle Haskell would be there too, for the first time, and Liz wouldn't be driving her truck and bringing up the rear of the parade.

She dug her ringing cell phone from her jacket pocket, checked the ID, and quickly answered it.

"Please tell me you found him and he's all right, Raylen."

"We've got him but he's got a nasty cut on his foreleg that is going to need a few stitches and he'll need a round of antibiotics. He's in the barn and the vet is on the way. Momma is with him, and Daddy is trying to figure out how he got out. Near as we can tell something spooked him and his gate stall wasn't fastened tightly. Once he was out he was running. We're lucky he's not banged up even worse. Found him in a mesquite thicket, limping back toward the house. He'd jumped three fences." Raylen's voice sounded worried.

"Is there anything I can do?" Liz asked.

"Not a thing. I just can't come help with the teardown business today. One of us will stay with him all day and night. I drew the shift from six to midnight. If you get home in time, you can come out to the barn and keep me company."

"I'll be there and I'll call before I leave so I can bring anything you need," she said.

"I just need you," he said softly.

His voice, going husky and sexy like that, turned her insides all mushy.

"I'll be there soon as I can. Call me with updates," she said.

"I will. I see the vet pulling in now. See you later then?"

"I promise," she said.

"You promise what?" Blaze cracked the door.

She stood up to let him open it all the way. "That I'll go by the barn and see about the horse that got out. Ever heard of Glorious Danny Boy?"

He stepped out and kept in step with her as she headed toward the Ferris wheel. "Hell, yeah! He's that famous quarter horse that won the Texas Heritage Stakes several years ago. When anyone talks about horse racing they say, 'as good as old Glorious Danny Boy' or 'never as good as.' Why are you asking?"

"That's the horse that got loose this mornin'. Glorious Danny Boy. The O'Donnells own him and Major Jack," she explained.

"Holy shit, Lizelle. They are real horse ranchers."

"Yes, they are. Hand me the stubby. I'll get the first board off since my hands are smaller," she said.

"And Colleen comes from that family," he groaned as he handed her the screwdriver.

Liz nodded.

"There's no way she'd ever be interested in a long-term relationship with me," Blaze said.

"Long-term or long-distance?"

"Either one," Blaze said. "What happened to the horse?"

"He got out of his stall and the horse barn, jumped a couple of fences, and they found him in a mesquite thicket with a torn foreleg. The vet had just gotten there. Raylen said he'd have stitches and they'd put him on antibiotics. The family will stay with him all day and Raylen's drawn the straw for first shift tonight."

"Hell, if that horse was mine, the whole damn family would stay with him tonight. I'd even call Colleen home from the casino. As smooth as her voice is, she could read bedtime stories to him and keep him calm."

Liz shook her head. "You are smitten."

"Yep, I am. Are you?"

"Oh, yeah! But I have been since I was a little girl," she answered.

Chapter 21

LIZ DROVE SLOWLY DOWN THE LANE. THE LIGHTS WERE on in the O'Donnell house. Colleen's truck was parked in the driveway, and halfway to the barn she found Colleen walking in the middle of the two-rut pathway. She'd been on the phone with Raylen the past five minutes and he was directing her to the barn.

She put on the brakes and said, "Just a minute. Your sister is in front of me. Is she supposed to relieve you?"

Raylen sighed. "I guess it's Colleen. Gemma just left and said that Colleen was on her way home for a few days."

"Looks like her red hair."

Colleen turned around when the truck didn't swerve out around her and walked back to the door. "Hi, Liz. I thought this was your truck. You on your way to the barn? I'll ride with you and show you the rest of the way."

"Got a passenger and a guide. See you in a minute," Liz said while Colleen made her way around the front of the truck and crawled inside.

She could see where Blaze would be taken with Colleen. With that deep red hair and those mossy green eyes, any man would be stone blind or else gay not to take a second glance.

"The vet said we didn't have to sit up with Danny Boy but Momma says different," Colleen said.

"Maddie loves that horse, doesn't she?" Liz asked.

"Yes, she does. He's been good to her. Straight ahead. You can see the lights already. We already took Raylen's supper to him. Dewar will relieve him at midnight and my shift starts at six in the morning. Momma will be out here most of the time with me, I'm sure. Gemma will take over at noon since she doesn't have to work on Mondays. Dewar said he'll do a stint tomorrow evening. By late tomorrow night, Momma says if he's doing well, we can stop baby-sitting. The vet will be here three times a day until we're sure his leg is healing right."

Liz nosed the truck in beside Raylen's vehicle. Before her hand reached the door handle, Raylen opened it.

"I'm so glad to see you." He leaned inside and planted a hot kiss on her lips right there in front of Colleen.

"Hello to you too, Brother," Colleen said.

"Hi," he said. "Y'all come on in. Danny Boy is doing fine. Vet said he could eat whatever he wanted, so he's getting spoiled. I've already fed him three carrots and two apples, so don't believe him when he gives you that 'poor pitiful me' look."

He laced his fingers in Liz's hand and led the way into the barn. "Vet put in six stitches and gave him a healthy dose of antibiotics, which he gets three times a day for three days, along with dressing changes. He assures us Danny Boy will be good as new and doesn't think he was out more than a couple of hours. The blood wasn't dried on his wound and he didn't have any scratches anywhere else."

Liz let go of his hand and went to the stall where Danny Boy had his head stuck and nickered. She walked right up to him, rubbed his nose, and crooned, "Poor baby boy. Now you have to stay in the stall and you won't get to see the Gypsy Vanners and flirt with my girls. That's what you get for givin' in to that rebellious streak. You want an apple? Well, I heard you already had two this evening, but I've got a carrot in my pocket that was left over when we loaded the Vanner ladies into the horse wagon. Will that do?" She reached into her jacket pocket, brought out the prize, and fed it to Danny Boy.

Colleen leaned against the stall on the other side of the midway from Danny Boy. "He's spoiled rotten and you're not helping."

"He's a pretty boy, yes he is," Liz said. "I love horses. We've got several out in Claude that have been put out to pasture. They're too old for the carnival and I spend a lot of time with them in the winter."

"Vanners? You have Vanners?" Colleen asked.

"Six mares," Raylen answered for her. "Fancy stock, let me tell you. They use them for pony rides, believe it or not. Dewar is going to drool."

"I might drool with him," Colleen said. "I didn't see them when I was there."

"The pony rides are at the far end of the carnival. Past the Ferris wheel. We keep them in a portable round pen. Blaze and Aunt Tressa take care of them. He's really good with them. Knows his horses well. He and Aunt Tressa flew to Pennsylvania last February to buy a stud. Brought home Sweet Diamond Jessie. Poppa is of the opinion the Vanners are too fancy for carnival work. He wants us to leave them home next year."

"I agree. Shetlands can do carnival work. Gypsy Vanners should be royalty," Colleen said.

Raylen took Liz's hand back in his and threw open a

stall door next to Danny Boy's. "Welcome to the baby-sitter's quarters."

Liz was amazed to see an army cot and two folding chairs. One chair held a laptop computer and one a baby monitor commonly used in baby cribs. She raised an eyebrow and Colleen laughed.

"There's one taped to Danny Boy's stall wall. We can hear him if he burps or whines," she explained.

Raylen tugged on her hand. "Sit by me."

She sat down on the cot and he settled close to her, keeping their entwined hands on his thigh. Colleen sat in the other metal chair and fidgeted with her fingers, lacing them together, then wringing them. She looked at the computer screen and then back at Raylen and Liz.

"I took a few days off work. Thought I'd better come home and help with Danny Boy. When Momma called she was frantic. Now I see y'all have it under control," she finally said.

It was evident that Colleen was nervous and wanted to talk but didn't know how to start the conversation.

Raylen reached across the space and patted Colleen's knee. "You work too hard. You need some time off anyway, and this is the week that Liz is having her big party. You'd hate to miss that. You goin' to lose any money?"

Colleen shook her head. "I've got four weeks paid vacation coming. I took a week of that."

"How did you get that much vacation?" Liz asked.

"I've been there six years now. It builds up. So did y'all get the carnival torn down and ready to move things onto your place tomorrow?"

"We did," Liz said. Aha! It was Blaze who was on Colleen's mind!

"I'd forgotten how much fun they are, and I really did have a good time the other night helping you set things up. How about you, Raylen? I heard you'd been down there every night," Colleen asked.

"Whole different view of carnivals now that I've helped get one ready to open. What time will they be here tomorrow? You going to light the place up for them?" Raylen asked Liz.

"Oh, yeah. I don't care if the sun is shining, it's going to be lit up. Momma is supposed to call me soon as they pull out so I'll have time to turn everything on. Y'all were supposed to bring the tables over tomorrow evening for the barn. I know where they're stored. Is it all right if I take Blaze and some of the guys over there and borrow them? You'll be busy with Danny Boy, I'm sure. Colleen, if you don't have to baby-sit, come on over and help us set up tables."

Colleen beamed. "I'd love to help. Do you have enough decorations? We could steal Momma's and then take them home. She's not putting up the tree until after Thanksgiving holiday."

"Got tons, but thank you. I kind of expect them to arrive about three, so come any time after that. I can use the help," Liz said.

"I'll be there. Well, since I've seen him, I'm going back to the house. Momma said to tell you she'll be out in a little while. She can't stay away from her Danny Boy. I'm surprised that Granny isn't here demanding that she do a shift with him." Colleen was all smiles.

The minute Colleen cleared the end of the stall, Raylen picked Liz up and settled her onto his lap. He didn't need to tip her chin for a real kiss. When he looked over at her, her lips were already on the way to his. That morning he'd had the feeling that something wasn't right, that maybe she was about to tell him they needed to talk, which in his past meant breakup time. But when their lips touched, everything was right and the doubts vanished.

His tongue found hers, and desire flooded his whole body. He had no doubt they could make love on the narrow cot as he unfastened her bra and moved a hand around to cup a breast. She gasped and ran her hands up under his knit shirt, toying with the soft hair on his chest and tasting his lips all at the same time.

And then his damned cell phone rang. He ignored it the first time, but when it set up a howl within seconds, he reached over and picked it up. "Dammit, Colleen! You just left," he said as he punched the button.

"Yes?" His tone was grouchy and short.

"I just passed Momma. Givin' you the heads up. She's probably almost there. Put Liz's bra back on and zip your britches," Colleen said and flipped her phone shut.

"Momma is almost at the barn door," he said.

Liz slapped a hand over her mouth and then both hands shot around her back. She'd barely refastened her bra when Maddie yelled from the doorway. "Y'all back here? How's my Danny Boy?"

Raylen yelled back as he pulled Liz down beside him and grabbed her hand. "We're in the baby-sittin' room. He's fine. Check him out and keep us company for a while."

"I'll have to remember to thank Colleen," Liz whispered.

"Just remember to give her the same warning if she

almost gets caught with Blaze these next few days. That's the real reason she took vacation time. She's dated a lot of cowboys in her day. Some guys I probably don't even know about up around Randlett where she lives, but she's never gone all tongue-tied over one like she has Blaze," Raylen said.

"And how do you feel about that?" Liz scooted over even closer so she could feel Raylen all up and down her body. She loved it when her shoulder, hip, thigh, and lower leg all touched his at the same time. That's when musical tingles two-stepped up and down her body.

"I didn't like it at all. I hated it because of what you've told me about him. But then your Aunt Tressa sent me to work with him, and he's a good man. But, and this is a big but…"

She giggled. "Big as an elephant's butt?"

"Oh, honey, an elephant is a tiny ballerina dancer compared to this but." Raylen laughed with her. "But if he's just in it for a one-night stand and breaks her heart, I'm going to break his ribs."

"He's not," Liz whispered.

Raylen cocked his head to one side and whispered back, "He talked to you?"

She nodded and motioned toward the monitor on the chair where they could hear Maddie crooning to Danny Boy. "She can hear us, can't she?"

"No, it's turned on so that we can hear him but he can't hear us so he won't get spooked if there's noise on this side of the wall," Raylen said.

"Right now, Blaze is as smitten as she is. What do you think of that?" Liz continued to whisper. She wasn't trusting that monitor one bit.

"I want Colleen to be happy and you said Blaze liked horses."

"Raylen, Blaze is a carnie to his core. He won't ever leave it."

"Oh!"

Liz snuggled in tighter to his side. "Yeah. Oh!"

Maddie settled into the metal chair in front of them. "He's lookin' good. I think he's goin' to be fine. Y'all get that carnival all packed up and ready to roll?" she asked Liz.

"It will be rolling by tomorrow afternoon. They had the majority of it done when I left, but carnies don't get in a hurry to get up in the morning," Liz said. "Don't forget about my dinner on Wednesday night."

Maddie tucked a strand of hair behind her ear. Worry was still etched into her face. Liz understood in a very small measure because when she thought about losing one of the six Vanner horses, she couldn't swallow down the baseball-sized lump in her throat. When she thought about losing Hooter or Blister, tears welled up behind her eyes. Maddie had raised Danny Boy from a newborn colt and had trained him. Liz couldn't imagine the pain of having to put him to sleep.

"I'm sorry," Liz said. "I don't mean to be thinking about a party when Danny Boy is hurt, but I want y'all to get acquainted with my family."

Maddie smiled and the worry eased up. "Honey, we need a party worse now than we did two days ago. Danny Boy is going to be fine, and by Wednesday night, he'll be almost new. And I couldn't forget if I wanted to. Mother has been buggin' me to death about it. She called four times this afternoon to see about Danny Boy and to talk about your party. She wants you and Raylen to play 'Fire on the Mountain' and 'The Devil Went Down to Georgia' together. She says that'll put the icing on any party."

"Well, if that's what she wants, it's what she'll get. Will she mind if some of the other folks bring their instruments and play?" Liz asked.

"Oh, no! The more the merrier. She loves music, and she's convinced you are Irish," Maddie said.

"When she sees Momma and Aunt Tressa, she'll believe it even more. They both have red hair and tempers. My dad was pure Latino, Eddie Garcia," Liz said.

"Was?"

"He died a few weeks before I was born. He and mother married on a whim. When the new wore off, he decided he didn't want a carnie wife. The divorce wasn't even final when he died. Momma gave me the Hanson name to avoid confusion, but if she'd given me his name I would be a Garcia."

Maddie nodded. "Well, he and your momma sure made a pretty daughter. I'm going back to the house. Now that I've seen Danny Boy one more time, I can sleep better. If you need anything, holler and I'll send one of the girls or Dewar down here with it."

"Thank you," Liz said.

When Maddie had been gone five minutes, she shifted her position and sat in Raylen's lap. "You reckon she could send one of the girls with a big king-sized bed and some satin sheets?"

He tangled his hands in her hair and brought her lips to him as if he was starving, and only her kisses would keep him alive. She was just as desperate for his touch, for his mouth on hers.

Not often was she able to think at all when he kissed her. Usually every sane thought left her head in a void that could only be refilled with thoughts of him after the love making had finished. But that night with the smell of horse and hay all around her, she realized something vital.

It was Raylen's touch and kisses that watered the roots she was growing in Montague County, Texas. And the pain of pulling up the roots would be worse than the pain of cutting off her wings. Every time she had doubts, all she needed to do was curl up in his arms and let him pour on the water.

"I see you every day but I miss you every hour I'm not with you," he said.

She laid her head on his shoulder. "But we saw each other this morning and we've slept together two nights."

"Slept. Not this. I missed having time to hold you without falling asleep, to kiss you until my brain goes to mush, and…"

She touched his zipper. "Looks like something else isn't mush."

He reached up above his head and flipped a switch. The stall went dark with the dim lights out in the center aisle barely letting him see the hot desire in her dark eyes. He kicked the stall door shut with his boot and grinned.

"Ever made love in a horse stall?"

"No, but I'm plannin' on it right now," she said as she slowly unbuckled his belt.

He deepened the kiss, making love to her lips and mouth with his tongue. She moaned and melted against him. He slipped a hand under her shirt and with two fingers undid her bra for the second time that night.

"Are you sure we won't get caught again?" She muttered words between passionate kisses.

He took his time standing up so that he wouldn't miss a single moment of tasting her lips and picked her up like a new bride.

"Where are we going?" she asked.

"Right here, but that cot is too narrow." He tossed the blanket he was supposed to use for cover while he napped onto the ground and laid her down on it. "It's not satin sheets but it's as big as a king-sized bed."

"Satin is overrated." She smiled.

"Your skin can be the satin for the night, and darlin', that's not overrated," he whispered as he removed her jacket and shirt and covered her skin with hot, steamy kisses.

She wiggled and undressed him in a hurry, pulled the side of the blanket up over them, and ducked under it to cover his hard body with nibbles, nips, tastes, and kisses. When she reached his toes she started back up the other side, stretching out on top of him when she got to his lips. She nibbled on his earlobe, and he wrapped his hands around her slim body and with one expert flip, she was under him and the blanket still covered them both like a cocoon.

If his kisses were the water that kept her tiny new Ringgold roots alive, then sex was the fertilizer, she thought just before his touch and kisses erased everything but that deep, hot, juicy desire to make love with Raylen. She arched against him and ran her hands down his back, digging her nails into his hips.

"God, Raylen," she said.

"Praying?" he panted.

"Oh, yeah," she said.

"For what?"

"For this to never end."

Raylen had found places that she never knew could make such intense heat, had already made her feel like she was teetering on the edge of a cliff. If she died right then, they'd find so many of those sexy chemicals in her body that there would be no doubt as to cause of death.

"That could be arranged," he said as he found another spot high on her inner thigh that fanned the already out-of-control blazing fire, making it even hotter. He began a long, easy rhythm that erased every word from her vocabulary: roots, wings, staying, carnivals, horses. They all disappeared, and the only word left in her brain was Raylen.

The crescendo built into panting breathlessness so intense that it would not be denied and had to be satisfied in that moment, and the barn lit up in a display of sizzling sparks. The monitor sitting above their head said they'd awakened Danny Boy with their noise.

"Guess we woke the baby," Raylen said as he rolled over to her side, keeping her hugged up to him in the cocoon.

"Need to check on him?" she panted.

"No, I think he was giving us his blessing," Raylen chuckled.

"I should go." She yawned.

"Stay a little while. I'll wake you up before midnight," he said.

"Oh, no. As tired as I am I'll fall asleep and Dewar would find us. I'll stay a few minutes but then I have to get out of here," she said.

"I wouldn't care if he did find us."

She wiggled until she was in position to kiss him. "That is so sweet. Now hold me until the bones come back in my knees."

"What if the bone comes back in all my joints?" he teased.

"Mmmm," she mumbled as she fell asleep.

She awoke at eleven thirty, eased out of Raylen's arms, and was fully dressed when he opened his eyes.

"Did Danny Boy wake you?"

"No, he's breathing easy." She dropped down in the straw and kissed him on the forehead. "Good night, darlin'. I'll see you tomorrow evening at the house."

"Oh?"

"It's an invitation. Bring Colleen. Aunt Tressa and Blaze are making Italian in my big kitchen."

He sat up. "You sure that's wise?"

"They like you. Momma even wondered if you'd like to travel."

He grinned. "No thank you. But wise about Colleen and Blaze?"

"Honey, she might find out that he's way too much for her to handle if they spend time together."

"Or he might find out the same thing."

He grabbed her hand and pulled her down for another searing kiss. She scrambled out of his embrace when his hand moved up her back toward her bra strap.

"Good night, Raylen. It's a quarter till twelve. If you don't want Dewar to find you strip stark naked, you'd better be gettin' your britches on!" She heard him scrambling as she made her way down the aisle toward the front door. And she and Dewar passed each other on the path from the house to the barn.

Chapter 22

LIZ, HOOTER, AND BLISTER STOOD ON THE PORCH AND watched the long carnival parade arrive. First the travel trailers and then the semis and last the flatbeds.

Marva Jo brought up the rear. When she saw Liz waving and smiling, she leaned out the window and yelled, "It's beautiful, Lizelle! Just beautiful!"

Liz could hardly believe her ears. That her mother had agreed to set foot on Haskell's land was a miracle. But for her to tell Liz that it was beautiful was acceptance and that was even more than a mere miracle; it bordered on magic. But then it wasn't Haskell's property anymore, it was Liz's. And denying a daughter would be tougher than denying a brother.

By the time the last flatbed had parked, Liz was making the rounds, showing them the barn, where the electrical outlets were, and where the Porta-Pottys were parked to the north of the barn. Her mother and Aunt Tressa were already in the barn, but they weren't looking at her tree or the multitude of presents under it. They were sizing up the barn and taking in the tack room.

"It's big enough," Tressa said.

"For what?" Liz slipped an arm around each of them.

"Winter," Marva Jo said.

"You are thinkin' about changing the winter site to here? Wow!" Liz's voice went high and squeaky and tears brimmed in her eyes.

"Not now. When you and Blaze take over the carnival. It would be ideal. Raylen could spend several months a year next to his folks and then y'all could travel the rest of it," Tressa said.

"Keep dreamin', ladies," she giggled. "It ain't happenin'. I wanted a cowboy for my Christmas present, not a carnie."

"And what's wrong with a carnie?" Blaze came up from behind and wrapped his big arms around all three of them.

"Not one thing. I love you all, but I've made up my mind. Don't matter if it's Thanksgiving or spring, Uncle Haskell is giving me this place. But I'd be glad for y'all to change your winter place when Poppa is gone."

"That will be for the next generation to talk about. Blaze will be in charge of making decisions if you are serious, Lizelle," Marva Jo said.

"I am very serious," Liz said slowly. Saying the words settled it in her heart forever.

"That's not for years and years. Tressa and Marva Jo are still going to be running the big show when they are ninety. Now show me and Tressa to the kitchen. It's been years since I had a big kitchen to work inside," Blaze said.

Liz spun around, kissed him on the cheek, and whispered, "Thank you!"

"Is it this way?" Tressa pointed toward the tack room.

"No, it's in my house where you two are sleeping tonight."

Marva Jo shook her head. "We've decided that we'll eat in your house and cook in your house and maybe even enjoy a bubble bath in a big tub, but we aren't sleeping there. Neither of us would be able to get a wink of rest with no wheels under us, and besides, look what sleeping in that house has done to you. Those roots might attack us in our sleep and never let us leave, and we've got a carnival to put on the road in four months."

Liz was only mildly disappointed. But it was a minor setback that she did not intend to argue. This year, she'd talked them into staying three nights and setting foot in her house. Next year, she might get them into a real bed. One baby step at a time and she could be a patient woman... in some things.

"Then lead the way," Blaze said.

"I will, but you don't get to play in the kitchen until after you round up some guys to haul a bunch of tables and folding chairs from Raylen's barn to mine. I'm borrowing them for our dinner on Wednesday night," she said.

Blaze gave her an extra squeeze. "I can do that. You show these two women the kitchen and then come back and take me to Raylen's barn. Can we make a side stop somewhere along the way and see Glorious Danny Boy and Major Jack?"

"No."

Blaze looked puzzled and hurt at the same time.

"I wouldn't deprive Colleen of that for anything. She's going to want to give you the tour of her folks' place. Think you can wait until after supper? I've invited her and Raylen to eat with us."

"Yes, ma'am!" Blaze's eyes looked like gold nuggets.

Liz talked nonstop the whole way to the house. "You should have been here when I first discovered that barn was on my property. I thought it belonged to Raylen.

And then we found the Christmas stuff up in the loft where Uncle Haskell had his wood shop, and Jasmine and Ace and Dewar and Gemma all pitched in to help me get it all up and lit before you got here. And I can't wait for you to meet Jasmine. She owns the café where I work. Don't look at me like that, Aunt Tressa. I know I'm rich and I don't have to work, but I want to. And I've invited everyone I know and a lot that I don't, since they know people I do know, to the party so you can meet the whole community. Oh, you are going to love Nellie and Ellen. They bicker and banter and the stories they tell are so funny. And you'd never believe that Jasmine left a high paying corporate job to be a cook in her own little café; or that Pearl was a high-powered banker and left that to run a motel over in Henrietta. And what do you think of this infatuation Blaze has with Colleen?"

Tressa giggled. "You threw that last question in there pretty slick, girl."

Liz led the way up the steps to the front door. "Oh, before you answer, meet Hooter and Blister. He's a terrible watchdog, and I understand she has kittens two or three times a year, but they are wonderful listeners. Now please answer that question, Aunt Tressa. I've been dying to ask you, and Blaze is always around, and he'll be back when he gets the guys all together to get the tables for me."

She slung open the door and stood back. Hooter and Blister followed Marva Jo and Tressa inside. Liz stepped in and shut the door behind her. "How do you like it?"

"Which question do you want answered first?" Tressa was taking in the whole huge living room in one glance.

"Blaze."

"He's a big boy and I like Colleen. My instincts tell me she's a quick study and I can already see her in costume."

Liz's dark eyes almost popped right out of her head. "For what?"

"Telling fortunes," Tressa said. "We lost the last one I trained, but I think I could get Colleen ready in a few weeks."

"You think she'd leave her family and her job?" Liz was astonished.

"You did. Now show me the kitchen and the pantry. You did remember to get fresh garlic, didn't you?" Marva Jo answered.

Liz nodded. "This way."

Marva Jo looped an arm around her daughter's waist. "I love the house. If I wasn't a carnie, it's exactly what I'd want. Big living room for the family. Big kitchen to cook in, and bedrooms on the other end. I can see why Haskell built it this way. Too bad he and Sara never had kids. I liked that woman. She would have made a good mother."

"You saying that means a lot to me. It can't be easy," Liz said.

"You'd better have more than one child. Have a house full, because at least one of my granddaughters is going inherit my traveling blood, and I'm going to make you pay for your raisin' one of these days," Marva Jo said. "Until then, know that I love you enough not to send you on a guilt trip."

Liz put both arms around her mother and hugged her fiercely. "You are the best mother in the whole world."

"Tell me that when I steal your favorite child and

make her a carnie. It'll be in her bloodline, Lizelle. Don't forget who you are."

"I can never forget that. Now let's go cook before you make me cry."

Tressa laughed. "You cook! Darlin', have you told Raylen that the extent of your cooking ability lies with whatever you can pour out of a can or heat up in a microwave?"

Liz pointed toward the end of the living room. "His momma lives one mile that way and she is an amazing cook. If I don't take her son off to the carnival, I'm bettin' I can wrangle a meal or two a week over there. And don't forget I'm a waitress at a café. Jasmine is an artist in the kitchen, and her prices are reasonable. I can take him up to the Chicken Fried when his momma ain't cookin'. And on the nights we want to stay in and have sex until our brains are fried, I betcha he doesn't mind canned soup and microwave pizza at all."

Tressa threw back her head and roared. "You raised a genius, Marva Jo!"

"Yes, I damn sure did, didn't I?" Marva laughed with her sister.

"Who's a genius? God, this is huge," Blaze said as he slipped in the kitchen door.

"Not really. Wait until you see the O'Donnell place. That's huge," Liz said.

Blaze's expression changed in the blink of an eye. "That big, huh?"

"Yes, it is," Liz said honestly. She tried to think of something that would make him feel better, but that was something he'd have to do on his own. "You ready to get those tables? Then while you help Aunt Tressa cook, the guys can set them up for us. That way if they want a place to gather up tonight they'll have it. I want them all to know I appreciate these few days. They could be halfway home."

"They all love you and they're ready for a rest and a big party," Blaze said. "Let's get this show on the road. I can't wait to mess up this big old kitchen."

"What you can't wait for is a glimpse of Colleen, and remember, the rule applies in a big kitchen the same as a little one: what you mess up you clean up. Only thing I like less than cooking is washing dishes," Liz teased on the way out the back door.

Chapter 23

RAYLEN ARRIVED EARLY WITH A BOTTLE OF AUSTIN'S watermelon wine. He was freshly shaven and smelled so good that Liz wanted to forget the lasagna, chicken Parmesan, and even the tiramisu for dessert and take him straight to bed. He wore starched and creased Wranglers stacked up perfectly on top of polished boots. His baby blue ironed shirt matched his eyes, and his big silver belt buckle was polished to a high shine.

"Can I take your hat?" Liz asked.

"Depends on what you intend to do with it." He removed the black felt dress hat from his head, tucked the bottle of wine under his arm, and finger combed his dark hair.

"I'll turn it upside down right there on the coffee table, and I promise I won't stomp it or sit on it," she said.

He handed it to her. "I'm putting a lot of trust in you, darlin'. I've seen what you can do to a man's good hat."

"What's that?" Blaze asked from the doorway into the living room.

Raylen handed the wine off to Blaze and slipped his arm around Liz. "She's got a hell of a temper. She threw my hat on the ground and then stomped it."

She looked up at him, opened her mouth to say something, and he kissed it soundly before she could utter a word.

"That's one way to shut her up, but she'll have her say or die, so it won't last long. That's the Latina in her." Blaze chuckled. "Thanks for the wine. Watermelon? I've never tasted that kind."

"I had to beg for that bottle. Austin wanted to send a bottle of Granny Lanier's because she's sure it's a good vintage. But I made her give me a bottle of her first year's crop to celebrate tonight."

"That's so romantic." Tressa walked up beside Blaze and took it from his hands. "I've only had it a couple of times but I really liked the flavor. It will go well with tonight's supper."

Raylen slipped his arm around Liz. "Thank you. Colleen said she'll be along in a little bit. She wasn't through primping and I have an idea she wants to bring her own vehicle tonight."

Liz scanned Blaze from boots to hair. He wore black Wranglers, boots, and a black shirt with two buttons open at the neck. A small drop of blood on his chin gave evidence that he'd shaved in that hour he'd spent in the bathroom, and his blond hair was feathered back with dew drops still clinging to a couple of hairs. She hoped Colleen wore a heavy sweater and a thick bra. Looking at Blaze was going to cause worse problems than icy wind going through a thin shirt.

"You two are certainly a couple of handsome fellers tonight," she said. "I suppose you've noticed that there's mistletoe over every doorway, and I don't know about Colleen, but I damn sure do not intend to waste any of it."

Blaze grinned, and his cat eyes glistened. "Thank you very much, Lizelle. And I forgot to tell you that the house is beautiful. It ought to be on one of those house tour things that they talk about in Amarillo."

"What I like most is that arrangement on the mantel," Tressa said. "Mother would have liked having a nativity in the house. She liked the spiritual side of the holiday and Poppa likes the silly side."

Raylen hugged Liz up to his side and squeezed. "What about you, darlin'? What do you like?"

"All of it. Nativity, Santa Claus, and we're doing the Chicken Fried in a country Christmas theme and I can't wait to do that too. You going to help me?"

"How cute is my butt?" He blushed scarlet. He hadn't meant to say the words out loud but to whisper them for her ears only.

"Cutest one in the house tonight. Don't look at us like that. It's an inside joke," Liz told her mother, Tressa, and Blaze.

The two tomcats weren't circling each other anymore. They'd reached a territorial understanding, but it didn't come with one hundred percent trust. Raylen's fear was doublefold: that Blaze in all his worldly charm would break his sister's heart and that he would convince Liz that the carnival needed her worse than Raylen did. Blaze wasn't afraid of Lucifer himself. But Liz had to have told Raylen about her best friend's womanizing, and that alone would make Raylen want to put Colleen in the nearest convent. And that scared the bejesus out of Blaze.

"Thank you," Raylen said.

"You look pretty damn fine yourself, sweetheart." Blaze jumped in with a compliment.

Raylen wanted to kick himself. "She always does.

She wore this the first time she came to Sunday dinner at my folks'. I thought she was a gypsy princess."

"She is." Blaze smiled. "You two go on in the living room and sit with Marva Jo. Tressa and I will finish up in here. I still have a few adjustments to make to the table. I need to put out glasses for the wine."

"He cooks?" Raylen whispered on the way to the living room.

"Yes, he is a chef in the kitchen and he's a neat freak and even does his own ironing because a laundry wouldn't to it to suit him."

"No wonder the women love him," Raylen said.

She shrugged. "Hadn't thought about it that way, but you are right."

Marva Jo caught the last of the conversation and pieced the rest together. "Liz does not cook. She knows how to do laundry and hates to iron. I made her learn so that she *can* do it. She had no choice but to keep things neat, but it's not by nature like it is with Blaze. It was by necessity because we lived in a small trailer."

Raylen sat down and hugged Liz up close to him. "You tryin' to scare me off?"

Liz patted him on the knee. "He's not a neat freak, but he's not sloppy. His biggest problem is that he's organized and a perfectionist."

"Then he'd better reconsider a relationship with you," Marva Jo said.

"It'll take more than that to scare me off," Raylen told her.

"How does Colleen fit into the picture? She's your sister?" Marva Jo asked.

"We are peas in a pod, but she only cooks when she has

to. Momma made all of us at home in the kitchen. Boys had to learn just like girls, but she also made sure they were able to run a ranch just like the boys. Goose and gander law, she called it. What was good for the goose was good for the gander. In the O'Donnell household, there is no division of men's and women's work." Raylen made lazy circles on the palm of Liz's hand with his thumb.

Liz vowed she'd get even later. It wasn't fair for him to heat her to the boiling point with nothing but his thumb, and right there in front of her mother. Oh, yeah, Raylen was going to get his just due.

The doorbell rang, and Liz started to hop up, but Raylen held her hand tightly and yelled, "Blaze, would you get that door?"

Liz shot him a look and he grinned at her. "Us guys got to stick together."

Marva Jo asked Raylen a question about Danny Boy, but Liz didn't hear his response. She was too busy watching Blaze and Colleen's interactions. Colleen wore a green skirt that stopped at her knee, a snug little sweater that barely made it to the waistband of the tight fitting skirt, and brown cowboy boots. Everything about her complimented her red hair and her clear complexion. And everything about her appealed to Blaze, who took her hand and led her to the kitchen.

"That's not fair. Why does she get to go to the kitchen?" Liz whispered.

Marva Jo shook her finger at Liz. "You've got all the pie you can eat right here in this living room, my child. Let Blaze have his in the kitchen. I guarantee you that Tressa won't let them do one thing more than I let you two get away with."

"Why do I feel like I'm sixteen and on my first date?" Liz asked.

Marva Jo smiled. "Next time we'll send Blaze over there to pick her up."

Liz giggled. "That sounds like a plan."

Blaze yelled from the kitchen, "I heard that last remark. Colleen has invited me over to her place to meet her parents tonight and to see those two famous horses. So don't be feeling all superior in there, sweetheart."

"Children, children! Forgive them, Colleen," Tressa said. "They've acted like siblings since the day I brought Blaze to the carnival. Marva Jo, bring your wayward daughter to the dinner table. We are ready to sit down."

Liz jerked the top sheet up over her and Raylen. A fine sheen of sweat covered them both, and the afterglow that surrounded them was almost as hot that night as the sex had been. She reached across the foot of bed space between them and clasped his hand in hers. How in the hell could she have ever doubted one second that she belonged in Ringgold? Raylen was her soul mate and Ringgold her home.

"That was fantastic. Good night, darlin'," she said breathlessly.

"Always is," he panted. "But I'm not spending the night."

"Why? Momma and Aunt Tressa are in their trailers."

"Did you want Dewar to catch us last night?" he asked.

"No!" she said quickly.

"I rest my case. I'm trying to show your momma and

aunt that I'm one of the good guys, not a bad boy who's only out for a romp in the hay, so as soon as my legs get bones in them, I'm going home."

She smiled at his expression. It was the same one she'd used the night before. She reached under the covers and walked her hand down the fine line of dark hair from his chest to his belly button and down to his penis.

"What if something else gets a bone?"

He rolled over but she hung on. He tickled her ribs, and she grabbed his hands with hers. In one swift movement he was off the bed and on his feet.

"You don't play fair," she said.

"That would be the pot calling the kettle black, darlin'." He slipped his arms into his shirt and picked up his underwear.

"Don't put them on. I like commando," she said. "You come commando to my party on Wednesday and I will too."

"Hell, no! I wouldn't be able to think about anything else all night. I have a helluva time every time I conjure up a picture of you in one of those dancin' outfits," he chuckled.

She sat up and wrapped the sheet under her arms. "You think Colleen made Blaze's trailer rock and roll?"

Raylen blushed. "Liz, she's my sister! God, I don't even want to think about that."

"You are her brother. You think she doesn't know we've been to bed? Hell, she was the one who warned us last night. Maybe they're out there in the horse stall next to Danny Boy using our blanket," she teased.

"Don't go there," Raylen said crossly.

She whipped the sheet back and jumped out of bed,

put her finger under his nose, and said, "Don't you talk to me in that tone. I was teasing you."

"Don't tease me about my sister. If you had a brother, would you want me to tease about him sleeping with Becca?"

She took a step forward. "That's different."

"How?"

"She's a witch. Blaze is just a womanizer."

"Which makes it all fine and good? My sister is infatuated with a womanizer, but since that's his only fault that makes it just fine?" Raylen said.

She folded her arms over her naked body and glared at him. "Go home. I guess I can't tease you. You can't take it."

He finished dressing, shoved his feet down in his boots, and stormed out of the house, slamming the door behind him. She threw herself back on the bed and pouted for five minutes before the tears started.

It was over. Raylen would never speak to her again. The whole reason fate let her come to Ringgold was so she could get Colleen and Blaze hooked up. It had nothing to do with her own happiness. Life wasn't fair.

Oh, hush your whining! You think you are the only one who is unsure of herself in this relationship? What about Raylen? You are a carnie and your whole carnie family is surrounding you right now. Ever think that he might be scared you'll go with them when they leave? Her conscience raked her over hot coals.

She wiped her eyes with the edge of the sheet and sniffled. "I'm not leaving. He's not running me off. I'm staying right here because it feels right," she said stoically. "But if Raylen isn't the one—" She broke down and wept again, burying her face in his pillow, inhaling the remnants of his aftershave. That made her cry even harder.

She couldn't call Blaze because he was probably romancing the hell out of Colleen and she wouldn't disturb that, but she sure needed a friend. She finally slung her legs over the edge of the bed, grabbed the first nightgown in her drawer, and put it over her head. She pushed her feet down into her cowboy boots and grabbed the truck keys from her purse, leaving everything else behind.

At the end of her lane she made a sharp left and gunned the motor the next mile, sliding around the O'Donnell lane and fishtailing on the gravel before she got control. She kept the speed down the rest of the way to Raylen's house, only to find the door locked. She rattled it until the window threatened to break loose when he didn't answer the doorbell immediately.

Finally he slung it open and stood before her in nothing but a towel. His wet hair stuck up every which way, and water dripped onto the floor.

"What do you want?" he asked gruffly.

She slung the door open and he took two steps backward. "Don't you ever leave in the middle of a fight. You stay until we settle it and then have makeup sex with me like we did in the shower that time, but don't you just walk away."

"You told me to leave."

"Well, I damn sure didn't mean it. You are supposed to stand up and fight for us if we are important enough. Are we, Raylen? Or are you tired of me already?"

"Don't you dare accuse me of being tired of you. I've wanted you since we were kids, dreamed about you, thought about you, and measured every other woman by the impossible yardstick you put in my mind. So don't you dare say I'm tired of you. I won't ever be tired of you. Maybe you just want to go back to the carnival and this is your way of doing it. Fight with me so it'll make it all right," he said.

She stepped right up into his space, her nose not six inches from his, and tiptoed so she could see right into his blue eyes. "You are an idiot if you think that. I was crying my eyes out and made up my mind that Ringgold is where I belong. So whether you are tired of me or not, I'm not leaving. You can just get used to having me for a neighbor, if that's all we are ever going to be to each other after tonight."

Gemma pushed her way into the living room and stared at them. "I don't even want to know. See you two in the morning." She went to her room, shut the door, and turned on the music loud enough that she couldn't hear them.

That two minutes gave them time enough to cool off.

Raylen reached out and pulled Liz to his wet chest. "I'm sorry. It was stupid."

"I'm sorry too. It was ugly of me to talk like that about Colleen. You were right. If I had a brother, I'd be livid if I thought he was with Becca. And you've been so good about Colleen even after all that stuff you know about Blaze. Forgive me."

"Of course I forgive you. I love you, Liz Hanson. I have since that day you were watching me ride. You were so beautiful leaning on the fence, but not as gorgeous as you are in that flannel gown. Lord, you are making me hot just holding you," he said.

"I love you too, and I have my whole life, it seems like. I'd like to rip that towel off your hips, but I'm going to turn around and go home," she said.

"Why? Gemma knows you are here."

"Because when we have our makeup sex it's not going to be with your sister across the hall."

He bookended her face with his big hands and kissed her hard. "I do love you."

"Me too!" She turned around and walked outside.

All the way home she singsonged, "Raylen loves me. Raylen loves me."

Chapter 24

IN TEXAS THEY CALL IT FOOTBALL WEATHER. CRISP enough for a jacket but not so cold that breath comes out in a fog every time a person exhales. Liz couldn't have asked for a better night for her party. The carnival folks had pulled the cinnamon bun wagon, the funnel cake wagon, and the gyro wagon off the flatbed and set them up inside the barn. Liz had made arrangements with Jasmine to cater in turkey and dressing and glazed ham. The rest was pure potluck. Bring whatever you like, put your name on the bottom of the dish, and go home with a full tummy and an empty dish.

"With all this food, why would you set up those wagons?" Gemma asked.

"Ovens. We needed more ovens," Liz explained.

Raylen slipped his arms around her waist and pulled her back to his chest. "Hello, darlin'."

"That sounded almost like Conway Twitty." Liz laughed.

Raylen buried his face in her hair and inhaled. "You smell good. Bet you'd taste even better."

She laughed again and turned around. "So do you on both counts."

He kissed her quickly and nodded toward the corner of the barn where the musicians were tuning up their instruments. "I didn't know so many of your friends played. Does Blaze?"

"Blaze can dance the leather off a woman's boot soles. He can almost carry a tune, but he can't play anything. Not even a washboard because his rhythm is off," she said.

Grandpa O'Malley's big booming voice sounded even louder coming from a microphone that had been set up in the musician's corner. "Franny tells me the food is ready so I'm announcing the party is officially open now. We are thankful for the opportunity for everyone to get to mingle and know each other. And whoever made those cinnamon rolls, would you hide one pan of them under the table for me to take home? Don't tell Franny. She and the doctor tell me I'm too fat, but those bathroom scales are the biggest damn liars in the world. Now load up your plates, and while you're doin' it Raylen and Liz are going to give us some fiddlin' to entertain us."

Liz looked at Raylen who shrugged. "Grandpa is the oldest in the family. He takes over the emcee jobs for us at everything. Is it a problem?"

She tucked her hand in his. "Not at all. I just didn't know we were supposed to play right now."

"Hungry?" he asked.

"Too nervous to eat," she answered.

"Might as well play then, hadn't we?"

She led him to the corner and picked up her fiddle.

He did the same.

She pulled the bow across the strings to make sure it was still in tune.

So did he.

"Ready?" she asked.

He winked.

"Then let's give 'em something to talk about," she said.

They locked eyes and she started the Bonnie Raitt tune, "Let's Give Them Something to Talk About." Liz stepped up to the microphone and sang as she played. The lyrics said that people were saying they were lovers kept under covers, that they laughed a little too loud, stood a little too close, stared a little too long. She sang that she was thinking about him every day and dreaming about him every night, and they were going to give them something to talk about and it was love, love, love.

Her voice was gravelly, sexy, and just listening to her shot desire through Raylen's body. When the last chords died, she whispered, "Is that yelling it from the rooftops?"

He nodded and mouthed, "My turn."

She recognized the Gene Watson tune "Love in a Hot Afternoon" from the first note and their fiddles became one as the instruments talked louder than the words if they had been singing. She hummed the lyrics about a lady sleeping like a baby in damp tangled sheets after love in a hot afternoon.

It brought memories of a blanket in a horse stall, and she smiled as their music blended perfectly and floated out over the barn.

"Give us some 'Devil Went Down to Georgia,'" Grandpa yelled when they'd finished that one.

Liz and Raylen's bows hit the fiddles at the same time and the whole barn went silent as they watched the show. Raylen stepped up to the microphone and sang as he played. Liz played into the song with her body language, and at the end the applause was deafening.

"Ready to give me that fiddle?" he asked Liz.

"You ready to give me yours?"

"I beat you that time. I sang and didn't miss a beat."

"I didn't either. Granny, who won?"

Franny stood up at the table where she and Tilman had settled in. "I'm callin' it a second tie. You two belong together, both with the fiddle and when you lay it down."

Raylen pulled the microphone to his mouth. "Yes, we do. Liz and I are together so all you other cowboys out there are out of luck."

"Well, praise the Lord! It's been announced to the whole county. Dewar, you'd better get your lazy ass in gear," Gemma yelled from across the barn. She was sitting at a table with Ace and Jasmine, Pearl and Wil, Blaze and Colleen, and Austin and Rye.

"I'm goin' to be the old bachelor uncle who raises Gypsy Vanners," he said.

He'd been close to Tressa all evening, the two of them discussing horses. He'd spent more than half the afternoon in the round pen with them and was more determined than ever to start a herd of his own.

"We're hungry so we're takin' a break. Rest of you can play when you want and maybe we'll join you later," Raylen said.

"You ain't goin' to do 'Earl's Breakdown' before you go?" Blaze asked.

"Maybe later. I've got something better to hold right now." Raylen slung his arm around Liz's shoulders. She fit there like God had taken his height, weight, and arm length into consideration before he made Liz. She was having her Christmas right there, even if it was before Thanksgiving. To him, every day was Christmas now that Liz had come into his life. He looked up where miles and miles of garland had been looped and hundreds of ornaments dangled in the air like the beads on her dancing costumes.

Whoa, boy, don't go there. Think about mistletoe, not toe rings.

"What are you looking for?" she asked.

"Mistletoe."

She led him to the doorway and pointed up to a ball of mistletoe attached to a beam with a red velvet ribbon. He grinned and gave her a kiss that curled her toenails and had her panting.

"It's beautiful," he said when he broke away.

"What?"

"You first. The barn, second."

"Yes, it is. I love it and all the fun we had making it look like this. Christmas at Thanksgiving time."

Red cloths covered all the tables, and cedar centerpieces with red candles and gold bows graced each one. The tree was a huge conversation piece, but not any more than all the other decorations, including an archway with cedar branches, lights, and garland woven into it, white wrought iron benches from Maddie's flower garden beside it, and Cash dressed as Santa Claus in a rocking chair in front of it.

Christmas music played in the background when the musicians weren't fired up, and the spirit in the barn was as jolly as if it were Christmas Eve instead of the month before.

Raylen led Liz to the food table where they fixed plates and carried them to the table that still had a few empty chairs. Blaze and Colleen sat side by side, their heads together in whispered tones most of the time.

Slade and Jane, Pearl and Wil, Austin and Rye, Gemma, Dewar, and Ace were all scattered around the rest of the table.

As soon as they sat down Blaze stood up.

"I've got a toast to give here in front of all these witnesses." Blaze held up his beer bottle. "I was wrong."

"Wow! Never heard that before," Liz said.

"Never was wrong before," Blaze grinned and went on, "I was wrong about you, sweetheart. You belong right here. Roots look good on you."

"Hear, hear." Colleen clinked her beer bottle with Blaze's.

"Raylen, be aware, she's got a temper," Blaze said.

"Oh, I've done seen that." Raylen laughed.

Colleen leaned over and whispered in Liz's ear, "You get ready to sell those wings of yours, I'll give you top dollar for them."

Pearl held up a glass of iced tea but kept her chair. "We're all here, so Wil and I have an announcement. It's twins and they're due in July. If they're girls they can have red hair but they're going to get Colleen's skin and no freckles. I don't care if we aren't blood kin, I'm claimin' shirttail kin."

Everyone started talking at once and didn't even see Marva Jo pulling out a chair at the end of the long table. "Sounds like you all have been doing a lot of toasting over here. Congratulations, Pearl. I can't imagine having two kids at once."

"I can't imagine having one." Pearl smiled. "But then I couldn't imagine being married to Wil the first time he came into my motel. He was cocky as hell, and the next morning the cops arrested him for murder."

"And?" Marva Jo asked.

"Mistaken identity," Wil said. "But she came to my rescue in her vintage Caddy, and I swear I was in love from that day."

"You were not! It took a shot contest to make you see you'd met your match," Pearl said.

Wil smacked a kiss on her cheek. "Red, darlin', that's just when I sort of admitted it to myself. My heart knew the first time your devil cat and Digger got into it."

"Red?" Marva Jo asked.

"Pearl to everyone else, believe me." Jasmine laughed. "But she lets Wil call her Red."

Marva Jo nodded. No wonder her child loved the area. They'd accepted her into their fold as tight as any carnie family. All but Colleen, and it looked like she was coming around, thanks going to Blaze.

Marva Jo looked at Blaze. "I heard your toast. After the way you carried on when Liz left, I know what that one cost you to deliver. But I agree. Roots look good on her. Y'all finish up your dinner and get Liz to introduce you to all our friends. Truth is, Raylen, I think you beat her on the fiddlin' contest, but I think the only way you'll get her fiddle is to take the woman that goes with it. That's goin' to take some doin'. Good luck, son."

Liz blushed. Raylen had said that he loved her that one time but he hadn't mentioned it again. He said they were together and that was enough for tonight. In a few months, maybe he'd be ready to take the fiddle and the girl. She'd been ready to take the man with or without a fiddle for a very long time.

Marva Jo went on to the next table where Franny and Tilman were entertaining a table full of carnies with stories about the O'Donnells. She stayed there a while before moving to the next one, where Maddie and Cash were laughing at something Tressa was telling about the year it snowed at their first gig.

Two families were blending very well. She couldn't ask for a better man than Raylen for her daughter. They were a perfect pair, and even if it did cost her more than it had cost Blaze to make his toast, she sincerely hoped that things worked out for them.

Thanksgiving was much, much better than she'd ever thought it could be that year. Only Liz could come up with such an idea as having a Christmas party at Thanksgiving. She looked up at the angel on the top of the tree and a tear formed on her eyelash. Her baby girl had given up her wings for love. She hoped that she was never disappointed.

Liz curled up in Raylen's lap in front of the fireplace. The clock above the mantel said that it was midnight. The party had begun to break up at eleven, but Liz had stayed until the last guest left. Tomorrow they'd reload the cinnamon roll, funnel cake, and gyro wagons back on the flatbed, and at two o'clock, all of them planned to start the final leg of their journey to Claude. They might have started earlier, but Liz had begged her mother and Tressa to stay until she finished her work day.

The trip would be over by six and the next day they'd winterize the travel trailers, unload the wagons in a long row beside the barn, and park the trucks. One by one, Poppa would use his little tractor to pull the wooden wagons inside for renovations throughout the winter months.

And all the people would be gone. A majority of the vendors lived within two hours of Amarillo. They'd unhook their trailers from their trucks and the exodus would begin by noon as they headed for their winter homes. One couple lived in Destin, Florida, and another in Willets, California. Marva would take them to the airport. Then the last week in February, they'd come driving in, a few each day, or making arrangements for Marva Jo to come get them. Everyone would be excited, and the new year would begin the same way the previous one ended with Poppa standing on the porch waving at everyone.

"It was a wonderful party," Raylen said.

She nodded. "But it's over."

He hugged her tightly. "Memories last forever. I remember this little girl who could stay on the fence longer than me. And one who watched me ride, and I wanted to show off for her but I was afraid Momma would kill me if I hurt her horse. Those memories were etched into my mind for years before she came back."

"Don't be sweet to me. Fight with me. I want to kick something or pitch a fit. It's like when the winter ended and it was time to go on the road. I was happy because everyone was so excited about a new year, but a little bit of me was angry because I didn't want to leave the horses and Poppa. It always made me cry to see him waving good-bye from the porch. I felt like I do now. Happy and sad at the same time," she said.

His cell phone rang in his shirt pocket so close to Liz's face that she jumped.

"It's Becca," he said.

Liz had found the perfect person to fight with even if she had to do it by phone.

"Hello. Why weren't you at Liz's party tonight? We missed you," he said.

Liz reached out and Raylen put the phone in her hand.

"This was a big thing for me and Raylen both tonight. If you were really Raylen's best friend then you should've been there instead of staying home pouting. Blaze came and Raylen wasn't too fond of him but you stayed home. Are you mad because I told you what the cards said? You knew that I wouldn't lie when I laid those cards out, and besides…"

"Shut up and listen to me," Becca said so loud that Raylen heard it.

Well, Liz had said she wanted a fight. That ought to do it!

"What did you say to me?" Liz raised her voice two octaves.

"I said shut up, Liz. I wasn't there because Taylor and I got married today. I wanted you and Raylen to be the first to know. I did what you said and Daddy said I could have the down payment for a house to be built on the ranch or a big, fancy wedding. Taylor and I decided to take the house and we flew to Las Vegas for three days. After that, I'm putting in ten-hour days at the ranch, learning what I should already know, so when the time comes I can keep it running. So shut up and wish me good luck."

"I'll be damned," Liz said.

"I finally got the best of you." Becca laughed.

"You did not!" Liz argued, but a grin spread across her face.

"Oh yes I did. Now give the phone to Raylen."

"He's going to be so disappointed, Becca. He

wanted to be your Maid of Honor, and now he's got this beautiful apricot-colored dress that he won't ever get to wear."

Becca's laughter shot through the phone and echoed off the walls.

Raylen wrested the phone from Liz's hand and shot her a dirty look.

"Congratulations, and I do not have a dress of any color," he said.

Becca lowered her voice. "She's a smart cookie. Hang on to her."

"Yes, ma'am."

"She'll make you toe the line like Taylor does me. Neither of us could ever be satisfied with a wimp."

"Yes, ma'am."

"Good night. Taylor was on the hotel phone ordering room service and he's finished. I love him, Raylen. Have for a long time. This will change things between me and you, won't it?"

"Sometimes change ain't too bad," he answered.

Liz looked at him with questions on her face when he turned the phone off and laid it on the arm of the sofa.

He raised a dark eyebrow and grinned. "What?"

"Yes, ma'am?" she said with both eyebrows raised.

"I was agreeing with my friend when she paid you a compliment."

She snuggled back against his chest. "I can't get a rousting good argument out of anyone."

"That's because we haven't had makeup sex from the last one yet. You can't work up the anger for another fight if you haven't completely settled the last one. Passionate people couldn't handle all that intense emotion at once. It would blow a fuse in their heart and they'd drop graveyard dead," he said.

"You are full of bullshit," she mumbled.

"So?" He wiggled his eyebrows.

"It's five hours until I have to go to work."

"Well, forget it," he said.

"Are we fighting?"

He grinned. "No. Five hours just isn't long enough for good makeup sex."

She shivered.

"My point is proven. If thinking about five whole hours of sex puts chills down your back, just think what enough to settle two fights would do to you."

She giggled. "Kiss me and go home, darlin'. I'm going to take a cold shower and go to bed. I'll see you tomorrow."

"I'll be here when the exodus begins." He kissed her hard on the lips, giving her a very small taste of what the future held when they got around to the making up business.

She walked him to the door, stole a dozen more kisses and a short, stand-up make-out session before she stumbled to the bathroom and took the fastest shower of her life. She was asleep two minutes after her head hit the pillow, but she was restless all night, tossing and turning, reaching out for Raylen, only to find an empty pillow beside her.

Chapter 25

Hugs were given.

Promises made.

Then it was time for Liz to stand on the porch like her Poppa had done for years and wave as the parade went down her lane. Flatbeds first, semis next, and then the pickup trucks pulling the living trailers. She'd flipped the lights on all the artwork even though the sun was bright and the day fairly warm.

Tears dripped off her cheeks and dropped onto her sweatshirt. She'd made up her mind and she was at peace with her decision. She liked her roots. She loved Raylen. But why did clipping her wings have to hurt so damn bad?

When the last taillight was out of sight, she tucked her head into Raylen's shoulder and sobbed. "I miss her already."

"She's four hours from here, Liz. You can go see her any weekend that you want to. You can take off when you get off at two on Saturday and come home the next day. It's not like you won't see her for a year." His tone was soothing.

"Oh, hush." Colleen rounded the end of the house and she was crying as hard as Liz.

Raylen held out his left arm to Colleen and she walked into it, laid her head on his other shoulder, and sobbed loudly. He didn't know what to do with one weeping woman and he had two hugged up to him, soaking his shirt.

"You still want those wings?" Liz asked.

"More than ever. What's the price?"

Liz wiped her cheeks with the back of her hands. "I'll sell them to you for your roots."

"Honey, today I'd rip them up and hand them to you on a silver platter. Watching him leave was the hardest thing I've ever done. How can I feel like this after only a week?"

Liz smiled through the tears. "Damnedest thing in the world, ain't it?"

"At least you don't have to have a long-distance relationship," Colleen said.

"Neither do you. Four hours out there. Take your vacation time and go spend it with him," Liz said.

Colleen swiped at her eyes with her denim jacket sleeve. "Momma will have a fit."

"Mine did. Didn't kill me. They come around when it's got to do with their kid's happiness," Liz said.

Colleen nodded and pulled out of Raylen's embrace. "I've got to go to Randlett. Got to be at work at four today. I'll call you, Liz."

Liz stepped away from Raylen and put a hand on Colleen's arm. "Think about going out there. He'll call you but…"

Colleen hugged Liz. "I know. He's cocky as hell, but there's a little insecurity there. I promise I'll think about it, but it takes at least a week after I put in a request for that kind of time. I'll call you when I figure it all out."

"I'll be right here or at work or riding horses to pay for all my help, but I'll have my phone," Liz said.

Colleen disappeared around to the backyard. Liz swallowed another lump in her throat just thinking about the decisions ahead of Colleen. If that had been Raylen driving away, her heart would have shattered.

"Well, that puts things in perspective," she mumbled.

"What's that?" Raylen asked.

"There could be a worse scenario than Momma and Aunt Tressa leaving," she said.

"And what would that be?" Raylen tucked her hand in his and started walking toward his truck.

"Watching you drive away," she answered honestly.

"That ain't happenin', darlin'," he whispered as he sealed that vow with a long, lingering kiss.

"Where are you takin' me?" she asked.

"Momma says Danny Boy needs a slow walk around the pasture and she wants me to do that. But there's about a dozen mares that need some exercise. Want to ride off those tears?" Raylen asked.

Liz nodded. "Let's go."

They rode to the horse barn in comfortable silence.

Two very different emotions rattled around in Raylen's soul. He was elated to hear Liz say that she wanted roots, and his heart floated when she said that about not wanting to watch him leave. But it was bittersweet, because his sister was pulling up her roots and growing carnival wings right before his eyes. He'd always figured all five of the O'Donnells would settle down right there close to Ringgold. They'd all come to Sunday dinner when Maddie called them in like a hen with her chickens. And raise their kids together. If Colleen and Blaze got really serious and wound up together, Rachel would hardly know her carnie cousins.

And Gemma? What did the future have in store for her? Would both of his sisters wind up living far away?

Maddie waved at them from the barn door where she leaned on a scoop shovel. She wore jeans and a gray sweatshirt. Both were stained with dirt, and her work boots left no doubt that she'd been mucking out stalls.

When Liz was close enough, Maddie hugged her tightly and said, "It can't be easy to watch your family leave like that. We've all lived in a pretty close pile. I'm not so sure how much longer that'll be the way it is. I saw the way Blaze looked at my daughter and it scares me. Colleen has always been the one with the..." She stumbled.

"The most pessimism." Raylen smiled.

"No, the one who took care of everyone else," Liz said.

"That's right." Maddie nodded. "I always thought she'd probably wind up with someone older who'd adore her."

"Blaze might not be older but he adores her," Liz said.

"And that is probably the most important part. But right now, this minute, I think you need some good old hard work. I understand you ride?"

"Yes, ma'am," Liz said.

"Well, start on the south side of the stables at the end. That'll be Missy. A couple of turns around the forty acres over there," Maddie pointed to her left, "should do it. You can ride as many as you have time for and I appreciate the help."

"Thank you, Maddie."

"I'll clean out her stall while you ride," she said.

Raylen draped an arm around Liz's shoulder and directed her to Missy's stall. "She's partial to that saddle." Raylen pointed to one on a sawhorse beside the stall door.

Liz picked a bridle from a nail up above the saddle and started talking softly to the horse. "You pretty doll. I bet you get tired of this old stall, don't you?"

Raylen backed up to the other side of the center aisle and crossed his arms over his chest. He'd make sure she had the hang of things before he went over to Danny Boy's stall. The saddle might be too heavy for her. She might have trouble getting Missy to stand still while she cinched it up. Or she might need a boost to get mounted up and ready.

Missy nudged Liz's shoulder and she giggled. "Impatient, are you? Well, we'll have us a good ride right after we get this bridle on you. Yes, baby girl, that's a good darlin'. I'm going to lead you out, and we'll get some good exercise, and then we'll have an apple or a carrot."

She bypassed the saddle and didn't respond to Raylen when he pointed at it. He followed her as she led the horse out into the sunshine and rubbed her ears for a minute before she grabbed a hunk of hair and swung up on the horse's bare back in one swift movement. She clamped her knees against Missy's flanks and the mare stepped high.

Maddie came out of the first stall and stared. "I'll be damned. Is she one of them horse whisperers?"

Raylen shook his head. "She's pretty good, isn't she?"

Liz's dark hair fluffed out behind her as she gave Missy more rein and let her go into a soft trot. "Fast enough, little girl. That's all you're going to get today. Any more and you'll work up too much sweat."

Maddie watched until she and Missy disappeared over a rise. "She don't need me to advise her on horses. I'm going back to work," Maddie said.

Raylen watched until they made the first circle and she waved at him, then he went back inside and brought Danny Boy out to walk him around the paddock a few times. The stallion looked disappointed that he couldn't have a good run, but Raylen reminded him that his leg wasn't healed and if he wanted to run, then he had to obey the rules.

"And besides all that, I'm still in shock at that woman of mine. I'm not sure I could keep up with you if we could take a jog around the pasture," Raylen said.

Liz finished the second round and brought Missy back to the front of the barn. She slid off her back, led her inside the barn, and grabbed up the equipment to rub her down before she put her back in the stall. Maddie had just finished mucking out and laying down fresh straw.

"You're pretty good ridin' bareback," she said.

"We got horses out in west Texas. I can saddle up if you want me to, but it's just extra time. Who's next?"

"Fire Red." She pointed to the name above the stall door.

"Her name mean she's got a temper?" Liz asked.

Maddie leaned on the shovel. "Gentlest mare I've got. She's birthed several of Danny Boy's colts for me. Got one that'll be in the sale this next fall. Beautiful boy that we haven't broken yet."

Liz itched to meet that horse. "Want me to start workin' with him?"

"Honey, Dewar would disown me as his mother if I

let anyone near that horse but him. But there'll be more colts and now that I've seen what you can do, you're goin' to have your hands full livin' next door to us, so you will get to break one eventually," Maddie said.

Liz and Fire Red had made it halfway around the pasture when her phone rang. She fished it out of her hip pocket and shifted the reins to one hand. Fire Red kept up a steady trot around the perimeter of the pasture.

"We're out past Wichita Falls," Marva Jo said. "Haskell called. Daddy is antsin' for us to get there."

"It wasn't easy, Momma," Liz said around the new lump in her throat.

"Change hurts sometimes, but I saw it in your eyes, you are where you should be. Dammit! I should have gotten involved with a carnie instead of a *gadjo*! It was his genes that keeps you in one place. A third-generation carnie would have given you good genes."

Liz giggled. "I'm riding bareback right now. I promised Raylen I'd help exercise horses if he'd help me take care of all my Christmas decorations and the party."

"You loved horses from the time you could walk. That's Daddy's genes coming out in you," Marva Jo said. "We're getting into Vernon and traffic is heavy. I'll call when we get there."

She'd barely flipped her phone shut when it rang again.

"I'm miserable," Blaze said when she answered, and she believed him. His tone sounded horrid.

"Good enough for you. When y'all left I cried my eyes out."

"I just now stopped snifflin' enough to call you. I'm in love, sweetheart."

"What are you going to do about it?"

"Hell if I know. It's a brand new territory for me. Got to go. Traffic is slowing us down. Call you tomorrow."

She flipped the phone shut and it rang a third time.

"Where'd you learn to ride like that?" Raylen asked when she answered. "Watchin' you makes me hot."

"What?" She giggled.

"Well, it does."

"I don't know how to answer that. Everything you do makes me hot. You can walk across the floor and I'm scalding hot. You can kiss me and flames shoot out my ears. But to answer your question, I started riding before Poppa or Momma knew it. I rescued an old wood stool from the barn and stood on it to mount up on the Shetland ponies. I was barely four, and Momma said I was too little to ride, but all I could think about was getting on that pony. I was too little to saddle up. I'd been riding a month or more when they figured out I wasn't playing with Barbie out there behind the barn."

"Stubborn little cuss, wasn't you," he said.

"Always," she said. "I'm bringing Fire Red in now. Who's next?"

"Glory. She's one of Major Jack's first colts. Spirited. She'll test you."

Liz giggled again. "As much as you do? Do I get makeup sex tonight?"

"It's a date," he said. "Starting with a long bath together. Not a shower."

"I'm looking forward to it," Liz said breathlessly.

"Me too," Raylen drawled.

She shivered at the idea of a bath with Raylen. Maddie was still mucking out the stall when she rode Fire Red into the barn. Liz slid off the mare's back and rubbed her down, but the visual of Raylen naked and wet kept a smile on her face until quitting time that evening. That cowboy sure knew how to rattle a girl's nerves, and Liz loved it.

The sun was a bright orange ball hanging right above the western horizon when they finished up. The inside of Raylen's truck smelled like hay, horses, and manure but neither Liz nor Raylen noticed. She wanted a long hot bath with Raylen. He could begin by massaging the aches from her upper thighs and butt cheeks. Tomorrow she was going to take the time to saddle the horses.

"Just so you know, Momma invited us to have supper with them. I told her that I'd promised to help you eat up some Italian leftovers," Raylen said.

Liz patted him on the leg. "And you will. After we have a long, hot steamy bath and then long, hot steamy sex."

"You don't stutter when it comes to speaking right up, do you?"

"I told you about riding that pony when I was four. I get something in my head, I do it. I got something to say, I say it."

"Then why didn't you tell me that summer when we were teenagers how you felt about me?"

She blushed. "At fourteen I barely knew what sex was or what that aching feeling down deep in my gut was. I do now."

She hopped out of the truck when he stopped it and hit the porch in a dead run. Hooter looked up, but she didn't invite him or Blister into the house. Raylen strutted up the steps and into the house, wondering why she was in such a big hurry. He found the answer when he opened the door. She stood in the middle of the foyer wearing nothing but a smile and a clamp in her hair.

"You sure are slow." She grinned.

With one swoop, he threw her over his shoulder, her bare butt too tempting, so he nibbled at it while he carried her back to the bedroom and flopped her down on the bed. He leaned down and kissed her long, hard, and passionately. When he broke the kiss and she opened her eyes, he'd kicked out of his boots and his jeans were down around his ankles. His lips found hers again and the next time she opened her eyes he was wearing nothing but a bit of straw in his dark hair.

"Who's slow?" he whispered.

He smelled like sweat and horses instead of shaving lotion and soap. She'd never had sex with anyone who wasn't showered and clean, but the idea was so heady that she was panting when he stretched out beside her and let his hands roam all over her body as he continued to make love to her mouth with his lips and tongue.

"I should've showered," she whispered. Maybe he didn't think heat and sweat were as sexy as she did.

"I've wanted you since you threw your leg over that horse this afternoon. God, you were so sexy. We'll shower later," he said.

"Five hours. You promised five hours."

"Not all at once, darlin'. This is the appetizer. Then we'll have a shower and the next course. Then maybe a bubble bath and the main entrée," he said.

"I like the way a sizzlin' hot cowboy thinks," she whispered as she ran her hands down his back.

He gasped when she cupped a firm butt cheek in each hand and squeezed.

"I like your body," she said.

"Oh, honey, I love your body," he whispered.

His breath on her neck was cool, she was so hot. Liquid spasms shot through her lower gut, and she arched against him. "Can that be a fast food appetizer, please?" she asked.

He raised up and looked deep into her dark eyes. They were filled with a mixture of want, need, and lust. It was a heady feeling, to know that Liz needed him as bad as he did her.

"Yes, ma'am," he said as he slipped inside her.

She rocked against him. "God that feels so good."

"Yes, ma'am," he agreed.

Her phone rang but her clothes were in the living room and she wouldn't have answered it if it had been lying between her naked breasts. Nothing mattered but Raylen and the next moment.

Chapter 26

"BLAZE, WHAT ARE YOU DOING HERE?" LIZ SQUEALED when she answered the doorbell.

"Standing out here in the rain freezing my ass off," he said.

She slung open the door and stood back. "Come in and warm your hands. There's a fire going in the fireplace, and I brought home leftovers from the café. They're on the stove if you are hungry."

"Hot coffee?" He stepped inside, gave her a hug, and shucked out of his heavy, work coat before heading to the warmth of the fire.

"In the pot. I'll pour us each a cup. Why didn't you tell me you were coming?"

He warmed his backside and then turned around and rubbed his hands. "For a fireplace I might..."

She carried two mugs of coffee to the living room and handed one to him. "No you wouldn't, so don't even think the words."

"I wasn't going to say I'd leave the carnival business. I was going to say that I'd consider building a house on the property for the winter months. Fireplace wouldn't do me a bit of good in the summertime anyway," he said.

She curled up in her favorite recliner and pulled a fluffy throw over her bare feet. Hooter had raised his head when Blaze came into the house, but he'd settled back down. Blister had barely opened one eye from her new bed on a pillow at the end of the sofa beside the bookcases.

"Talk to me," Liz said.

"Colleen invited me for the weekend and she took next week off. I'm scared out of my mind, Liz. I don't know whether to take her to Claude or what? She says she wants to get to know the carnival business, but I want her to get to know me first," Blaze said.

"Sit." Liz gestured toward the other recliner.

He settled into the chair and sipped his coffee. "What do I do? And where is Raylen?"

"I helped exercise the mares all afternoon. I'd just come in, got a shower, and was waiting on Raylen to heat up leftovers. You hungry? There's plenty in there for all of us. Jasmine sent them home with me."

"I haven't eaten. Don't know if I could swallow, I'm so nervous. I'm a carnie, Liz. I can't change that. You can, but I can't."

"Hello!" Raylen yelled at the door.

"In here. Blaze is here," Liz said.

Raylen removed his coat on the way to the living room.

"Hey, Raylen. Have I stolen your chair?" Blaze asked.

Raylen kissed Liz and slumped down on the end of the sofa. "No, but what are you doing here? Colleen is over there jumping every time she hears a truck door slam. She's got my old room all fixed for you."

"I'm scared," Blaze admitted.

"That's understandable," Raylen said. "I'd be scared of Colleen too."

Blaze set his coffee on the table. "We were talkin' about what Colleen and I should do this next week. She's taken a week off work and Haskell told me he was looking forward to helping Poppa so I should take her somewhere. She said she'd be happy in Claude in my trailer but…"

"Go on," Raylen said.

"There's this place off the coast of the state of Washington that I've been looking at. I've got plane tickets and the room on reserve but I have to confirm by midnight. I wanted Liz's opinion before I went over to your folks' place," Blaze said.

"What's your heart tell you?" Liz asked.

"It says I don't want to share her. It says that I want to spend a whole week in a place where neither of us knows another soul. But I don't know if that's what she wants," Blaze said.

"Confirm your reservations and tell her it's a surprise. Is it that place we've looked at that you have to go out to it by ferry?"

He nodded.

"Tell her pack a warm coat. It'll be a chilly ride," Liz said.

"Thank you." Blaze breathed a sigh of relief. He left half a mug of coffee on the end table and put his coat back on. "I knew talkin' to you would help."

"Don't tell her that you talked to me, Blaze. If I was her, I'd rather think it was all your idea and didn't need a second opinion." Liz walked him to the door and hugged him good-bye. "Guess I'll see you tomorrow at Sunday dinner?"

"Oh, yeah. Our flight is at six o'clock tomorrow evening out of Dallas. We'll have to leave Ringgold about three."

Liz went back to the living room and curled up in Raylen's lap. "Think we'll ever get them raised?"

Raylen didn't answer, so she leaned back and looked into his eyes.

"What are you worried about? Something happen at the barn? Are the horses all right?" she asked.

"It's not that. It's…"

It sounded so silly in Raylen's head that he wasn't sure he could put his feelings into words, but he felt the necessity to try to get it out even if it did sound crazy. He remembered when Rye fell head over heels in love with Austin; and now Colleen called him daily wanting to talk about nothing but Blaze McIntire.

It hadn't happened like that with him and Liz. It was as if they'd been put on the earth especially for each other, so they'd been comfortable from the time he slung open the door and found her on Haskell's porch. He hadn't needed to call Gemma or Dewar and talk about it every day. It didn't mean he wasn't in love with her or that he took that love for granted.

Liz waited for a full minute but he didn't say anything else. "Okay, now you are worrying me. Are you about to tell me that this is over and I'm going to be sitting on the porch tonight all by myself for the first night of the light show?"

"Hell, no! Liz, I'm in this for a long relationship. But I work all year for a living, sometimes from daylight to way past dark like today. I've got land and a house but I don't have the time or money to book a flight to some remote island for a whole week, as bad as I'd like to. It sounds romantic and I…"

Liz cupped his cheeks in her hands and stared right into his eyes. "Look at me, Raylen. I've had the traveling scene my whole life. Sitting here with you after a hard day's work, having Jasmine's leftovers for supper, looking forward to tomorrow with your family, and cuddling down in your arms tonight is living my dream."

He leaned forward and the kiss they shared was more passionate than any that preceded it. "I love you," he said simply.

"And I love you. Did you ever see a baby chicken fresh hatched?" she asked.

He shook his head. "Can't say that I have. Is that anything like a newborn colt?"

She kissed him again. "Not at all. Poppa raises a few chickens out on the property. He likes fresh eggs. Little chicken comes out of the egg with these little wings that don't look they'd ever be good for anything, but give them six weeks and they're flapping them and flying."

"What does that have to do with spending a week on an island with no one but me and you?"

She kissed him harder. "Colleen just came out of the egg. She needs to grow her own wings. Mine won't fit. She has to get used to a different lifestyle, but she has to know that Blaze loves her enough to keep her safe and protected while she's sprouting her wings."

"I'm not sure I understand it all," he said.

"Okay, cowboy, here's the deal. Right now. Right here. There's no one else around here and this house is our island."

"That I understand just fine." He picked her up like a bride and carried her to the porch. "Thank you."

"For what? Forcing you to sit with me two hours every night for the light show?"

"For making this our island," he said.

"No fortune-teller is an island unto herself. She must

have a sexy cowboy before it's a real island," she whispered as she plastered herself to him in a fierce embrace.

The first car lights brought the kiss to an abrupt end.

"Here they come," she said.

"Didn't you think they would?"

"I didn't know, Raylen. I really didn't know."

"Honey, in these parts folks have to drive a long way to get a little Christmas light show. You got a write-up on the front page of the Bowie paper and one in the Ryan paper. People want to see what they read about, and besides, it's free and you are giving out candy canes. Pretty impressive."

He grabbed her hand and hurried around the end of the house to the barn. People would turn around and go back out to the road on the south side of the fence. He had opened the gates on his property out onto the highway and strung lights along the top of her yard fence.

"And I'm entered in the Montague County Christmas contest for the best property decorations," she said. "Aren't they ever going to get here?"

"No, they're takin' it slow and easy, probably talking about each one of those exhibits. You got the candy canes ready?"

He sat down on one of Maddie's cast iron benches and pulled her down beside him. A smaller version of Santa's sack filled with candy canes sat between them.

"Right here. All ready," she said.

The first car arrived and the window on the passenger's side slowly lowered. "This is so pretty. The kids had a wonderful time," a lady said.

"It'll be open nightly until Christmas Eve. Come back and here's candy canes for everyone," Liz said.

The kids in the backseat of the van squealed.

The next car was there before she could sit down. The third pickup pulled off to one side and three elderly cowboys crawled out.

"We want the whole tour, not just the drive-thru," one said.

"Yes, sir." Liz grinned and looked over at Raylen. "You are on candy cane duty. This way, guys. The whole tour is the light show and the barn, which is still decorated because I didn't want to give it up after a big party we had at Thanksgiving."

"Read about this in the paper. Them fool reporters didn't give it the right credit, though. I know you. You are the waitress up at the café who always keeps my coffee cup full. Man alive, Roy, would you look at that tree. Place looks prettier than that mall over at Wichita Falls, don't it?"

"Momma would've liked the angel on the tree," Roy said softly. His shoulders sagged and white stubble on his face said that Momma wasn't around anymore to fuss at him to shave.

"You and Raylen keepin' company?" the third fellow asked.

Liz nodded.

"We heard that, didn't we, Buddy? Raylen needs a good woman. You be good to him," Roy said.

Buddy, a tall, lanky cowboy in bib overalls, nodded. "This is a fine put-on for a town like Ringgold. Must've took you a spell to put it all together. I got a feeling that you are happy here in Ringgold."

"Yes, it did take a lot of work, but I had a lot of good friends that helped me. And I enjoyed it all. And I am very happy here. I plan to stay forever. Y'all know Haskell? He's my uncle," she said.

"Yes, ma'am, we surely do. Our wives and Miz Sara was good friends in the day. He made all them pretty things, didn't he?" Buddy asked.

Liz nodded.

"Well, guess we'll be on our way. We might come back another day," Roy said.

"It'll be open all month," she said.

Raylen smiled when she sat back down on the bench with him. "I was busy. Was that Roy and Buddy?"

"I guess so. But I'm going to remember them as the three wise men. Look up there." She pointed.

A star was shining brighter than all the others and it hung right above her barn.

Sunday dinner was at the O'Donnell's place and Blaze still wasn't completely comfortable. He kept touching Colleen's hand, her hair, and her cheek for assurance.

Liz had loved that first rush phase of excitement with Raylen, but she loved the new phase even better. The one where she knew he'd be at her house as soon as he finished work, that if she had a nightmare she could back up into his embrace and it would disappear. Most of all, she loved the confidence in knowing not one ounce of the sizzle was going to fade each time they took their relationship to the next phase.

Everyone was talking all around her and Raylen, but suddenly she felt as if they really were an island unto themselves. His fingertips gently massaging her neck muscles sent her mind to an imaginary clear river where they were skinny-dipping and making love in the water. When he looked down into her dark eyes, she joined souls with him right there in all the noise and confusion of getting everyone gathered around in the kitchen so Grandpa could say grace, and everything and everyone disappeared.

"What are you thinking about? I think Blaze is doing pretty good, don't you?" he asked.

"I was thinking how wonderful family and friends are, and yes, Blaze is doing fine," she whispered.

He kissed her softly on the lips.

"Our Father in heaven." Grandpa's voice brought the last few whispers to a halt.

Liz bowed her head, but she didn't hear the prayer. She was too busy letting her imagination run full like she did Missy the afternoon before. In her vision, she and Raylen weren't skinny-dipping; they were making passionate love again the first time. She'd never guessed that she could endure such heat and come out on the other side without a visible mark on her body. Of course, there was that brand on her heart.

"Liz?" Raylen said.

She opened her eyes and raised her head. Prayer was over and everyone was lining up around the food tables.

"Where were you?" Raylen asked.

She pulled his head down and whispered, "Making love with you in the shower."

Colleen saw the red creeping up on his neck. "Raylen is blushing. What did Liz just say to you?"

The high color that had reached his cheeks deepened.

"She said she's starving. So will you hurry up and get your turkey? You are holding up the line," he told Colleen.

"I don't believe you," Colleen said.

"Believe it. Food isn't the only thing a woman can hunger after, is it?" Liz leaned forward and whispered into Colleen's ear.

Colleen's translucent complexion looked as if she'd walked through a forest fire. "You got it, sister! You know anything about this big surprise Blaze has in store for me?"

"Now I wonder what I said that made you think of Blaze?" Liz asked.

Colleen's face turned darker crimson. "Hush! Surprise?"

"Yes, I do know."

"Tell me," Colleen said.

"Take a warm coat."

Colleen gave her a stern look.

Liz giggled. "It won't work. You don't scare me anymore."

Blaze grinned. "But you did at first, darlin'. She called me every night and whined about how you wouldn't ever accept her."

"I still might not if she doesn't tell me what you two cooked up," Colleen said.

"Don't care if you do or not, I'm not sayin' another word other than pack a warm coat and have a good time," Liz said.

"You've met your match," Austin told Colleen. "She scared the bejesus out of me too, Liz, but she comes around even if she is almighty slow about it."

Liz looked up at Austin, who was several inches taller than her. "She's worse than Maddie."

"I am not," Colleen argued.

"Yeah, you are," Austin said. "But I think it's about time for payback. Call me tonight and tell me what is going on, Liz. I won't tell her a thing."

Liz smiled.

Raylen waited until they were seated and kissed Liz on the ear. His warm breath sizzled when he whispered, "I love you."

Chapter 27

DEER SEASON OPENS THE FIRST WEEK IN NOVEMBER in the northern counties of Texas and it stays open until the first week of January. The first day might as well be written down on the calendar as a national holiday and the last is as sad as a funeral. But during the two months it is open season on anything with antlers with at least a thirteen-inch spread. The great deer hunters of Montague County had drifted in and out of the café all day in their camouflage gear bringing their tall tales with them. By closing time, Liz was ready for them to go back to the woods. She didn't even care if they were big tippers or if they died of pure boredom sitting up in their deer stands. She could think of at least one way to use a deer stand that was a hell of a lot more fun than waiting, and waiting, and then waiting some more for a deer.

When the last hunters finally left, Jasmine locked the door and Liz grabbed the salt and pepper to get her jobs done quickly. Raylen would be there any minute.

"Give me a room full of girls and gossip over deer hunters any day of the week," Liz grumbled.

Jasmine laughed. "You are in north Texas, honey. Up here men folks have three main holidays. First day of deer season. Second day of deer season, and last day of deer season. The first is bigger than Christmas. The second is kin to Thanksgiving. The last one is a funeral wake because they won't get to drag out their bows, guns, and muzzle loaders for another year."

"I believe it. I've heard nothing but tall tales today. One bionic deer as big as a good-sized Angus bull ran off into the woods with sixteen arrows sticking out of his heart and one right through his brain, ear to ear."

"Heard them all," Jasmine said. "What are you and Raylen doing with your weekend?"

"It's a surprise," she said. "I think it's payback for not telling Colleen about the surprise that Blaze had for her, which, by the way, was a huge success. Now she's taking another week at Christmas and going out to Claude to spend it with him there."

"I knew I'd miss out on all the fun by going to Sherman for Thanksgiving, but Momma would have bitched me to death if I'd stayed here. I wish she would have had ten kids."

Liz nodded seriously. "I hear you loud and clear. Momma says I'd better have a dozen because she's going to steal at least one to make into a carnie."

"What do you *want* to do this weekend?" Jasmine asked. "Besides take a pizza and a six-pack to bed and not leave except to go to the bathroom."

"That sounds fine to me, especially if we could get a couple dozen buffalo wings tossed in with the pizza order. And thank you and Ace again for taking care of my light drive tonight. If you run out of candy canes…"

"I know, Liz. They are in the barn in the tack room."

Raylen knocked on the door and pressed his nose against the glass before Jasmine could say anything else. Liz unlocked it and tiptoed for a quick kiss.

"Ready?"

"We're runnin' late. Deer hunters had to talk a buck into falling down dead out there in front of their trucks in the parking lot before they could leave," she said.

"Did they get the job done?" Raylen asked.

"I don't think so, but they'll be back next week to give it another try. Where are y'all off to?" Jasmine asked.

Raylen grinned.

Jasmine thought he was cute.

Liz wondered how the paint stayed on the walls. Surely as hot as Raylen was when he smiled it would have at least blistered part of it.

"You aren't telling, are you?" Jasmine asked.

Raylen shook his head.

"Go on. I'll get this one and you can pay me back later when I want to leave early," Jasmine said.

"You sure?" Liz asked.

Jasmine took the salt container from her hands.

"Got your bag ready?" Raylen said.

"It's in my truck. You said casual. I hope you meant it."

"I did. I fed Hooter and Blister, and Dewar is going to check on them in the morning," Raylen said.

"Then my fate is in your hands." Liz untied her apron and laid it over the back of a chair, picked up her purse, and looped her arm through his.

"Have fun," Jasmine said.

Raylen put a Christmas CD in the player when they were in the truck and headed north. Liz was surprised when he made a right turn on Highway 82 instead of turning left. She'd thought she had the whole trip figured out by looking at Colleen and Blaze's plans. They'd had a trip to an island and were planning another trip to Claude so she figured Raylen was taking her to west Texas.

A twinge of disappointment flashed through her but it was soon replaced with excitement. Knowing that he wasn't following in Blaze's footsteps made it even more exciting, and she began to envision all kinds of scenarios, most of which involved very little clothing and lots of touching.

"Hungry?" he asked when they reached the second red light in Nocona.

"Little bit. I usually grab something from the kitchen before I leave. I was in a hurry," she said.

He put on the left blinker and pointed. "That Dairy Queen makes the best nachos. How about a couple of orders of those to hold us until supper?"

She nodded, and when the light turned green he whipped across the highway, stopping at the drive-by window. Sugarland was singing about pretending a snowman was Parson Brown who would ask them if they were married. The lyrics said that they'd tell him that they weren't but that he could do the job when he was in town. Liz didn't even know what kind of wedding she wanted, but she did know that someday she wanted to be married to Raylen and spend every Christmas with him for the rest of her life.

"What do you think of them?" Raylen pulled back out on the highway, ate with one hand, and drove with the other.

"They are great! Almost as good as the ones Freddy and Martha make at the carnival." She picked up a paper napkin and wiped his fingers for him when he held them out.

He pulled into the parking lot of a Mexican restaurant and stopped the truck. "Maybe not such a good idea to drive and eat at the same time."

She leaned across the seat and kissed him. "No, it's not but please eat faster. I can't wait to see where we are going."

They stayed on Highway 82 all the way to Whitesboro where he turned north and crossed the Red River into the little border town of Willis.

"Aha! Sin awaits us in Oklahoma," she said.

He shot her a smile that said sin wouldn't begin to cover what awaited them.

"Still not tellin'?" she asked.

"No, but it's not far now," he said.

Twenty minutes later, he made a right turn at the first red light they came to in Madill, Oklahoma, and she saw another Dairy Queen sign.

"Bathroom stop, please!" She pointed.

"You got it. Want some coffee while we're stopped?"

"How much further to our destination?"

"Half an hour."

"Got a coffee pot there?"

"Among other things," he said with another wicked grin.

"Half an hour from Madill going east is nothing but water, Raylen. We played this little town several times and there's a long bridge over a big lake. Where are we going?" she asked.

"To that lake. Want to go skinny-dippin'?"

Her eyes popped wide open. "In December? I don't think so."

"Party pooper. I'd planned a picnic on the edge of the water and some serious skinny-dippin'. Hot as we are together it should warm up the whole lake," he said as he parked the truck.

"Honey, we'd kill all the fish. The water would boil like a hot tub and they'd wash up on the banks already cooked," she bantered.

"Got a good point. Guess my idea wasn't so good. We'll just have to see what else they've got over there for us to do this weekend."

She dashed inside and hurried to the restroom. As she washed her hands, she hummed the Conway tune they'd just heard. Could he really hear the echoes of her thoughts? Had he gotten so far into her soul and mind that he knew what she was thinking? The lyrics said that she'd never been this far before, and that was the gospel according to Conway written about Lizelle Hanson. She'd never been that far before.

"There's a resort on this side of that bridge. I bet that's where he's taking me," she muttered. "A place where no one knows us."

He was sitting patiently in a booth when she opened the bathroom door. He stood up and threw an arm around her waist when he saw her. "Sure you don't want coffee?"

"I'm sure," she said.

Half an hour later they made a right turn into Lake Texoma Resort. She bit her lip to keep from smiling. She'd figured it out and they were going to stay in that big hotel... but he drove right past it. She wasn't a bit disappointed when she saw the little cabins right on the waterfront... but he drove past all of them.

He made a few more turns and then braked in a small, concrete parking lot. She looked out ahead at a marina. Surely to goodness, he wasn't serious about skinny-dipping.

He pointed. "See that houseboat out there with *Sinful Pleasure* written on the side?"

She nodded.

"She's ours until six o'clock tomorrow evening," he said.

"Oh, my! Do we get to go out into the water in it?" she asked breathlessly.

"Darlin', we can do anything we want. Tomorrow we'll take it around the lake. Today I have other plans."

"Then lead me on into sinful pleasures," she said.

He carried their bags onto the boat, unlocked the door, and led the way down to the bedroom and bathroom. It was everything that the rental agency said it would be and more. He dropped the bags beside the round bed covered in gold satin with dozens of pillows and picked up the remote control on the stand beside it. He pushed a button and soft country music came through the ceiling speakers.

He held out a hand. "May I have this dance, Miz Hanson?"

She took two steps and looped both her arms around his neck. He removed his hat and held it at the small of her back while they danced.

"Guess letting the hat dance with us will make up for abuse," she whispered when she could find her voice.

He chuckled. "It might. Have I told you today that you are one hot lady?"

"Have I told you that you are the one who makes me hot?"

When the song ended, he kissed her with so much

passion that her insides ached with desire, but angels walking on a barbed wire fence and singing her favorite country song wouldn't make her hurry the process. She would enjoy each and every second of it.

"Is your dance calendar full, or can I ask for another?" he asked huskily.

"It's got your name on every page, Raylen O'Donnell." She locked gazes with him.

He tossed his hat on the bed and held her close as they danced around the big bed that beckoned to them both. It would be so easy to fall back on the bed and make love to her, but Raylen had other things in mind. When the second song ended, he led her to the heart-shaped tub and started running water. He picked up a jar of bubble bath, added a generous amount, and pulled her back into his embrace for another dance.

Oh, Becca, thank God you never found out what kind of man your best friend really is and what a romantic he is or you'd have wrangled him to the altar right out of high school, she thought.

The kiss at the end of the dance was so soft and sensuous that she felt as if she were falling off a tall building in slow motion. But she wasn't afraid, because Raylen would be here to catch her.

"Are we planning on skinny-dippin' in that big old tub?" she asked.

"Oh, yes, darlin', but it will take a while to fill up," he said.

Two songs later he turned off the water.

She pulled her shirt up over her head and he pulled it back down. "Let me."

His touch on her skin as the clothing came off a piece

at a slow time might not have boiled the lake and killed all the fish, but it damn sure could have turned the big heart into a hot tub.

When he finished he quickly tossed his clothing to one side and picked her up, holding her naked body tightly to his chest.

"I love you," he said.

"And I love you," she said.

He eased her into the bubbles and then joined her, pulling her into his lap and slipping his wet hands all over her body.

"You are so soft and beautiful," he whispered.

Her soft skin was an aphrodisiac more powerful than anything pills or food could produce. He wanted to touch everything at once, and every time she gasped he was more and more aroused at his power over her body.

Her hands worked their way across the tight muscles on his chest and downward to his erection. He gasped when she touched him. He'd never get used to the sizzle that shot through him whenever she touched any part of his body.

"First time we did this in the shower, I couldn't believe how sensual it was. This is even better."

"Ready?" He kissed her long and hard.

"Oh, yeah." She wrapped her arms around his back, and together they began a rocking rhythm. She'd never felt so uninhibited, so totally into sex, as she did right then. She had tunnel vision that had only one thing in sight and that was satisfaction when she reached the bright burning light at the end.

His mouth covered hers in a string of passionate kisses that fanned the flames and she gave herself absolutely and totally to him.

"Mercy!" he gasped when she started to do the work, bringing him right up to the edge of passion and then slowing down.

"Liz, you are really going to make this water boil," he said.

"It was getting a little cold and we won't kill any fishes," she said.

Then suddenly they were working in unison and Liz couldn't hold back another minute.

"Please, darlin'." Her voice had more gravel and more intensity than he'd ever heard before.

"Welcome to *Sinful Pleasure*," he said when he could utter a word.

"Can we stay forever?" she asked breathlessly.

Chapter 28

RAYLEN AWOKE BEFORE LIZ THE NEXT MORNING. HE propped up on an elbow and drank in her dark beauty against the gold satin. She slept on her side with one arm under the pillow. Her black hair fanned out everywhere, even covering her face. Lizelle Hanson belonged in a satin atmosphere, not wrapped in a quilt in a tack room. One day she'd realize that; he just hoped she was so much in love with him when she did that it wouldn't matter what kind of sheets she and Raylen slept on. What mattered was what went on between them. He carefully pushed it back so he could see her delicate features.

She felt a touch and opened her eyes to see Raylen not a foot from her.

"Good morning, beautiful," he said.

"I wasn't dreaming," she said.

"No, but you look like a dream."

"Hold me until I get awake. Then can we take this out on the water and pretend we are the only two people in the whole world."

He cradled her into his arms, her head resting on his shoulder and her hair tickling his nose. "We are the only two left. Last night the aliens came and took them all away."

She giggled. "We'd better make the most of the day. My poppa and your granny and grandpa will wage a war and they'll bring the population back by nightfall."

He hugged her tightly. "Amen. Breakfast first?"

"Which is?" It was Sunday so her thoughts went to canned cinnamon rolls and bacon.

"It's in the refrigerator and marked 'breakfast.' You cook and I'll get the boat ready to move. We can eat on deck," he said.

"I was dreaming about gold satin sex all day," she whispered.

He ran his hand down her naked back. "Are you sure?"

She giggled and wiggled out of his embrace, pulling a gold sheet around her when she stood up, reminding him of an exotic statue in an Italian setting.

"Nice outfit there, Madam Whammy," he said.

She did a few belly dance moves, but when she raised her arms, the sheet fell to the floor and she stood before him strip stark naked. "I'm going for a quick shower and then I'll cook breakfast if the directions aren't too tough."

"Want some company in the shower?"

She put a finger on her chin. "Hmmm. If I get in the shower with you, this big old boat will never get out of the marina. Do I want you in the shower or do I want to putter about on the water?"

He chuckled. "Go take your shower, woman."

She pointed at him. "Don't boss me, Raylen."

"Is that an order? Is the lioness cranky?"

"It's an order and the lioness is cranky. She wants to kiss you until your brain goes to mush. She wants to roll around on that bed all day. But she wants to go out on the boat, and feel the wind in her face, and she can't have both. So, she's cranky. And besides all that, my breath is horrid after that champagne we had last night. While I was dancing, I breathed on your hat, and it almost shriveled up into nothing but a little pile of straw. I'm afraid to kiss you for fear it would fog your blue eyes."

Raylen laughed. "You don't have a bit of problem speaking your mind, do you?"

"No, I do not." She disappeared behind the tiny bathroom door.

He slung his legs over the edge of the bed and got dressed. He'd love to rent the boat again next week, but Dewar, Cash, and Maddie had to be away from the ranch for a horse show in Conroe, Texas. So the best he could do that weekend was a late dinner date on Saturday night. Maybe he'd order takeout from that Chinese place in Bowie and rent a movie. After a weekend on the *Sinful Pleasure*, it would be a big letdown and he hoped Liz wasn't disappointed.

Liz had finished a quick shower and wrapped a towel around her body when she heard the engine kick into gear and the boat begin to sway even more than it had all night. When she first saw the houseboat she'd had a moment of panic, fearing that she'd spoil Raylen's beautiful plan, that the constant movement would make her queasy. She'd never been on anything bigger than a worn out old canoe, and that was with Blaze when they paddled out into the middle of the farm pond to fish for bass.

The gentle movement hadn't been any worse than the travel trailer in a good wind storm. And Raylen's strong arms around her had steadied the whole world. Now she was in love with the boat and wondered how much one cost. Maybe she'd put some of her money into one and she and Raylen could get away from the whole world several times a year. Only her houseboat was going to be named *Madam Whammy*.

She dressed in jeans, boots, and a turtleneck sweater before she opened the refrigerator. Breakfast was in two aluminum pans with direction that involved preheating the small oven and cooking for twenty minutes. One container was marked quiche, the other cinnamon rolls. While the oven preheated, she read the rest of the instructions on the cinnamon roll pan: *Serve with juice (in the door of the refrigerator) and coffee. Use tray in cabinet beside the stove if you are taking it topside.*

"Well, duh! I thought I'd ignore the heat and take it up there without even a hot pad," she grumbled.

She slid the food into the oven, made a pot of coffee, and removed two single serving bottles of juice. The boat moved slowly, leaving the noise and smells of a marina coming awake behind. She looked at the clock on the microwave: seven o'clock.

The last time she looked at the clock last night it had been well past midnight. As a carnie, she would have slept until midmorning. She poured a cup of coffee the minute it stopped dripping and backed up against the cabinet beside the tiny sink.

"I'm not a carnie anymore," she whispered.

What do you want to be when you grow up? that niggling little voice in her head asked.

"I want to be a horse rancher," she answered without hesitation. "I want to be a Maddie."

"Do I hear talking down there? Are you fighting off aliens?" Raylen called down the hatch.

"No, the aliens are arguing with Poppa and your

grandpa. They don't have time to fight with me. They've got their hands full. I heard the engine. Are we on the way to the end of the world, where we'll drop off into fantasy land?" she said.

"We went there last night," he said.

She poured a cup of coffee and carried it up to him. "Kiss me, Captain Sexy Cowboy."

She tiptoed and he leaned.

"I love you, Liz," he whispered.

"You must. You didn't throw me overboard when I was cranky. Is this thing on autopilot or something?"

He laughed. "No, and it's time for me to get back to the wheel. Breakfast about ready?"

"Five minutes. We worked up a pretty damn good appetite, didn't we?"

Raylen brushed another kiss across her forehead before he took over the wheel again. She went back to the galley, located the tray, and pulled the food from the oven.

"Juice and coffee on the tray. Two forks. Don't have a rose in a vase," she talked as she worked. She added the coffee pot and a couple of napkins, and carried it up to the deck.

The wind was still and the water was a mirror beneath them, barely leaving a wave in their wake as the boat inched along toward the bridge up ahead. She set the tray on the table and rushed back down to get her coat. Even though the sun was shining brightly, the temperature hovered around fifty degrees, and with the movement of the boat, that was downright chilly.

When she returned, the boat had come to a standstill and Raylen was sitting at the table. He'd removed the aluminum covers from the food and the aroma of sausage and eggs and cinnamon blended to make her stomach growl.

"Plates?" he asked.

"They're down there, but..." She shrugged.

He picked up a fork and dug into the quiche. "Sharing, are we? This is good. Momma makes them sometimes for special breakfast."

Liz dug to the bottom and blew on the steaming egg mixture before she put it in her mouth. She rolled her eyes. "God, that's good. It beats the hell out of Blaze's attempt to make it."

Raylen smiled. "Try the cinnamon rolls."

She did and moaned. "They're as good as what they sell at the carnival."

"Good as canned ones?" he asked.

"Oh, no! They are the best in the world. They mean the gig is up and it's time to move to the next one," she said.

"Then don't ever serve them to me, Liz," he said seriously.

"Why?"

"Because I don't ever want this gig to end."

She reached across the table and touched his hand. "Me either."

He brought her fingertips to his lips and kissed them. Not proposing to her right then and there was the hardest thing he'd ever done.

They barely made it home Sunday night when the cars began to drive down the lane. The very first car load brought two elderly people who parked and headed for the barn. They were dressed in plaid men's robes, belted at the waist and hanging to their ankles. Dark blue towels were held down on their heads with stretchy black headbands, but kinky gray curls had escaped around their ears.

"We didn't have time to go home and change. We just came from a Christmas play at the church. Didn't have enough men to be the shepherds so we stepped in. Hell, the congregation don't know if they're lookin' at men or women by the time we get our towels on our heads and our Goodwill store bathrobes on," one of them giggled.

Liz followed them into the barn. "Welcome to the Ringgold light show."

"Would you look at that, Agnes? That's the prettiest damn tree I've ever seen. Folks don't use real ones much no more. And look at that angel up there. Can't buy them like that no more. It's an antique for sure."

"Belonged to Uncle Haskell," she said. "Aunt Sara liked Christmas and she must've had a lot of her decorations passed down by her parents because some of the stuff I found isn't available in the stores today. But I love Christmas and I wanted to share it with everyone."

"I knew I recognized that angel. It was Sara Hanson's grandmother's topper. I saw it once when I was a kid," the tall shepherd said.

"Shit, Mavis, you can't remember that far back." Agnes slapped her playfully on the shoulder.

"Don't be hittin' on me, woman. Just because you're two years younger than me and was Momma's favorite don't mean you can hit on me now," Mavis said.

"You are sisters?" Liz asked.

"Hell, yeah," Agnes said. "Oh, we forgot to tell you,

we're the judges for the Montague County contest. We are supposed to tell the folks when we first get there but sometimes we forget."

"Don't be usin' that *we* word. *You* forget. I got my tally sheet right here under my robe." Mavis pulled out a small clipboard from inside her robe and fumbled in her pocket for a pencil.

Agnes fished one from her pocket and handed it to Mavis. "Here's one. See, she does forget."

"Good damn thing we ain't real shepherds, ain't it? We'd be them kind that lose their sheep for sure." Mavis giggled.

"If you don't watch your foul talk, God is going to strike you graveyard dead. All dressed up like a shepherd that went to see the baby Jesus and talkin' like a sailor." Agnes frowned.

"Don't you be bossin' me around. I'll talk anyway I damn well please. I was good up there on the stage with that squallin' kid they got to be baby Jesus. Lord have mercy, but if I was him, I woulda squalled too. Havin' to lay there in that straw in nothin' but a blanket wrapped around him."

Liz giggled.

"It's the God's honest truth, he was," Mavis said.

"I don't doubt it," Liz said.

"We was so glad to be done with that play that we couldn't get out of there fast enough. Next year somebody else can wear our Goodwill robes and our towels. We're going to be on the refreshment committee."

"I'm going back outside. You ladies call me if you need me," Liz said.

"We'll just take our notes and be gone. But honey,

as far as I'm concerned, this is the biggest splash in the county," Mavis said.

"Thank you. Don't forget to get a candy cane."

"We won't. Agnes here does love candy canes. I swear she's been sittin' on Santa's lap for ninety-two years just to get a damned candy cane. She says the ones at Christmas taste better than the ones you can buy any other time of year," Mavis said.

"Ninety-one years. You can't remember a damn thing," Agnes said.

Liz giggled. "See you outside. If you need anything holler at me."

"Where's your shepherds?" Raylen whispered.

"The world is a new place this year. They are women," she whispered back.

"Cross-dressers in reverse?"

"You got it, darlin', and the judges for the county decoration prize too, so be very nice to them," she said.

Chapter 29

MONDAY MORNING STARTED OFF WITH A BANG. THE electricity had blinked off during the night, and Liz woke up fifteen minutes late. Raylen had already gone, so she didn't even get a good morning kiss, and when she got to work that morning, a dozen coffee drinkers followed her inside when she opened the door at exactly six o'clock. That meant she hit the floor in a dead run without even a second to get a cup of coffee.

By midmorning she was dragging and thinking about one of those crazy energy drinks that she'd seen advertised on television. She finally had time to pour a cup of coffee but barely got a sip before the door opened again.

"Wait," Jasmine said. "That's Lucy. She'll come right back here."

The woman was tiny, just over five feet tall and slim built. Her brown hair was pulled up in a ponytail, and her face round. But her eyes were enormous and stood out like the pictures of those little kids that were popular thirty years before. They were even lighter blue than a summer sky and much lighter than Raylen's. When she smiled, they sparkled like diamonds.

"Hi, Jasmine." Lucy went straight for the coffee pot and poured a cup. "You must be Liz. I've heard good things about you."

"Well, with what I've heard about you, I expected

you to be as tall as Austin and able to wrestle an Angus bull to the ground with your bare hands," Liz said.

Lucy shook her head. "Not me."

"What brings you out today? I haven't seen you in a couple of months. I missed you, girl," Jasmine said.

"Been busy with the new therapy group, and the motel is going really good. I started to call this morning, but we only had five rooms to clean and Tasha said she'd take care of them if I wanted to get out. Thought I'd run down to the used bookstore in Bowie and stock up for a month or so. I've got two strays I need to find jobs for." Lucy sipped her coffee.

"I'm not in the market…" Jasmine started.

"You could be," Liz said.

"Oh?"

"I talked to Maddie last night about… well, when this day came. I only said I'd work until Lucy found someone. I've never had a job. I don't know how to do this," Liz said.

"You're doin' fine," Lucy said.

"I kind of figured out over the weekend that I want to work with the horses or on the ranch. That's what I want to be when I grow up. It's like fate that Lucy came today. I'll move over and let one of Lucy's girls have my waitress job," Liz said.

"Thank you," Lucy said. "Bridget is twenty-one. She's got waitress experience. She's living with her folks in Petrolia. I'm afraid if she doesn't get a job, she'll fall right back into her abusive husband's web. If she's got a routine and her own money, she'll be fine with our weekly meetings."

"What meetings?" Jasmine asked.

"Started them a month ago. That's another reason I don't get out much. Sunday afternoons, those that can, we all meet in the Baptist church fellowship hall. It's like AA only for abused women. It's our support group," Lucy said.

"When does she want to start work?" Liz asked.

"She's sittin' out there in my truck. Thought we'd check here first since it's closest to her folks' farm," Lucy said.

Jasmine looked at Liz. "You sure about this, Liz?"

"I'll miss you but I figured out what I want to be and Maddie said I could work with the horses. I'll give Bridget my apron and start work on the ranch tomorrow morning."

"Then bring her on in. She can work with Liz all afternoon and start full-time tomorrow morning," Jasmine said.

Lucy didn't waste a minute as she fairly well danced across the floor.

"She takes her mission very seriously. That's a good thing you did, but I'm going to miss you like crazy," Jasmine said.

"It's the right thing and the right time," Liz said. "And we're friends. I'll see you often."

Bridget was a short woman, carrying about twenty extra pounds and a few faint yellow bruises around her eyes. She wore a chambray shirt out over her tight jeans. She held out her hand to Jasmine and said, "Thank you for givin' me a chance. I did some work over at the Dairy Queen when I was in high school, but that was a while ago. I'll learn fast though."

"Minimum wage to start," Jasmine said.

"The tips are really good, though," Liz said.

"I would work for minimum and give the tips to you," Bridget said.

"That isn't the way it works. You keep the tips. Some days they'll be better than your wages. I pay on Saturday at quittin' time. You need a fifty dollar advance on your first paycheck for gas to get you to work the rest of the week?"

Bridget nodded. "Daddy said I can use his old work truck until I can get something better. He'd probably fill it up with gas, but if I can do it on my own, I'd like that."

"Then get an apron and follow Liz everywhere she goes today. Lucy, you want to pick her up on your way back home?" Jasmine asked.

"I'll be here at two," Lucy said.

"Hey, Lucy, you said you had two women needing work. What's the other lady looking for?" Liz asked.

"She's fifty years old and never worked outside the home. We got her set up in a little garage apartment in Henrietta, but rent is due at the end of the month. We could only help her get situated and pay one month. She's not qualified for anything."

Liz's mind went into overdrive. "Cooking and cleaning."

Lucy nodded. "She could sure do that. She takes care of cleaning the fellowship hall when we leave."

"Does she have transportation?"

Lucy nodded again. "She's got a car. Have you heard about anything?"

"I might have something. Send her down to my house this afternoon. We'll talk. I hate to clean and I damn sure hate to cook. We might work up a deal," Liz said.

"What time?" Lucy asked.

"Three. I'm supposed to be at the horse barn at four," she said.

"She'll be there," Lucy said.

Bridget fell right into the work, and Liz had five minutes of free time just before the lunch rush. She called Maddie and told her what she'd done that morning.

"That's a good thing you did, Liz. Then you were serious about working more?" Maddie asked.

"Were you serious about me working as much as I want?" Liz asked.

"I was. Dewar, Cash, and I are leaving tomorrow morning and we'll be gone a week. The hired help will be helping Raylen and he'll be your boss. Think you can handle that?"

"I'll do my best not to piss him off and get fired before you get back," Liz said.

"If you can do that, I'll start you at a quarter above minimum."

"Better make it minimum wage, then." Liz laughed.

Raylen waved from the horse barn when he saw Liz drive up. She hopped out of the truck and gave him a quick kiss on the cheek. "Did Maddie talk to you?"

"Not since breakfast. I meant to run up to the café for dinner, but Granny made fried chicken and it would have hurt her feelings if I didn't take an hour and eat with her and Grandpa. How'd your day go?"

"I quit my job."

Raylen's heart fell to the ground. The other shoe had dropped. The weekend on the boat had proved to her that she wasn't ready for ranch life.

"Aren't you going to say anything?" Liz asked.

"I'm afraid of what I'll hear."

"Lucy needed places for a couple of her abused women. One is working for Jasmine. I quit and gave her my job. Kind of like fate tossed them women in my path. Aunt Tressa says when opportunity knocks, invite it in for a cup of coffee before you send it on its way. So I did. Bridget is working for Jasmine, and she's a hard worker. She'll do all right. The other one is my new housekeeper and cook. She'll be at my house at eight in the morning and she's going to clean, wash, and iron and all those things I hate. And hot damn, she likes to cook. She'll have our dinner ready at noon and she'll leave at two. She's working five days a week. As of this minute, I'm working for O'Donnell's Horses and you are my boss."

The grin that split Raylen's face lit up the whole north part of Texas. "What's her name?"

"Who?"

"The new lady."

"Oh, that'll be Wilma. She's Hispanic and has put up with years of mental abuse from a rascal husband, but she doesn't want to talk about it. She says that's behind her now and she wants to go on with her life."

Raylen took off his hat and slapped the dust out of it on his leg. "How can you afford that?"

"I'm going to pay her with what I make working for you," she said.

She wanted to spit it all out right then but she couldn't make herself do it. She'd tell Raylen about her finances someday but not that day.

"I suppose we'll be out of the house by the time she gets there every day," he said.

"We'd better be if we want to be finished before dark. I'm a horse woman now, not a carnie. I can't sleep until noon. So what are my orders?"

"Kiss me and then exercise horses until dark." He continued to grin.

Chapter 30

CHRISTMAS EVE WASN'T EXCEPTIONALLY COLD BUT IT was nippy. The O'Donnell family had decided to have their dinner and present exchange that day, and then on Christmas Austin and Rye could take Rachel to Tulsa to spend the day with the other side of the family; Liz and Raylen and Blaze and Colleen could all go to Claude.

"Got to be accommodatin' to the other folks," Cash had said.

Liz awoke in a state of excitement. She'd already wrapped ten presents for Raylen and hid them in a spare bedroom. In the living room, piled up on the sofa and waiting for Raylen to arrive, she had at least one present for everyone in the O'Donnell family and one for Blaze who would be there also.

There was a pretty shawl for Colleen, a sweater for Gemma, several baby toys for Rachel, who had stolen her heart. A lovely crystal bowl for Maddie, and a Christmas CD for Cash, and a big box of Dewar's favorite Christmas chocolate covered cherries from a special candy factory in Wichita Falls. She'd chosen a silver picture frame for Austin and Rye with a gift certificate to a fancy photography shop to have a family portrait done. Today Raylen got a silver belt buckle with the ranch brand engraved in the middle in gold, and Blaze got the biggest bottle of his favorite shaving lotion that she could find.

Raylen was running a little late that morning. A mare was down in the horse barn trying to deliver a foal too early and he'd called the vet in for an opinion. Medicine had been given, but the vet didn't think it would save the foal brought on by one of Danny Boy's escapes.

"Merry Christmas Eve," he said with a sweet kiss. "You ready?"

"Once we get all these presents out to the truck."

"That's a lot of presents," he said.

"Buying them was so much fun. I love shopping and I got to buy so many this year. Usually it's one for Momma, one for Aunt Tressa, for Poppa, and for Blaze. I love Ringgold," she said.

"Did you buy something for everyone in town?" he asked as she stacked presents in his arms.

"I would have if they were coming to Christmas at your folks." She giggled.

Colleen met them at the door and helped Liz unload the presents from Raylen's arms and arrange them under the tree.

"So how are things between you and Raylen?" she whispered.

"First, tell me about you and Blaze," Liz said.

"I'm in love."

"Me too," Liz said.

Dinner was loud and noisy just like all affairs at the ranch. Presents afterwards left the room covered in paper and ribbons and more noise and laughter. Liz opened her presents slowly, savoring every single moment and enjoying watching others open what she'd shopped for.

Gemma gave her a lovely horseshoe pendant dangling from a chunky bead chain. Colleen's present was a snow globe with an angel inside and a note that said she'd still be glad to buy Liz's wings. Austin and Rye gave her two bottles of Austin's watermelon wine in a crystal wine bucket. Dewar's gift was a set of horse head bookends and a gift certificate to the nearest bookstore. Maddie and Cash gave her a quilt rack to sit in the corner of her living room, and Granny and Grandpa's present was a hand quilted throw to put on it.

She loved all of the presents and the thought that went into them, but they would never know how much fun she'd had agonizing over what she gave them that year. To have friends so close that she knew what they would like was the biggest gift of all.

Raylen looked strange when he opened her gift, as if he didn't like it or she'd intruded on some kind of private ground by commissioning a silversmith in Amarillo to make the buckle. He kissed her on the cheek and thanked her, but something wasn't right.

Before she could ask him what was wrong, Maddie dug her phone from her hip pocket and answered it. "Oh, no!" she said.

"What?" Raylen asked.

"It's that mare we've been watching. She's delivering early. I knew she was too old to breed. Damn that horny Danny Boy," she fussed.

"You stay here. Liz and I will take care of her," Raylen said. "Everyone doesn't need to go."

"Get rid of those shoes and use my boots, and, darlin', you'd better shuck out of that fancy dress and put on my coveralls too. They're hangin' on a hook by the clothes dryer," Maddie told Liz.

Liz was a little disappointed that she couldn't finish

the day in the glow of the family in full Christmas spirit, but she nodded in agreement. She hurried into the utility room and changed into the coveralls, kicked her high heels off, and donned a pair of worn cowboy boots. They were half a size too big but they beat ruining her expensive high heels.

The mare was down in one of the stalls with a hired hand standing over her when they reached the stables.

"I'm on stall duty every two hours. When I left last time she was fine," he said.

"The vet checked her early, Carl. We both thought we had it under control. It's not your fault. Go on home to your family. We're here and we'll take care of her." Raylen knelt beside the black horse. "And Merry Christmas, Carl."

"Same to you and Miz Liz." Carl headed out of the barn.

"Come on, girl," he said softly.

Liz dropped to her knees and wrapped her arms around the mare's neck. "We won't ever let Danny Boy close to you again if you'll have this foal and not die."

"How do you plan to keep that promise?" Raylen asked. His tone was edgy but he'd felt terrible when he didn't have a present for her. Now she'd think he was a total jerk and in front of his whole family. Even Blaze had thought to bring something for Colleen which made matters even worse. But he'd been so wrapped up in his present for the next day he'd forgotten about the gift exchange among the family that day. He gave gift cards every year to everyone. To fancy restaurants for Rye and Austin, to Toys"R"Us for Rachel, to a spa for each of his sisters, and a cruise for his parents. Dewar got one to a George Strait concert and...

"Shit!" he said. He hadn't gotten Blaze a damn thing either. Now Colleen would be mad at him too.

"What is the matter with you? Didn't you like my present?" Liz snapped.

"Hell, yes. It's beautiful and I love it. But I didn't have a thing for you or Blaze. Dammit!"

Liz walked across the stall on her knees and wrapped her arms around Raylen. "Tell me you love me."

"You know I do."

"Tell me."

"I love you."

"That's the best Christmas present in the world. Now let's take care of this horse. She's just about ready. Look at those little hooves coming out."

"It's premature, so it's probably not going to make it."

"Oh, yes it will. Little or not, it's not going to die. That momma horse has worked too hard not to have her baby, and it will live," Liz declared as the next contraction pushed more of the foal out into the world.

It was black except for one white ear and a white splotch on the forehead that faintly resembled a star. When it was fully out Raylen was everywhere at once, wiping its nose, shaking it gently to make it suck in air, and cussing under his breath the whole time.

Liz stayed out of his way until the newborn finally heaved and started breathing, then she helped wipe it down with warm towels. "What now?"

"We baby-sit for a while. See if it can stand on its own and hope his momma survives," he said.

"Do we call the vet?"

"No, nothing he can do that we can't now," Raylen said.

"Where'd that blaze come from? His momma and daddy are both solid black."

"He's thrown one other one with a blaze. He's won two major races and is almost as famous as Danny Boy," Raylen said.

At midnight, the mare was standing on her own and everything looked fine. The tiny little horse had fed even though it had to stretch its neck to the full extent to reach his mother's teats.

"I'm going to get a shower and grab a few hours sleep," Raylen said.

"Me too. Santa Claus is coming at five in the morning, right?"

Raylen grinned. "Leave milk and cookies."

Liz woke up Christmas morning to the aroma of coffee wafting down the hallway. Without opening her eyes she patted Raylen's side of the bed, only to find a pillow and cold sheets. Then she remembered that he was going to his house after the foal had been born. He'd promised to be at her house at five o'clock because Santa was coming that morning. She jumped out of bed, pulled the curtains back, and gave a sigh of relief. The weatherman had said there was a slim possibility of freezing rain, but the sun was peeking up over the eastern horizon. After presents, she and Raylen should have dry roads all the way to Claude where they were having Christmas with her family.

Raylen slipped his arms around her from behind, clasping them under her breasts and pulling her back to his chest. "Merry Christmas, darlin'."

"Merry Christmas to you." She wiggled in closer and sniffed the air. "Do I smell cinnamon rolls? Does that mean the gig is up? Did you find the milk and cookies on the bar, Santa?"

"I found my milk and cookies. Blister talked me out of the milk and Hooter begged for the cookie so that was their Christmas present. The cinnamon rolls are *not* canned. Wilma had them in the refrigerator with a note on top that said to heat for ten minutes on Christmas morning."

"Guess that rules out a quickie," she teased.

"They've been in the oven seven minutes. Three minutes is even too fast for me unless you want to dance for me this morning. It *is* Christmas," he said.

He nuzzled into her neck, nibbling gently at the sweetness offered there before he clasped her hand in his and led her to the kitchen. Coffee, juice, and two forks were already on the table. He brought the cinnamon rolls from the oven and put them on a hot pad in the middle of the table.

Excitement and a tiny edge of fear mixed together to curb his appetite. This was the day, and he hoped he had planned it well enough.

Excitement reigned in her heart. She'd gotten what she wanted for Christmas. A house that wasn't on wheels and not just any old cowboy picked up under a tumbleweed or behind a mesquite tree, but Raylen O'Donnell. Miracles did happen. She had living proof.

She nibbled at the cinnamon rolls but was too nervous to eat more than a few bites. She'd put out all ten of his presents before she went to bed the night before, had awakened at two o'clock and checked to make sure they were arranged just right and to see if he'd snuck one in for her. At four she woke up again and padded up to the Christmas tree to rearrange them one more time. Still nothing from Raylen.

"All finished?" she asked.

He pushed back the coffee cup. Butterflies the size of half-grown buzzards flittered about in his stomach. It was time.

"Wait right here," he said.

He disappeared down the hallway and into the spare bedroom where she'd kept all her presents until the night before. When he returned he was carrying something wrapped in an old quilt.

"What is it?" she asked.

"Your Christmas present," he whispered.

He laid it in her lap, and a little white head and two black hooves shot out from under the quilt. The foal made a noise that reminded her of a baby and looked up at her with big, round black eyes.

"Oh!" Other than one word she was totally speechless.

"His momma died about an hour ago. He's going to need lots of care to make it. So Merry Christmas, Liz. If he lives, it'll be because you made a miracle."

Tears filled her eyes and spilled down her cheeks.

"The first of my own herd. And he's staying in the bedroom until he's big enough to go outside in the yard. Did you put some hay in there for him to sleep on?"

Raylen grinned. "Yes, and the quilt which will have to be washed every day. And formula in the refrigerator which will have to be warmed so he can eat every four hours. Momma says she'll take care of him today and tomorrow morning, but we're on our own after that."

"Do I get to name him?"

"He's your baby," Raylen said.

"His name is Glorious Christmas Star because of the star on his forehead, and because all winners have to have three names. I'm calling him Star."

Raylen cocked his head to one side. "Sounds fine to me, but are you sure that's a star? It looks more like a lightning streak to me."

"It's a star that got smeared a little, but it's still a star." Her tone left no room for argument.

"You are going to be a fine racer, aren't you, Star, and we're going to win the same prize that Danny Boy did. Your momma didn't die for nothing, darlin'." She crooned to the foal and used her nose to pet the white splotch on his forehead.

Raylen kissed her on the top of her head and smiled.

She looked up and meant to kiss him on the lips but missed and got the side of his mouth. "Now it's your turn. I'm going to sit right here and hold Star while you open your presents. The big, round one first with the red paper and gold bow."

Raylen's eyes widened. "All of these for me?"

He didn't have a single present under the tree for her. He should have bought a hundred presents for her to unwrap in addition to the unwrapped ones out in the yard.

He ripped into a box with a brand new Stetson.

She hugged Star and said, "I promise not to stomp it or throw it on the ground."

The next present was a bottle of Stetson.

"That scent turns me on," she said with a smile.

He could hardly wait to give her the rest of his Christmas present. Anxiety, hoping that she would like it, made him open faster so he could take her to the backyard and show her how much he loved her.

Liz was suddenly worried that she'd overdone it. He had only given her the horse because the momma died, and he'd think she was smothering him. Dammit!

The last present was a long, black silk scarf.

"It's actually for me when I dance for you," she said.

"Very nice," he mumbled.

How in the devil did she afford all those expensive gifts? She used what she made working at the ranch for Wilma's salary; she had said so herself. So where did the money come from for a new hat, Stetson aftershave, a hundred-dollar scarf, and all the rest?

But the idea of her finances quickly took a backseat when he thought about what he'd planned for the rest of her Christmas. He was almost giddy with excitement at that point. "Thank you, darlin'. You did way too much, but I love every one of my gifts."

"So did you. This horse is a son of Glorious Danny Boy. I can't wait to tell Blaze what I got. Someday when Danny Boy can't even get it up with Viagra, Star is going to take his place on the ranch." She smiled.

"Well, darlin', can Star get back in his baby bed for now? The rest of your presents are outside." He stood up, bent down, and kissed her hard.

They carried Star back to his room and settled him into the middle of a pile of clean hay as big as a full-sized bed.

"Look, Raylen, he's happy. Our new baby is happy in his bed," she whispered.

Raylen slipped his arm around Liz, and they stood there several minutes gazing down at the new baby horse lying in a bed of hay and a frayed old quilt.

Star shut his eyes and sighed.

"Yes, he is. While he's sleeping, I have a surprise for you, darlin'. Close your eyes," Raylen said.

She didn't have to be told twice. She loved surprises. She was so excited she had trouble standing still. "What is it?"

"Santa Claus came last night and left you a present," he said.

"Is it a new puppy?"

"No, darlin'. I thought about us getting one but I thought you'd want to help me pick him or her out."

He took her hands in his and pulled her up to a standing position. When they passed the living room, he picked up the folded quilt he'd left on the sofa and fluffed it out.

She heard a snapping noise and felt a whoosh of air. "What was that?"

"You'll get cold so I'm wrapping you up." He scooped her up into his arms and carried her out the back door.

When the cold air hit her nose, she cuddled closer to him. "Are you sure it's not a puppy?"

They didn't go far before he sat down with her in his lap and suddenly, they were swinging. "Now open your eyes."

She gasped. "You bought it!"

They were cuddled up together in the swing that she'd coveted on their first real date. And there was the picnic table and two Adirondack chairs to match.

"I can't believe it. It's a wonderful, wonderful present. I love it, darlin'. It's perfect. It means you want me to stay in Ringgold as long as this wood holds up, doesn't it?" she gushed.

"Longer than that," Raylen said.

Something a rancher would have. Something a carnie could never, ever tote around, she thought.

"When I went back to get my keys, that old feller told me that you could swing the new babies in it and your grandbabies would eat off that table," he said.

The idea of having children with Raylen and then grandchildren brought tears to her eyes and put a lump in her throat the size of a grapefruit. It was what she'd said she wanted when she saw Granny and Grandpa together that first Sunday she spent at the O'Donnell's.

Raylen deposited her on the other side of the swing. He dropped down on one knee in front of her and took her hands in his.

She looked down into his blue eyes and saw her future. Love, fights, makeup sex, horses, kids, and grandkids in a flash. Her heart swelled up so big that she had trouble catching a breath.

Raylen looked up into her black eyes and saw his soul mate looking back at him. "Liz Hanson, I've loved you since we were kids. I want to be the father of those babies that you swing in this swing. I want to sit on those two chairs when we are old and watch our grandbabies eat off that table. Will you marry me?"

"Yes!" she answered without a second's hesitation, locked her arms around his neck, and pulled his lips up to hers in a sizzling kiss.

⁓

February is a petulant child in Texas. It can be happy, sunny, bright, and beautiful or it can spend the day pouting in the corner not knowing what it wants. It was a happy-go-lucky kid on the last Saturday of the month. The sun was out and only a few white clouds floated across the sky above Claude, Texas.

The big barn had been cleaned from top to bottom under Poppa and Haskell's supervision and transformed into a thing of beauty for the wedding. The barn was full with the carnival family, the O'Donnells, and all the friends from the Ringgold area that could make the trip. They were seated in folding chairs when the fiddle music began.

Blaze took his place beside the minister. He was the luckiest man in the whole world. Hell, he was even luckier than Dewar and Rye and Poppa, his best men, all supporting him on the most important and most nervous day of his life.

The fiddle music blended together beautifully and Gemma, Jasmine, and Pearl, all dressed in bright red satin, made their way to the front of the barn. Then the fiddles struck the first note of the traditional wedding march, and the bride appeared on her father's arm at the back of the barn. Everyone stood up, and Blaze's heart absolutely left his chest in one enormous beat when he saw Colleen in that long, white velvet dress. White roses were scattered in her red hair, and she wore the silver heart necklace he'd bought her on Orcas Island.

When Cash and Colleen reached the front of the barn, Cash put his daughter's hands in Blaze's and said, "Be good to her. I'm trustin' you with my precious daughter, son."

"You have my promise, sir," Blaze said.

Colleen took the microphone from the preacher. Liz and Raylen's bows hit the fiddle strings at the same time and she looked deep into Blaze's eyes and sang, "Bless the Broken Road," a song made popular by Rascal Flatts.

Liz locked eyes with Raylen's as they made the fiddles whine to lyrics saying that every long lost dream led her to where he was and that God blessed the broken road that led her straight to him.

When Colleen finished singing, she handed the microphone back to the preacher. Liz and Raylen laid their fiddles down. Raylen joined the groomsmen, and Liz the bridesmaids. When the ceremony ended, the preacher announced that the wedding party would have a few pictures taken.

"But feel free to partake of the food tables and when the pictures are done, the bride and groom will cut the cake so you can have dessert," he said.

While the photographer did his job, Liz parked herself in Raylen's lap on a front row chair and waited for their turn to have pictures with the bride and groom.

"I'm glad we did it different," she whispered.

"I was sure nervous about giving you an envelope rather than a ring," he said.

"I loved it. A proposal with a marriage license! Bet no one else has ever got that." She held up her left hand and admired the wide gold band. A ring for a rancher's wife who mucked out stalls, saddled up horses, drove a tractor, and hauled hay.

"And I will always love my ring." She laughed.

Jasmine sat down beside Liz. "It's a beautiful wedding. I love that it's in a barn even if this scarcely looks like a barn. Colleen is beautiful and Blaze can't take his eyes off her. But if I ever get married I'm doing it the way y'all did, Liz. Propose. Get married in an hour. Put on a nice wide gold band and be married. I suppose my mother would throw a hissy if I did. She's been plannin' my wedding for years."

Ace sat down next to Raylen and patted him on the shoulder. "Blaze has been branded. No doubt about it. His prowlin' days are done. But I got to admit, Raylen, you're the smart one. You'll never forget your anniversary. Been meanin' to ask you, how did you get a judge to marry you on Christmas day? And how did you work up the nerve to give Liz a marriage license instead of an engagement ring?"

"First chance at a horse he wants to buy got the judge. I wanted to be a husband, not a fiancé, and I had a pretty good idea that Liz felt the same way but I got pretty nervous right there at the end." Raylen smiled.

It was time for Jasmine and Ace to have pictures taken with the bride and groom, so they left and Marva Jo and Tressa sat down beside Raylen and Liz.

"Did you tell him?" Marva Jo whispered.

"I did after we were married. That way it could never be said he married me for my money. I told him all about my inheritance from my father, and I even let him glance at my portfolio and my checkbook." She laughed.

"I married her for twenty acres, not her bank account," Raylen teased.

Tressa patted him on the shoulder. "And you got a sassy piece of baggage with it. We leave in a week for the new carnival year. I'll miss her, but Colleen is a quick study. I swear with that red hair she's a born gypsy. She can lay out the cards and tell a fortune better than I ever could. Too bad she can't belly dance."

"I offered her my costumes, but she turned me down," Liz said.

"Parents of the groom, please," the photographer said.

"That's me. Come on, Marva Jo. You're going to stand on one side and me the other." Tressa motioned to Marva Jo.

Lucy sat down beside Liz.

"Wilma is so excited about the move. You are a good woman, Liz," she said.

"I'm a selfish woman. I don't want to lose her so I settled her in more permanently. And besides, we had two houses. We decided to live in Raylen's house and Gemma moved in with Dewar. So one house was empty. We opened the fence and put a cattle guard between the two places so on nice days she can walk from one place to the other."

"Well, she's a happy woman. She's been telling your Uncle Haskell all about how much she loves Hooter and Blister and how they refused to move with you and I heard her tellin' him that she'd already bought five used Louis L'Amour books for the bookcases," Lucy said.

Lucy meandered away and Pearl and Wil settled in beside Liz and Raylen.

"I heard you bought a couple of Gypsy Vanner mares," Wil said.

Liz nodded. "I sure did. Star needed some company since he's gotten big enough to go live in the barn."

Raylen chuckled. "And Dewar spends more time with them than she does."

Liz smiled. "He's got more time than I do. When he finds a good woman, the Vanners will take a backseat. Isn't this pretty close to your first anniversary, Pearl?"

"Wil and I were married a year a couple of weeks ago. Colleen doesn't know how lucky she has it. Maddie is so laid back and calm about everything. Momma about drove me bonkers on my wedding day. You two did it the right way. Get married and then tell Momma. Only if I'd done that we'd have had a funeral instead of a wedding."

"Yours or hers?" Liz asked.

Wil patted Pearl on the thigh. "Red's, to be sure. Her momma was determined to have a wedding."

Liz pointed at Pearl's belly and asked, "How are those twins coming along?"

Pearl patted her stomach. "Doc says they're doin' fine. Twins. Identical boys. We just found out yesterday. Daddy is ecstatic and so is Wil. I don't know jack shit about raising boys but I guess I'll learn. I'm just glad Colleen didn't wait until June to get married. I'd have had to have Omar the Tentmaker design my dress."

"And now the whole wedding party," the photographer said.

"That's our cue," Liz said.

Later, after pictures and after the bride and groom had danced to "I Cross My Heart" by George Strait, Raylen and Liz laid down their fiddles, and he led her to the dance floor.

He wrapped his arms around her, letting them rest on the small of her back. "You really aren't disappointed that you didn't have all this?"

"Hell, no! Our wedding was perfect and I got exactly what I wanted. A house with no wheels and a sexy cowboy. I had a darn good cowboy Christmas. Now kiss me, please. Weddings, a sexy cowboy, and good fiddlin' always turn a girl on," she whispered.

THE END

About the Author

Carolyn Brown is a *New York Times* and *USA Today* bestselling author with more than fifty books published. Her books include the cowboy trilogy *Lucky in Love, One Lucky Cowboy*, and *Getting Lucky*, the Honky Tonk series, *I Love This Bar, Hell Yeah, Honky Tonk Christmas*, and *My Give a Damn's Busted*, and her new Spikes & Spurs series beginning with *Love Drunk Cowboy* and *Red's Hot Cowboy*. She was born in Texas but grew up in southern Oklahoma where she and her husband, Charles, a retired English teacher, make their home. They have three grown children and enough grandchildren to keep them young.

Love DRUNK COWBOY

BY CAROLYN BROWN

She's a self-made city girl...

High-powered career woman Austin Lanier suddenly finds herself saddled with an inherited watermelon farm deep in the countryside. She's determined to sell the farm, until her new, drop-dead sexy neighbor Rye O'Donnell shows up...

He's as intoxicating as can be...

Rancher Rye O'Donnell thinks he's going to get a good deal on his dream property—until he meets the fiery new owner. Rye is knocked sideways when he realizes that not only is Granny Lanier's city-slicker granddaughter a savvy businesswoman, she's also sexy as hell...

Suddenly Rye is a whole lot less interested in real estate and a whole lot more focused on getting Austin to set aside her stiletto heels...

Praise for *Love Drunk Cowboy*:

"Brown revitalizes the Western romance with this fresh, funny, and sexy tale filled with likable, down-to-earth characters."

—Booklist

978-1-4022-5358-4 • $7.99 U.S. / £4.99 UK